In Convent Walls

By

Emily Sarah Holt

Double 9
BOOKS

In Convent Walls
by Emily Sarah Holt

Copyright © 2023

All Rights reserved.

ISBN: 978-93-60466-36-7
Published by

DOUBLE 9 BOOKS

2/13-B, Ansari Road
Daryaganj, New Delhi – 110002
info@double9books.com
www.double9books.com
Tel. 011-40042856

ABOUT THE AUTHOR

Emily Sarah Holt was an English author who lived from 1836 to 1893. She was born on April 25, 1836, in Stubbylee, Bacup, Lancashire. She was the oldest daughter of John Holt and Judith Mason of Greens, whose husband was a judge for Lancashire and the West Riding. She is said to have gone to school at Oxford. She got sick in late 1893 while she was in Harrogate and went to go live with her brother in Balham, London. She died there on Christmas Day. An obelisk marks the spot where she was buried in the Church of St. Saviour's, Bacup. Holt had written more than fifty books, most of them for kids. The BML catalogue lists 52 of Holt's books as historical stories, which is what most of her work is. Protestantism is a theme in Holt's work.

CONTENTS

Preface

The historical portion of this tale has been partially narrated in one of my previous volumes, "In All Time of our Tribulation," in which the Despenser story is begun, and its end told from another point of view. That volume left Isabelle of France at the height of her ambition, in the place to reach which she had been plotting so long and so unscrupulously. Here we see the Nemesis come upon her and the chief partner of her guilt; the proof that there is a God that judgeth in the earth. It is surely one of the saddest stories of history—sad as all stories are which tell of men and women whom God has endowed richly with gifts, and who, casting from them the Divine hand which would fain lift them up into the light of the Golden City, deliberately choose the pathway of death, and the blackness of darkness for ever. Few women have had grander opportunities given them than Isabelle for serving God and making their names blessed and immortal. She chose rather to serve self: and thereby inscribed her name on one of the blackest pages of England's history, and handed down her memory to eternal execration. For "life is to do the will of God"—the true blessedness and glory of life here, no less than the life hereafter.

> "Oh, the bitter shame and sorrow,
> That a time should ever be
> When I let the Saviour's pity
> Plead in vain, and proudly answered—
> 'All of self, and none of Thee!'
>
> "Yet He found me; I beheld Him
> Bleeding on the accursed tree,—
> Heard Him pray, 'Forgive them, Father!'
> And my wistful heart said faintly,
> 'Some of self, and some of Thee!'
>
> "Day by day, His tender mercy,
> Healing, helping, full and free,
> Sweet and strong, and, ah! so patient,

Brought me lower, while I whispered,
'Less of self, and more of Thee!'

"Higher than the highest heaven,
Deeper than the deepest sea,
Lord, Thy love at last hast conquered:
Grant me now my heart's desire—
'None of self, and all of Thee!'"

PART 1

Chapter 1
Wherein Dame Cicely de Chaucombe scribeth soothliness (1360)

Wherein Commence the Annals of Cicely

"Heaven does with us, as we with torches do—
Not light them for themselves."

Shakespeare.

"It is of no use, Jack," quoth I. "I never did love her, I never can, and never shall."

"And I never bade you, Sissot," answered he. "Put that in belike, prithee."

"But you bade me write the story out," said I. "Ay, I did so. But I left you free to speak your mind of any body that should come therein, from a bishop to a baa-lamb," said he.

"Where shall I go for mine ink?" I made answer: "seeing that some part of my tale, to correspond to the matter, should need to be writ in vernage, (Note 1) and some other in verjuice."

"Keep two quills by you," saith he, "with inkhorns of the twain, and use either according to the matter."

"Ay me!" said I. "It should be the strangest and woefullest tale ever writ by woman."

"The more need that it should be writ," quoth Jack, "by them that have lived it, and can tell the sooth-fastness (truth) thereof. Look you, Sissot, there are men enough will tell the tale of hearsay, such as they may win of one and another, and that is like to be full of guile and contrariousness. And many will tell it to win favour of those in high place, and so shall but the half be told. Thou hast lived through it, and wist all the inwards thereof, at least from thine own standing-spot. Let there be one tale told just as it was, of one that verily knew, and had no purpose to win gold or favour, but only to speak sooth-fastness."

"You set me an hard task, Jack!" I said, and I think I sighed.

"Easier to do, maybe, than to reckon on," saith he, in his dry, tholemode (Note 2) way. "Thou needest write but one word at once, and thou canst take thine own time to think what word to write."

"But I have no parchment," said I. I am a little afraid I coveted not any, for I fancied not the business at all. It was Jack who wanted the story writ out fair, not I.

"Well, I have," saith Jack calmly.

"Nor any quills," said I.

"I have," saith Jack, after the same fashion.

"And the ink is dried-up."

"Then will we buy more."

"But—" I stayed, for I thought I had better hold my tongue.

"But— I have no mind to it," saith Jack. "That might have come first, Sissot. It shows, when it doth, that thou hast come to an end of thine excuses. Nay, sweet heart, do but begin, and the mind will have after."

"Lack-a-daisy!" said I, trying to laugh, though I felt somewhat irked (worried, irritated): "I reckon, then, I had best do mine husband's bidding without more ado."

"There spake my Sissot," saith he. "Good dame!"

So here am I, sat at this desk, with a roll of parchment that Jack hath cut in even leches (strips) for to make a book, and an inkhorn of fresh ink, and divers quills—O me! must all this be writ up?

Well, have forth! I shall so content Jack, and if I content not myself, that shall pay me.

It was through being one of Queen Isabel's gentlewomen that I came to know these things, and, as Jack saith, to live through my story. And I might go a step further back, for I came to that dignity by reason of being daughter unto Dame Alice de Lethegreve, that was of old time nurse to King Edward. So long as I was a young maid, I was one of the Queen's sub-damsels; but when I wedded my Jack (and a better Jack never did maiden wed) I was preferred to be damsel of the chamber: and in such fashion journeyed I with the Queen to France, and tarried with her all the time she dwelt beyond seas, and came home with her again, and was with her the four years following, until all brake up, and she was appointed to keep house at Rising Castle. So the whole play was played before mine own eyes.

I spake only sooth-fastness when I told Jack I could never love her. How can man love whom he cannot trust? It would have been as easy to put faith in a snake because it had lovesome marks and colouring, as in that fair, fair face—ay, I will not deny that it was marvellous fair—with the gleaming eyes, which now seemed to flash with golden light, and now to look like the dark depths of a stagnant pool. Wonderful eyes they were! I am glad I never trusted them.

Nor did I never trust her voice. It was as marvellous as the eyes. It could be sweet as honey and sharp as a two-edged sword; soft as dove's down, and hard as an agate stone. Too soft and sweet to be sooth-fast! She meant her words only when they were sword and agate.

And the King—what shall I say of him? In good sooth, I will say nothing, but leave him to unfold himself in the story. I was not the King's foster-sister in sooth, for I was ten years the younger; and it was Robin, my brother, that claimed kin with him on that hand. But he was ever hendy (amiable, kindly, courteous) to me. God rest his hapless soul!

But where shall my tale begin? Verily, I have no mind to set forth from the creation, as chroniclers are wont. I was not there then, and lived not through that, nor of a long while after. Must I then begin from my creation? aswhasay (as who should say—that is to say), as near it as my remembrance taketh me. Nay, I think not so: for then should I tell much of the reign of King Edward of Westminster (Edward the First), that were right beside the real story. I think I shall take date from the time of the Queen's first departure to France, which was the year of our Lord God, 1324.

I was a young maid of seventeen years when I entered the Queen's household,—her own age. But in another sense, I was tenfold the child that she was. Indeed, I marvel if she ever were a child. I rather think she was born grown-up, as the old heathen fabled Minerva to have been. While on waiting, I often used to see and hear things that I did not understand, yet which I could feel were disapproved by something inside me: I suppose it must have been my conscience. And if at those times I looked on my mother's face, I could often read disapproval in her eyes also. I never loved the long secret discourses there used to be betwixt the Queen and her uncle, my Lord of Lancaster: they always had to me the air of plotting mischief. Nor did I ever love my Lord of Lancaster; there was no simplicity nor courtesy in him. His natural manner (when he let it be seen) was stern and abrupt; but he did very rarely allow it to be seen; it was nearly always some affectation put on. And I hate that, and so doth Jack.

At that time I loved and hated instinctively, as I think children do; and at seventeen years, I was a child in all things save by the almanac. I could rarely tell why I did not love people—only, I did not love them. I knew oftener why I did. I never thought much of Sir Piers de Gavaston, that the King so dearly affected, but I never hated him in a deadly fashion, as some did that I knew. I loved better Sir Hugh Le Despenser, that was afterwards Earl of Gloucester, for he—

"Sissot," saith a voice behind me, "what is the name of that chronicle?"

"I cannot tell, Jack," said I. "What wouldst have it called?"

"'The Annals of Cicely,'" quoth he; "for she is beginning, middle, and end of it."

I felt as though he had cast a pitcher of cold water over me. I sat looking at my parchment.

"Read it over, prithee," saith he, "and count how many great I's be therein."

So did I, and by my troth there were seventy-seven. Seventy-seven of me! and all in six leaves of parchment, forsooth. How many soever shall there be by the time I make an end?

"That's an ill beginning, Jack!" said I, and I felt ready to cry. "Must I begin over again?"

"Sissot," quoth he, "nothing is ever undone in this world."

"What mean you?" said I.

"There was man died the year before thou wert born," he made answer, "that was great friend of my father. He was old when my father was young, yet for all that were they right good friends. He was a very learned man; so wise in respect of things known but to few, that most men accounted him a very magician, and no good Christian. Howbeit, my father said that was but folly and slander. He told my father some of the strange matters that he found in nature; and amongst them, one thing, which hath ever stuck by me. Saith Friar Roger, Nothing is ever destroyed. Nothing that hath once had being, can ever cease to be."

"Why, Jack!" cried I. "Verily that must be folly! I cast this scrap of parchment on the chafer, and it burneth up. It is gone, see thou. Surely it hath ceased to be?"

"No," saith he. "It is gone into ashes and smoke."

"What be ashes and smoke?" asked I, laughing.

"Why, they be ashes and smoke," he made answer. "And the smoke curleth up chimney, and goeth out into the air: and the air cometh up Sissot's nose-thirls, and feedeth her bodily life; and Sissot maketh seventy-seven I's to six pages of parchment."

"Now, Jack, softly!" said I.

"So it is, my dame," pursueth he. "Every thing that dieth, feedeth somewhat that liveth. But I can go further an' thou wilt. Friar Roger thought (though he had not proved it) that every word spoken might as it were dwell in the air, and at bidding of God hereafter, all those words should return to life and be heard again by all the world."

I could not help but laugh.

"Why, what a din!" said I. "Do but think, all the words, in all languages, buzzing about man's ears, that were ever spoken since Adam dwelt in the Garden of Eden!"

"Wouldst thou like all thy words repeated thus, Sissot?"

"I would not mind, Jack."

"Wouldst not? Then I am worser than thou, which is like enough. I would not like to hear all my foolish words, all my angry words, all my sinful words, echoed back to me from the starry walls of heaven. And suppose, Sissot—only suppose that God should do as much with our thoughts! I dare say He knows how."

I covered my face with mine hands.

"That would be dreadful!" I whispered.

"It will be, in very deed," softly said Jack, "when the Books are opened, and the names read out, in the light of that great white Throne which shall be brighter than noon-day. I reckon in that day we shall not be hearkening for Sir Piers de Gavaston's name, nor for Sir Hugh Le Despenser's, but only for those of John and Cicely de Chaucombe. Now, set again to thy chronicling, my Sissot, and do it in the light of that Throne, and in the expectation of that Book: so shall it be done well."

And so Jack left me. But to speak sooth, seeing the matter thus makes me to feel as though I scarce dared do it at all. Howsobe, I have it to do: and stedfast way maketh stedfast heart.

There were plenty of people who hated Sir Hugh Le Despenser, but I and my mother Dame Alice were not amongst them. He had been brought up with the King from his youth, but the King never loved him till after the death of Sir Piers de Gavaston. The Queen loved him, just so long as the King did not. That was always her way; the moment that she saw he cared for anything which was not herself, she at once began to hate it. And verily he never gave her cause, for he held her ever dearest of any mortal thing.

Sir Hugh was as goodly a gentleman as man's eyes might see. Those who loved him not called him proud—yea, the very spirit of pride. But the manner they thought pride seemed to me rather a kind of sternness or shortness of speech, as if he wished to have done with the matter in hand. Some people call every thing pride; if man talk much, they say he loves to hear his own voice; if he be silent, he despises his company. Now it seems to me that I often speak and am silent from many other causes than pride, and therefore it may be the like with other folk. Do those which are ever accusing other of pride, do all their actions for that reason? If not so, how or why should they suspect it in other men? I do not think Sir Hugh was so much prouder than other. He knew his own value, I dare say; and very like he did not enjoy being set at nought—who doth so? Other said he was ambitious: and there might be some sooth-fastness in the accusation; yet I fancy the accusers loved a slice of worldly grandeur no less than most men. And some said he was wicked man: that did I never believe.

As for his wife, Dame Alianora, I scarcely know what to say of her. She was a curious mixture of qualities. She clung to the King her uncle when others forsook him, she was free-handed, and she could feel for man in trouble: those were her good points. Yet she seemed to feel but what she saw; it was "out of sight, out of mind," with her; and she loved new faces rather too well to please me. I think, for one thing, she was timid; and that oft-times causes man to appear what he is not. But she was better woman than either of her sisters—the Lady Margaret Audley and the Lady Elizabeth de Clare. I never saw her do, nor heard her say, the heartless acts and speeches whereof I knew both of them guilty. I dare say, as women go, she was not ill woman. For, alas! I have lived long enough to know that there be not many good ones.

Well, I said—no did I?—that I would begin with the year 1324 of our Lord God. But, lack-a-day! there were matters afore 1324, like as there were men before Agamemnon. Truly, methinks there be a two-three I did well not to omit: aswhasay, the dying of Queen Margaret, widow of King Edward of Westminster, which deceased seven years earlier than so. I shall never cease to marvel how it came to pass that two women of the same nation, of the same family, being aunt and niece by blood, should have been so strangely diverse as those two Queens. All that was good, wise, and gentle, was in Queen Margaret: what was in Queen Isabel will my chronicle best tell. This most reverend lady led a very retired life after her husband's death, being but a rare visitor to the Court, dwelling as quietly and holily as any nun might dwell, and winning love and respect from all that knew her. Very charitable was she and most devout: and (if it be lawful to say thus) had I been Pope, I had sooner canonised her than a goodly number that hath been. But I do ill to speak thus, seeing the holy Father is infallible, and acts in such matters but by the leading of God's Spirit, as saith the Church. Good lack, but there be queer things in this world! I saw once Father Philip screw up his mouth when one said the same in his hearing, and saith he—

"The Lord Pope is infallible when he speaketh *ex cathedrâ*, but so only."

"But how," saith he that spake, "shall we know when he is sat in his chair and when he is out of it?"

An odd look came into Father Philip's eyes.

"Master," saith he, "when I was a little lad, my mother told me divers times that it was not seemly to ask curious questions."

But I guess what the good Friar thought, though it be not always discreet to speak out man's thoughts. Ah me! will the time ever come when man may say what he will, with no worse thereafter than a sneer or a sharp rebuke from his neighbour? If so were, I would I had been born in those merry days—but I should want Jack to be born then belike.

"Sissot," saith a voice over my shoulder, "wist thou the full meaning of thy wish?"

Jack is given to coming in quietly—I never knew him make a noise— and peeping over my shoulder to see how my chronicle maketh progress: for he can well read, though he write not.

"What so, Jack?" said I.

"I reckon we should be the younger by some centuries," quoth he, "and perchance should not be at all. But allowing it, dost thou perceive that such a difference should mean a change in all things?—that no fear should in likelihood mean no reverence nor obedience, and might come to mean more than that?"

"That were dread!" said I. "What manner of times should they be?"

"I think," saith he, "those very '*tempora periculosa*' whereof Saint Paul speaketh, when men shall love their own selves, and be proud, unthankful, without affection, peace, or benignity, loving their pleasures rather than God. And if it serve thee, I would not like to live in those times."

"Dear heart, nor would I!" quoth I. "Yet surely, Jack, that seemeth a gainsaying. Were all men free to speak what they would, and not be called to account therefor, it were soothly to love their neighbours and show benignity."

"Ay, if it were done for that end," he made answer. "But the heart of man is a cage of deceits. Much must befall the world, I take it, ere that cometh to pass: and while they that bring it about may be good men that mean well, they that come to use it may be evil, and mean ill. The Devil is not come to an end of his shifts, be thou sure. Let man run as fast and far as he will, Satan shall wit how to keep alongside."

I said nought. Jack is very wise, a deal more than I, yet I cannot always see through his eye-glasses. Mayhap it is not always because I am wiser of the twain.

"Freedom to do good and be good is a good thing," then saith he: "but freedom to be ill, and do ill, must needs be an ill thing. And man being what he is, how makest thou sure that he shall always use his freedom for good, and not for ill?"

"Why, that must man chance," said I.

"A sorry chance," answereth he. "I were liever not to chance it. I thought I heard thee deny Fina this last week to go to the dance at Underby Fair?"

"So thou didst," said I. "She is too young, and too giddy belike, to trust with a bevy of idle damosels as giddy as she."

"Well, we are none of us so far grown-up in all wisdom that it were safe to trust us with our own reins in all things. Hast never heard the saw, 'He that ruleth his own way hath a fool to his governor'?"

"Well!" said I; "but then let the wise men be picked out to rule us, and the fools to obey."

"Excellent doctrine, my Sissot!" quoth Jack, smiling in his eyes: "at least, for the fools. I might somewhat pity the wise men. But how to bring it about? Be the fools to pick out the wise men? and are they wise enough to do it? I sorely fear we shall have a sorry lot of governors when thy law comes to be tried. I think, Wife, thou and I had better leave God to rule the world, for I suspect we should do it something worser than He."

Let me fall back to my chronicling. Another matter happed in the year 1319, the which I trow I shall not lightly forget. The Queen abode at Brotherton, the King being absent. The year afore, had the Scots made great raids on the northern parts of England, had burned the outlying parts of York while the King was there, and taken the Earl of Richmond prisoner: and now, hearing of the Queen at Brotherton, but slenderly guarded, down they marched into Yorkshire, and we, suspecting nought, were well-nigh caught in the trap.

Well I mind that night, when I was awoke by pebbles cast up at my casement, for I lay in a turret chamber, that looked outward. So soon as I knew what the sound meant, I rose from my bed and cast a mantle about me, and opened the casement.

"Is any there?" said I.

"Is that thou, Sissot?" quoth a voice which I knew at once for my brother Robert's, "Lose not one moment, but arouse the Queen, and pray her to take horse as speedily as may be, or she shall be captured of the Scots, which come in great force by the Aire Valley, and are nearhand (nearly) at mine heels. And send one to bid the garrison be alert, and to let me in, that I may tell my news more fully."

I wis not whether I shut the casement or no, for ere man might count ten was I in the Queen's antechamber, and shaking of Dame Elizabeth by the shoulders. But, good lack, she took it as easy as might be. She was alway one to take matters easy, Dame Elizabeth de Mohun.

"Oh, let be till daylight," quoth she, as she turned on her pillow. "'Tis but one of Robin Lethegreve's fumes and frets, I'll be bound. He is for ever a-reckoning that the Scots be at hand or the house o' fire, and he looks for man to vault out of his warm bed that instant minute when his fearsome news be spoken. Go to sleep, Cicely, and let folks be."

And round turned she, and, I warrant, was asleep ere I could bring forth another word. So then I fell to shaking Joan de Vilers, that lay at tother end of the chamber. But she was right as bad, though of another fashion.

"Wherefore rouse me?" saith she. "I can do nought. 'Tis not my place. If Dame Elizabeth arise not, I cannot. Thou wert best go back abed, dear heart. Thou shalt but set thyself in trouble."

Well, there was no time to reason with such a goose; but I longed to shake her yet again. Howbeit, I tarried no longer in the antechamber, but burst into the Queen's own chamber where she lay abed, with Dame Tiffany in the pallet—taking no heed that Joan called after me—

"Cicely! Cicely! how darest thou? Come back, or thou shall be mispaid or tint!" (Held in displeasure or ruined.)

But I cared not at that moment, whether for mispayment or tinsel. I had my duty to do, and I did it. If the news were true, the Queen was little like to snyb (blame) me when she found it so: and if no, well, I had but done as I should. And I knew that Dame Tiffany, which tended her like a hen with one chicken, should hear my tidings of another fashion from the rest. Had Dame Elizabeth lain that night in the pallet, and Dame Tiffany in the antechamber, my work had been the lighter. But afore I might win to the pallet—which to do I had need to cross the chamber,—Queen Isabel's own voice saith from the state bed—"Who is there?"

"Dame," said I,—forgetting to kneel, in such a fluster was I—"my brother hath now brought tidings that the Scots come in force by the Aire Valley, with all speed, and are nearhand at the very gate; wherefore—"

The Queen heard me no further. She was out of her bed, and herself donning her raiment, ere I might win thus far.

"Send Dame Elizabeth to me," was all she said, "and thyself bid De Nantoil alarm the garrison. Well done!"

I count I am not perfect nor a saint, else had I less relished that second shake of Dame Elizabeth—that was fast asleep—and deliverance of the Queen's bidding. I stayed me not to hear her mingled contakes and wayments (reproaches and lamentations), but flew off to the outermost door, and unbarring the same, spake through the crack that wherewith I was charged to Oliver de Nantoil, the usher of the Queen's chamber, which lay that night at her outer door. Then was nought but bustle and stir, both within and without. The Queen would have up Robin, and hearkened to his tale while Alice Conan combed her hair, the which she bade bound up at the readiest, to lose not a moment. In less than an hour, methinks, she won to horse, and all we behind, and set forth for York, which was the contrary way to that the Scots were coming. And, ah me! I rade with Dame Elizabeth, that did nought but grieve over her lost night's rest, and harry poor me for breaking the same. I asked at her if she had better loved to be taken of the Scots; since if so, the Queen's leave accorded, we might have left her behind.

"Scots!" quoth she. "Where be these ghostly (fabulous, figurative) Scots? I will go bail they be wrapped of their foldings (plaids) fast asleep on some moor an hundred miles hence. 'Tis but Robin, the clown! that is so clumst (stupid) with his rashness, that he seeth a Scot full armed under every bush, and heareth a trumpeter in every corncrake: and as if that were not enough, he has a sister as ill as himself, that must take all for gospel as if Friar Robert preached it. Mary love us! but I quoke when thou gattest hold on me by the shoulders! I count it was a good hour ere I might sleep again."

"Dear heart, Dame!" cried I, "but it was not two minutes! It is scantly an hour by now."

"Then that is thy blame, Cicely, routing like a bedel (shouting like a town-crier), and oncoming (assaulting) folks as thou dost. I marvel thou canst not be peaceable! I alway am. Canst mind the night that ever I shaked thee awake and made thee run out of thy warm bed as if a bear were after thee?"

I trust I kept out of my voice the laughter that was in my throat as I said, "No, Dame: that cannot I." The self notion of Dame Elizabeth ever doing thus to any was so exceeding laughable.

"Well! then why canst—Body o' me! what ever is yonder flaming light?"

Master Oliver was just alongside, and quoth he drily—

"Burden not your Ladyship; 'tis but the Scots that have reached Brotherton, and be firing the suburbs."

"Holy Mary, pray for us!" skraighs Dame Elizabeth, at last verily feared: "Cicely, how canst thou ride so slow? For love of all the saints; let us get on!"

Then fell she to her beads, and began to invoke all the Calendar, while she urged on her horse till his rapid trotting brake up the *aves* and *oras* into fragments that man might scarce hear and keep him sober. I warrant I was well pleased, for all my weariness, when we rade in at Micklebar of York; and so, I warrant, was Dame Elizabeth, for all her impassibility. We tarried not long at York, for, hearing that the Scots came on, the Queen removed to Nottingham for safer keeping. And so ended that year.

But no contakes had I, save of Dame Elizabeth, that for the rest of that month put on a sorrowful look at the sight of me. On the contrary part, Robin had brave reward from the King, and my Lady the Queen was pleased to advance me, as shall now be told, shortly thereafter: and ever afterwards did she seem to affy her more in me, as in one that had been tried and proved faithful unto trust.

Thus far had I won when I heard a little bruit behind me, and looking up, as I guessed, I saw Jack, over my shoulder.

"Dear heart, Jack!" said I, "but thou hast set me a merry task! Two days have I been a-work, and not yet won to the Queen's former journey to France; yet I do thee to wit, I am full disheartened at the stretch of road I see afore me. Must I needs tell every thing that happed for every year? Mary love us! but I feel very nigh at my wits' end but to think of it. Why, my Chronicle shall be bigger than the Golden Legend and the Morte Arthur put together, and all Underby Common shall not furnish geese enow to keep me in quills!"

I ended betwixt laughter and tears. To say sooth, I was very nigh the latter.

"Take breath, Sissot," saith Jack, quietly.

"But dost thou mean that, Jack?"

"I mean not to make a nief (serf) of my wife," saith he. I was something comforted to hear that.

"As for time, dear heart," he pursueth, "take thou an hour or twain by the day, so thou weary not thyself; and for events, I counsel thee to make a diverse form of chronicle from any ever yet written."

"How so, Jack?"

"Set down nothing because it should go in a chronicle, but only those matters wherein thyself was interested."

"But that, Jack," said I, laughing as I looked up on him, "shall be the 'Annals of Cicely' over again; wherewith I thought thou wert not compatient." (Pleased, satisfied; the adjective of compassion.)

"Nay, the Annals of Cicely were Cicely's fancies and feelings," he made answer: "this should be what Cicely heard and saw."

I sat and meditated thereon.

"And afore thou wear thy fingers to the bone with thy much scribing," saith he, with that manner of smile of his eyes which Jack hath, "call thou Father Philip to write at thy mouth, good wife."

"Nay, verily!" quoth I. "I would be loth to call off Father Philip from his godly meditations, though I cast no doubt he were both fairer scribe and better chronicler than I."

To speak sooth, it was Father Philip learned me to write, and the master should be better than the scholar. I marvel more that have leisure learn not to write. Jack cannot, nor my mother, and this it was that made my said mother desirous to have me taught, for she said, had she wist the same, she could have kept a rare chronicle when she dwelt at the Court, and sith my life was like to be there also, she would fain have me able to do so. I prayed Father Philip to learn my discreet Alice, for I could trust her not to make an ill use thereof; but I feared to trust my giddy little Vivien with such edged tools as Jack saith pen and ink be. And in very sooth it were a dread thing if any amongst us should be entrapped into intelligence with the King's enemies, or such treasonable matter; and of this are wise men ever afeared, when their wives or daughters learn to write. For me, I were little feared of such matter as that: and should rather have feared (for such as Vivien) the secret scribing of love-letters to unworthy persons. Howbeit, Jack is wiser than I, and he saith it were dangerous to put such power into the hands of most men and women.

Lo! here again am I falling into the Annals of Cicely. Have back, Dame Cicely, an' it like you. Methinks I had best win back: yet how shall I get out of the said Annals, and forward on my journey, when the very next thing that standeth to be writ is mine own marriage?

It was on the morrow of the Epiphany, 1320, that I was wedded to my Jack in the Chapel of York Castle. I have not set down the inwards of my love-tale, nor shall I, for good cause; for then should I not only fall into the Annals of Cicely, but should belike never make end thereof. Howbeit, this will I say,—that when King Edward bestowed me on my Jack, I rather count he had his eyes about him, and likewise that there had been a few little passages that might have justified him in so doing: for Jack was of the household, and we had sat the one by the other at table more than once or twice, and had not always held our tongues when so were. So we were no strangers, forsooth, but pretty well to the contrary: and verily, I fell on my feet that morrow. I am not so sure of Jack. And soothly, it were well I should leave other folks to blow my trumpet, if any care to waste his breath at that business.

I was appointed damsel of the chamber on my marriage, and at after that saw I far more of the Queen than aforetime. Now and again it was my turn to lie in that pallet in her chamber. Eh, but I loved not that work! I used to feel all out (altogether) terrified when those great dark eyes flashed their shining flashes, and there were not so many nights in the seven that they did not. She was as easy to put out as to shut one's eyes, but to bring in again—eh, that was weary work!

I am not like to forget that July even when, in the Palace of Westminster, my Lord of Exeter came to the Queen, bearing the Great Seal. It was a full warm eve, and the Queen was late abed. Joan de Vilers was that night tire-woman, and I was in waiting. I mind that when one scratched on the door, we thought it Master Oliver, and instead of going to see myself, I but bade one of the sub-damsels in a whisper. But no sooner said she,—"Dame, if it shall serve you, here is my Lord of Exeter and Sir Robert de Ayleston,"—than there was a full great commotion. The Queen rose up with her hair yet unbound, and bade them be suffered to enter: and when my Lord of Exeter came in, she—and after her all we of her following—set her on her knees afore him to pray his blessing. This my Lord gave, but something hastily, as though his thoughts were elsewhere. Then said he—

"Dame, the King sends you the Great Seal, to be kept of you until such time as he shall ask it again."

And he motioned forward Sir Robert de Ayleston, that held in his arms the great bag of white leather, wherein was the Great Seal of gold.

Saw I ever in all my life face change as hers changed then! To judge from her look, she might have been entering the gates of Heaven. (A sorry Heaven, thought I, that gold and white leather could make betwixt them.) Her eyes glowed, and flashed, and danced, all at once: and she sat her down in a chair of state, and received the Seal in her own hands, and saith she—

"Bear with you my duty to the King my lord, and tell him that I will keep his great charge in safety."

So her words ran. But her eyes said—and eyes be apt to speak truer than voices—"This day am I proudest of all the women in England, and I let not go this Seal so long as I can keep it!"

Then she called Dame Elizabeth, which received the Seal upon the knee, and the Queen bade her commit it to the great cypress coffer wherein her royal robes were kept.

Not long after that, the Queen took her chamber at the Tower afore the Lady Joan was born; and the Great Seal was then returned to the King's Wardrobe. Master Thomas de Cherleton was then Comptroller of the Wardrobe: but he was not over careful of his office, and left much in the hands of his clerks; and as at that time Jack was clerk in charge, he was truly Keeper of the Great Seal so long as the Queen abode in the Tower. He told me he would be rare thankful when the charge was over, for he might not sleep o' nights for thinking on the same. I do think folks in high place, that be set in great charge, should do their own work, and not leave it to them beneath, so that Master Comptroller hath all the credit when things go well, and poor John Clerk payeth all the wyte if things go wrong. But, dear heart! if man set forth to amend all the crooked ways of this world, when shall he ever have done? Maybe if I set a-work to amend me, Cicely, it shall be my best deed, and more than I am like to have done in any hurry.

Now come I to the Queen's journey to France in 1324, and my tale shall thereupon grow more particular. The King sent her over to remonstrate with the King of France her brother for his theft of Guienne—for it was no less; and to conclude a treaty with him to restore the same. It was in May she left England and just before that something had happened wherein I have always thought she had an hand. In the August of the year before, Sir Roger de Mortimer brake prison from the Tower, and made good his escape to Normandy; where, after tarrying a small season with his mother's kinsmen, the Seigneurs de Fienles, he shifted his refuge to Paris, where he was out of the King's jurisdiction. Now in regard of that matter it did seem to me that King Edward was full childish and unwise. Had his father been on the throne, no such thing had ever happed: he wist how to deal with traitors. But now, with so slack an hand did the King rule, that not only Sir Roger gat free of the Tower by bribing one of his keepers and drugging the rest, but twenty good days at the least were lost while he stale down to the coast and so won away. There was indeed a hue and cry, but it wrought nothing, and even that was not for a week. There was more diligence used to seize his lands than to seize him. And at the end of all, just afore the Queen's journey, if my Lady Mortimer his wife, that had gone down to Southampton thinking to join him, was not taken and had to Skipton Castle, and the young damsels, her children, that were with her, sent to separate convents! I have ever believed that was the Queen's doing. It was she that loved not the Lady Mortimer should go to France: it should have interfered with her game. But what weakness and folly was it that the King should hearken her! Well—

"Soft you, now!"

"O Jack, how thou didst start me! I very nigh let my pen fall."

"Then shouldst thou have inked thy tunic, Sissot; and it were pity, so good Cologne sindon as it is. But whither goest thou with thy goose-quill a-flying, good wife? Who was Sir Roger de Mortimer? and what like was he?"

"Who was he, Jack?" quoth I, feeling somewhat took aback. "Why, he was—he was Sir Roger de Mortimer."

"How like a woman!" saith Jack, setting his hands in the pockets of his singlet.

"Now, Jack!" said I. "And what was he like, saidst thou? Why, he was as like a traitor, and a wastrel, and every thing that was bad, as ever I saw man in all my life."

"Horns, belike—and cloven feet—and a long tail?" quoth Jack. "I'll give it up, Sissot. Thou wert best write thy chronicle thine own way. But it goeth about to be rarely like a woman."

"Why, how should it not, when a woman is she that writeth it?" said I, laughing. But Jack had turned away, with that comical twist of his mouth which shows him secretly diverted.

Verily, I know not who to say Sir Roger was, only that he was Lord of Wigmore and Ludlow, and son of the Lady Margaret that was born a Fienles, and husband of the Lady Joan that was born a Geneville; and the proudest caitiff and worst man that ever was, as shall be shown ere I lay down my pen. He was man that caused the loss of himself and of other far his betters, and that should have been the loss of England herself but for God's mercy. The friend of Sathanas and of all evil, the foe of God and of all good—this, and no less, it seemeth me, was Sir Roger de Mortimer of Wigmore. God pardon him as He may (if such a thing be possible)!

Note 1. A very sweet, luscious wine. Verjuice was the most acid type of vinegar.

Note 2. Quiet, calm, patient. In Lowland Scotch, to *thole* is still to endure; and *thole-mood* must mean calm endurance.

Chapter 2
Wherein Cicely begins to see

"Tempt not the Tempter; he is near enough."

Dr Horatius Bonar.

Now can any man tell what it is in folks that causeth other folks to fancy them? for I have oft-times been sorely pestered to find out. Truly, if man be very fair, or have full winning ways, and sweet words, and so forth, then may it be seen without difficulty. I never was puzzled to know why Sir Roger or any other should have fallen o' love with Queen Isabel. But what on earth could draw her to him, that puzzled me sore. He was not young—about ten years elder than she, and she was now a woman of thirty years. Nor was he over comely, as men go,—I have seen better-favoured men, and I have seen worser. Nor were his manners sweet and winning, but the very contrary thereof, for they were rough and rude even to women, he alway seemed to me the very incarnation of pride. Men charged Sir Hugh Le Despenser with pride, but Sir Roger de Mortimer was worse than he tenfold. One of his own sons called him the King of Folly: and though the charge came ill from his lips that brought it, yet was it true as truth could be. His pride showed every where—in his dress, in the way he bore himself, in his words,—yea, in the very tones of his voice. And his temper was furious as ever I saw. Verily, he was one of the least lovesome men that I knew in all my life: yet for him, the fairest lady of that age bewrayed her own soul, and sold the noblest gentleman to the death. Truly, men and women be strange gear!

I had written thus far when I laid down my pen, and fell a-meditating, on the strangeness of such things as folks be and do in this world. And as I there sat, I was aware of Father Philip in the chamber, that had come in softly and unheard of me, so lost in thought was I. He smiled when I looked up on him.

"How goeth the chronicle, my daughter?" saith he.

"Diversely, Father," I made answer. "Some days my pen will run apace, but on others it laggeth like oxen at plough when the ground is heavy with rain."

"The ground was full heavy when I entered," saith he, "for the plough was standing still."

I laughed. "So it was, trow. But I do not think I was idle, Father; I was but meditating."

"Wise meditations, that be fruitful in good works, be far away from idlesse," quoth he. "And on what wert thou thinking thus busily, my daughter?"

"On the strange ways of men and women, Father."

"Did the list include Dame Cicely de Chaucombe?" saith Father Philip, with one of his quiet smiles.

"No," I made answer. "I had not reached her."

"Or Philip de Edyngdon? Perchance thou hadst not reached him."

"Why, Father, I might never think of sitting in judgment on you. No, I was thinking of some I had wist long ago: and in especial of Dame Isabel the Queen, and other that were about her. What is it moveth folks to love one another, or to hate belike?"

"There be but three things can move thee to aught, my daughter: God, Satan, and thine own human heart."

"And my conscience?" said I.

"Men do oftentimes set down to conscience," saith he, "that which is either God or Satan. The enlightened conscience of the righteous man worketh as God's Holy Spirit move him. The defiled conscience of the evil man listeneth to the promptings of Satan. And the seared conscience is as dead, and moveth not at all."

"Father, can a man then kill his conscience?"

"He may lay it asleep for this life, daughter: may so crush it with weights thereon laid that it is as though it had the sickness of palsy, and cannot move limb. But I count, when this life is over, it shall shake off the weight, and wake up, to a life and a torment that shall never end."

"I marvel if she did," said I, rather to myself than him.

"Daughter," he made answer, "whoso *she* be, let her be. God saith not to thee, *He*, and *she*, but *I*, and *thou*. When Christ knocketh at thy door, if thou open not, shall He take it as tideful answer that thou wert full busy watching other folks' doors to see if they would open?"

"Yet may we not learn, Father, from other folks' blunders?"

"Hast thou so learned, daughter?"

"Well, not much," said I. "A little, now and then, maybe."

"I never learned much," saith he, "from the blunders of any man save Philip de Edyngdon. What I learned from other folks' evil deeds was mostly to despise and be angered with them—not to beware for myself. And that lore cometh not of God. Thou mayest learn from such things set down in Holy Writ: but verily it takes God to pen them, so that we may indeed profit and not scorn,—that we may win and not lose. Be sure that whenever God puts in thine hand a golden coin of His realm, with the King's image stamped fair thereon, Satan is near at hand, with a gold-washed copper counterfeit stamped with his image, and made so like that thou hast need to look close, to make sure which is the true. 'Hold not all gold that shineth'—a wise saw, my daughter, whether it be a thing heavenly or earthly."

"I will endeavour myself to profit by your good counsel, Father," said I. "But mine husband bade me write this chronicle, though, sooth to say, I had no list thereto. And if I shall leave to deal with he and she, how then may my chronicle be writ?"

"Write thy chronicle, my daughter," he answered. "But write it as God hath writ His Chronicles. Set down that which men did, that which thou sawest and heardest. Beware only of digging into men's purposes where thou knewest them not, and sawest but the half thereof. And it is rarely possible for men to see the whole of that which passeth in their own day. Beware of setting down a man as all evil for one evil thing thou mayest see him to do. We see them we live amongst something too close to judge them truly. And beware, most of all, of imagining that thou canst get behind God's purposes, and lay bare all His reasons. Verily, the wisest saint on earth cannot reach to the thousandth part thereof. God can be fully understood, only of God."

I have set down these wise words of good Father Philip, for though they be too high and wide for mine understanding, maybe some that shall read my chronicle may have better brains than she that writ.

So now once again to my chronicling, and let me endeavour to do the same as Father Philip bade me.

It was on the eve of Saint Michael, 1325, that the Queen and her meynie (I being of them) reached Paris. We were ferried over the Seine to the gate of Nully (Note 1), and thence we clattered over the stones to the Hotel de Saint Pol (Note 2), where the Queen was lodged in the easternmost tower, next to our Lady Church, and we her meynie above. Dame Isabel de Lapyoun and I were appointed to lie in the pallet by turns. The Queen's bedchamber was hung with red sindon, broidered in the border with golden swans, and her cabinet with blue say, powdered with lily-flowers in gold, which is the arms of France, as every man knoweth, seeing they are borne by our King that now is, in right of this same Queen Isabel his mother. He, that was then my Lord of Chester, was also of the cortege, having sailed from Dover two days before Holy Cross (Note 3), and joined the Queen in Guienne; but the Queen went over in March, and was all that time in Guienne.

Dear heart! but Jack—which loveth to be square and precise in his matters—should say this were strange fashion wherein to write chronicles, to date first September and then the March afore it! I had better go back a bit.

It was, then, the 9th of March the Queen crossed from Dover to Whitsand, which the French call Guissant. She dwelt first, as I said, in Guienne, for all that summer; very quiet and peaceful were we, letters going to and fro betwixt our Queen and her lord, and likewise betwixt her and the King of France; but no visitors (without there were one that evening Dame Isabel lay in the pallet in my stead, and was so late up, and passed by the antechamber door with her shoes in her hands, as little Meliora the sub-damsel would have it she saw by the keyhole): and we might nearhand as well have been in nunnery for all the folks we saw that were not of the house. Verily, I grew sick irked (wearied, distressed) of the calm, that was like a dead calm at sea, when ships lie to, and can win neither forward nor backward. Ah, foolish Cicely! thou hadst better have given thanks for the last peace thou wert to see for many a year.

Well, my Lord of Chester come, which was the week after Holy Cross, we set forth with few days' delay, and came to Paris, as I said, the eve of Michaelmas. Marvellous weary was I with riding, for I rade of an horse the whole way, and not, as Dame Isabel did, with the Queen in her char. I was so ill tired that I could but eat a two-three wafers (Note 4), and drink a cup of wine, and then hied I to my bed, which, I thank the saints, was not the pallet that night.

The King and Queen of France were then at Compiegne, King Charles having been wed that same summer to his third wife, Dame Jeanne of Evreux: and a good woman I do believe was she, for all (as I said aforetime) there be but few. But I do think, and ever shall, that three wives be more than any man's share. The next morrow, they came in from Compiegne, to spend Michaelmas in Paris: and then was enough noise and merriment. First, mass in our Lady Church, whereto both Dame Isabel and I waited on the Queen; and by the same token, she was donned of one of the fairest robes that ever she bare, which was of velvet blue of Malyns (Malines), broidered with apple-blossom and with diapering of gold. It did not become her, by reason of her dark complexion, so well as it should have done S—

"Hold! Man spelleth not Cicely with an S."

"Jack, if thou start me like this any more, then will I turn the key in the lock when I sit down to write," cried I, for verily mine heart was going pitter-patter to come up in my throat, and out at my mouth, for aught I know. "Thou irksome man, I went about to write 'some folks,' not 'Cicely.'"

"But wherefore?" saith Jack, looking innocent as a year-old babe. "When it meaneth Cicely, then would I put Cicely."

"But I meant *not* Cicely, man o' life, bless thee!"

"I thank thee for thy blessing, Sissot; and I will fain hope thou didst mean that any way. I will go bail thy pen meant not Cicely, good wife; but if it were not in thine heart that Sissot's fair hair, and rose-red complexion, and grey eyes, should have gone better with that blue velvet gown than Queen Isabel's dusky hair and brown eyes, then do I know little of man or woman. And I dare be bound it would, belike."

And Jack lifteth his hat to me right courteously, and is gone afore I well know whether to laugh or to be angered. So I ween I had better laugh.

Where was I, trow? Oh, at mass in our Lady Church of Paris, where that day was a miracle done on two that were possessed of the Devil, whose names were Geoffrey Boder and Jeanne La Petite; and the girdle of Saint Mary being shown on the high altar, they were allowed to touch the same, whereon they were healed straightway. And the Queen, with her own hands, gave them alms, a crown; and her oblation to the image of Saint Mary in the said church, being a festival, was a crown (her daily oblation being seven-pence the day); and to the said holy girdle a crown, and to the holy relics, yet another. Then came we home by the water of Seyne, for which the boatman had twelve pence. (Note 5.)

We dwelt after this full peacefully at Paris for divers weeks, saving that we made short journeys to towns in the neighbourhood; as, one day to the house of the Sisters Predicants of Poissy, and another to God's House of Loure (Note 6), and another to Villers, where tarried the Queen of France, and so forth. And some days spent we likewise at Reyns and Sessouns. (Note 7.)

At Paris she had her robes made, of purple and colour of Malbryn, for the feast of All Saints, and they were furred with miniver and beasts ermines. And to me Cicely was delivered, to make my robe for the same, three ells rayed (striped) cloth and a lamb fur, and an hood of budge.

The Queen spent nigh an whole day at Sessouns, and another at Reyns, in visiting the churches; and the last can I well remember, by reason of that which came after. First, we went to the church of Saint Nicholas, where she offered a cloth of Turk, price forty shillings; and to Saint Remy she gave another, price forty-five shillings; and to the high altar of the Cathedral one something better. And to the ampulla (Note 7) and shrine of Saint Remy a crown, and likewise a crown to the holy relics there kept. Then to the Friars Minors, where at the high altar she offered a cloth of Lucca bought in the town, price three and an half marks (Note 8). And (which I had nearhand forgot) to the head of Saint Nicasius in the Cathedral, a crown.

The last night ere we left Sessouns, I remember, as I came into the Queen's lodging from vespers in the Cathedral,—Jack, that went with me, having tarried at the potter's to see wherefore he sent not home three dozen glasses for the Queen's table (and by the same token, the knave asked fifteen pence for the same when they did come, which is a price to make the hair stand on end)—well, as I said, I was a-coming in, when I met one coming forth that at first sight I wist not. And yet, when I meditated, I did know him, but I could not tell his name. He had taken no note of me, save to hap his mantle somewhat closer about his face, as though he cared not to be known—or it might be only that he felt the cold, for it was sharp for the time of year. Up went I into the Queen's lodging, which was then in the house of one John de Gyse, that was an honester man than Master Bolard, with whom she lodged at Burgette, for that last charged her three shillings and seven-pence for a worser lodging than Master Gyse gave her for two shillings.

I had writ thus far when I heard behind me a little bruit that I knew.

"Well, Jack?" said I, not looking up.

"Would thou wert better flyer of falcons, Sissot!" saith he.

"Dear heart! what means that, trow?" quoth I.

"Then shouldst thou know," he made answer, "that to suffer a second quarry to turn thee from thy first is oft-times to lose both."

"Verily, Jack, I conceive not thy meaning."

"Why, look on yon last piece. It begins with thee coming home from vespers. Then it flieth to me, to the potter and his glasses, to the knavery of his charges, and cometh back to the man whom thou didst meet coming forth of the door—whom it hath no sooner touched, than it is off again to the cold even; then comest thou into the Queen's lodging, and down 'grees' (degrees, that is, stairs) once more to the landlord's bill. Do, prithee, keep to one heron till thou hast bagged him."

"*Ha, chétife!*" cried I. "Must I have firstly, secondly, thirdly, yea, up to thirty-seventhly, like old Father Edison's homilies?"

"Better so," saith he, "than to course three hares together and catch none."

"I'll catch mine hare yet, as thou shall see," saith I.

"Be it done. Gee up!" saith he. (Note 9).

Well, up came I into the Queen's antechamber, where were sat Dame Elizabeth, and Dame Isabel de Lapyoun, and Dame Joan de Vaux, and little Meliora. And right as I came in at the door, Dame Joan dropped her sewing off her knee, and saith—

"Lack-a-day! I am aweary of living in this world!"

"Well, if so," saith Dame Elizabeth, peacefully waxing her thread, "you had best look about for a better."

"Nay!" quoth she, "how to get there?"

"Ask my Lord of Winchester," saith Dame Isabel.

"I shall lack the knowledge ill ere I trouble him," she made answer. "Is it he with the Queen this even?"

"There's none with the Queen!" quoth Dame Isabel, as sharp as if she should have snapped her head off.

Dame Joan looked up in some astonishment.

"Dear heart!" said she, "I thought I heard voices in her chamber."

"There was one with her," answereth Meliora, "when I passed the door some minutes gone."

"Maybe the visitor is gone," said I. "As I came in but now, I met one coming forth."

"Who were it, marry?" quoth Dame Joan.

"It was none of the household," said I. "A tall, personable man, wrapped in a great cloak, wherewith he hid his face; but whether it were from me or from the November even, that will I not say."

"There hath been none such here," saith Dame Elizabeth.

"Not in this chamber," saith Meliora.

"Meliora Servelady!" Dame Isabel made answer, "who gave thee leave to join converse with thy betters?" (Note 10).

The sub-damsel looked set down for a minute, but nought ever daunted her for long. She was as pert a little maid as ever I knew, and but little deserved her name of Meliora. (Ah me, is this another hare? Have back.)

"There hath been none of any sort come to the Queen to-day," said Dame Isabel, in so angered a tone that I began at once to marvel who had come of whom she feared talk.

"Nay, but there so hath!" makes response Dame Joan: "have you forgot Master Almoner that was with her this morrow nigh an hour touching his accounts?—and Ralph Richepois with his lute after dinner?"

"Marry, and the Lady Gibine, Prioress of Oremont," addeth Dame Elizabeth.

"And the two Beguines—" began Meliora; but she ended not, for Dame Isabel boxed her ears.

"Ay, and Jack Bonard, that she sent with letters to the Queen of France," saith Dame Joan.

"Yea, and Ivo le Breton came a-begging, yon poor old man that had served her when a child," made answer Dame Elizabeth.

"And Ma—" Poor Meliora got no further, for Dame Isabel gave her a buffet on the side of her head that nigh knocked her off the form. I could not but think that some part of that buffet was owing to us three, though Meliora had it all. But what so angered Dame Isabel, that might I not know.

At that time came the summons to supper, so the matter ended. But as supper was passing, Dame Joan de Vaux, by whom I sat, with Master Almoner on mine other hand, saith to me—

"Pray you, Dame Cicely, have you any guess who it were that you met coming forth?"

"I have, and I have not," said I. "There was that in his face which I knew full well, yet cannot I bethink me of his name."

"It was not Master Madefray, trow?"

"In no wise: a higher man than he, and of fairer hair."

"Not a priest neither?"

"Nay, certes."

"Leave not to sup your soup, Dame Cicely, nor show no astonishment, I pray, while I ask yet a question. Was it—Sir Roger the Mortimer of Ludlow?"

For all Dame Joan's warnful words, I nigh dropped my spoon, and I never knew how the rest of the soup tasted.

"Wala wa!" said I, under my breath, "but I do believe it was he."

"I saw him," saith she, quietly. "And take my word for it, friend—that man cometh for no good."

"Marry!" cried I in some heat, "how dare he come nigh the Queen at all? he, a banished man! Without, soothly, he came humbly to entreat her intercession with the King for his pardon. But e'en then, he might far more meetly have sent his petition by some other. Verily, I marvel she would see him!"

"Do you so?" saith Dame Joan in that low quiet voice. "So do not I. She will see him yet again, or I mistake much."

"*Ha, chétife!*" I made answer. "It is full well we be on our road back to Paris, for there at least will he not dare to come."

"Not dare?"

"Surely not, for the King of France, which himself hath banished him, should never suffer it."

Dame Joan helped herself to a roasted plover with a smile. When the sewer was gone, quoth she—

"I think, Dame Cicely, you know full little whether of Sir Roger de Mortimer or of the King of France. For the last, he is as easily blinded a man as you may lightly see; and if our Queen his sister told him black was white, he should but suppose that she saw better than he. And for the other—is there aught in all this world, whether as to bravery or as to wickedness, that Sir Roger de Mortimer would *not* dare?"

"Dear heart!" cried I. "I made account we had done with men of that order."

"You did?" Dame Joan's tone, and the somewhat dry smile which went with it, said full plainly, "In no wise."

"Well, soothly we had enough and to spare!" quoth I. "There was my Lord of Lancaster—God rest his soul!—and Sir Piers de Gavaston (if he were as ill man as some said)."

"He was not a saint, I think," she said: "yet could I name far worser men than he."

"And my sometime Lord of Warwick," said I, "was no saint likewise, or I mistake."

"Therein," saith she, "have you the right."

"Well," pursued I, "all they be gone: and soothly, I had hoped there were no more such left."

"Then should there be no original sin left," she made answer; "yea, and Sathanas should be clean gone forth of this world."

The rest of the converse I mind not, but that last sentence tarried in my mind for many a day, and hath oft-times come back to me touching other matters.

We reached Loure on Saint Martin's Day (November 11th), and Paris the next morrow. There found we the Bishops of Winchester and Exeter, (Stratford and Stapleton), whom King Edward had sent over to join the Queen's Council. Now I never loved overmuch neither of these Reverend Fathers, though it were for very diverse causes. Of course, being priests, they were holy men; but I misdoubt if either were perfect man apart from his priesthood—my Lord of Winchester more in especial. Against my Lord of Exeter have I but little to say; he was fumish (irritable, captious) man, but no worse. But my Lord of Winchester did I never trust, nor did I cease to marvel that man could. As to King Edward, betray him to his enemies to-day, and he should put his life in your hands again to-morrow: never saw I man like to him, that no experience would learn mistrust. Queen Isabel trusted few: but of them my said Lord of Winchester was one. I have noted at times that they which be untrue themselves be little given to trust other. She trusted none save them she had tried: and she had tried this Bishop, not once nor twice. He never brake faith with her; but with King Edward he brake it a score of times twice told, and with his son that is now King belike. I wis not whether at this time the Queen was ready to put affiance in him; I scarce think she was: for she shut both Bishops out of her Council from the day she came to Paris. But not at this time, nor for long after did I guess what it signified.

November was nigh run out, when one morrow Dame Joan de Vaux brought word that the Queen, being a-cold, commanded her velvet mantle taken to her cabinet: and I, as the dame in waiting then on duty, took the same to her. I found her sat of a chair of carven wood, beside the brasier, and two gentlemen of the other side of the hearth. Behind her chair Dame Elizabeth waited, and I gave the mantle to her to cast over the Queen's shoulders. The gentlemen stood with their backs to the light, and I paid little note to them at first, save to see that one was a priest: but as I went about to go forth, the one that was not a priest turned his face, and I perceived to mine amaze that it was Sir Roger de Mortimer. Soothly, it needed all my courtly self-command that I should not cry out when I beheld him. Had I followed the prompting of mine own heart, I should have cried, "Get thee gone, thou banished traitor!" He, who had returned unlicenced from Scotland ere the war was over, in the time of old King Edward of Westminster; that had borne arms against his son, then King, under my Lord of Lancaster; that, having his life spared, and being but sent to the Tower, had there plotted to seize three of the chief fortresses of the Crown—namely, the said Tower, and the Castles of Windsor and Wallingford,—and had thereupon been cast for death, and only spared through the intercession of the Queen and the Bishop of Hereford: yet, after all this, had he broken prison, bribing one of his keepers and drugging the rest, and was now a banished felon, in refuge over seas: *he* to dare so much as to breathe the same air with the wife of his Sovereign, with her that had been his advocate, and that knew all his treacheries! Could any worser insult to the Queen have been devised? But all at once, as I passed along the gallery, another thought came in upon me. What of her? who, knowing all this and more, yet gave leave for this man— not to kneel at her feet and cry her mercy—that had been grace beyond any reasonable hope: but suffered him to stand in her presence, to appear in her privy cabinet—nay, to act as though he were a noble appointed of her Council! Had she forgot all the past?

I travelled no further for that time. The time was to come when I should perceive that forgetfulness was all too little to account for her deeds.

That night, Dame Tiffany being appointed to the pallet, it so fell out that Dame Elizabeth, Dame Joan, and I, lay in the antechamber. We had but began to doff ourselves, and Dame Elizabeth was stood afore the mirror, a-combing of her long hair—and rare long hair it was, and of a fine colour (but I must not pursue the same, or Jack shall find in the hair an hare)— when I said to her—

"Dame Elizabeth, pray you tell me, were you in waiting when Sir Roger de Mortimer came to the Queen?"

"Ay," saith she, and combed away.

"And," said I, "with what excuse came he?"

"Excuse?" quoth she. "Marry, I heard none at all."

"None!" I cried, tarrying in the doffing of my subtunic. "Were you not ill angered to behold such a traitor?"

"Dame Cicely," saith she, slowly pulling the loose hairs forth of the comb, "if you would take pattern by me, and leave troubling yourself touching your neighbours' doings, you should have fewer griefs to mourn over."

Could the left sleeve of my subtunic, which I was then a-doffing, have spoke unto me, I am secure he should have 'plained that he met with full rough treatment at my hands.

"Good for you, Dame, an' you so can!" said I somewhat of a heat. "So long as my neighbours do well, I desire not to mell (meddle) nor make in their matters. But if they do ill—"

"Why, then do I desire it even less," saith she, "for I were more like to get me into a muddle. Mine own troubles be enough for me, and full too many."

"Dear heart! had you ever any?" quoth I.

"In very deed, I do ensure you," saith she, "for this comb hath one of his teeth split, and he doth not only tangle mine hair, but giveth me vile wrenches betimes, when I look not for them. And 'tis but a month gone, at Betesi (Béthizy), that I paid half-a-crown for him. The rogue cheated me, as my name is Bess. I could find in mine heart to give him a talking."

"Only a talking?" saith Dame Joan, and laughed. "You be happy woman, in good sooth, if your worsest trouble be a comb that hath his teeth split."

"Do but try him!" quoth Dame Elizabeth, and snorked (twisted, contorted) up her mouth, as the comb that instant moment came to a spot where her hair was louked (fastened) together. "Bless the comb!" saith she, and I guess she meant it but little. "Wala wa! Dame Joan, think you 'tis matter for laughter?"

"More like than greeting," (weeping), she made answer.

"Verily," said I, "but I see much worser matter for tears than your comb, Dame Elizabeth. Either the Queen is sore ill-usen of her brother, that such ill companions should be allowed near her, or else—"

Well for me, my lace snapped at that moment, and I ended not the sentence. When I was laid down beside Dame Joan, it came to me like a flash of lightning—"Or else—what?" And at that minute Dame Joan turned her on the pillows, and set her lips to mine ear.

"Dame Cicely," quoth she, "mine heart misdoubts me it is the 'or else.' Pray you, govern your tongue, and use your eyes in time to come. Trust not her in the red bed too much, and her in the green-hung chamber not at all."

The first was Dame Elizabeth, and the last Dame Isabel de Lapyoun, that lay in a chamber hung with green, with Dame Tiffany. I was secure she meant not the other, but to make certain I whispered the name, and she saith, "She."

I reckoned it not ill counsel, for mine own thoughts assented thereto, in especial as touched Dame Isabel.

After that day wherein Sir Roger de Mortimer was in the Queen's cabinet, I trow I kept mine eyes open.

For a few days he came and went: but scarce more than a sennight had passed ere I learned that he had come to dwell in Paris all out; and but little more time was spent when one even, Dame Isabel de Lapyoun came into our chamber as we were about to hie us abed, and saith she, speaking to none in especial, but to all—

"Sir Roger de Mortimer is made of the Prince's following, and shall as to-morrow take up his abode in the Queen's hostel."

"Dear heart!" saith Dame Elizabeth, making pause with one hand all wet, and in the other the napkin whereon she went about to dry it. "Well, no business of mine, trow."

I could not help to cry, "*Ha, chétife!*"

Dame Isabel made answer to neither the one nor the other, but marched forth of the door with her nose an inch higher than she came in. She was appointed to the pallet for that night, so we three lay all in our chamber.

"This passeth!" saith Dame Elizabeth, drying of her fingers, calm enough, on the napkin.

"Even as I looked for," saith Dame Joan, but her voice was not so calm. There was in it a note of grief (a tone of indignation).

"*I* ne'er trouble me to look for nought," quoth Dame Elizabeth. "What good, trow? Better to leave folks come and go, as they list, so long as they let (hinder) you not to come and go likewise."

"I knew not you were one of Cain's following, Dame Bess."

"Cain's following!" saith she, drawing off her fillet. "Who was Cain, trow? Wala wa! but if my fillet be not all tarnished o' this side. I would things would go right!"

"So would I, and so did not Cain," Dame Joan makes answer. "Who was he, quotha? Why, he that slew his brother Abel."

"Oh, some of those old Scripture matters? I wis nought o' those folks. But what so? I have not slain my brother, nor my sister neither."

"It looks as though your brother and your sister too might go astray and be lost ere you should soil your fingers and strain your arms a-pulling them forth."

"Gramercy! Every man for himself!" saith Dame Elizabeth, a-pulling off her hood. "Now, here's a string come off! Alway my luck! If a body might but bide in peace—"

"And never have no troubles, nor strings come off, nor buttons broke, nor stitches come loose—" adds Dame Joan, a-laughing.

"Right so—man might have a bit of piece of man's life, then. Why, look you, the string is all chafen, that it is not worth setting on anew; and so much as a yard of red ribbon have I not. I must needs don my hood of green of Louvaine."

She said it in a voice which might have gone with the direst calamity that could befall.

"Dame Elizabeth de Mohun, you be a full happy woman!"

"What will the woman say next?"

"That somewhat hangeth on what you may next say."

"Well, what I next say is that I am full ill-used to have in one hour a tarnished fillet and a broken string, and—Saint Lucy love us! here be two of my buttons gone!"

I could thole no longer, and forth brake I in laughter. Dame Joan joined with me, and some ado had we to peace Dame Elizabeth, that was sore grieved by our laughing.

"Will you leave man be?" quoth she. "They be right (real) silver buttons, and not one more have I of this pattern: I ensure you they cost me four shillings the dozen at John Fairhair's in London (a London goldsmith). I'll be bound I can never match them without I have them wrought of set purpose. Deary, deary me!"

"Well!" saith Dame Joan, "I may break my heart afore I die, but I count it will not be over buttons."

"Not o'er your buttons, belike," saith Dame Elizabeth. "And here, this very day, was Hilda la Vileyne at me, begging and praying me that I would pay her charges for that hood of scarlet wrought with gold and pearls the which I had made last year when I was here with the Queen. Truly, I forgat the same at that time; and now I have not the money to mine hand. But deary me, the pitiful tale she told!—of her mother ill, and her two poor little sisters without meet raiment for winter, and never a bit of food nor fuel in the house—I marvel what maids would be at, to make up such tales!"

"It was not true, trow?"

"True?" saith Dame Elizabeth, pulling off her rings. "It might be true as Damascus steel, for aught I know. But what was that to me? I lacked the money for somewhat that liked me better than to buy fuel for a parcel of common folks like such. They be used to lack comforts, and not I. And I hate to hear such stories, belike. Forsooth, man might as well let down a black curtain over the window on a sunshine day as be plagued with like tales when he would fain be jolly. I sent her off in hot haste, I can tell you."

"With the money?"

"The saints be about us! Not I."

"And the little maids may greet them asleep for lack of food?" saith Dame Joan.

"How wis I there be any such? I dare be bound it was all a made-up tale to win payment."

"You went not to see?"

"I go to see! I! Dame Joan, you be verily—"

"I am verily one for whom Christ our Lord deigned to die on the bitter rood, and so is Hilda la Vileyne. Tell me but where she dwelleth, and *I* will go to see if the tale be true."

"Good lack! I carry not folks' addresses in mine head o' that fashion. Let be; she shall be here again in a day or twain. She hath granted me little peace these last ten days."

"And you verily wis not where she dwelleth?"

"I wis nought thereabout, and an' I did I would never tell you to-night. Dear heart, do hie you abed and sleep in peace, and let other folks do the like! I never harry me with other men's troubles. Good even!"

And Dame Elizabeth laid her down and happed the coverlet about her, and was fast asleep in a few minutes.

The next even, when we came into hall for supper, was Sir Roger de Mortimer on the dais, looking as though the world belonged to him. Maybe he thought it was soon to do the same; and therein was he not deceived. The first day, he sat in his right place, at the high table, after the knights and barons of France whom the King of France had appointed to the charge of our Queen: but not many days were over ere he crept up above them—and then above the bishops themselves, until at last he sat on the left hand of Queen Isabel, my Lord of Chester being at her right. But this first night he kept his place.

Note 1. Neuilly. Queen Isabelle's scribe is responsible for the orthography in this and subsequent places.

Note 2. The old Palace of the French Kings, the remaining part of which is now known as the Conciergerie.

Note 3. September 12th.

Note 4. Cakes made with honey. Three pennyworth were served daily at the royal table.

Note 5. Wardrobe Account, 19 Edward the Second, 25/15.

Note 6. Rheims and Soissons. An idea of the difficulties of travelling at that time maybe gathered from the entry of "Guides for the Queen between Paris and Rheims, 18 shillings."

Note 7. The vessel containing the oil wherewith the Kings of France were anointed, oil and ampulla being fabled to have come from Heaven.

Note 8. 2 pounds 13 shillings 4 pence.—Wardrobe Account, 19 Edward the Second, 25/15.

Note 9. Gee. This is one of the few words in our tongue directly derivable from the ancient Britons.

Note 10. "Avice Serueladi" occurs on the Close Roll for 1308.

Chapter 3
How Dame Elizabeth's Bill was paid

"And yet it never was in my soul
To play so ill a part:
But evil is wrought by want of thought
As well as by want of heart."

Thomas Hood.

As I came forth of hall, after supper, that even, and we were entered into the long gallery whereinto the Queen's degrees opened, I was aware of a full slender and white-faced young maid, that held by the hand a small (little child) of mayhap five or six years. She looked as though she waited for some man. The Queen had tarried in hall to receive a messenger, and Dame Joan de Vaux was in waiting, so Dame Elizabeth, Dame Isabel, Dame Tiffany, and I were those that passed along the gallery. Dame Isabel and Dame Tiffany the maid let pass, with no more than a pitiful look at the former, that deigned her no word: but when Dame Elizabeth came next, on the further side, I being betwixt, the maid stepped forward into the midst, as if to stay her. Her thin hands were clasped over her bosom, and the pitifullest look ever I saw was in her eyes.

"*Dame, ayez pitié!*" was all she said; and it was rather breathed than spoken.

"Bless us, Saint Mary!—art thou here again?" quoth Dame Elizabeth of a testier fashion than she was wont. "Get thee gone, child; I have no time to waste. Dear heart, what a fuss is here over a crown or twain! Dost think thy money is lost? I will pay thee when it liketh me; I have not my purse to mine hand at this minute."

And on she walked, brushing past the maid. I tarried.

"Are you Hilda la Vileyne?" I said unto her.

"Dame, that is my name, and here is my little sister Iolande. She hath not tasted meat (food) this day, nor should not yesterday, had not a kindly gentleman, given me a denier to buy soup. But truly I do not ask for charity— only to be paid what I have honestly earned."

"And hadst thou some soup yesterday?"

"Yes—no—Oh, I am older; I can wait better than the little ones. The mother is sick: she and the babes must not wait. It does not signify for me."

Oh, how hungered were those great eyes, that looked too large for the white face! The very name of soup seemed to have brought the craving look therein.

I turned to the small. "Tell me, Iolande, had Hilda any of the soup yesterday?"

"No," said the child; "I and Madeleine drank it, every drop, that our mother left."

"And had Hilda nothing?"

"There was a mouldy crust in the cupboard," said the child. "It had dropped behind the cup, and Hilda found it when she took the cup down. We could not see it behind. We can only just reach to take the cup down, and put it up again. That was what Hilda had, and she wiped the cup with one end of it."

"The cup that had held the soup?"

"Yes, surely," said the child, with a surprised look. "We only have one,—does not Madame know?"

"It is an esquelle (porringer; a shallow bowl), not a cup," said Hilda, reddening a little: "the child hardly knows the difference."

I felt nearhand as though I could have twisted Dame Elizabeth's neck for meat for those children.

"And are you, in good sooth, so ill off as that?" said I. "No meat, and only one esquelle in all the house?"

"Dame," said Hilda meekly, as in excuse, "our father was long ill, and now is our mother likewise; and many things had to be sold to pay the apothecary, and also while I waited on them could I not be at work; and my little sisters are not old enough to do much. But truly it is only these last few weeks that we have been quite so ill off as to have no food, and I have been able to earn but a few deniers now and then—enough to keep us alive, but no more."

"How much oweth you Dame Elizabeth?" said I.

"Dame, it is seven crowns for the hood I wrought, and three more for a girdle was owing aforetime, and now four for kerchiefs broidering: it is fourteen crowns in all. I should not need to ask charity if I could but be paid my earnings. The apothecary said our mother was sick rather from sorrow and want of nourishment than from any malady; and if the good Dame would pay me, I might not only buy fresh matter for my work, but perchance get food that would make my mother well—at least well enough to sew, and then we should have two pairs of hands instead of one. I do not beg, Dame!"

She louted low as she spoke, and took her little sister again by the hand. "Come, Iolande; we keep Madame waiting."

"But hast thou got no money?" pleaded the barne. "Thou saidst to Madeleine that we should bring some supper back. Thou didst, Hilda!"

"I did, darling," allowed her sister, looking a little ashamed. "I could not peace the babe else, and—I hoped we should."

I could bear no more. The truth of those maids' story was in the little one's bitter disappointment, and in poor Hilda's hungry eyes. Eyes speak sooth, though lips be false.

"Come," said I. "I pray you, tarry but one moment more. You shall not lose by it."

"We are at Madame's service," said Hilda.

I ran up degrees as fast as ever I could. As the saints would have it, that very minute I oped the door, was Dame Elizabeth haling forth silver in her lap, and afore her stood the jeweller's man awaiting to be paid. Blame me who will, I fell straight on those gold pieces and silver crowns.

"Fourteen crowns, Dame Elizabeth!" quoth I, all scant of breath. "Quick! give me them—for Hilda la Vileyne—and if no, may God forgive you, for I never will!"

Soothly, had the Archangel Raphael brake into the chamber and demanded fourteen crowns, Dame Elizabeth could have gazed on him no more astonied than she did on me, Cicely, that she had seen nearhand every day of her life for over a dozen years. I gave her leave to look how it listed her. From the coins in her lap I counted forth nine nobles and a French crown, and was half-way down degrees again ere she well knew what I would be at. If I had had to pay her back every groat out of mine own purse—nay, verily, if I had stood to be beheaden for it—I would have had that money for Hilda la Vileyne that night.

They stood where I had left them, by the door of the long gallery, near the *porte-cochère*, but now with them was a third—mine own Jack, that had but now come in from the street, and the child knew him again, as she well showed.

"O Hilda!"

I heard her say, as I came running down swiftly—for I was dread afraid Dame Elizabeth should overtake me and snatch back the money—and I might have spared my fears, for had I harried the Queen's crown along with her crowns, no such a thing should ever have come in her head—"O Hilda!" saith the child, "see here the good Messire who gave us the denier to buy soup."

I might have guessed it was Jack. He o'erheard the child, and stayed him to pat her on the head.

"Well, little one, was the soup good?"

"So good, Messire! But Hilda got none—not a drop."

"Hush!" saith Hilda; but the child would go on.

"None at all! why, how was that?" saith Jack, looking at Hilda.

I answered for her. "The sick mother and helpless babes had the soup," said I; "and this brave maid was content with a mouldy crust. Jack, a word in thine ear."

"Good!" saith he, when I had whispered to him. "Go thy ways, sweetheart, and so do."

"Nay, there is no need to go any ways," said I, "for here cometh Meliora down degrees, and of a truth I somewhat shrink from facing Dame Elizabeth after my robbery of her, any sooner than must be—Meliora, child, wilt run above an instant, and fetch my blue mantle and the thicker of mine hoods?"

Meliora ran up straightway; for though she was something too forward, and could be pert when she would, yet was she good-natured enough when kindly used. I turned to Hilda.

"Hold thy palm, my maid," said I. "Here is the money the lady ought (owed) thee." And I haled into her hand the gold pieces and the silver crown.

Verily, I could have greeted mine eyes sore to see what then befell. The barne capered about and clapped her hands, crying, "Supper! supper! now we shall have meat!" but Hilda covered her eyes with her void hand, and sobbed as though her heart should break.

"God Almighty bless you, kind Dame!" said she, when as she could speak again. "I was nearhand in utter mishope (nearly in despair). Now my mother can have food and physic, and maybe, if it please God, she shall recover. May I be forgiven, but I was beginning to think the good God cared not for poor folks like us, or maybe that there was no God to care at all."

Down came Meliora with my hood and mantle, which I cast all hastily about me, and then said I to Hilda—

"My maid, I would fain see thy mother; maybe I could do her some good; and mine husband here will go with us for a guard. Lead on."

"God bless you!" she said yet again. "He *must* have heard me." The last words were spoken lowly, as to herself.

We went forth of the great gates, and traversed the good streets, and came into divers little alleys that skirt the road near Saint Denis' Gate. In one of these Hilda turned into an house—a full poor hut it was—and led me up degrees into a poor chamber, whither the child ran gleefully afore. Jack left me at the door, he and I having covenanted, when we whispered together, what he should do whilst I visited Hilda's mother.

Little Iolande ran forward into the chamber, crying, "Supper! supper! Mother and Madeleine, Hilda has money for supper!"

What I then beheld was a poor pallet, but ill covered with a thin coverlet, whereon lay a pale, weak woman, that seemed full ill at ease, yet I thought scarce so much sick of body as sick at heart and faint with fasting and sorrow. At the end of the pallet sat a child something elder than Iolande, but a child still. There was no form in the chamber, but Hilda brought forward an old box, whereon she cast a clean apron, praying me to sit, and to pardon them that this should be the best they had to offer. I sat me down, making no matter thereof, for in very deed I was full of pity for these poor creatures.

The mother, as was but like, took me for Dame Elizabeth, and began to thank me for having paid my debts—at long last, she might have said. But afore I could gainsay it, Hilda saith warmly—

"Oh no, Mother! This is not the lady that ought the money. Madame here is good—so good! and that lady—she has no heart in her, I think."

"Not very good, Hilda," said I, laughing, "when I fell on the dame that ought thee the money, and fairly wrenched it from her, whether she would or no. Howbeit," I continued to the poor woman, "*I* will be good to you, if I can."

By bits and scraps I pulled her story forth of her mouth. It was no uncommon tale: a sickly wife and a selfish husband,—a deserted, struggling wife and mother—and then a penniless widow, with no friends and poor health, that could scant make shift to keep body and soul together, whether for herself or the children. The husband had come home at last but to be a burden and sorrow—to be nursed through a twelve months' sickness and then to die; and what with the weariness and lack of all comfort, the poor widow fell sick herself soon after, and Hilda, the young maid, had kept matters a-going, as best she might, ever sithence.

I comforted the poor thing to my little power; told her that I would give Hilda some work to do (and pay her for it), and that I would come and see her by times whilst the Queen should abide in Paris; but that when she went away must I go likewise, and it might be all suddenly, that I could not give her to wit. Hilda had sent the children forth to buy food, and there were but her and her mother. Mine husband was longer in return than I looked for.

"My maid," said I to Hilda, "prithee tell me a thing. What didst thou signify by saying to thyself, right as we set forth from the Palace, that God must have heard thee?"

A great wave of colour passed over her face and neck.

"Dame," she said, "I will speak soothliness. It was partly because I had prayed for money to buy food and physic: but partly also, because I was afraid of something, and I had asked the good God to keep it away from me. When you said that you and Messire would condescend to come with me, it delivered me from my fear. The good God must have heard me, for nobody else knew."

"Afraid!" said I. "Whereof, my maid? Was it the porter's great dog? He is a gentle beast as may be, and would never touch thee. What could harm thee in the Queen's Palace?"

The wave of colour came again. "Madame does not know," she said, in a low voice. "There are men worse than brutes: but such great ladies do not see it. One stayed me and spoke to me the night afore. I was afraid he might come again, and there was no one to help me but the good Lord. So I called to Him to be my guard, for there was none else; and I think He sent two of His angels with me."

Mine own eyes were full, no less than Hilda's.

"May the good Lord guard thee ever, poor maid!" said I. "But in very sooth, I am far off enough from an angel. Here cometh one something nearer thereto"—for I heard Jack's voice without. "But tell me, dost thou know who it was of whom thou wert afraid?"

"I only know," she said, "that his squire bare a blue and white livery, guarded in gold. I heard not his name."

"Verily!" said I to myself, "such gentlemen be fair company for Dame Isabel the Queen!"

For I could have no doubt that poor Hilda's enemy was that bad man, Sir Roger de Mortimer. Howbeit, I said no more, for then oped the door, and in came Jack, with a lad behind, bearing a great basket. Jack's own arms were full of fardels (parcels), which he set down in a corner of the chamber, and bade the lad empty the basket beside, which was charged with firewood, "There!" saith he, "they be not like to want for a day or twain, poor souls! Come away, Sissot; we have earned a night's rest."

"Messire!" cried the faint voice of the poor woman. "Messire is good as an angel from Heaven! But surely Messire has not demeaned himself to carry burdens—and for us!"

She seemed nearhand frightened at the thought.

"Nay, good woman," saith Jack, merrily—"no more than the angel that carried the cruse of water for the Prophet Elias. Well-a-day! securely I can carry a fardel without tarnishing my spurs? I would I might never do a worse deed."

"Amen!" said I, "for both of us."

We bade the woman and Hilda good even, and went forth, followed by blessings till we were in the very street: and not till then would I say—

"Jack, thou art the best man ever lived, but I would thou hadst a little more care for appearances. Suppose Sir Edmund or Master de Oxendon had seen thee!"

"Well?" saith Jack, as calm as a pool in a hollow. "Suppose they had."

"Why, then should they have laughed thee to scorn."

"Suppose they did?"

"Jack! Dost thou nothing regard folks' thoughts of thee?"

"Certes. I regard thine full diligently."

"But other folks, that be nought to thee, I would say."

"If the folks be nought to me, wherefore should the thoughts be of import? Securely, good wife, but very little. I shall sleep the sweeter for those fardels: and I count I should sleep none the worser if man laughed at me. The blessing of the poor and the blessing of the Lord be full apt to go together: and dost thou reckon I would miss that—yea, so much as one of them—out of regard for that which is, saith Solomon, '*sonitum spinarum sub olla*'? (Ecclesiastes chapter seven, verse 6). *Ha, jolife!* let the thorns crackle away, prithee; they shall not burn long."

"Jack," said I, "thou *art* the best man ever lived!"

"Rhyme on, my fair *trouvere*," quoth he. (Troubadour. Their lays were usually legends and fictitious tales.) "But, Sissot, to speak sooth, I will tell thee, if thou list to hearken, what it is keepeth my steps from running into many a by-way, and mine heart from going astray after many a flower sown of Satan in my path."

"Do tell me, Jack," said I.

"There be few days in my life," saith he, "that there cometh not up afore mine eyes that Bar whereat I shall one day stand, and that Book out of the which all my deeds shall be read afore men and angels. And I have some concern for the thoughts of them that look on, that day, rather than this. Many a time—ay, many a time twice told—in early morn or in evening twilight, have I looked up into heaven, and the thought hath swept o'er me like a fiery breeze—'What if our Lord be coming this minute?' Dost thou reckon, Sissot, that man to whom such thoughts be familiar friends, shall be oft found sitting in the alebooth, or toying with frothy vanities? I trow not."

"But, Jack!" cried I, letting all else drop, "is that all real to thee?"

"Real, Sissot? There is not another thing as real in life."

I burst forth. I could not help it.

"O Jack, Jack! Don't go and be a monk!"

"Go and be a monk!" saith Jack, with an hearty laugh. "Why, Wife, what bees be in thine hood? I thought I was thine husband."

"So thou art, the saints be thanked," said I. "But thou art so good, I am sore afraid thou wilt either die or be a monk."

"I'll not be a monk, I promise thee," quoth he. "I am not half good enough, nor would I lose my Sissot. As to dying, be secure I shall not die an hour afore God's will is: and the Lord hath much need of good folks to keep this bad world sweet. I reckon we may be as good as we can with reasonable safety. I'll try, if thou wilt."

So I did, and yet do: but I shall never be match to Jack.

Well, by this time we had won back to the Queen's lodging; and at foot of degrees I bade good-night to Jack, being that night appointed to the pallet—a business I never loved. I was thinking on Jack's last words, as I went up, and verily had for the nonce forgat that which went afore, when all at once a voice saith in mine ear—

"Well, Dame Cicely! Went you forth in such haste lest you should be clapped into prison for stealing? Good lack, but mine heart's in my mouth yet! Were you wood (mad), or what ailed you?"

"Dame Elizabeth," said I, as all came back on me, "I have been to visit Hilda's mother."

"Dear heart! And what found you? Was she a-supping on goose and leeks? That make o' folks do alway feign to be as poor as Job, when their coffers be so full the lid cannot be shut. You be young, Dame Cicely, and know not the world."

"Maybe," said I. "But if you will hearken me, I will tell you what I found."

"Go to, then," saith she, as she followed me into our chamber. "Whate'er you found, you left me too poor to pay the jeweller. I would fain have had a sapphire pin more than I got, but your raid on my purse disabled me thereof. The rogue would give me no credit."

"Hear but my tale," said I, "and if when it be told you regret your sapphire pin, I beseech you say so."

So I told her in plain words, neither 'minishing nor adding, how I had found them, and the story I had heard from the poor woman. She listened, cool enough at first, but ere I made an end the water stood in her eyes.

"*Ha, chétife!*" said she, when I stayed me. "I'll pay the maid another time. Trust me, Dame Cicely, I believed not a word. If you had been cheated as oft—! Verily, I am sorry I sent not man to see how matters stood with them. Well, I am fain you gave her the money, after all. But, trust me, you took my breath away!"

"And my own belike," said I.

I think Hilda and hers stood not in much want the rest of that winter. But whenever she came with work for me, either Margaret my maid, or Jack's old groom, a sober man and an ancient, walked back with her.

Meantime Sir Roger de Mortimer played first viol in the Court minstrelsy. Up and yet higher up he crept, till he could creep no further, as I writ a few leaves back. On the eve of Saint Pancras was crowned the new Queen of France in the Abbey of Saint Denis, which is to France as Westminster Abbey to us: and there ramped my Lord of Mortimer in the very suite of the Queen herself, and in my Lord of Chester's own livery. Twice-banished traitor, he appeared in the self presence of the King that had banished him, and of the wife of his own natural Prince, to whom he had done treason of the deepest dye. And not one voice said him nay.

Thus went matters on till the beginning of September, 1326. The Queen abode at Paris; the King of France made no sign: our King's trusty messenger, Donald de Athole, came and went with letters (and if it were not one of his letters the Queen dropped into the brasier right as I came one day into her chamber, I marvel greatly); but nought came forth that we her ladies heard.

On the even of the fifth of September, early, came Sir John de Ostrevant to the Palace, and had privy speech of the Queen—none being thereat but her confessor and Dame Isabel de Lapyoun: and he was scarce gone forth when, as we sat in our chamber a-work, the Queen herself looked in and called Dame Elizabeth forth.

I thought nought of it. I turned down hem, and cut off some threads, and laid down scissors, and took up my needle to thread afresh—in the Hotel de Saint Pol at Paris. And that needle was not threaded but in the Abbey of Saint Edmund's Bury in Suffolk, twenty days after. Yet if man had told me it should so be, I had felt ready to laugh him to scorn. Ah me, what feathers we be, that a breath from God Almighty can waft hither or thither at His will!

Never but that once did I see Dame Elizabeth to burst into a chamber. And when she so did, I was in such amaze thereat that I fair gasped to see it.

"Good lack!" cried I, and stared on her.

"Well may you say it!" quoth she. "Lay by work, all of you, and make you ready privily in all haste for journeying by night. Lose not a moment."

"Mary love us!" cries Isabel de la Helde. "Whither?"

"Whither the Queen's will is. Hold your tongues, and make you ready."

We lay that night—and it was not till late—in the town of Sessouns, in the same lodging the Queen had before, at Master John de Gyse's house. The next night we lay at Peronne, and the third we came to Ostrevant.

Dame Isabel told us the reason of this sudden flight. The Queen had heard that her brother the King of France—who for some time past had been very cool and distant towards her—had a design to seize upon her and deliver her a prisoner to King Edward: and Sir John of Hainault, Count of Ostrevant, who came to bring her this news, offered her a refuge in his Castle of Ostrevant. I believed this tale when Dame Isabel told it: I have no faith in it now. What followed did away entirely therewith, and gave me firm belief that it was nothing save an excuse to get away in safety and without the King of France's knowledge. Be it how it may, Sir Roger de Mortimer came with her.

We were not many days at Ostrevant: only long enough for the Count to raise his troops, and then, when all was ready, the Queen embarked for England. On the 22nd of September we came ashore at Orwell, and had full ill lodging; none having any shelter save the Queen herself, for whom her knights ran up a shed of driftwood, hung o'er with carpets. Never had I so discomfortous a night—the sea tossing within a few yards, and the wind roaring in mine ears, and the spray all-to beating over me as I lay on the beach, lapped in a mantle. I was well pleased the next morrow, when the Queen, whose rest had been little, gave command to march forward to Bury. But afore we set forth, come nearhand an army of peasants into the presence, 'plaining of the Queen's officers, that had taken their cows, chickens, and fruits, and paid not a penny. The Queen had them all brought afore her, and with her own hands haled forth the money due to each one, bidding them bring all oppressions to her own ears, and straitly commanding her officers that they should take not so much as an egg without payment. By this means she won all the common people to her side, and they were ready to set their lives in pledge for her truth and honour.

At that time I was but little aware how matters verily stood. I said to Dame Joan de Vaux that the Queen showed her goodness hereby—for though I knew the Mortimer by then to be ill man, I wist not that she knew it, and reckoned her yet as innocent and beguiled woman.

"Doth she so?" answered Dame Joan. "How many grapes may man gather of a bramble?"

"Nay!" said I, scarce perceiving her intent, "but very grapes come not of brambles."

"Soothly," saith she: "neither do very brambles bear grapes."

Three days the Queen tarried at Bury: then, with banners flying, she marched on toward Essex. I thought it strange that even she should march with displayed banners, seeing the King was not of her company: but I reckoned she had his order, and was acting as his deputy. Elsewise had it been dread treason (Note 1), even in her. I was confirmed in my thought when my Lord of Lancaster, the King's cousin, and my Lord of Norfolk, the King's brother, came to meet her and joined their troops to her company; and yet more when the Archbishop of Dublin, and the Bishops of Hereford, Lincoln, and Ely, likewise joined them to her. Verily, such holy men could not countenance treason.

Truth enough: but that which was untrue was not the treason, but the holiness of these Caiaphases.

And now began that woeful Dolorous Way, which our Lord King Edward trod after his Master Christ. But who knoweth whither a strange road shall lead him, until he be come to the end thereof? I wis well that many folk have said unto us—Jack and me—since all things were made plain, How is it ye saw not aforetime, and wherefore followed ye the Queen thus long? They saw not aforetime, no more than we; but now that all is open, up come they with wagging heads and snorkilling noses, and—

"Verily, we were sore to blame for not seeing through the mist"—the mist through the which, when it lay thick, no man saw. *Ha, chétife!* I could easily fall to prophesying, myself, when all is over. Could we have seen what lay at the end of that Dolorous Way, should any true and loyal man have gone one inch along it?

And who was like to think, till he did see, what an adder the King nursed in his bosom? Most men counted her a fair white dove, all innocent and childlike: that did I not. I did see far enough, for all the mist, to see she was no child in that fashion; yet children love mischief well enough betimes; and I counted her, if not white, but grey—not the loathly black fiend that she was at the last seen to be. I saw many a thing I loved not, many a thing I would not have done in her place, many a thing that I but half conceived, and feared to be ill deed—but there ended my seeing. I thought she was caught within the meshes of a net, and I was sorry she kept not thereout. But I never guessed that the net was spread by her own hands.

My mother, Dame Alice de Lethegreve, I think, saw clearer than I did: but it was by reason she loved more,—loved him who became the sacrifice, not the miserable sinner for whose hate and wickedness he was sacrificed.

So soon as King Edward knew of the Queen's landing, which was by Michaelmas Eve at latest, he put forth a proclamation to all his lieges, wherein he bade them resist the foreign horde about to be poured upon England. Only three persons were to be received with welcome and honour: which was, the Queen herself, Edward her son (his father, in his just ire, named him not his son, neither as Earl of Chester), and the King's brother, the Lord Edmund of Kent. I always was sorry for my Lord of Kent; he was so full hoodwinked by the Queen, and never so much as guessed for one moment, that he acted a disloyal part. He was a noble gentleman, a kindly and a generous; not, maybe, the wisest man in the realm, and something too prone to rush after all that had the look of a noble deed, ere he gave himself time enough to consider the same. But if the world held no worser men at heart than he, it were marvellous better world than now.

One other thing did King Edward, which showed how much he had learned: he offered a great price of one thousand pounds (about 18,000 pounds, according to modern value), for the head of the Mortimer: and no sooner did the Queen hear thereof, than she offered double—namely, two thousand pounds—for the head of Sir Hugh Le Despenser—a man whose little finger was better worth two thousand than the Mortimer's head was worth one. Two days later, the King fortified the Tower, and appointed the Lord John of Eltham governor thereof; but he being only a child of ten years, the true governor was the Lady Alianora La Despenser, who was left in charge of the King's said son. And two days afore Saint Francis (October 2nd) he left the Tower, and set forth toward Wallingford, leaving the Bishop of Exeter to keep the City: truly a thankless business, for never could any man yet keep the citizens of London. Nor could he: for a fortnight was not over ere they rose in insurrection against the King's deputies, invested the Tower, wrenched the keys from the Constable, John de Weston, to whom the Lady Alianora had confided them, brought her out with the young Lord, and carried them to the Wardrobe—not without honour—and then returning, they seized on the Bishop, with two of his squires, and strake off their heads at the Standard in Chepe. And this will I say for the said Bishop, though he were not alway pleasant to deal withal, for he was very furnish—yet was he honest man, and loved his master, ay, and held to him in days when it was little profit so to do. And seeing how few honest men there be, that will hold on to the right when their profit lieth to the left, that is much to say.

With the King went Sir Hugh Le Despenser—I mean the younger, that was create Earl of Gloucester by reason of his marriage; for the Lady Alianora his wife was eldest of the three sisters that were coheirs of that earldom. And thereanent—well-a-day! how different folks do from that I should do in their place! I can never tell wherefore, when man doth ill, the penalty thereof should be made to run over on his innocent sons. Because Sir Hugh forfeited the earldom, wherefore passed it not to his son, that was loyal man and true, and one of the King's best councillors all his life? On the contrary part, it was bestowed on Sir Hugh de Audley, that wedded the Lady Margaret (widow of Sir Piers de Gavaston), that stood next of the three coheirs. And it seemeth me scarce just that Sir Hugh de Audley, that had risen up against King Edward of old time, and been prisoned therefor, and was at best but a pardoned rebel, should be singled out for one of the finest earldoms in England, and not Sir Hugh Le Despenser, whose it was of right, and to whose charge—save the holding of the Castle of Caerphilly against Queen Isabel, which was in very loyalty to his true lord King Edward—no fault at all could be laid. I would I had but the world to set right! Then should there be justice done, and every wrong righted, and all crooked ways put straight, and every man and woman made happy. Dear heart, what fair and good world were this, when I had made an end of—

Did man laugh behind me?

"Jack! Soothly, I thought it must be thou. What moveth thy laughter?"

"Dame Cicely de Chaucombe," saith he, essaying to look sober—which he managed but ill. "The Annals of Cicely, likewise; and the imaginings of Cicely in especial."

"Well, what now mispayeth (displeases) thee?" quoth I.

"There was once man," saith Jack, "thought as thou dost. And seeing that the hollyhocks in his garden were taller than the daisies, he bade his gardener with a scythe cut short the hollyhocks, that all the flowers should be but of one height."

"Well, what happed?" said I.

"Why, next day were there no hollyhocks. And then the hollyhock stems and the daisies both laid 'plaint of the gardener."

"Both?" said I.

"Both. They alway do."

"But what 'plaint had the daisies to offer?"

"Why, that they had not been pulled up to the height of the hollyhocks, be sure."

"But how could they so?"

"Miscontent hath no 'can' in his hornbook. Not what thou canst, but what he would, is his measure of justice."

"But justice is justice," said I—"not what any man would, but what is fair and even."

"Veriliest. But what is fair and even? If thou stand on Will's haw (hillock), the oak on thy right hand is the largest tree; if thou stand on Dick's, it shall be the beech on thy left. And thine ell-wand reacheth not. How then to measure?"

"But I would be on neither side," said I, "but right in the midst: so should I see even."

"Right in the midst, good wife, is where God standeth; and few men win there. There be few matters whereof man can see both to the top and to the bottom. Mostly, if man see the one end, then he seeth not the other. And that which man seeth not, how shall he measure? Without thou lay out to follow the judge which said that he would clearly man should leave to harry him with both sides of a matter. So long as he heard but the plaintiff, he could tell full well where the right lay; but after came the defendant, and put him all out, that he wist not on which side to give judgment. Maybe Judge Sissot should sit on the bench alongside of him."

"Now, Jack," said I, "thou laughest at me."

"Good discipline for thee, sweetheart," saith he, "and of lesser severity than faulting thee. But supposing the world lay in thine hands to set right, and even that thou hadst the power thereto, how long time dost think thy work should abide?"

"*Ha, chétife!*" cried I. "I ne'er bethought me of that."

"The world was set right once," quoth Jack, "by means of cold water, and well washed clean therein. But it tarried not long, as thou wist. Sin was not washed away; and Satan was not drowned in the Flood: and very soon thereafter were they both a-work again. Only one stream can wash the world to last, and that floweth right from the rood on Calvary."

"Yet there is enough," said I, "to wash the whole world."

"Verily. But how, if the world will not come and wash? 'He that will'— *qui vult*—'let him take water of life freely.' But he that is not athirst for the holy water, shall not have it forced down his throat against his will."

"How shall man come by the thirst, Jack, if he hath it not? For if the gift shall be given only to him that thirsteth for it, it seemeth me the thirst must needs be born ere we shall come for the water."

"Nay, sweetheart, we all desire happiness and wealth and honour; the mistake is that we be so ready to slake our thirst at the pools of muddy water which abound on every hand, rather than go to the fount of living water. We grasp at riches and honours and pleasures of this life: lo, here the blame, in that we are all athirst for the muddy pool, and have no desire for the holy water—for the gold of the royal mint stamped with the King's image, for the crown of everlasting life, for the bliss which shall endure unto all ages. We cry soothly for these things; but it is aswhasay, Give me happiness, but let it end early; give me seeming gold, but let it be only tinsel; give me a crown, but be it one that will fade away. Like a babe that will grip at a piece of tin whereon the sun shineth, and take no note of a golden ingot that lieth by in shadow."

"But who doth such things, Jack?"

"Thou and I, Sissot, unless Christ anoint our eyes that we see in sooth."

"Jack!" cried I, all suddenly, "as I have full many times told thee, thou art better man than many a monk."

"Now scornest thou at me," saith he. "How can I be perfect, that am wedded man? (Note 2.) Thou wist well enough that perfect men be only found among the contemplative, not among them that dwell in the world. Yet soothly, I reckon man may dwell in the world and love Christ, or he may dwell in cloister and be none of His."

Well, I know not how that may be; but this do I know, that never was there any Jack even to my Jack; and I am sore afraid that if I ever win into Heaven, I shall never be able to see Jack, for he shall be ten thousand mile nearer the Throne than I Cicely am ever like to be.

Note 1. At this time it was high treason for any subject to march with banners displayed, unless he acted as the King's representative by his distinct commission.

Note 2. The best men then living looked on the life of idle contemplation as the highest type of Christian life, to which no married man could attain.

Chapter 4
The Glamour of the Queen

"Hast thou beheld thyself, and couldst thou stain
So rare perfection? Even for love of thee
I do profoundly hate thee."

Lady Elizabeth Carew.

So I was got into the Annals of Cicely, was I? Well then, have back. Dear heart! but what a way have I to go back ere I can find where I was in my story!

Well the King left the Tower for Wallingford, and with him Sir Hugh Le Despenser, and Hugh his young son, Archdeacon Baldok, Edward de Bohun the King's nephew, and divers of his following. I know not whether he had with him also his daughters, the young Ladies Alianora and Joan, or if they were brought to him later. By Saint Denis' Eve (October 7th) he had reached Wallingford.

The Queen was in march to London: but hearing that the King had left, she altered her course, and went to Oxford. There tarried we one day, and went to our duties in the Church of Saint Martin (Note 1), where an homily was preachen by my Lord of Hereford (Note 2). And a strange homily it was, wherein Eva our mother stood for the Queen, and I suppose Adam for the King, and Sir Hugh Le Despenser (save the mark!) was the serpent. I stood it out, but I will not say I goxide (gaped) not. The next day went the Queen on toward Gloucester, pursuing the King, which had been there about ten days afore her. She put forth from Wallingford, on her way between Oxford and Gloucester, a letter wherein she earnestly prayed the King to return, and promised that he should receive the government with all honour if he would conform him to his people. I had been used to hear of the people obeying the King, as in duty bound to him whom God had set over them; and this talk of the King obeying the people was marvellous strange to mine ears. Howbeit, it was talk only; for what was really meant was that he should conform himself to his wife. And considering how much wives be bidden of God to obey their lords, that surely was as ill as the other. Which the King saw belike, for instead of coming nearer he went further away, right over the Severn, and strengthened himself, first in the strong Castle of Chepstow, and after in the Castle of Caerphilly. For us, we went on, though not so quick as he, to Gloucester, and thence to Bristol, where Sir Hugh de Despenser the father was governor, and where the citizens, on the Queen's coming, opened the gates to her, and Sir Hugh on perceiving it retired into the Castle. But she summoned the Castle also to surrender, which was done speedily of the officers, and Sir Hugh delivered into her hands. Moreover, the two little ladies, the King's daughters, whom he had sent from Gloucester on his retreat across the Severn, were brought to her (Note 3), and she welcomed them motherly, or at least seemed to do so. Wala wa! I have no list to set down what followed, and will run by the same as short as shall serve truth.

The morrow of Saint Crispin, namely, the 26th day of October, the Queen and her son, now Duke of Aquitaine—whom man whilome called Earl of Chester—came into the great hall of Bristol Castle, and sat in state: I Cicely being behind the Queen's chair, and Jack in waiting on my Lord the Duke. Which done, they called council of the prelates and nobles of the realm, being the Archbishop of Dublin and five bishops; the King's two brothers, my Lords of Norfolk and Kent; my Lord of Lancaster their cousin; and all the nobles then present in Bristol town: thus they gathered, the Duke on the right hand of the throne and the Queen on the left, the throne all empty. Then a marvellous strange thing happened: for the Queen rose up and spake, in open Council, to the prelates and nobles of England. When she first arose (as afterwards I heard say) were there some murmurs that a woman should so speak; and divers up and down the hall rowned (whispered) one the other in the ear that it had been more seemly had she kept to her distaff. But when she ended, so great was the witchery of her fair face, and the gramary (magic) of her silver voice, that scarce man was in the hall but was ready to live and die with her. *Ha, chétife!* how she witched the world! yet never did she witch me.

How can it be, I marvel at times, that men—and women too—will suffer themselves to be thus led astray, and yet follow on, oft knowing whither they go, after some one man or woman, that casteth over them a manner of gramary? There be some that can witch whom they will, that God keepeth not. And 'tis not alway a fair face that witcheth; I have known full unbright (plain, ugly) folks that have this charm with them. And I note moreover, that many times he that wields it doth use it for evil, and not for good. I dare not say no good man ever hath the same; for securely I know not all folks in this world: yet of them I do know, I cannot call to mind a verily good man or woman that hath seemed me to possess this power over his fellows. I have known some metely good folk that had a touch thereof; but of such as I mean, that do indeed wield it in power, and draw all manner of men to them, and after them, nearhand whether they choose or no—of such I cannot call to mind one that was true follower of our Lord. Therefore it seems me an evil power, and one that may come of Satan, sith it mostly is used in his service. And I pray God neither of my daughters may ever show the same, for at best it must be full of peril of pride to him that possesseth it. Indeed, had it so been, I think they should have shown it afore now.

But now to have back to the hall of Bristol Castle, lest Jack, coming in to look stealthily over my shoulder as he doth betimes, should say I have won again into the Annals of Cicely.

Well, all the prelates and nobles were full witched by Dame Isabel the Queen, and agreed unto all her plans, the which came ready cut and dried, as though all had been thought on and settled long afore. Verily, I dare say it so had. First, they elected the Duke of Aquitaine to the regency—which of course was the self thing as electing his mother, since he, being a mere lad, was but her mouthpiece, and was buxom (submissive) unto her in all things: and all present sware to fulfil his pleasure, as though he had been soothly king, under his privy seal, for there was no seal meet for the regency. And incontinent (immediately) thereafter, the said Duke, speaking doubtless the pleasure of the Queen, commanded Sir Hugh Le Despenser the father to be brought to his trial in the hall of the Castle.

Then was he led in, an old white-haired man, (See note in Appendix, on the Despensers), stately and venerable, who stood up before the Council as I would think none save innocent man should do, and looked the Queen straight in the face. He was not witched with her gramary; and soothly I count in all that hall he was the sole noble that escaped the spell. A brave man was he, of great probity, prudent in council, valiant in war: maybe something too readily swayed by other folks (the Queen except), where he loved them (which he did not her), and from this last point came all his misfortunes (Note 4).

Now stood he up to answer the charges laid against him (whereof there were nine), but answer such as man looked for made he none. He passed all by as of no account, and went right to the heart and verity of the whole matter. I could not but think of a Prisoner before him who had answered nothing; and I crede he knew that in like case, "per invidiam tradidissent eum." (Note 5). Moreover, he spake not to them that did the will of other, but to her that was at the core of the whole matter.

"Ah, Dame!" quoth he, bowing low his white, stately head, "God grant us fair trial and just judge; and if we may not find it in this world, we look for it in another."

I trust he found it in that other world—nay, I know he must have done. But in this world did he not find it. Fair trial had he none; it was an end foregone from the beginning. And as to just judge—well, she is gone now to her judgment, and I will leave her there.

I had forgot to say in due order that my Lord of Arundel was he that was tried with him, but he suffered not till later. (This appears to be the case from comparison of the best authorities.) He, therefore, was had back to prison; but Sir Hugh was hung on the common gallows in his coat armour, in strong cords, and when he was cut down, after four days, his head was struck off and his quarters cast to the dogs. On whose soul God have mercy! Amen. In very deed, I think he deserved a better fate. Secure am I, that many men be hung on gallows which might safely be left to die abed, and many more die abed that richly demerit the gallows. This world is verily a-crooked: I reckon it shall be smoothed out and set straight one day. There be that say that day shall last a thousand years; and soothly, taking into account all the work to be done ere the eve droppeth, it were small marvel an' it did so.

This done, we tarried not long at Bristol. Less than a month thereafter was the King taken at Neath Abbey in Wales, and all that yet obeyed him were either taken with him or dispersed. The news found the Queen at Hereford, whither she had journeyed from Bristol: and if I had yet a doubt left touching her very nature (real character), I think it had departed from me when I beheld how she received that news. Sir Thomas Le Blount, his Steward of the Household, was he that betrayed him: and may God pardon him easier than I could. But my Lord of Lancaster (whom I can pray God pardon with true heart, seeing he afterward repented bitterly), the Lord Zouche of Ashby, and Rhys ap Howel—these were they that took him. With him they took three other—Sir Hugh Le Despenser the son, and Archdeacon Baldok, and Sir Simon de Reading. The good Archdeacon, that was elect (*Bishop* is understood) of Norwich, was delivered over to the tender mercies (which, as saith the Psalmist, were cruel) of that priest of Baal, the Bishop of Hereford, whom indeed I cannot call a priest of God, for right sure am I that God should never have owned him. If that a man serveth be whom he worshippeth, then was Sir Adam de Orleton, Bishop of Hereford, priest of Sathanas and none other. The King was had to Kenilworth Castle, in ward of my Lord of Lancaster—a good though mistaken man, that used him not ungently, yet kept him straitly. Sir Hugh and Sir Simon were brought to the Queen at Hereford, and I was in waiting when they came into her presence. I had but one glimmer of her face (being behind her) when she turned her head for a moment to bid me send Oliver de Nantoil to fetch my Lord of Lincoln to the presence: but if ever I beheld pictured in human eyes the devilish passions of hate, malice, and furious purpose, I beheld them that minute in those lovely eyes of hers. Ay, they were lovely eyes: they could gleam soft as a dove's when she would, and they could shoot forth flames like a lioness robbed of her prey. Never saw I those eyes look fiercer nor eviller than that night when Sir Hugh Le Despenser stood a captive at her feet.

For him, he was full calm: stately as his father—he was comelier of the twain, yea, the goodliest man ever mine eyes lit on: but I thought not on that in that hour. His chief fault, man deemed, was pride: not the vanity that looketh for applause of man, but rather the lofty-mindedness that is sufficient to himself, and despiseth other. I beheld no trace thereof as he there stood. All that had been—all that was of earth and earthy—seemed to have dropped away from him: he was calm and tranquil as the sea on a summer eve when not a breath stirreth. Wala wa! we have all our sins: and what be we, to throw the sins of another in his face? Sir Hugh did some ill deeds, belike; and so, God wot, hath done Cicely de Chaucombe; and whose sins of the twain were worser in His sight, He knoweth, not I. Verily, it was whispered that he had taint of heresy, the evillest thing that may be: but I trust that dread charge were untrue, and that he was but guilty of somewhat more pride and ambitious desires than other. Soothly, pride is one of the seven deadly sins—pray God save us all therefrom!—yet is heresy, as the Church teacheth, an eighth deadlier than all the seven. And if holy Church hath the words of God, and is alonely guided of His Spirit, then must it be an awful and deadly sin to gainsay her bidding. There be that take in hand to question the same: whom holy Church condemneth. I Cicely cannot presume to speak thereof, not being a priest, unto whom alone it appertaineth to conceive such matter. 'Tis true, there be that say lay folk can as well conceive, and have as much right as any priest; but holy Church agreeth not therewith. God be merciful to us all, whereinsoever we do err!

But now was the Queen in a sore strait: for that precious treasure that had once been in her keeping—to wit, the Great Seal—was no longer with her. The King had the same; and she was fain to coax it forth of his keeping, the which she did by means of my said Lord of Hereford. I know not if it were needful, but until she had this done, did not Sir Hugh Le Despenser suffer.

It was at Hereford, the eve of Saint Katherine, that he died. I thank the saints I was not there; but I heard dread stories of them that were. Dame Isabel de Lapyoun was in waiting that day; I think she was fittest for it.

I ween it was on that morrow, of the eve of Saint Katherine, that mine eyes first began to ope to what the Queen was in very deed. Wherefore was she present at that deed of blood? Dame Tiffany reckoned she deemed it her duty: and truly, to behold what man can deem his duty, is of the queerest things in this queer world. I never knew a cow that reckoned it duty to set her calf in peril, and herself tarry thereout; nor a dog that forsook his master's company by reason of his losing of worldly gear; nor an horse that told falsehoods to his own profit. I have wist men that would do all these things, and more; because, forsooth, it was their duty! Now, after what manner it could be duty to Dame Isabel the Queen to preside in her own person at the execution of Sir Hugh, that cannot I Cicely tell. Nay, the saints love us! what need was there of an execution at all? Sir Hugh was dying fast. Since he was taken would he never open his lips, neither to speak nor yet to eat; and that eve of Saint Katherine had seen his end, had they left him die in peace. Veriliest, I wis not what he had done so much worser than other men, that so awesome an ensample should be made of him. I do trust the rumour was not true that ran of his heresy; for if so, then must not man pity him. And yet—

Virgo sanctissima! what is heresy? The good Lord wot.

My Lord of Lincoln was he, as I heard, which brought tidings to the Queen that Sir Thomas Wager had done him to wit Sir Hugh would die that day. Would die—whether man would or no. Holy Mary, the pity of it! Had I been Sir Thomas, never word would I have spoken till the breath was clean gone out of him, and then, if man coveted vengeance, let him take it on the silent dust. But no sooner was it known to the Queen—to her, a woman and a mother!—than she gave command to have the scaffold run up with all speed, and that dying man drawn of an hurdle through the city that all men might behold, with trumpets going afore, and at last hanged of the gallows till he were dead. Oh, the pity of it! the pity of it!

The command was obeyed—so far as man could obey. But ere the agony were full over, God Almighty stepped in, and bare him away from what she would have had him suffer. When they put him on the hurdle, he lay as though he wist not; when they twined a crown of nettles and pressed it on his brow, he was as though he felt not; when, the torture over, they made ready to drag him to the gallows, they saw that he was dead. God cried to them, "Let be!"

God assoil that dead man! Ay, maybe he shall take less assoiling than hath done that dead woman.

Man said that when my Lord of Lincoln came to tell her of this matter, she was counting the silver in my Lord of Arundel his bags, that were confiscate, and had then been brought to her: and but a few days later, at Marcle, Sir William de Blount brought from the King the Great Seal in its leathern bag sealed with the privy seal, and delivered it unto the Queen and her Keeper (Chancellor) the Bishop of Norwich. Soothly, it seemed to me as though those canvas bags that held my Lord of Arundel's silver, and the white leathern bag that held the Great Seal, might be said to be tied together by a lace dipped in blood. And somewhat later, when we had reached Woodstock, was Sir Hugh Le Despenser's plate brought to the Wardrobe, that had been in the Tower with the Lady Alianora his wife—five cups and two ewers of silver, and twenty-seven cups and six ewers of gold; and his horses and hers delivered into the keeping of Adam le Ferrour, keeper of the Queen's horses: and his servants either cast adrift, or drafted, some of them, into the household of the Lord John of Eltham. Go to! saith man: was all this more than is usual in like case? Verily, nay: but should such things be usual in Christendom? Was it for this our Lord came to found His Church—that Christian blood should thus treat his Christian brother? And if no, what can be said of such as called themselves His priests, and passed by on the other side?—nay, rather, took into their own hands the arrows of Sathanas, and wounded their brother with their own fingers? *"Numquid adhaeret Tibi sedes iniquitatis?"* (Psalm 94, verse 20). Might it not have been said to Dame Isabel the Queen like as Moses said to Korah, "Is it nothing to you that you have been joined to the King, and set by his side on the throne, and given favour in his eyes, so that he suffereth you to entreat him oftener and more effectually than any other, but you must needs covet the royal throne theself?" (Itself.)

Ah, what good to write such words, or to speak them? When man hath no fear of God before his eyes, what shall he regard the reasonings of men? But the day of doom cometh, and that sure.

The morrow of that awesome day, to wit, Saint Katherine, departed we from Hereford, and came to Gloucester and Cirencester, going back on the road we had come. By Woodstock (where Dame Margery de Verdon joined us from Dover) we came to Wallingford: where was the Lord John of Eltham, that had come from London, and awaited the Queen his mother. So, by Reading and Chertsey, came we to Westminster Palace, on the fourth day of January (1327). And here was Dame Alice de Lethegreve, mine honoured mother, whom I was full fain to see after all the long and somewhat weariful time that I had been away from England.

My mother would have me tell her all I had seen and heard, in the which she oft stayed me by tears and lamentations. And saith she—

"I bid thee well to note, Cicely, how much ill can come of the deeds of one woman. Deeds, said I? Nay, but of the thoughts and feelings; for all deeds are but the flowers whereto man's thoughts be the seed. And forget not, daughter, that there must ever be one first thought that is the beginning of it all. O Cis, take thou heed of the first evil thought in thine heart, and pray God it lead not to a second. They that fear not God be prone to ask, What matter for thoughts? Deeds be the things that signify. My thoughts are mine own; who shall govern me therein? Ah, verily, who shall, without God doth, and thou dost? He that makes conscience of his thoughts, men reckon a great saint. I would say rather, he that maketh not conscience of his thoughts cannot serve God at all. Pray God rule thee in thine innermost heart; then shall thy deeds please Him, and thy life shall be a blessing to thy fellows."

"Dame," said I, "would you signify that the Queen is not ruled of God?"

"He governeth better than so, Cis," saith she.

"Yet is she Christian woman," quoth I.

"A Christian woman," made answer my mother, "is a woman that followeth Christ. And thou followest not Jack, Cis, when thou goest along one road, and Jack goeth another. Man may follow near or far; but his face must be set the same way. Christ's face was ever set to do the will of God. If thou do thy will, and I do mine, our faces be set contrary."

"Then must we turn us around," said I.

"Ay, and flat round, too," she saith. "When thou standest without Aldgate, ready to pass within, 'tis but a full little turn shall take thee up to Shoreditch on the right hand, or down Blanche Chappleton on the left. Thy feet shall be set scarce an inch different at beginning. Yet pursue the roads, and the one shall land thee at York, and the other at Sandwich. Many a man hath reckoned he set forth to follow Christ, whose feet were scarce an inch out of the way. 'Go to,' quoth he; 'what can an inch matter? what difference shall it make?' Ah me, it maketh all the difference between Heaven and Hell, for the steps lead to diverse roads. Be well assured of the right road; and when thou so art, take heed to walk straight therein. Many a man hath turned a score out of the way, by reason that he walked a-crooked himself."

"Do we know alway when we walk straight?" said I.

"Thou hast thy Psalter and thine Evangelisterium," made she answer: "and thou hast God above. Make good use of the Guide and the map, and thou art not like to go far astray. And God pardon the souls that go astray! Ay, God forgive us all!"

She sat and span a while, and said nought.

"Cicely," then quoth she, "I shall not abide here."

"Whither go you, Dame?"

"Like Abraham of old," she saith, "to the land which God shall show me. If I could serve my dear master,—the lad that once lay in mine arms—by tarrying hither, I could bear much for his sake. But now can I do nought: and soothly I feel as though I could not bear to stand and look on. I can pray for him any whither. Cicely, this will go on. Man that setteth foot on slide shall be carried down it. Thou mayest choose to take or let be the first step; but oft-times thou canst not choose touching the second and all that be to follow. Or if thou yet canst choose, it shall be at an heavy cost that thou draw back thy foot. One small twinge may be all the penalty to-day, when an hour's deadly anguish shall not pay the wyte to-morrow. Thou lookest on me aswhasay, What mean you by this talk? I mean, dear heart, that she which hath entered on this road is like to pursue it to the bitter end. A bitter end it shall be—not alone to her. It means agony to him and all that love him: what maimer of agony God wot, and in His hand is the ell-wand to measure, and the balances to weigh. Lord! Thou wilt not blunder to give an inch too much, nor wilt Thou for all our greeting weigh one grain too little. Thou wilt not let us miss the right way, for the rough stones and the steep mountain-side. Thou hast trodden before us every foot of that weary road, and we need but to plant our steps in Thy footmarks, which we know well from all others by their blood-marked track. O blessed Jesu Christ! it is fair journeying to follow Thee, and Thou leadest Thy sheep safe to the fold of the Holy Land."

I mind her words well. For, woe is me! they were nearhand the last that ever I heard of her.

"Dame," said I, "do you bid me retreat belike?"

"Nay, daughter," quoth she, and smiled, "thou art no longer at my bidding. Ask thine husband, child."

So I told Jack what my mother had said. He sat and meditated thereon afore the fire, while I made ready my Christmas gown of blue kaynet guarded with stranling. (Note 6.)

"Sissot," saith he, his meditation ended, "I think Dame Alice speaks wisely."

"Then wouldst thou depart the Court, Jack?" said I.

"I? Nay, sweet heart. The young King hath about him no more true men than he needeth. And as I wait at his *coucher*, betimes I can drop a word in his ear that may, an' it please God, be to his profit. He is yet tender ground, and the seed may take root and thrive: and I am tough gnarled old root, that can thole a blow or twain, and a rough wind by now and then."

"Jack!" cried I, laughing. "'A tough gnarled old root,' belike! Thou art not yet of seven-and-thirty years, though I grant thee wisdom enough for seventy."

"I thank you heartily, Dame Cicely, for that your courtesy," quoth he, and made me a low reverence. "Ay, dear heart, a gnarled root of cross-grained elm, fit for a Yule log. I 'bide with the King, Sissot. But thou wist, that sentence (argument) toucheth not thee, if thou desire to depart with Dame Alice. And maybe it should be the best for thee."

"I depart from the Court, Jack, on a pillion behind thee," said I, "and no otherwise. I say not I might not choose to dwell elsewhere the rather, if place were all that were in question; but to win out of ill company at the cost of thy company, were to be at heavier charge than my purse can compass. And seeing I am in my duty therein, I trust God shall keep me from evil and out of temptation."

"Amen!" saith Jack, and kissed me. "We will both pray, my dear heart, to be kept out of temptation; but let us watch likewise that we slip not therein. They be safe kept that God keepeth; and seeing that not our self-will nor folly, but His providence, brought us to this place, I reckon we have a right to ask His protection."

Thus it came that I tarried yet in the Queen's household. And verily, they that did so, those four next years, had cause to seek God's protection.

On the first of February was—but, wala wa! my pen runneth too fast. I must back nearhand a month.

It was the seventh of January, being the morrow of the Epiphany, and three days after we reached Westminster, that the Queen met the King's Great Council, the which she had called together on the eve of Saint Barbara (December 3rd), the Duke sitting therein in state as keeper of the kingdom. Having opened the said Parliament, the Duke, by his spokesmen, my Lords of Hereford and Lincoln, laid before them all that had taken place since they last met, and bade them deliberate on what was now to be done for the safety of the realm and Church of England. (Note 7). Who at once adjudged the throne void, and the King to be put down and accounted such no longer: appointing certain nobles to go with the Duke to show these things unto the Queen.

Well do I mind that morrow of the Epiphany. The Queen sat in the Painted Chamber, spinning amongst us, when the nobles waited upon her. She had that morrow been full furnish, sharply chiding Joan de Vilers but a moment ere the Duke entered the presence: but no sooner came he in than she was all honey.

"Dame," saith he, "divers nobles of the Council pray speech of you."

The Queen looked up; she sighed, and her hand trembled. Then pulled she forth her sudary (handkerchief), and wiped her cheek: I am somewhat unsure of the tears thereon. Yet maybe they were there, for verily she could weep at will.

Dame Elizabeth, that sat in the casement, saith to Dame Joan, that was on the contrary side thereof, I being by her, — "Will the Queen swoon, think you?"

"She will come to an' she do," answered she.

I was ready at one time to reckon Dame Joan de Vaux somewhat hard toward the Queen: I saw later that she had but better sight than her neighbours.

Then came in the prelates and nobles which were deputed of the Parliament to convey the news, and the Queen bowed her head when they did reverence.

My Lord of Winchester it was that gave her the tidings that the Parliament then sitting had put down King Edward, and set up the Duke, which there stood, as King. All innocent stood he, that had been told it was his father's dearest wish to be free of that burden of state, and himself too true and faithful to imagine falsehood or unfaithfulness in her that spake it.

Soothly, she played her part full well. She greet plenteously, she wrung her hands, she tare off the hood from her head, she gripped her hair as though to tear that, yea, she cast her down alow on the rushes, and swooned or made believe thereto. The poor young Duke was full alarmed, and kneeling beside her, he would have cast his arms about her, but she thrust him away. Until at the last he arose, and with mien full princely, told the assembled nobles that he would never consent to that which so mispaid (displeased, distressed) his dear mother, without his father should himself command the same. She came to, it seemed me, full soon thereafter.

Then was sent my Lord of Lancaster and other to the King to hear his will thereon. Of these was my Lord of Hereford one, and man said he spake full sharply and poignantly to the King, which swooned away thereunder (somewhat more soothly, as I guess); and the scene, said man that told me, was piteous matter. Howbeit, the King gave full assent, and resigned the crown to his son, who was now to be king, he that had so been being thenceforth named only Sir Edward of Caernarvon. This was the eve of Saint Agnes (January 20th, 1327), the twentieth year of the said King.

Note 1. Better known as Carfax. The exact church is not on record, but it was likely to be this.

Note 2. Adam de Orleton. He and Henry Burghersh, Bishop of Lincoln, are the two Bishops whom Thomas de la Moor, King Edward's squire, brands as "priests of Baal" and "Caiaphases."

Note 3. I have here given the version of events which seems best to reconcile the accounts of the chroniclers with the testimony of contemporary documents. See Appendix.

Note 4. This is the character sketched of him by De La Moor, to whom he was personally known.

Note 5. "For envy they had delivered Him." Matthew, twenty-seven, verse 18.

Note 6. Kennet, a coarse Welsh cloth, trimmed with stranling, the fur of the squirrel taken between Michaelmas and Christmas.

Note 7. The idea of some persons that the Church of England began to exist at the Reformation would have astonished the medieval reckoners "according to the computation of the Church of England," who were accustomed to hear Parliaments summoned to debate "concerning the welfare of the kingdom and Church of England." The former notion is purely modern.

Chapter 5
The Reign of King Roger

"She is no sheep who goes walking with the wolf."

Russian Proverb.

And now, were I inditing a very chronicle, should I dip my quill next in the red ink, and write in full great letters—"Here beginneth the reign of King Edward of Windsor, the Third after the Conquest."

But, to scribe soothliness, I cannot do so. For not for four years thereafter did he in verity begin to reign. And what I should write, if I writ truth, should be—"Here beginneth the reign of King Roger de Mortimer, the First in England."

Now, here cometh an other matter I have noted. When man setteth him up to do that whereto he was not born, and hath not used himself, he is secure to do the same with never so much more din and outrage (extravagance) than he to whom it cometh of nature. If man be but a bedel (herald, crier) he shall rowt (Shout) like a lion the first day; and a prince's charetter (charioteer) shall be a full braver (finer, more showy) man than the prince his master. Sir Roger made a deal more bruit than ever the King himself; that during all these four years was meek and debonair (humble and gentle), as though he abode his time. He wrought what he would (which was mostly ill), and bare him like those of whom the Psalmist speaketh, that said, "Our lips are of us, who is our lord?" (Psalm 9 4, Rolle's translation.) He held up but a finger, and first the King, and all else after, followed along his path. Truly, I fault not the King; poor lad, he was in evil case, and might well enough have found hard to know the way he should go. But I do fault them that might have oped his eyes, and instead thereof, as being smoother way, chose to run after King Mortimer with his livery on their backs.

"How many of them knew the man, thinkest?" saith Jack, that had come in while I writ the last piece.

"Jack!" cried I. "What, to see him do that he did, more in especial when his pride was bolned (swollen, pulled up) by being create Earl of March— when he had larger following than the King himself, having nine score knights at his feet; when he arose from the King's table ere the King stirred, as though he were lord and master of all; when he suffered the King to rise on his coming into the presence, all meekly and courteously, yet himself, when the King entered, kept his seat as he micht afore a servitor; when he walked even with the King, and sometimes afore him; when he was wont to put him down, and mock at him, and make him a laughing-stock. I have heard him myself say to the King—'Hold thy peace, lad!' and the King took it as sweetly as if he had been swearing of allegiance."

"I have eyes in mine head, my fair warrior, and ears belike. I saw so much as thou—maybe a little more, since I was something oftener in my Lord's company than thou."

"But thou sawest what he was?" said I.

"So did I; and sorry am I to have demerited the wrath of Dame Cicely de Chaucombe, for that I oped not the King my master's even."

"Nay, Jack! I never meant thee. I have somewhat more reverence for mine husband than so."

"Then art thou a very pearl amongst women. Most dames' husbands find not much reverence stray their way—at least from that quarter. I misdoubt if Vivien's husband ever picks up more than should lightly slip into his pocket."

"Sir James Le Bretun is not so wise as thou," said I. "But what I meant, Jack, was such as my Lord of Lancaster and my Lord of Kent, and my Lord of Hereford—why did never such as these tell the King sooth touching the Mortimer?"

"As for my Lord of Hereford," saith Jack, "I reckon he was too busied feeling of his pulse and counting his emplastures, and telling his apothecary which side of his head ached worser since the last draught of camomile and mallows. Sir Edmund de Mauley was wont to say he had a grove of aspens at Pleshy for to make his own populion (Note 1), and that he brake his fast o' dragons' blood and dyachylon emplasture. Touching that will I not say; but I reckon he thought oftener on his tamarind drink than on the public welfare. He might, perchance, have bestirred him to speak to the King had he heard that he had a freckle of his nose, for to avise him to put white ointment thereon; but scarce, I reckon, for so small a matter as the good government of the realm."

"Now, Jack!" said I, a-laughing.

"My Lord of Kent," went he forth, "was he that, if he thought he had hurt the feelings of a caterpillar, should have risen from his warm bed the sharpest night in winter to go and pray his pardon of his bare knees. God assoil him, loving and gentle soul! He was all unfit for this rough world. And the dust that Sir Roger cast up at his horse-heels was in my Lord of Kent's eyes as thick as any man's. He could not have warned the King, for himself lacked the warning."

"Then my Lord of Lancaster—why not he?"

"He did."

"Ay, at long last, when two years had run: wherefore not long ere that? The dust, trow, was not in his eyes."

"Good wife, no man's eyes are blinder than his which casts the dust into his own. My Lord of Lancaster had run too long with the hounds to be able all suddenly to turn him around and flee with the hare."

"Soothly, I know he met the Queen on her landing, and likewise had the old King in his ward: but—"

"I reckon, Sissot, there were wheels within wheels. We need not judge my Lord of Lancaster. He did his duty at last. And mind thou, between him and his duty to King Edward the father, stood his brother's scaffold."

"Which never man deserved richer."

"Not a doubt thereof: but man may scarce expect his brother to behold it."

"Then," said I, "my Lord Zouche of Mortimer—but soothly he was cousin to the traitor. Jack, I never could conceive how it came about that he ever wedded the Lady Alianora. One of the enemies of her own husband, and she herself set prisoner in his kinsman's keeping, and to wed her gaoler's cousin, all against the King's pleasure and without his licence—canst solve the puzzle?"

"I can tell thee why he wed her, as easy as say 'twice two be four.' She was co-heir of the earldom of Gloucester, and his sword was nearhand his fortune."

"Then wherefore wed she him?"

"Kittle (ticklish, delicate) ground, Sissot, for man to take on him to account for the doings of woman. I might win a clap to mine ears, as like as not."

"Now, Jack, thou wist well I never demean me so unbuxomly. Tell me thy thought."

"Then I think," saith he, "that the Lady Alianora La Despenser was woman of that manner that fetch their souls from the vine. They must have somewhat to lean on. If an oak or a cedar be nigh, good: but if no, why then, a bramble will serve their turn. The one thing that they cannot do is to stand alone. There be not only women of this fashion; there be like men, but too many. God help them, poor weak souls! The woman that could twine round the Lord Zouche the tendrils torn from Sir Hugh Le Despenser must have been among the very weakest of women."

"It is sore hard," said I, "to keep one from despising such weakness."

"It is full hard, soothly. I know but one way—to keep very near to Him that never spurned the weakest that prayed His help, and that tholed weakness amidst other meeknesses (humiliations), by reason that it behoved Him to resemble His brethren in all things. And some of His brethren are very weak. Sissot, when our daughters were babes, I was wont to think thou lovedst better Alice than Vivien, and I am nearhand secure that it was by reason she was the weaker of the twain, and gave thee the more thought."

"Surely," said I; "that alway holdeth good with a mother, that the barne which most needeth care is the dearest."

Jack's answer, I knew, came from Holy Writ.

"'As by him whom his mother blandisheth, thus will I comfort you.'"

The Sunday after the Conversion of Saint Paul (February 1st, 1327) was the young King crowned in Westminster Abbey before the high altar, by Walter (Reynolds) Archbishop of Canterbury, that had been of old a great friend of King Edward the father, and was carried away like the rest by the glamour of the Queen. But his eyes were opened afore most other, and he died of a broken heart for the evil and unkindness which himself had holpen, the day of Saint Edmund of Pontigny (November 16th) next thereafter. Also present were nine bishops, the King's uncles, and many nobles: yea, and Queen Isabel likewise, that caused us to array her in great doole (mourning), and held her sudary at her eyes nearhand all the office (Service) through. And it was no craft, for she could weep when it listed her—some women have that power—and her sudary was full wet when she returned from the Abbey. And the young King, that was but then full fourteen years of age, took oath as his father and all the kings had done afore him, that he would confirm to the people of England the laws and the customs to them granted by the ancient Kings of England his predecessors, the rights and offerings of God, and particularly the laws, customs, and liberties granted to the clergy and people by the glorious King, Saint Edward, his predecessor. He sware belike to keep unto God and holy Church, unto the clergy and the people, entire peace and concord to his power; to do equal and true justice in all his judgments, and discretion in mercy and truth; to keep the laws and righteous customs which the commons of his realm should have elected

(*Auera estu* are the rather singular words used), and to defend and enforce them, to the honour of God and to his power. (Note 2.)

Six sennights we tarried at Westminster: but, lack-a-day! what a time had we at after! All suddenly the Queen gave order to depart thence. She controlled all things, and the King her son was but a puppet in her hands. How did we trapes up and down all the realm!

To Canterbury the first round, a-pilgrimage to Saint Thomas; then right up as far as York, where we tarried a matter of five weeks. Then to Durham, which we had scarce reached ere we were aflight again, this time to Auckland, and a bit into that end of Yorkshire; back again to Durham, then away to York, and ten days later whisked off to Nottingham; there a fortnight, off again to Lincoln. I guess well now, what I wist not then, the meaning of all this. It was to let the young King from taking thought touching his father, and all that had happed of late. While he was cheerful and delectable (full of enjoyment), she let him be; but no sooner saw she his face the least downfell (cast down) than she plucked him away, and put turn to his thoughts by sending him some other whither. It paid (Note 3) for a time.

It was while we were at Lincoln, where we tarried from the morrow of Holy Cross to Michaelmas Eve (September 15th to 28th), that Donald the Scots messenger came from the southern parts with tidings. For some time— divers weeks, certes—afore that, had the Queen been marvellous unrestful and hard to serve. That which liked her yesterday was all out this morrow, and each matter man named for her plesance was worser than that had gone afore. I was nearhand driven out of senses that very morrow, so sharp (irritable) was she touching her array. Not a gown in her wardrobe would serve the turn; and when at last she chose which she would don, then were her hoods all awry; and then would she have no hood, but only a wimple of fair cloth of linen. Then, gramercy! such pains had we to find her a fillet: this was too deep, and that too narrow, and this set with amethysts should ill fit with her gown of rose-colour, and that wrought of lily-flowers should catch in her hair.

I wished me at the further end of the realm from Lincoln, ay, a dozen times twice told.

At long last we gat her filleted; and then came the mantle. First, Dame Elizabeth brought one of black cloth of Stamford, lined with fox fur: no, that served not. Then brought Dame Joan de Vaux the fair mantle of cloth of velvet, grey, that I ever reckoned the fairest in the Queen's wardrobe, guarded with black budge, and wrought in embroidery of rose-colour and silver: she waved it away as though the very sight 'noyed (disgusted) her.

Then fetched Isabel de la Helde the ray mantle, with corded ground, of blue, red, and green; and the Queen chid her as though she had committed one of the seven deadly sins. At the last, in uttermost wanhope (despair), ran I and brought the ugsomest of all, the corded olive green with border of grey; and forsooth, that would she have. Well-a-day, but I was fain when we had her at last arrayed!

When the Queen had left the chamber, Dame Elizabeth cast her on the nearest bench, and panted like a coursed hare.

"Deary, deary me!" crieth she: "I would I were abed."

"Abed!" crieth Isabel de la Helde. "Abed at five o'clock of a morrow!"

"Ay, or rather, I would I had never gat out. Gramercy, but how fractious is the Queen! I counted we ne'er should have her donned."

"She never spoke to me so sharp in her life," saith Isabel.

"I tell you, I am fair dog-weary!" quoth Dame Elizabeth.

"Whatever hath took the Queen?" saith Joan de Vilers.

"Foolish childre, all of you!" saith old Dame Tiffany, looking on us with a smile. "When man is fractious like to this, with every man and every matter, either he suffereth pain, or else he hath some hidden anguish or fear that hath nought to do with the matter in hand. 'Tis not with you that my Lady is wrathful. There is something harrying her at heart. And she hath not told me."

In hall, during dinner. I cast eyes from time to time on the Queen, and I could not but think Dame Tiffany spake sooth. She looked fair haggard, as though some bitter care were eating out her heart. I never loved her, as I said at the first: but that morn I felt sorry for her.

Sorry for *her*! Ah, I soon knew what sore cause there was to be sorry to the very soul for some one else!

It was while we were sat at supper that Donald came. I saw him enter from the high table where I sat, and I knew in an instant that he brought some fearsome tidings. I lost him in the crowd at the further end, and then Mereworth, one of the varlets of the King's chamber, came all in haste up the hall, with a face that had evil news thereon writ: and Sir John de Ros, that was then Seneschal, saw him, and guessing, as I think, the manner of word he brought, stepped down from the dais to meet him. Then, in an other minute, I saw Donald brought up to the King and to the Queen.

I watched them both. As Donald's news was told, the young King's face grew ashen pale, and he cried full dolefully "*Dieu eit mercie!*" The news troubled him sore and sure enough. But the Queen's eyes, that a moment before had been full of terror and untholemodness (impatience), shot out one flash of triumphant gladness: and the next minute she had hidden her face in her sudary, and was greeting as though her heart had broke. I marvelled what tidings they could be, that were tene (grief) to the King, and blisfulhed (happiness) to the Queen. Sir John de Gaytenby, the King's confessor, was sat next to me at the table, and to him I said—

"Father, can you guess what manner of news Donald de Athole shall have brought?"

"Ay, daughter," he made answer. "Would I were in doubt!"

"You think—?" I asked him, and left him to fill up.

"I think," he saith in a low voice somewhat sorrowful of tone, "that God hath delivered from all labour and sorrow one of His servants that trust in Him."

"Why, that were nought to lament o'er!" I was about to say; but I stayed me when half through. "Father, you mean there is man dead?"

"We call it death," saith Sir John de Gaytenby—"we of this nether world, that be ever in sickness and weariness, in tene and in temptation. Know we what they call it which have forded the Rubicon, and stand safe on the pavement of the Golden City? '*Multo magis melius,*' saith the Apostle (Philippians One verse 23): 'much more better' to dissolve and to be with Christ. And the colder be the waters man hath to ford, the gladder and welcomer shall be the light of the Golden City. They were chill, I cast no doubt: and all the chiller for the hand that chilled them. With how sharp thorns and briers God hath to drive some of His sheep! But once in the Fold, there shall be time to forget them all. 'When thou passest through the waters, I will be with thee' (Isaiah 43 verse 2)—that is enough now. We can stay us upon that promise till we come through. And then there shall be no more need for Him to be with us in tribulation, since we shall reign with Him for ever and ever."

Old Sir Simon de Driby came up behind us as the Confessor ended.

"Have you guessed, Sir John, our dread news?—and you, Dame Cicely?"

"I have guessed, and I think rightly," answered Sir John. "For Dame Cicely I cannot say."

I shook mine head, and Sir Simon told me.

"Sir Edward of Caernarvon is dead."

"Dead—the King!"

"'The King' no longer," saith Sir Simon sorrowfully.

"O Sir Simon!" cried I. "How died he?"

"God knoweth," he made answer. "I misdoubt if man shall know."

"Or woman?" quoth Sir John, significantly.

"The schoolmaster learned me that man includeth woman," saith Sir Simon, smiling full grimly.

"He learned you not, I reckon, that woman includeth man," saith Sir John, somewhat after the same manner.

"Ah, *woe* worth the day!" Sir Simon fetched an heavy sigh. "Well, God forgive us all!"

"Amen!" Sir John made answer.

I think few men were in the realm that did not believe the King's death was murder. But nought was done to discover the murderers, neither to bring them to justice. It was not until after the Mortimer was out of the way that any such thing was done. When so it was, mandate was issued for the arrest of Sir Thomas de Gournay, Constable of Bristol Castle, and William de Ocle, that had been keepers of the King at Berkeley Castle. What came of Ocle know I not; but Sir Thomas fled beyond seas to the King's dominions of Spain (Note 3), and was afterwards taken. But he came not to trial, for he died on the way: and there were that said he knew too much to be permitted to make defence. (Note 4.)

The next thing that happed, coming under mine eyes, was the young King's betrothal and marriage. The Lady Philippa of Hainault, that was our young Queen, came over to England late in that same year, to wit, the first of King Edward, and was married the eve of the Conversion of Saint Paul, the year of our Lord 1327, after the computation of the Church of England (Note 5). Very praisable (lovely) and fulbright (beautiful) was the said lady, being sanguine of complexion, of a full fair face, and fair hair, having grey (grey) cyen and rosen colour of her cheeks. She was the same age as the King, to wit, fifteen years. They were wed in York Minster.

"Where hast reached to, Sissot?" saith Jack, that was sat by the fire, as I was a-bending the tail of my Y in York.

"Right to the King's wedding," said I.

"How many more skins o' parchment shall I bring thee for to set forth the gowns?"

"Dear heart!" cried I, "must I do that for all that were there?"

"Prithee use thy discretion. I wist not a woman could write a chronicle without telling of every gown that came in her way."

"Go thy ways, Jack!" said I. "Securely, if I set down the King's, and the Queen's, and thine and mine, that shall serve well enough."

"It should serve me, verily," quoth he. "Marry, I hope thou mindest what manner of raiment I had on, for I ensure thee I do not a whit."

"Dost thou ever, the morrow thereof?" said I. "Nay, I wis I must pluck that out of mine own memory."

The King, then, was donned of a robe of purple velvet, with a pair of sotlars of cloth of gold of Nakes silk; the said velvet robe wrought with the arms of England, of golden broidery. The Queen bare a robe of green cloth of velvet, with a cape thereto, guarded with miniver, and an hood of miniver; her hair falling full sweetly over from under her golden fillet, sith she put not on her hood save to leave the Minster. And at the feast thereafter, she ware a robe of cloth of samitelle, red and grey, with a tunic and mantle of the same. (Note 6.)

As for Jack, that was then clerk of the Wardrobe (Note 7), he ware a tabard of the King's livery (the arms of France and England) of mine own broidering, and hosen of black cloth, his hood being of the same. I had on a gown of grey cloth of Northampton, guarded with gris, and mine hood was of rose-colour say (Note 8) lined with black velvet.

But over the inwards of the wedding must I not linger, for much is yet to write. The latter end of February was the Lady La Despenser loosed from the Tower, and in April was all given back to her. All, to wit, that could be given. Her little children, that the Queen Isabel had made nuns without any leave given save her own, could come back to her never more. I misdoubt if she lamented it greatly. She was one from whom trouble and sorrow ran lightly, like the water from a duck's back: and I reckon she thought more on her second marriage, which had place secretly about a year after her release, than she ever did for her lost children. And here may I say that those sisters, coheirs of Gloucester, did ever seem to me the queerest mothers I wist. The Lady Margaret Audley gave up her little Kate (a sweet child she was) to the Ankerage at Ledbury with scarce a sigh; and the Lady Alianora, of whom I write, took but little thought for her maids at Sempringham, or I err. I would not have given up my Alice after that fashion: and I did sore pity those little barnes, of which the eldest was not seven years old. Folk said it was making of gift to God, and was an holy and blessed thing. Soothly, I marvel if God setteth store by such like gifts, when men do but cast at his feet that whereof they would be rid! The innermost sanctuary of the Temple, it seemeth me, is scarce the fittest place to shoot rubbish. And when the rubbish is alive, if it be but vermin, I cannot slack to feel compassion for it.

Methinks the Lady Alianora felt it sorer trouble of the twain, when she suffered touching certain jewels reported to be missing from the Tower during her governance thereof—verily a foolish charge, as though the Lady of Gloucester should steal jewels! Howbeit, she was fined twenty thousand pound, for the which she rendered up her Welsh lands, with the manors of Hanley and Tewkesbury, being the fairest and greatest part of her heritage. The King allowed her to buy back the said lands if she should, in one and the same day, pay ten thousand marks: howbeit, one half the said fine was after remitted at the intercession of the Lords and Commons.

That autumn was the insurrection of my Lord of Lancaster—but a bit too soon, for the time was not ripe, but I reckon they knew not how longer to bear the ill thewis (manners, conduct) of the Mortimer, which ruled every thing at his will, and allowed none, not even my Lord of Lancaster, to come nigh the King without his leave, and then he had them watched of spies. The Parliament was held at Salisbury that Michaelmas, whereto all men were forbidden to come in arms. Thither, nathless, came the said Mortimer, with a great rabble of armed men at his heels. My Lord of Lancaster durst not come, so instead thereof he put himself in arms, and sent to expound matters to the King. He was speedily joined by all that hated the Mortimer (and few did not), among whom were the King's uncles, the Bishops of Winchester and London, the Lord Wake, the Lord de Beaumont, Sir Hugh de Audley, and many another that had stood stoutly for Queen Isabel aforetime. Some, I believe, did this out of repentance, seeing they had been deceived; other some from nought save hate and envy toward the Mortimer. The demands they put forth were no wise unskilwise (unreasonable). They were chiefly that the King should hold his revenues himself (for the Queen had so richly dowered herself that scarce a noble was left to the King); that the Queen should be dowered of the third part, as queens had been aforetime; and that the Mortimer should live on his own lands, and make no encroachments. They charged him with divers evil deeds, that he had avised the King to dissolve his Council appointed of twelve peers, he had wasted the royal treasure, he had counselled the King to give up Scotland, and had caused the Lady Joan to wed beneath her dignity.

"Make no encroachments!" grimly quoth old Sir Simon, when he heard of this; "verily, an' this present state of matters go on but a little longer, the Mortimer can make no encroachments, for he shall have all England to his own."

The Mortimer, that had yet the King's ear (though I think he chafed a bit against the rein by now and then), avised him that the Lords sought his crown, causing him to ride out against them as far as Bedford, and that during the night. Peace was patched up some way, through the mediating of Sir Simon de Mepham, the new Archbishop of Canterbury, my Lord of Lancaster being fined eleven thousand pounds—though, by the same token, he never paid it. (Note 9.) That same Michaelmas was the King's uncle, the Lord Edmund de Woodstock, create Earl of Kent (marry, I named him my Lord of Kent all through, seeing he should so best be known, but he was not so create until now), and King Roger, that was such, but was not so-called, had avancement to the dignity of Earl of March. There was many a lout and courtesy and many a leg made, when as my Lord's gracious person was in presence; and when as he went forth, lo! brows were drawn together, and lips thrust forth, and words whispered beneath the breath that were not all of praise.

Now, whether it be to fall into the Annals of Cicely or no, this must I needs say—and Jack may flout me an' he will (but that he doth never)—that I do hate, and contemn, and full utterly despise, this manner of dealing. If I love a man, maybe I shall be bashful to tell him so: but if I love him not, never will I make lout nor leg afore him for to win of him some manner of advantage. I would speak a man civilly, whether I loved him or no; that 'longeth to my gentlehood, not his: but to blandish and losenge him (coax and flatter), and say 'I love thee well' and 'Thou art fairest and wisest of all' twenty times in a day, when in mine heart I wished him full far thence, and accounted of him as fond and ussome (foolish and ugly)—that could I never demean me to do, an' I lived to the years of Methuselah.

And another thing do I note—I trust Jack shall have patience with me—that right in proportion as a man is good, so much doth an ill man hate him. My Lord of Lancaster was wise man and brave, as he oft showed, though he had his failings belike; and he did more than any other against the Mortimer, until the time was full ripe: my Lord of Kent was gent, good, and sweet of nature, and he did little against him—only to consort with my said Lord of Lancaster: yet the Mortimer hated my Lord of Kent far worser than my Lord of Lancaster, and never stayed till he had undone him. Alas for that stately stag of ten, for the cur pulled him down and worried him!

My Lord of Kent, as I writ afore, had dust cast in his eyes by the Queen. He met her on her landing, and marched with her, truly believing that the King (as she told him) was in thrall to the old and young Sir Hugh Le Despenser, and that she was come to deliver him. Nought less than his brother's murder tare open his sealed eyes. Then he woke up, and aswhasay looked about him, as a man roughly wakened that scarce hath his full sense.

Bitter was his lamentation, and very sooth his penitence, when he saw the verity of the matter. Now right as this was the case with him, the Queen and the Mortimer, having taken counsel thereon, (for they feared he should take some step that should do them a mischief), resolved to entangle him. They spread a rumour, taking good care it should not escape his ears, that King Edward his brother yet lived, and was a prisoner in Corfe Castle. He, hearing this, quickly despatched one of his chaplains, named Friar Thomas Dunhead, a Predicant—for all the Predicants were on the King's side—to see if the report were as it was said: and Sir John Deveroil, then Keeper of the Castle, having before his instructions, took the Friar within, seeming nothing loth, and showed unto him the appearance of a king seated at supper in hall, with his sewers (waiters) and other officers about him. This all had been bowned (prepared) afore, of purpose to deceive my Lord of Kent, and one chosen to present (represented) the King that was like enough to him in face and stature to pass well. On this hearing went my Lord of Kent with all speed to Avignon, to take counsel with Pope John (John Twenty-Two) who commended him for his good purpose to deliver his brother, and bade him effect the same by all means in his power: moreover, the said Pope promised himself to bear all charges—which was a wise deed of the holy Father, for my Lord of Kent was he that could never keep money in his pocket, but it flowed out of all sides. Then my Lord returned back, and took counsel with divers how to effect the same. Many an one promised him help—among other, the Archbishop of York, and the Lord Zouche of Mortimer (that wedded the Lady Alianora, widow of Sir Hugh Le Despenser), the Lord Wake (which had wrought much against the King of old, and was brother unto my Lady of Kent), and Sir Ebulo L'Estrange, (that wedded my Lady of Lancaster, widow of Earl Thomas), and the young Earl of Arundel, and others of less sort. My said Lady of Kent was likewise a-work in the matter, for she was not woman to let either tongue or hand lie idle.

Now, wherefore is it, that if man be rare sweet, gent, and tender, beyond other men, he shall sure as daydawn go and wed with woman that could hold castle or govern army if need were? 'Tis passing strange, but I have oft noted the same. And if he be rough and fierce, then shall he take fantasy to some soft, nesh (Note 10), bashful creature that scarce dare say nay to save her life. Right as men of high stature do commonly wed with small women, and the great women with little men. Such be the ways of Providence, I take it.

Jack saith—which I must not forget to set down—that he credeth not a whit that confession set forth as made of my Lord of Kent, nor any testimony of Friar Dunhead, but believeth the whole matter a pack of lies, saving only that my Lord believed the report of his brother prisoner in Corfe Castle. Howbeit, my Lord of Kent writ a letter as to the King his brother, offering his deliverance, which he entrusted to Sir John Deveroil: who incontinently carried the same to the Mortimer, and he to the Queen. She then showed it to the young King, saying that herein might he see his uncle was conspiring to dethrone him and take his life and hers. The King, that dearly loved his mother, allowed inquiry into the same, pending the which my said Lord was committed to prison.

The next morrow came the Mortimer to the Queen as she sat at dinner, and prayed instant speech of her, and that full privy: and the Queen, arising from the table, took him into her privy closet. Dame Isabel de Lapyoun alone in waiting. I had learned by then to fear mischief whensoever the Queen bade none follow her save Dame Isabel, for I do verily believe she was in all the ill secrets of her mistress. They were in conference maybe ten minutes, and then hastened the Mortimer away, nor would he tarry so long as to drink one cup of wine. It was not many minutes after that the young King came in; and I perceived by their discourse that the Queen his mother had sent for him. Verily, all that day (which was Saint Joseph (March 19th)) she watched him as cat, mouse. He could not leave the chamber a moment but my Lord of March crept after. I reckoned some mischief was brewing, but, *purefoy*! I guessed not how much. That day died my Lord of Kent, on the scaffold at Winchester. And so beloved was he that from noon till four of the clock they had to wait, for no man would strike him, till at last they persuaded one in the Marshalsea, that had been cast for (sentenced to) death, to behead him as the price of his own life.

A little after that hour came in Sir Hugh de Turpington, that was Marshal of the Hall to the King.

"Sir," saith he to the King, "I am required of the Sheriff to tell you that my Lord of Kent hath paid wyte on the scaffold. So perish all your enemies!"

Up sprang the King with a face wherein amaze and sore anguish strave for the mastery.

"My uncle Edmund is dead on scaffold!" cried he in voice that rang through hall. "Mine enemies! *He* was none! What mean you? I gave no mandate for such, nor never should have done. *Dieu eit mercie*! mine enemies be they that have murdered my fair uncle, that I loved dear. Where and who be they? Will none here tell me?"

Wala wa! was soul in that hall brave enough to tell him? One of those two chief enemies stale softly to his side, hushing the other (that seemed ready to break forth) by a look.

"Fair Son," saith the Queen, in her oiliest voice, "hold you so light your own life and your mother's? Was your uncle (that wist full well how to beguile you) dearer to you than I, on whose bosom you have lain as babe, and whose heart hath been rent at your smallest malady?"

(Marry, I marvel when, for I never beheld less careful mother than Dame Isabel the Queen. But she went forth.)

"The proofs of what I say," quoth she, "shall be laid afore you in full Parliament, and you shall then behold how sorely you have been deceived in reckoning on a friend in your uncle. Meanwhile, fair Son, trust me. Who should seek your good, or care for your safety, more than your own mother?"

Ah verily, who should! But did she so? I could see the King was somewhat staggered by her sweet words, yet was he not peaced in a moment. His anger died down, but he brake forth in bitter tears, and so left the hall, greeting as he went.

Once more all passed away: and they that had hoped for the King to awake and discover truth found themselves beguiled.

Order was sent to seize my Lady of Kent and her childre, that were then in Arundel Castle. But the officers, there coming, told her the dread tidings, whereat she fell down all in swoon, and ere the eve was born the Lord John her son, and baptised, poor babe, in such haste in the Barefooted Friars' Church, that his young brother and sister, no more than babes themselves, were forced to stand sponsors for him with the Prior of the Predicants (Note 11). Howbeit he lived to grow to man's estate, yea, longer than the Lord Edmund his brother, and died Earl of Kent a matter of eight years gone.

The Castle of Arundel, and the lands, that had been given to my Lord of Kent when my Lord of Arundel was execute, were granted to Queen Isabel shortly after his 'heading. I think they were given as sop to keep him true to the Queen: not that he was man to be bought, but very like she thought all men were. Dear heart, what strange gear are we human creatures! I marvel at times whether the angels write us down greater knaves or fools.

Note 1. The crystallised juice of the aspen. Earl John of Hereford seems to have been a valetudinarian.

Note 2. Close Roll, 1 Edward the Third, Part One. The exact wording of the coronation oath is of some importance, since it has sometimes been stated that our sovereigns have sworn to maintain religion precisely as it existed in the days of

Edward the Confessor. The examination of the oath shows that they promised no such thing. They engaged only to keep and defend to the people, clerical and lay, the laws, customs, rights, and liberties granted by their predecessors, and by Edward more especially. "To his power" means "to the best of his power."

Note 3. Then not an unusual way of saying "the King of Spain's dominions."

Note 4. In my former volume, *In All Time of our Tribulation*, I committed the mistake of repeating the popular error that the Queen took immediate vengeance, by banishment, on the murderers of her husband. It was only Gournay and Ocle who were directly charged with the murder: the others who had a share in it were merely indicted for treason. Gournay was Constable of Bristol in December, 1328; and the warrant for his apprehension was not issued until December 3, 1330—after the fall of Mortimer, when Edward the Third, not his mother, was actually the ruler.

Note 5. By this phrase was meant the reckoning of the year from Easter to Easter, subsequently fixed for convenience' sake at the 25th of March.

Note 6. I have searched all the Wardrobe Accounts in vain for the wedding attire of this royal pair. The robes described are that worn by the King for his coronation; that in which the Queen rode from the Tower to Westminster the day before her coronation; and that in which she dined after the same ceremony. These details are given in the Wardrobe Accounts, 33/2, and 34/13. It was the fashion at this time for a bride's hair to be left flowing straight from head to foot.

Note 7. Chaucombe was in the Household, but of his special office I find no evidence.

Note 8. A coarse variety of silk, used both for garments and upholstery.

Note 9. Dr Barnes tells his readers that Lancaster was at this time so old as to be nearly decrepit; and two years later, that he was "almost blind for age." He was exactly forty-one, having been born in 1287 (Inq. Tho. Com. Lane, 1 Edward the Third 1. 88), and 53 years had not elapsed since the marriage of his parents. We may well say, after Chancellor Oxenstiern, "See with how little accuracy history is written!"

Note 10. Tender, sensitive, either in body or mind. This word is still a provincialism in the North and West.

Note 11. *Prob. aet. Johannis Com. Kant.*, 23 Edward the Third 76, compared with *Rot. Pat.*, 4 Edward the Third, Part 1, and *Rot. Claus.*, 4 Edward the Third.

Chapter 6
Nemesis

"The mills of God grind slowly, but they grind exceeding small."

Longfellow.

After this, the Queen kept the King well in hand. To speak sooth, I should say the old Queen, or Queen Isabel, for now had we a young Queen. But verily, all this time Queen Philippa was treated as of small account; and she, that was alway sweet and gent, dwelt full peaceably, content with her babe, our young Prince of Wales, that was born at Woodstock, at Easter of the King's fourth year (Note 1) and the old Queen Isabel ruled all. She seemed fearful of letting the King out of her sight. When he journeyed to the North in August, she went withal, and came back with him to Nottingham in October. It was she that writ to my Lord of Hereford that he should not fail to be at the Colloquy (note 2) to be held in that town the fifteenth of October. With her was ever my Lord of March, that was as her shadow: my Lady of March, that might have required to have her share of him with some reason, being left lone with her childre in Ludlow Castle. It was the 13th of October that we came to Nottingham. My Lord of Hereford, that was Lord High Constable, was at that time too sick to execute his office (or thought he was); maybe he desired to keep him well out of a thing he foresaw: howbeit, he writ his excuse to the King, praying that his brother Sir Edward de Bohun might be allowed his deputy. To this the King assented: but my Lord of March, that I guess mistrusted more Sir Edward than his brother (the one having two eyes in his head, and the other as good as none), counselled the Queen to take into her own hand the keys of the Castle. Which she did, having them every night brought to her by Sir William Eland, then Constable thereof, and she laid them under her own pillow while the morning.

The part of my tale to follow I tell as it was told to me, in so far as matters fell not under mine eye.

The King, the old Queen, the Earl of March, and the Bishop of Lincoln, were lodged in the Castle with their following: and Sir Edward de Bohun, doing office for his brother, appointed my Lord of Lancaster to have his lodging there likewise. Whereat my glorious Lord of March was greatly angered, that he should presume to appoint a lodging for any of the nobles so near the person of Queen Isabel. (He offered not to go forth himself.) Sir Edward smiled something grimly, and appointed my Lord of Lancaster his lodging a mile forth of the town, where my Lord of Hereford also was.

That night was dancing in the hall; and a little surprised was I that Sir William de Montacute (Note 3) should make choice of me as his partner. He was one of the bravest knights in all the King's following—a young man, with all his wits about him, and lately wed to the Lady Katherine de Grandison, a full fair lady of much skill (Note 4) and exceeding good repute. It was the pavon (Note 5) we danced, and not many steps were taken when Sir William saith—

"Dame Cicely, I have somewhat to say to you, under your good leave."

"Say on, Sir William," quoth I.

"Say I well, Dame, in supposing you true of heart to the old King, as Dame Alice de Lethegreve's daughter should be?"

"You do so, in good sooth," I made answer.

"So I reckoned," quoth he. "Verily, an' I had doubted it, I had held my peace. But now to business:—Dame, will you help me?"

I could not choose but laugh to hear him talk of business.

"That is well," saith he. "Laugh, I pray you; then shall man think we do but discourse of light matter. But what say you to my question?"

"Why, I will help you with a very good will," said I, "if you go about a good matter, and if I am able, and if mine husband forbid me not."

"Any more ifs?" quoth he—that I reckon wished to make me to laugh, the which I did.

"Not at this present," made I answer.

"Then hearken me," saith he. "Can you do a deed in the dark, unwitting of the cause—knowing only that it is for the King's honour and true good, and that they which ask it be true men?"

I meditated a moment. Then said I,—"Ay; I can so."

"Will you pass your word," saith he, "to the endeavouring yourself to keep eye on the Queen and my Lord of March this even betwixt four and five o' the clock? Will you look from time to time on Sir John de Molynes, and if you hear either of them speak any thing as though they should go speak with the King, will you rub your left eye when Sir John shall look on you? But be you ware you do it not elsewhere."

"What, not though it itch?" said I, yet laughing.

"Not though it itch to drive you distraught."

"Well!" said I, "'tis but for a hour. But what means it, I pray you?"

"It means," saith he, "that if the King's good is to be sought, and his honour to be saved, you be she that must help to do it."

Then all suddenly it came on me, like to a levenand (lightning) flash, what it was that Sir William and his fellows went about to do. I looked full into his eyes. And if ever I saw truth, honour, and valour writ in man's eyes, I read them there.

"I see what you purpose," said I.

"You be marvellous woman an' you do," answered he.

"Judge you. You have chosen that hour to speak with the King, and to endeavour the opening of his eyes. For Queen Isabel or my Lord of March to enter should spoil your game. Sir John de Molynes is he that shall give you notice if such be like to befall, and I am to signify the same to him."

Right at that minute I had to take a volt (jump), and turn to the right round Sir John Neville. When I returned back to my partner, saith he, so that Sir John could hear—

"Dame Cicely, you vault marvellous well!"

"That was not so ill as might have been, I reckon," quoth I.

"Truly, nay," he made answer: "it was right well done."

I knew he meant to signify that I had guessed soothly.

"Will you try it yet again?" saith he.

"That will I," I said: and I saw we were at one thereon.

"Good," saith he. "I reckoned, if any failed me at this pinch, it should not be Dame Alice's daughter."

That eve stood I upon tenterhooks. As the saints would have it, the Queen was a-broidering a certain work whereon Dame Elizabeth wrought with her: and for once in my life I thanked the said hallows (saints) for Dame Elizabeth's laziness.

"Dame Cicely," quoth she, "an' you be not sore pressed for time, pray you, thread me a two-three needles. I wis not how it befalleth, but thread a neeld can I never."

I could have told her well that *how*, for whenso she threadeth a neeld she maketh no bones of the eye, but thrusteth forward the thread any whither it shall go, on the chance that it shall hit, which by times it doth: I should not marvel an' she essayed to thread the point. Howbeit, her ill husbandry was right then mine encheson (Note 6).

"Look you," said I, "I can bring my work to that end of the chamber; then shall I be at hand to thread your neeld as it shall be voided."

"Verily, you be gent therein," saith she.

The which I fear I was little. Howbeit, there sat I, a-threading Dame Elizabeth her neeld, now with red silk and now with black, as she lacked, and under all having care that I rubbed not my left eye, the which I felt strong desire to frote (rub). I marvel how it was, for the hour over, I had no list to touch it all the even.

My task turned out light enough, for my Lord of March was playing of tables (backgammon) with Sir Edward de Bohun, and never left his seat for all the hour: and the Queen wrought peacefully on her golden vulture, and moved no more than he. When I saw it was five o' the clock (Note 7), I cast an eye on Sir John de Molynes, which threw a look to the clock, and then winked an eye on me; and I saw he took it we had finished our duty.

The next morrow, which was Saint Luke's even (October 17th), came a surprise for all men. It was found that the Constable of the Castle, with Sir William de Montacute, Sir Edward de Bohun, Sir John de Molynes, the Lord Ufford, the Lord Stafford, the Lord Clinton, and Sir John Neville, had ridden away from the town the night afore, taking no man into their counsel. None could tell wherefore their departure, nor what they purposed. I knew only that the King was aware thereof, though soothly he counterfeited surprise as well as any man.

"What can they signify?" saith Sir Edmund de Mortimer, the eldest son of my Lord of March—a much better man than his father, though not nigh so crafty.

"Hold thy peace for a fool as thou art!" saith his father roughly. "They are afraid of me, I cast no doubt at all. And they do well. I could sweep them away as lightly as so many flies, and none should miss them!"

He ended with a mocking laugh. Verily, pride such as this was full ready for a fall.

We knew afterward what had passed in that hour the day afore. The King had been hard to insense (cause to understand: still a Northern provincialism) at the first. So great was his faith in his mother that he ne could ne would believe any evil of her. As to the Mortimer, he was ready enough, for even now was he a-chafing under the yoke.

"Be he what he may—the very foul fiend himself an' you will," had he said to his Lords: "but she, mine own mother, my beloved—Oh, not she, not she!"

Then—for themselves were lost an' they proved not their case—they were fain to bring forth their proofs. Sir William de Montacute told my Jack it was all pitiful to see how our poor young King's heart fought full gallantly against the light as it brake on his understanding. Poor lad! for he was but a lad; and it troubled him sore. But they knew they must carry the matter through.

"Oh, have away your testimonies!" he cried more than once. "Spare her—and spare me! Mother, my mother, mine own dear Lady! how is this possible?"

At the last he knew all: knew who had set England in flame, who had done Sir Hugh Le Despenser and his son to death, who had been his own father's murderer. The scales were off his eyes; and had he list to do it, he could never set them on again. They said he covered his face, and wept like the child he nearhand was. Then he lifted his head, the tears over, and in his eyes was the light of a settled purpose, and in his lips a stern avisement. No latsummes (backwardness, reluctance) was in him when once fully set.

"Take the Mortimer," quoth he, firm enough.

"Sir," quoth Sir William de Montacute, "we, not being lodged in the Castle, shall never be able to seize him without help of the Constable."

"Now, surely," saith the King, "I love you well: wherefore go to the Constable in my name, and bid him aid you in taking of the Mortimer, on peril of life and limb."

"Sir, then God grant us speed!" saith Sir William.

So to the Constable they went, and brake the matter, only at first bidding him in the King's name (having his ring for a token) to aid them in a certain enterprise which concerned the King's honour and safety. The Constable sware so to do, and then saith Sir William—

"Now, surely, dear friend, it behoved us to win your assent, in order to seize on the Mortimer, sith you are Keeper of the Castle, and have the keys at your disposal."

Then the Constable, having first lift his brows and made grimace of his mouth, fell in therewith, and quoth he—

"Sirs, if it be thus, you shall wit that the gates of the Castle be locked with the locks that Queen Isabel sent hither, and at night she hath all the keys thereof, and layeth them under the pillow of her bed while morning:

and so I may not help you into the Castle at the gates by any means. But I know an hole that stretcheth out of the ward under earth into the Castle, beginning on the west side (still called Mortimer's Hole), which neither the Queen nor her following nor Mortimer himself, nor none of his company, know anything of; and through this passage I will lead you till you come into the Castle without espial of enemies."

Thereupon went they forth that even, as though to flee away from the town, none being privy thereto save the King. And Saint Luke's Day passed over quiet enough. The Queen went to mass in the Church of the White Friars, and offered at the high altar five shillings, her customary offering on the great feasts and chief saints' days. All peaceful sped the day; the Queen gat her abed, and the keys being brought of the Constable's deputy, I (that was that night in waiting) presented them unto her, which she received in her own hands and laid under the pillow of her bed. Then went we, her dames and damsels, forth unto our own chambers in the upper storey of the Castle: and I, set at the casement, had unlatched the same and thrown it open (being nigh as warm as summer), and was hearkening to the soft flow of the waters of the Leene, which on that side do nearhand wash the Castle wall. I was but then thinking how peaceful were all things, and what sore pity it were that man should bring in wrong, and bitterness, and anguish, on that which God had made so beautiful—when all suddenly my fair peace changed to fierce tumult and the clang of armed men—the tramp of mail-clad feet and the hoarse crying of roaring voices. I was as though I held my breath: for I could well guess what this portended. Then above all the routing and bruit (shouting and noise), came the voice of Queen Isabel, clear and shrill.

"Now, fair Sirs, I pray you that you do no harm unto his body, for he is a worthy knight, our well-beloved friend, and our dear cousin."

"They have him, then!" quoth I, scarce witting that I spake aloud, nor who heard me.

"'Have him!'" saith Dame Joan de Vaux beside me: "whom have they?"

Then, suddenly, a word or twain in the King's voice came up to where we stood; on which hearing, an anguished cry rang out from Queen Isabel.

"Fair Son, fair Son! have pity on the sweet Mortimer!" (Note 8.)

Wala wa! that time was past. And she had shown no pity.

I never loved her, as in mine opening words I writ: yet in that dread moment I could not find in mine heart to leave her all alone in her agony. I have ever found that he which brings his sorrows on his own head doth not suffer less thereby, but more. And let her be what she would, she was a woman, and in sorrow, not to say mine own liege Lady: and signing to Dame Joan to follow me, down degrees ran I with all haste, and not staying to scratch on the door (Note 9), into the chamber to the Queen.

We found her sitting up in her bed, her hands held forth, and a look of agony and horror on her face.

"Cicely, is it thou?" she shrieked. "Joan! Whence come ye? Saw ye aught? What do they to him? who be the miscreants? Is my son there? Have they won him over—the coward neddirs (serpents) that they be! Speak I who be they?—and what will they do? Ah, Mary Mother, what will they do with him?"

Her voice choked, and I spake.

"Dame, the King is there, and divers with him."

"What do they?" she wailed like a woman in her last agony.

"There hath been sharp assault, Dame," said I, "and I fear some slain; for as I ran in hither, I saw that which seemed me the body of a dead man at the head of degrees."

"Who?" She nearhand screamed.

"Dame," I said, "I think it was Sir Hugh de Turpington."

"But what do they with *him*?" she moaned again, an accent of anguish on that last word.

I save no answer. What could I have given?

Dame Joan de Vaux saith, "Dame, the King is there, and God will be with the King. We may well be ensured that no wrong shall be done to them that have done no wrong. This is not the conteks (quarrel) of a rabble rout; it is the justice of the Crown upon his enemies."

"His enemies?—whose? Mine enemies are dead and gone. All of them— all! I left not one. Who be these? who be they, I say? Cicely, answer me!"

Afore I could speak word, I was called by another voice. I was fain enough of the reprieve. Leaving Dame Joan with the Queen, I ran forth into the Queen's closet, where stood the King.

What change had come over him in those few hours! No longer a bashful lad that was nearhand afraid to speak for himself ere he were bidden. This was a young man (he was now close on eighteen years of age) that stood afore me, a youthful warrior, a budding Achilles, that would stand to no man's bidding, but would do his will. King of England was this man. I louted low before my master.

He spake in a voice wherein was both cold constrainedness, and bitterness, and stern determination—yet under them all something else—I think it was the sorely bruised yet living soul of that deep unutterable tenderness which had been ever his for the mother of his love, but could be the same never more. Man is oft cold and bitter and stern, when an hour before he hath dug a grave in his own heart, and hath therein laid all his hopes and his affections. And they that look on from afar behold the sheet of ice, but they see not the grave beneath it. They only see him cold and silent: and they reckon he cares for nought, and feels nothing.

"Dame Cicely, you have been with the Queen?"

"Sir, I have so."

"Take heed she hath all things at her pleasure, of such as lie in your power. Let my physician be sent for if need arise, as well as her own; and if she would see any holy father, let him be fetched incontinent (immediately). See to it, I charge you, that she be served with all honour and reverence, as you would have our favour."

He turned as if to depart. Then all suddenly the ice went out of his voice, and the tears came in.

"How hath she taken it?" saith he.

"Sir," said I, "full hardly as yet, and is sore troubled touching my Lord of March, fearing some ill shall be done him. Moreover, my Lady biddeth me tell her who these be. Is it your pleasure that I answer the same?"

"Ay, answer her," saith he sorrowfully, "for it shall do no mischief now. As for my Lord of March, no worser fate awaits him than he hath given better men."

He strade forth after that kingly fashion which was so new in him, and yet sat so seemly upon him, and I went back to the Queen's chamber.

"Cicely, is that my son?" she cried.

"In good sooth, Dame," said I.

"What said he to thee?"

I told her the King had bidden me answer all her desire; that if she required physician she should be tended of his chirurgeon beside her own, and she should speak with any priest she would. I had thought it should apay (gratify) her to know the same; but my words had the contrariwise effect, for she looked more frightened than afore.

"Nought more said he?"

"Dame," said I, "the Lord King bade me to serve you with all honour and reverence. And he said, for my Lord of March—"

"Fare forth!" (go on) she cried, though I scarce knew that I paused.

"He answered, that no worser should befall him than he had caused to better men than he."

"Mary, Mother!"

I thought I had scarce ever heard wofuller wail than she made then. She sank down in the bed, clutching the coverlet with her hands, and casting it over her, as she buried her face in the pillows. I went nigh, and drew the coverlet full setely (properly, neatly) over her.

"Let be!" she saith in a smothered voice. "It is all over. Life must fare forth, and life is of no more worth. My bird is flown from the cage, and none can win him back. Is there so much as one of the saints will speak for me? As I have wrought, so hast Thou paid me, God!"

Not an other word spake she all the livelong day. Never day seemed longer than that weary eve of Saint Ursula (October 20th). That morrow were taken in the town the two sons of my Lord of March, Sir Edmund and Sir Geoffrey, beside divers of his friends—Sir Oliver Byngham, Sir Simon de Bereford, and Sir John Deveroil the chief. All were sent that same day under guard to London, with the Mortimer himself.

No voice compassionated him. Nay, "my Lord of March" was no more, but in every man's mouth "the Mortimer" as of old time. Some that had seemed his greatest losengers (flatterers) now spake of him with the most disdain, while they that, while they allowed him not (did not approve of him), had yet never abused ne reviled him, were the least wrathful against him. I heard that when he was told of all, my Lord of Lancaster flung up his cap for joy.

Some things afterward said were not true. It was false slander to say, as did some, that the Mortimer was taken in the Queen's own chamber. He was arrest in the Bishop of Lincoln's chamber (which had his lodging next the Queen), and in conference with the said Bishop. They took not that priest of Baal; I had shed no tears had they so done. Sir Hugh de Turpington and Sir John Monmouth, creatures of the Mortimer, were slain; Sir John Neville, on the other side, was wounded.

Fourteen charges were set forth against the Mortimer. The murder of King Edward was one; the death of my Lord of Kent an other. One thing was not set down, but every man knew how to read betwixt the lines, when the indictment writ that other articles there were against him, which in respect of the King's honour were not to be drawn up in writing. Wala wa! there was honour concerned therein beside his own: but he was very tender of her. His way was hard to walk and beset with snares, and he walked it with cleaner feet than most men should. Never heard I from his lips word unreverent toward her; and if other lips spake the same to his knowing, they forthank (regretted) it.

That same day the King departed from Nottingham for Leicester, on his way to London. He left behind him the Lord Wake de Lydel, in whose charge he placed Queen Isabel, commanding that she should be taken to Berkhamsted Castle as soon as might be. I know not certainly if he spake with her afore he set forth, but I think rather nay than yea.

October was not out when we reached Berkhamsted. The Queen's first anguish was over, and she scarce spake; but I could see she hearkened well if aught was said in her hearing.

The King sent command to seize all lands and goods of the Mortimer into his hands; but the Lady of March he bade to be treated with all respect and kindliness, and that never a jewel nor a thread of her having should be taken. Indeed, I heard never man nor woman speak of her but tenderly and pitifully. She was good woman, and had borne more than many. For the Lady Margaret her mother-in-law, so much will I not say; for she was a firebrand that (as saith Solomon) scattered arrows and death: but the Lady Joan was full gent and reverend, and demerited better husband than the Fates gave her. Nay, that may I not say, sith no such thing is as Fate, but only God, that knoweth to bring good out of evil, and hath comforted the Lady Joan in Paradise these four years gone.

But scarce three weeks we tarried at Berkhamsted, and then the Lord Wake bore to the Queen tidings that it was the King's pleasure she should remove to Windsor. My time of duty was then run out all but a two-three days; and the Queen my mistress was pleased to say I might serve me of those for mine own ease, so that I should go home in the stead of journeying with her to Windsor. At that time my little maid Vivien was not in o'er good health, and it paid me well to be with her. So from this point mine own remembrances have an end, and I serve me, for the rest, of the memory of Dame Joan de Vaux, mine old and dear-worthy friend, and of them that abode with Queen Isabel till she died. For when her household was 'minished and again stablished on a new footing, it liked the King of his grace to give leave to such as should desire the same to depart to their own homes, and such as would were at liberty to remain—one except, to wit, Dame Isabel de Lapyoun, to whom he gave congé with no choice. I was of them that chose to depart. Forsooth, I had seen enough and to spare of

Court life (the which I never did much love), and I desired no better than to spend the rest of my life at home, with my Jack and my little maids, and my dear mother, so long as God should grant me.

My brother Robert (of whom, if I spake not much, it was from no lack of loving-kindness), on the contrary part, chose to remain. He hath ever loved a busy life.

I found my Vivien full sick, and a weariful and ugsome time had I with her ere she recovered of her malady. Soothly, I discovered that diachylum emplasture was tenpence the pound, and tamarinds fivepence; and grew well weary of ringing the changes upon rosin and frankincense, litharge and turpentine, oil of violets and flowers of beans, *Gratia Dei*, camomile, and mallows. At long last, I thank God, she amended; but it were a while ere mine ears were open to public matter, and not full filled of the moaning of my poor little maid. So now, to have back to my story, as the end thereof was told me by Dame Joan de Vaux.

Queen Isabel came to Windsor about Saint Edmund the King (November 20th); and nine days thereafter, on the eve of Saint Andrew (November 29th), was the Mortimer hanged at Tyburn. He was cast (sentenced) as commoner, not as noble, and was dragged at horse's tail for a league outside the city of London to the Elms. But the penalties that commonly came after were not exacted, seeing his body was not quartered, nor his head set up on bridge ne gate. His body was sent to the Friars Minors' Church at Coventry, whence one year thereafter, it was at the King's command delivered to the Lady Joan his widow and Sir Edmund his son, that they might bury him in the Abbey of Wigmore with his fathers. His mother, the Lady Margaret, overlived him but four years; but the Lady Joan his wife died four years gone, the very day and month that he was taken prisoner, to wit, the nineteenth day of October, 1356, nigh two years afore Queen Isabel.

The eve of Saint Andrew, as I writ, was the Mortimer hanged, without defence by him made (he had allowed none to Sir Hugh Le Despenser and my Lord of Kent): and four days hung his body in irons on the gibbet, as Sir Hugh's the father had done. Verily, as he had done, so did God apay him, which is just Judge over all the earth.

And the very next day, Saint Andrew, came His dread judgment upon one other—upon her that had wrought evil and not good, and that had betrayed her own lord to his cruel death. All suddenly, without one instant's warning, came the bolt out of Heaven upon Isabel of France. While the body of the Mortimer hung upon the gibbet at the Elms of Tyburn, God stripped that sinful woman of the light of reason which she had used so ill, and she fell into a full awesome frenzy, so dread that she was fain to be strapped down, and her cries and shrieks were nearhand enough to drive all wood that heard her. While the body hung there lasted this fearsome frenzy. But the hour it was taken down, came change over her. She sank that same hour into the piteous thing she was for long afterward, right as a little child, well apaid with toys and shows, a few glass beads serving her as well as costly jewels, and a yard of tinsel or fringe bright coloured a precious treasure. The King was sore troubled; but what could he do? At the first the physicians counselled that she should change the air often; and first to Odiham Castle was she taken, and thence to Hertford, and after to Rising. But nothing was to make difference to her any more for many a year,—only that by now and then, for a two-three hours, she hath come to her wit, and then is she full gent and sad, desiring ever the grace of our Lord for her ill deeds, and divers times saying that as she hath done, so hath God requited her. I have heard say that as time passed on, these times of coming to her wit were something oftener and tarried longer, until at last, a year afore she died, she came to her full wit, and so abode to the end.

The King, that dealt full well with her, and had as much care of her honour as of his own (and it was whispered that our holy Father the Pope writ unto him that he should so do), did at the first appoint her to keep her estate in two of her own castles, to wit, Hertford and Rising: and set forth a new household for her, appointing Sir John de Molynes her Seneschal, and Dame Joan de Vaux her chief dame in waiting. Seldom hath she come to Town, but when there, she tarried in the Palace of my Lord of Winchester at Southwark, on the river side, and was once in presence when the King delivered the great Seal to Sir Robert Parving. Then she was in her wit for a short time. But commonly, at the King's command, she hath tarried in those two her castles,—to wit, Hertford and Rising—passing from one to the other according to the counsel of her physicians. The King hath many times visited her (though never the Queen, which he ever left at Norwich when he journeyed to Rising), and so, at times, have divers of his children. Ten years afore her death, the King's adversary of France, Philippe de Valois, that now calleth him King thereof, moved the King that Queen Isabel should come to Eu to treat with his wife concerning peace: and so careful is the King, and hath ever been, of his mother's honour, that he would not answer him with the true reason contrary thereto, but treated with him on that footing, and only at the last moment made excuse to appoint other envoys. Poor soul! she had no wit thereto. I never saw her after I left her service saving once, which was when she was at Shene, on Cantate Sunday (April 29th), an eleven years ere her death, at supper in the even, where were also the King, the Queen of Scots (her younger daughter), and the Earl of March (grandson of the first Earl); and soothly, for all the ill she wrought, mine heart was woe for the caged tigress with the beautiful eyes, that was wont to roam the forest wilds at her pleasure, and now could only pace to and fro, up and down her cage, and toy with the straws upon the floor thereof. It was pitiful to see her essaying, like a babe, as she sat at the board, to cause a wafer to stand on end, and when she had so done, to clap her hands and laugh with childish glee, and call her son and daughter to look. Very gent was the King unto her, that looked at her bidding, and lauded her skill and patience, as he should have done to his own little maid that was but three years old. Ah me, it was piteous sight! the grand, queenly creature that had fallen so low! Verily, as she had done, so God requited her.

She died at Hertford Castle, two days afore Saint Bartholomew next thereafter (August 22nd, 1358. See Note in Appendix). I heard that in her last hours, her wit being returned to her as good as ever it had been, she had her shriven clean, and spake full meek (humble) and excellent words of penitence for all her sins, and desired to be buried in the Church of the Friars Minors in London town, and the heart of her dead lord to be laid upon her breast. They have met now in the presence above, and he would forgive her there. *Lalme de qui Dieux eit mercie!* Amen.

Here have ending the Annals of Cicely.

> Note 1. The chroniclers (and after them the follow-my-leader school of modern historians) are unanimous in their assertion that the Black Prince was born on June 15th. If this be so, it is, to say the least, a little singular that the expenses of the Queen's churching were defrayed on the 24th and 28th of April previous (Issue Roll, Easter, 4 Edward the Third). On the 3rd, 5th, and 13th of April, the King dates his mandates from Woodstock; on the 24th of March he was at Reading. This looks very much as if the Prince's birth had taken place about the beginning of April. The 8th of that month was Easter Day.
>
> Note 2. Modern writers make no difference between a Colloquy and a Parliament. The Rolls always distinguish them, treating; the Colloquy as a lesser and more informal gathering.
>
> Note 3. Second son of the elder Sir William de Montacute and Elizabeth de Montfort. He appears as a boy in the first chapter of the companion volume, *In All Time of our Tribulation.*
>
> Note 4. Discretion, wisdom.

Note 5. The pavon was a slow, stately dance, but it also included high leaps.

Note 6. Occasion, opportunity. Needles, at this time, were great treasures; a woman who possessed three or four thought herself wealthy indeed.

Note 7. Striking clocks were not invented until about 1368.

Note 8. Had the Queen spoken in English, she would certainly have said *sweet*, not *gentle*, which last is an incorrect translation of *gentil*. This latter speech, though better known, is scarcely so well authenticated as the previous one.

Note 9. Royal etiquette prescribed a scratch on the door, like that of a pet animal; the knock was too rough and plebeian an appeal for admission.

PART 2

Chapter 1
Wherein Agnes the Lady of
Pembroke telleth tale (1348)

The Children of Ludlow Castle

"O little feet, that, such long years,
Must wander on through hopes and fears,
Must ache and bleed beneath your load:
I, nearer to the wayside inn
Where toil shall cease and rest begin,
Am weary, thinking of your road."

Longfellow.

Hereby I promise, and I truly mean to execute it, to give my new green silk cloth of gold piece, bordered with heads of griffins in golden broidery, to the Abbey of Saint Austin at Canterbury, if any that liveth, man or woman, will tell me certainly how evil came into this world. I want to know why Eva plucked that apple. She must have plucked it herself, for the serpent could not give it her, having no hands. And if man—or woman—will go a step further, and tell me why Adam ate another, he shall have my India-coloured silk, broidered with golden lions and vultures, whereof I had meant to make me a new gown for this next Michaelmas feast. It doth seem as if none but a very idiot could have let in evil and sin and sorrow and pain all over this world, for the sake of a sweet apple. It must have been sweet, I should think, because it grew in Eden. But was there never another in all the garden save only on that tree? Or did man not know what would happen? or was it that man would not think? That is the way sometimes with some folks, else that heedless Nichola had not broken my favourite comb.

The question has been in my head many a score of times; but it came just now because my Lady, my lord's mother, was earnest with me to write in a book what I could remember of mine early days, when my Lady mine own mother was carried to Skipton and Pomfret. If those were not evil days, I know not how to spell the word. And I am very sure it was evil men that made them; and evil women. I believe bad woman is far worse than bad man. So saith the Lady Julian, my lord's mother; and being herself woman, and having been thrice wed, she should know somewhat of women and men too. Ay, and I were ill daughter if I writ not down also that a good woman is one of God's blessedest gifts to this evil world; for such is mine own mother, the Lady Joan de Geneville, that was sometime wife unto the Lord Roger Mortimer, Earl of March, whose name men of this day know but too well.

Well-a-day! if a thing is to be, it is best over. It is never any good to sit on the brink shivering before man plunge in. So, if I must needs write, be it done. Here is a dozen of parchment, and a full inkhorn, and grey goose-quills: and I need nothing else save brains; whereof, I thank the saints, I have enough and to spare. And indeed, it is as well I should, for in this world—I say not, in this house—there be folks who have none too many. But I reckon, before I begin my tale, I had best say who and what I am, else shall those who read my book be like men that walk in a mist, which is not pleasant, as I found this last summer, when for a time I lost my company— and thereby, myself—on the top of a Welsh mountain.

I, then, who write, am Agnes de Hastings, Countess of Pembroke and Lady of Leybourne: and I am wife unto the Lord Lawrence de Hastings, Earl and Baron of the same. My father and mother I have already named, but I may say further that my said mother is a Princess born, being of that great House of Joinville in France—which men call Geneville in England— that are nobles of the foremost rank in that country. These my parents had twelve children, of whom I stand right in the midst, being the seventh. My brother Edmund was the eldest of us; then came Margaret, Joan, Roger, Geoffrey, Isabel, and Katherine; then stand I Agnes, and after me are Maud, John, Blanche, and Beatrice (Note 1). And of them, Edmund and Margaret have been commanded to God. He died young, my poor brother Edmund, for he set his heart on being restored to the name and lands which our father had forfeited, and our Lord the King thought not good to grant it; so his heart broke, and he died. Poor soul! I would not say an unkind word over his grave; where the treasure is, there will the heart be; but I would rather set my heart on worthier treasure, and I think I should scarce be so weak as to die for the loss. God assoil him, poor soul!

I was born in the Castle of Ludlow, on the morrow of the Translation of Saint Thomas, in the year of King Edward of Caernarvon the eleventh (Note 2), so that I am now thirty years of age. I am somewhat elder than my lord, who was born at Allesley, by Coventry town, on Saint Cuthbert's

Day, in the fourteenth year of the same (March 20th, 1321). I might say I was wiser, and not look forward to much penance for lying; for I should be more likely to have it set me if I said that all the wits in this world were in his head. Howbeit, there is many a worse man than he: a valiant knight, and courteous, and of rarely gentle and gracious ways; and maybe, if he were wiser, he would give me more trouble to rule him, which is easy enough to do. Neverthelatter, there be times when it should do me ease to take him by the shoulders and give him an hearty shake, if I could thereby shake a bit more sense into him: and there be times when it comes over me that he might have been better matched, as our sometime Lord King Edward meant him to have been, with the Lady Alianora La Despenser, that Queen Isabel packed off to a nunnery in hot haste when she came in. Poor soul! He certainly is not matched with me, unless two horses be matched whereof one is black and of sixteen handfuls, and steppeth like a prince, and the other is white, and of twelve handfuls, and ambles of a jog-trot. I would he had a bit more stir in him. Not that he lacks knightly courage—never a whit; carry him into battle, and he shall quit him like a man; but when all is said, he is fitter for the cloister, for he loveth better to sit at home with Joan of his knee, and a great clerkly book afore him wherein he will read by the hour, which is full well for a priest, but not for a noble of the King's Court. He never gave me an ill word (veriliest (truly), I marvel if ever he said 'I won't!' in all his life), yet, for all his hendihood (courtesy, sweetness), will he have his own way by times, I can never make out how. But he is a good man on the whole, and doth pretty well as he is bid, and I might change for a worse without taking a long journey. So, take it all in all, there are many women have more to trouble them than I, the blessed saints be thanked, and our sweetest Lady Saint Mary and my patron Saint Agnes in especial. Only I do hope Jack shall have more wit than his father, and I shall think the fairies have changed him if he have not. *My* son should not be short of brains.

But now, to have back, and begin my story: for I reckon I shall never make an end if I am thus lone: in coming to the beginning.

We were all brought up in the Castle of Ludlow, going now and then to sweeten (to have the house thoroughly cleaned) to the Castle of Wigmore. Of course, while we were little children, we knew scarce any thing of our parents, as beseemed persons of our rank. The people whom I verily knew were Dame Hilda our mistress (governess), and Maud and Ellen our damsels, and Master Terrico our Chamberlain, and Robert atte Wardrobe, our wardrobe-keeper, and Sir Philip the clerk (I cry him mercy, he should have had place of Robert), and Stephen the usher of the chamber, and our four nurses, whose names were Emelina, Thomasia, Joan, and Margery, and little Blaise the page. They were my world. But into this world, every now and then, came a sweet, fair presence—a vision of a gracious lady in velvet robes, whose hand I knelt to kiss, and who used to lay it on my head and bless me: and at times she would take up one of us in her arms, and sit down with the babe on her velvet lap, and a look would come into her eyes which I never saw in Dame Hilda's; and she would bend her fair head and kiss the babe as if she loved her very much. But that was mostly while we were babies. I cannot recollect her doing that to me—it was chiefly to Blanche and Beatrice. Until one day, and then—

Nay, I have not come to that yet. And then, at times, we should hear a voice below—a stern, deep voice, or a peal of loud laughter—and in an instant the light and the joy would die out of the tender eyes of that gracious vision, and instead would come a frightened look like that of a hunted hare, and commonly she would rise suddenly, and put down the babe, and hasten away, as if she had been indulging in some forbidden pleasure, and was afraid of being caught. I can remember wishing that the loud laugh and the stern angry voice would go away, and never come back, but that the gracious vision would stay always with us, and not only pay us a rare visit. Ay, and I can remember wishing that she would take *me* on that velvet lap, and let me nestle into her soft arms, and dare to lay my little head on her warm bosom. I think she would have done it, if she had known! I used to feel in those days like a little chicken hardly feathered, and longed to be under the soft brooding wings of the hen. The memory of it hath caused me to pet my Jack and Joan a deal more than I should without it.

Then, sometimes, we had a visit from a very different sort of guest. That was an old lady—about a hundred and fifty, I used to fancy her—dressed in velvet full as costly, but how differently she wore it! She never took us on her lap—not she, indeed! We used to have to kneel and kiss her hand—and Roger whispered to me once that if he dared, he would bite it. This horrid old thing (who called herself our grandmother) used to be like a storm blowing through the house. She never was two minutes in the room before she began to scold somebody; and if she could not find reasonable fault with any body, that seemed to vex her more than anything else. Then she scolded us all in a lump together. "Dame Hilda, what an untidy chamber!"—she usually began in that way—"why don't you make these children put their playthings tidy? (Of course Dame Hilda did, at the end of the day; but how could we have playthings tidy while we were playing with them?) Meg, your hair is no better than a mop! Jack, how got you that rent in your sleeve? (I never knew Jack without a rent in some part of his clothes; I should not have thought it was Jack if he had come in whole garments.) Joan, how ungainly you sit! pluck yourself up this minute. Nym, take your elbows off the table. Maud, your chaucers (slippers) are down at heel. How dirty your hands are, Roger! go and wash them. Agnes, that wimple of yours is all awry; who pinned it up?"

So she went on—rattle and scold, scold and rattle—as long as she stayed in the room. Jack, always the saucy one, asked her one day, when he was very little—

"Are you really Grandmother?"

"Certes, child," said she, turning to look at him: "why?"

"Because I wish you were somebody else!"

Ha, chétife! did Jack forget that afternoon? I trow not.

I had a sound whipping once myself from Dame Hilda, because I said, right out, that I hated the Lady Margaret: and Joan,—poor delicate Joan, who was perpetually scolded for stooping—looked at me as if she wished she dared say it too. Roger had his ears boxed because he drawled out, "Amen!" I think we all said Amen in our hearts.

Sometimes the Lady Margaret did not come upstairs, but sent for some of us down to her. That was worse than ever. There were generally a number of gentlemen there, who seemed to think that children were only made to be teased: and some of them I disliked, and others I despised. Only of one I was terribly afraid: and that was—mercy, Jesu!—mine own father.

I should have found it difficult to say what it was in him that frightened me. I used to call it fear then; but when I look back on the feeling from my present state, I think it was rather a kind of ungovernable antipathy. He did not scold us all round as Lady Margaret did. The worst thing, I think, that I remember his saying to me was a sharp—"Get out of the way, girl!" And I wished I only could get out of his way, for ever and ever. Something made me feel as if I could not bear to be in the same room with him. I used to shiver all over, if I only heard his voice. Yet he never ill-used any of us; he scarcely even looked at us. It was not any thing he did which made me feel so; it was just himself.

Surely never did man dress more superbly than he. I recollect thinking that the King was not half so fine; yet King Edward liked velvet and gold as well as most men. My Lord my father never wore worsted summer tunics or woollen winter cloaks, like others. Silk, velvet, samite, and cloth of gold, were his meanest wear; and his furs were budge, ermine, miniver, and gris. I can remember hearing how once, when the furrier sent him in a robe of velvet guarded with hare's fur, he flung it on one side in a fury, and ordered the poor man to be beaten cruelly. He always wore much golden broidery, and buttons of gems or solid gold; and he never would wear a suit of any man's livery—not even the King's,—save once, when he wore the Earl of Chester's at the coronation of the Queen of France, just to vex King Edward—as it sorely did, for he was then a proscribed fugitive, who had no right to use it.

It is a hard matter when a child is frightened of its own father. It is yet harder when he makes it hate him. Ah, it is easy to say, That was wicked of thee. So it was: and I know it. But doth not sin lead to sin?—spring out of it, like branches from a stem, like leaves from a branch? And when one man's act of sin creates sin in another man, and that again in a third, whose is the sin—the black root, whereof came the rotten branches and the withered leaves? Are we not all our brothers' and our sisters' keepers? Well, it will not answer to pursue that road: for I know well I should trace up the sin too high, to one of whom it were not meet for me to speak in the same breath with ugly words. Ay me! what poor weak things we mortal creatures are! Little marvel, little marvel for the woe that was wrought!—so fair, so fair she was! She had the soul of a fiend with the face of an angel. Was it any wonder that men—ay, and some women—were beguiled with that angel face, and fancied but too rashly that the soul must be as sweet as it? God have mercy on all Christian souls! Verily, I myself, only this last spring-time, was ready to yield to the witch's spell—never was woman such enchantress as she!—and athwart all the past, despite all I knew, gazing on that face, even yet fairer than the faces of younger women, to think it possible that all the tales were false, and all the past a vision of the night, and that the lovely face and the sweet, soft voice covered a soul white as the saints in Heaven! And men are easier deluded by such dreams than women—or at least I think it. My poor father! If only he had never seen her that haled him to his undoing! he might, perchance, have been a better man. Any way, he paid the bill in his heart's blood. So here I leave him. God forgive us all!

And now to my story. While I was but a little child, we saw little of our mother: little more, indeed, than we did of our father. I think, of the two, we oftener saw our grandmother. And little children, as God hath wisely ordered it, live in the present moment, and take no note of things around them which men and women see with half an eye. Now, looking back, I can recall events which then passed by me as of no import. It was so, and there was an end of it. But I can see now why it was so: and I know enough to guess the often sorrowful nature of that wherefore.

So it was nothing to us children, unless it were a relief, that after I was about four years old, we missed our father almost entirely. We never knew why he tarried away for months at a time. We had not a notion that he was first in the prison of the Tower, and afterwards a refugee over seas. And we saw without seeing that our mother grew thin and white, and her sweet eyes were heavy with tears which we never saw her shed. All we perceived was that she came oftener to the nursery, and stayed longer with us, and petted the babies more than had been her wont. And that such matters had a meaning,—a deep, sad, terrible meaning—never entered our heads. Later on we knew that during those lonely years her heart was being crucified, and crucifixion is a dying that lasts long. But she never let us know it. I think she would not damp our fresh childish glee by even the spray of that roaring cataract wherein her life was overwhelmed. Mothers—such mothers as she—are like a reflection of God.

I remember well, though I was but just seven years old, the night when news came to Ludlow Castle that my father had escaped from the Tower. It was a very hot night in August—too hot to sleep—and I lay awake, chattering to Kate and Isabel, who were my bedfellows, about some grand play we meant to have the next afternoon, in the great gallery—when all at once we heard a horse come dashing up to the portcullis, past our chamber wall, and a horn crying out into the night.

Isabel sat up in bed, and listened.

"Is it my Lord coming home?" I said.

"What, all alone, with no company?" answered Isabel, who is four years elder than I. "Silly child! It is some news for my Lady my mother. The saints grant it be good!"

Of course we could hear nothing of what passed at the portcullis, as our window opened on the base court. But in a few minutes we heard the horse come trotting into our court, and the rider 'lighted down: and Isabel, who lay with her head next the casement, sat up again and put her head out of the curtain. It was a beautiful moonlight night, almost as bright as day.

"What is it, Ibbot?" said Kate.

"It is a man in livery," answered Isabel; "but whose livery I know not. It is not ours."

Then we heard the man call to the porter, and the door open, and the sound of muffled voices to and fro for a minute; and then Master Inge's step, which we knew—he was then castellan—coming in great haste past our door as if he were going to my Lady's chamber. Then the door of the large nursery opened, and we heard Dame Hilda within, saying to Tamzine, "Thou wert better run and see." And Tamzine went quickly along the gallery, as if she, too, were going to my Lady.

For a long, long time, as it seemed to us—I dare say it was not many minutes—we lay and listened in vain. At length Tamzine came back.

"Good tidings, or bad?" we heard Dame Hilda ask.

"The saints wot!" whispered Tamzine. "My Lord is 'scaped from the Tower."

"*Ha, chétife!* will he come here?" said Dame Hilda: and we saw that it was bad news in her eyes.

"Forsooth, nay!" replied Tamzine. "There be hues and cries all over for him, but man saith he is fled beyond seas."

"Amen!" ejaculated Dame Hilda. "He may win to Cathay (China) by my good will; and if he turn not again till mine hair be white, then will I give my patron saint a measure in wax. But what saith my Lady?"

"Her I saw not," answered Tamzine; "but Mistress Robergia, who told me, said she went white and red both at once, and her breast heaved as though her very heart should come forth."

"Gramercy!" said Dame Hilda. "How some folks do set their best pearls in copper!"

"Eh, our Lady love us!" responded Tamzine. "That's been ever sith world began to run, Dame, I can tell you."

"I lack no telling, lass," was Dame Hilda's answer. "Never was there finer pearl set in poorer ore than that thou and I wot of."

I remember that bit of talk because I puzzled myself sorely as to what Dame Hilda could mean. Kate was puzzled, too, for she said to Isabel—

"What means the Dame? I never saw my Lady wear a pearl set in copper."

"Oh, let be!" said Isabel. "'Tis but one of the Dame's strange sayings. She is full of fantasies."

But whether Isabel were herself perplexed, or whether she understood, and thought it better to shut our mouths, that cannot I tell to this day.

Well, after that things were quiet again for a while: a very long while, it seemed to me. I believe it was really about six months. During that time, we saw much more of our mother than we used to do; she would come often into the nursery, and take one of the little ones on her lap—it was oftenest Blanche—and sit there with her. Sometimes she would talk with Dame Hilda; but more frequently she was silent and sad, at times looking long from the casement as if she saw somewhat that none other eyes could see. Jack said one day—

"Whither go Mother's eyes when she looks out of the window?"

"For shame, Damsel (Note 3) John!" cried Dame Hilda. "'Mother,' indeed! Only common children use such a word. Say 'my Lady' if you please."

"She is my mother, isn't she?" said Jack stubbornly. "Why shouldn't I call her so, I should like to know? But you haven't answered me, Dame."

"I know not what you mean, Damsel."

"Why, when she sits down in that chair, and takes Blanchette on her knee,—her eyes go running out of the window first thing. Whither wend they?"

"Children like you cannot understand," replied Dame Hilda, with one of those superior smiles which used to make me feel so very naughty. It seemed to say, "My poor, little, despicable insect, how could you dream of supposing that your intellect was even with Mine?" (There, I have writ that a capital M in red ink. To have answered to Dame Hilda's tone when she put that smile on, it should have been in vermilion and gold leaf.) Howbeit, Jack never cared for all the airs she put on.

"Then why don't you make us understand it?" said he.

I do not remember what Dame Hilda said to that, but I dare say she boxed Jack's ears.

Deary me, how ill doth my tale get forward! Little things keep a-coming to my mind, and I turn aside after them, like a second deer crossing the path of the first. That shall never serve; I must keep to my quarry.

All this time our mother grew thinner and whiter. Poor soul, she loved him well!—but so sure as the towel of the blessed Nicodemus is in the sacristy of our Lady at Warwick, cannot I tell for why. Very certain am I that he never gave her any reason.

We reckoned those six months dreary work. There were no banquets in hall, nor shows came to the Castle, nor even so much as a pedlar, that we children saw; only the same every-day round, and tired enough we were of it. All the music we ever heard was in our lessons from Piers le Sautreour; and if ever child loved her music lessons, her name was not Agnes de Mortimer. All the laughter that was amongst us we made ourselves; and all the shows were when Jack chose to tumble somersaults, or Maud twisted some cold lace round her head, and said, "Now I am Queen Isabel." Dreary work, in good sooth! yet was it a very Michaelmas show and an Easter Day choir to that which lay ahead.

And then, one night,—ah, what a night that was! It was near our bed-time, and Jack, Kate, and I, were playing on the landing and up and down the staircase of our tower. I remember, Jack was the stag, and Kate and I were the hunters; and rarely did Jack throw up his head, to show off his branching horns—which were divers twigs tied on his head by a lace of Dame Hilda's, for the use whereof Jack paid a pretty penny when she knew it. Kate had just made a grab at him, and should have caught him, had his tunic held, but it gave way, and all she won was an handful of worsted and a slip of the step that grazed her shins; and she was rubbing of her leg and crying "Lack-a-day!" and Jack above, well out of reach, was making mowes (grimaces) at us—when all at once an horn rang loud through the Castle, and man on little ambling nag came into the court-yard. Kate forgat her leg, and Jack his mowes, and all we, stag and hunters alike, ran to the gallery window for to gaze.

I know not how long we should have tarried at the window, had not Emelina come and swept us afore her into the nursery, with an impatient— "Deary me! here be these children for ever in the way!"

And Jack cries, "You always say we are in the way; but mustn't we be any where?"

Whereto she makes answer—"Go and get you tucked into bed; that's the only safe place for the like of you!"

Jack loudly resented being sent to bed before the proper time, whereupon he and Emelina had a fight (as they had most nights), and Kate and I ran into the nursery to get out of the way. Here was Margery, turning down the beds, but Dame Hilda we saw not till, an half-hour after, as we were doffing us for bed, she came, with her important face which she was wont to wear when some eventful thing had befallen her or us.

"Are the damsels abed, Emelina?" saith she.

"The babes be, Dame; and the elders be a-doffing them."

Dame Hilda came forward into the night nursery.

"Hold you there, young ladies!" saith she: "at the least, I would say my three elder young ladies—Dame Margaret, Dame Joan, and Dame Isabel. Pray you, don you once more, but of your warmest gear, for a journey by night."

"Are we not to go to bed?" asked Joan in surprise: but our three sisters donned themselves anew, as Dame Hilda had said, of their warmest gear. Dame Hilda spake not word till they were all ready. Then Meg saith—

"Whither be we bound, Dame?—and with whom?"

"With my Lady, Dame Margaret, to Southampton."

I think we all cried out "Southampton!" in diverse tones.

"There is news come to her Ladyship, as she herself may tell you," said Dame Hilda, mysteriously.

"Aren't we to go, Dame?" saith Blanche's little voice.

Dame Hilda turned round sharply, as if she went about to snap Blanche's head off; and Blanche shrank in dismay.

"Certainly not, Dame Blanche! What should my Lady do to be worried with babes like you? She has enough else on her mind at this present, without a pack of tiresome children—holy saints be her help! Eh dear, dear, this world!"

"Dame, is this world so bad?" saith Jack, letting his nose appear above the bed-clothes.

"Go to sleep, the weary lot of you!" was Dame Hilda's irritable answer.

"Because," saith Jack, ne'er a whit daunted—nothing ever cowed Jack—"if it is so bad, hadn't you better be off out of it? You'd be better off, I suppose, and we shouldn't miss you,—that I'll promise. Do go, Dame!"

Jack spake these last words with a full compassionate air, as though he were seriously concerned for Dame Hilda's happiness; but she, marching up to the bed where Jack lay, dealt him a stinging slap for his impudence.

"Ah!" saith Jack in a mumbled voice, having disappeared under the bed-clothes, "this is a bad world, I warrant you, where folks return evil for good o' this fashion!"

We heard no more of Jack beyond divers awesome snores, which I think were not altogether sooth-fast: but before many minutes had passed, the door of the antechamber opened, and my Lady, donned in travelling gear, entered the nursery.

Dame Hilda's words had given me the fancy that some sorrowful, if not shocking news, had come to her; and I was therefore much astonished to see a faint flush in her cheeks, and a brilliant light in her eyes, which looked as though she had heard good news.

"My children," said our mother, "I come to bid you all farewell—may be a long farewell. I have heard that—never mind what; that which will take me away. Meg, and Joan, and Ibbot, must go with me."

"Take me too!" pleaded little Blanche.

"Thee too!" repeated our mother, with a loving smile. "Nay, sweetheart! That cannot be. Now, my children, I hope you will all be good and obedient to Dame Hilda while I am away."

It was on Kate that her glance fell, being the next eldest after Isabel; and Kate answered readily—

"We will all be good as gold, Dame."

"Nym, and Hodge, and Geoffrey," she went on, "go also with me; so thou, Kate, wilt be eldest left here, and I look to thee to set a good ensample to thy brethren,—especially my little wilful Jack."

Jack's snoring had stopped when she came in, and now, as she went over and sat her down by the bed wherein Jack lay of the outside, up came Jack's head from under the blue velvet coverlet. Our mother laid her hand tenderly upon it.

"My dear little Jack!" she said; "my poor little Jack!"

"Dame, I'm not poor, an't like you!" made answer Jack, in a tone of considerable astonishment. "I've got a whole ball of new string, and two battledores and a shuttlecock, and a ball, and a bow and arrows."

"Yes, my little Jack," she said, tenderly.

"There are lots of lads poorer than me!" quoth Jack. "Nym himself hasn't got a whole ball of string, and Geoff hasn't a bit. I asked him. Master Inge gave it me yesterday. I'm going to make reins with it for Annis and Maud, and lots of cats' cradles."

"You're not going to make reins for *me*," said Maud from our bed. "Dame, it is horrid playing horses with Jack. He wants you to take the string in your mouth, and you don't know where he's had it. I don't mind having it tied to my arms, but I won't have it in my mouth."

"Did you ever see a horse with his reins tied to his arms?" scornfully demanded Jack. "You do as you are bid, my Lady Maud, or I'll come and make you."

"Children!" said our mother's soft voice, before Maud could answer, "are you going to quarrel this last night when I have come to say farewell? For shame, Maud! this was thy blame."

"Oh, of course, it is always me," muttered Maud, too angry for grammar. "Jack's always the favourite; I never do any thing right."

"Yes, you do—now and then, by accident," responded Joan, who was sitting at the foot of our bed; a speech which did not better Maud's temper, and it was never angelic.

Jack seemed to have forgotten his passage-at-arms with Maud. He was always good-tempered enough, though he did tease outrageously.

"Why am I poor, Dame?" quoth Jack.

"Little Jack, thou must shortly go into the wars, and thou hast no armour."

"But you'll get me a suit. Dame?"

"I cannot, Jack. Not for these wars. Neither can I give thee the wealth to make thee rich, as I fain would."

"Then, Dame, you will petition the King for a grant, will you not?" saith Meg.

"True, my daughter," saith our mother softly. "I must needs petition the King, both for the riches from His treasury, and for the arms from His armoury." And then she bent down to kiss Jack. "O my boy, lay not up treasure for thyself, and thus fail to be rich in God."

I began then to see what she meant; but I rather wondered why she said it. Such talk as that, it seemed to me, was only fit for Sunday. And then I remembered that she was going away for a long, long time, and that therefore Sunday talk might be appropriate.

I do not recollect any thing she said to the others, only to Jack and me. Jack and I were always fellows. We children had paired ourselves off, not altogether according to age, but rather according to tastes. Edmund and Meg should have gone together, and then Hodge and Joan, and so forth: whereas it was always Nym and Joan, and Meg and Hodge. Then Geoffrey and Isabel made the right pair, and Kate, Jack, and I, went in a trio. Maud was by herself; she paired with nobody, and nobody wanted her, she was so cross. Blanche was every body's pet while she was the baby, and Beatrice came last of all.

Our mother went round, and kissed and blessed us all. I lay inside with Kate and Maud, and when she said, "Now, my little Agnes,"—I crept out and travelled over the tawny silk coverlet, to those gentle velvet arms, and she took me on her lap, and lapped me up in a fur mantle that Meg bare on her arm.

"And what shall I say to my little Agnes?"

"Mother, say you love me!"

It came out before I knew it, and when I had said it, I was so frightened that I hid my face in the fur. It did not encourage me to hear Dame Hilda's exclamation—

"Lack-a-day! what next, trow?"

But the other voice was very tender and gentle.

"Didst thou lack that told thee, mine own little Annis? Ay me! Maybe men are happier lower down. Who should love thee, my floweret, if not thine own mother? Kiss me, and say thou wilt be good maid till I see thee again."

I managed to whisper, "I will try, Dame."

"How long will it be?" cries Jack.

"I cannot tell thee, Jack," she saith. "Some months, I fear. Not years—I do trust, not years. But God knoweth—and to Him I commit you." And as she bent her head low over the mantle wherein I was lapped, I heard her say—"*Agnus Dei, qui tollis peccata mundi, miserere nobis, Jesu!*"

I knew that, because I always had to repeat it in my evening prayers, though I never could tell what it meant, only, as it seemed to say "Agnes" and "Monday," I supposed it had something to do with me, and was to make me good after some fashion, but I saw not why it must be only on a Monday, especially as I had to say it every day. Now, of course, I know what it means, and I wonder children and ignorant people are not taught what prayers mean, instead of being made to say them just like popinjays. I wanted to teach my Joan what it meant, but the Lady Julian, my lord's mother, commanded me not to do so, for it was unlucky. I begged her to tell me why, and she said the Latin was a holy tongue, known to God and the saints, and so long as they understood our prayers, we did not need to understand them.

"But, Dame," said I, "saving your presence, if I say prayers I understand not, how can I tell the way to use them? I may be asking for a basket of pears when I want a pair of shoes."

"Wherefore trouble the blessed saints for either?" saith she. "Prayers be only for high and holy concerns—not for base worldly matter, such as be pears and shoes."

"But I am worldly matter, under your leave, Dame," said I. "And saith not the Paternoster somewhat touching daily bread?"

"Ay, the food of the soul—'*panem supersubstantialem da nobis*'" quoth she. "It means not a loaf of bread, child."

"That's Saint Matthew," said I. "But Saint Luke hath it '*panem quotidianum*,' and saith nought of '*supersubstantialem*.' And surely common food cometh from God."

"Daughter!" saith she, somewhat severely, "thou shouldst do a deal better to leave thy fantasies and the workings of thine own brain, and listen with meek submission to the holy doctors that can teach thee with authority."

"Dame, I cry you mercy," said I. "But surely our Lord teacheth with more authority than they all; and if I have His words, what need I of theirs?"

Ha, chétife! she would not listen to me,—only bade me yet again to beware of pride and presumption, lest I should fall into heresy, from the which Saint Agnes preserve me! But it doth seem strange that folks should fall into heresy by studying our Lord's words; I had thought they should rather thereby keep them out of it.

Well—dear heart, here again am I got away from my story! this it is to have too quick a wit—our mother blessed us, and kissed us all, and set forth, the six eldest with her, for Southampton. I know now, though I heard not then, that she was on her way to join our father. News had come that he was safe over seas, in France, with the Sieurs de Fienles, the Lady Margaret's kin, and no sooner had she learned it than she set forth to join him. I doubt greatly if he sent for her. Nay, I should rather say he would scarce have blessed her for coming. But she got not thus far on her way, as shall be seen.

His tarrying with the Sieurs de Fienles was in truth but a blind to hide his true proceedings. He stayed in Normandy but a few weeks, until the hue and cry was over, and folks in England should all have got well in their heads that he was there: then, or ever harm should befall him by tarrying there too long, he made quiet departure, and ere any knew of it he was safe in the King of France's dominions. At this time the King of France was King Charles le Bel, youngest brother of our Queen. I suppose he was too much taken up with the study of his own perfections to see the perfections or imperfections of any body else: otherwise had he scarce been so stone-blind to all that went on but just afore his nose. There be folks that can see a mouse a mile off, and there be others that cannot see an elephant a yard in front of them. But there be a third sort, and to my honest belief King Charles was of them, that can see the mouse as clear as sunlight when it is their own interest to detect him, but have not a notion of the elephant being there when they do not choose to look at him. When he wanted to be rid of his first wife Queen Blanche, he could see her well enough, and all her failings too, as black as midnight; but when his sister behaved herself as ill as ever his wife did or could have done, he only shut his eyes and took a comfortable nap. Now King Charles had himself expelled my father from his dominions, for some old grudge that I never rightly understood; yet never a word said he when he came back without licence. Marry, but our old King Edward should not have treated thus the unlicenced return of a banished man! He would have been hung within the week, with him on the throne. But King

Charles was not cut from that stuff. He let my father alone till the Queen came over—our Queen Isabel, his sister, I mean—and then who but he in all the French Court! Howbeit, they kept things pretty quiet for that time; nought came to King Edward's ears, and she did her work and went home. Forsooth, it was sweet work, for she treated with her brother as the sister of France, and not as the wife of England. King Charles had taken Guienne, and she, sent to demand restitution, concluded a treaty of peace on his bare word that it should be restored, with no pledge nor security whatever: but bitter complaints she laid of the King her husband, and the way in which he treated her. Well, it is true, he did not treat her as I should have done in his place, for he gave in to all her whims a deal too much, where a good buffet on her ear should have been ever so much more for her good—and his too, I will warrant. Deary me, but if some folks were drowned, the world would get along without them! I mention no names (only that weary Nichola, that is for ever mashing my favourite things). So the Queen came home, and all went on for a while.

But halt, my goose-quill! thou marchest too fast. Have back a season.

Note 1. This is the probable order of birth. The date assigned to the birth of Agnes is fictitious, but that of her husband is taken from his *Probatio Aetatis*.

Note 2. July 8th, 1317; this is about the probable time. The Countess is supposed to be writing in the spring of 1348.

Note 3. This word was then used of both sexes, and was the proper designation of the son of a prince or peer not yet arrived at the age of knighthood.

Chapter 2
The Lady of Ludlow

"Toil-worn and very weary—
For the waiting-time is long;
Leaning upon the promise—
For the Promiser is strong."

So were we children left alone in the Castle of Ludlow, and two weary months we had of it. Wearier were they by far than the six that ran afore them, when our mother was there, and our elder brethren, that she had now carried away. Lessons dragged, and play had no interest. It had been Meg that devised all our games, and Nym that made boats and wooden horses for us, and Joan that wove wreaths and tied cowslip balls—and they were all away. There was not a bit of life nor fun anywhere except in Jack, and if Jack were shut in a coal-hole by himself, he would make the coals play with him o' some fashion. But even Jack could fetch no fun out of *amo, amas, amat*; and I grew sore weary of pulling my neeld (needle) in and out, and being banged o'er the head with the fiddlestick when I played the wrong string. If we could swallow learning as we do meat, what a lessening of human misery should it be!

No news came all this while—at least, none that we heard. Winter grew into spring, and May came with her flowers. Ay, and with something else.

The day rose like the long, dreary days that had come before it, and nobody guessed that any thing was likely to happen. We ate eggs and butter, and said our verbs and the commandments of God and the Church, to Sir Philip, and played some weary, dreary exercises on the spinnet to Dame Hilda, and dined (I mind it was on lamb, finches, and flaunes (custards)), and then Kate, I, and Maud, were set down to our needles. Blanche was something too young for needlework, saving to pull coloured silks in and out of a bit of rag for practice. We had scarce taken twenty stitches, when far in the distance we heard a horn sounded.

"Is that my Lady a-coming home?" said I to Kate.

"Eh, would it were!" quoth she. "I reckon it is some hunters in the neighbourhood."

I looked to and fro, and no Dame Hilda could I see—only Margery, and she was easy enough with us for little things; so I crept out on tiptoe into the long gallery, and looked through the great oriel, which I could well reach by climbing on the window-seat. I remember what a sweet, peaceful scene lay before me,—the fields and cottages lighted up with the May sunshine, which glinted on the Teme as it wound here and there amid the trees. I looked right and left, but saw no hunters—nothing at all, I thought at first. And then, as I was going to leave the oriel, I saw the sun glance on something that moved, and looked like a dark square, and I heard the horn ring out again a little nearer. I watched the square thing grow—from dark to red, from an indistinct mass to a compact body of marching men, with mounted officers at their head; and then, forgetting Dame Hilda and every thing else except the startling news I brought, I rushed back into the nursery, crying out—

"The King's troops! Jack, Kate, the King's troops are coming! Come and see!"

Dame Hilda was there, but she did not scold me. She turned as white as the sindon in her hand, and stood up.

"Dame Agnes, what mean you? Surely 'tis never thus! Holy Mary, shield us!"

And she hurried forth to the oriel window, where Jack was already perched.

The square had grown larger and plainer now. It was evident they were marching straight for the Castle.

Dame Hilda hastened away—I guessed, to confer with Master Inge—and having so done, she came back to the nursery, bade us put aside our sewing and wash our hands, and come down with her to hall. We all trooped after, Beatrice led by her hand, and she ranged us afore her in the great hall, on the dais, standing after our ages,—Kate at the head, then I, Maud, and Jack. And so we awaited our fate.

I scarce think I was frighted. I knew too little what was likely to happen, to feel so. That something was going to happen, I had uncertain fantasy; but our life had been colourless for so long, that the idea of any thing to happen which would make a change was rather agreeable than otherwise.

We heard the last loud summons of the trumpet, which in our ignorance we had mistaken for a hunting-horn, and the trumpeter's cry of "Open to the King's troops!" We heard the portcullis lifted, and the steady tramp of the soldiers as they marched into the court-yard. There was a little parleying outside, and then two officers in the King's livery (Note 1) came forward into the hall, bowing low to us and Dame Hilda.

The Dame spoke first. "Sir Thomas Gobioun, if I err not?"

"He, and your servant, Dame," answered one of the officers.

"Then I must needs do you to wit, Sir, that in this castle is neither Lord nor Lady, and I trust our Lord the King wars not with little children such as you see here."

"Stale news, good Dame!" answered Sir Thomas, with (as methought) a rather grim smile. "We know something more, I reckon, than you, touching your Lord and Lady. Sir Roger de Mortimer is o'er seas in Normandy, and the Lady Joan at Skipton Castle."

"At Southampton, you surely mean?" said Master Inge, who stood at the other end of the line whereof I made the midmost link.

The knight laughed out. "Nay, worthy Master Inge, I mean not Southampton, but Skipton. 'Tis true, both begin with an *S*, and end with a *p* and a *ton*; but there is a mile or twain betwixt the places."

"What should my Lady do at Skipton?" saith Dame Hilda.

"Verily, I conceive not this!" saith Master Inge, knitting his brows. "It was to Southampton my Lady went—at least so she told us."

"Your Lady told you truth, Master Castellan. She set forth for Southampton, and reached it. But ere a fair wind blew for her voyage, came a somewhat rougher gale in the shape of a command from the King's Grace to the Sheriff to take her into keeping, and send her into ward at Skipton Castle, whither she set forth a fortnight past. Now, methinks, Master Inge, you are something wiser than you were a minute gone."

"And our young damsels?" cries Dame Hilda. "Be they also gone to Skipton?"

I felt Kate's hand close tighter upon mine.

"Soft you, now, good Dame!" saith Sir Thomas—who, or I thought so, took it all as a very good joke. "Your damsels be parted in so many as they be, and sent to separate convents,—one to Shuldham, one to Sempringham, and one to Chicksand—and their brothers be had likewise into ward."

To my unspeakable amazement, Dame Hilda burst into tears, and catched up Beatrice in her arms. I had never seen her weep in my life: and a most new and strange idea was taking possession of me—did Dame Hilda actually care something for us?

"Sir," she sobbed, "you will never have the heart to part these babes from all familiar faces, and send them amongst strangers that may use them hardly, to break their baby hearts? Surely the King, that is father of his people, hath never commanded such a thing as that? At the least leave me this little one—or put me in ward with her."

I was beginning to feel frightened now. I looked at Kate, and read in her face that she was as terrified as I was.

"Tut, tut, Dame," saith the other officer (Sir Thomas, it seemed to me, enjoyed the scene, and rather wished to prolong it, but this other was of softer metal), "take not on where is no cause, I pray you. The little ones bide here under your good care. Only, as you may guess, we be commanded to take to the King's use this Castle of Ludlow and all therein, and we charge you—" and he bowed to Dame Hilda, and then to Master Inge—"and you, in the King's name, that you thwart not nor hinder us, in the execution of his pleasure. Have here our commission."

Master Inge took the parchment, and scrutinised it most carefully, while Dame Hilda wiped her eyes and put Beatrice down with a fervent "Bless thee, my jewel!"

Now out bursts Jack, with a big sob that he could contain no longer. "Does the King want my new ball of string, and my battledores?"

"Certes," answered Sir Thomas: but I saw a twinkle in his eye, though his mouth was as grave as might be.

Jack fell a-blubbering.

"No, no—nonsense!" saith the other officer. "Don't spoil the fun, man!" quoth Sir Thomas. "Fun! it is no fun to these babes," answered the other. "I've a little lad at home, and this mindeth me of him. I cannot bear to see a child cry—and for no cause!—Nay, my little one," saith he to Jack, "all in this Castle now belongs to the King, as aforetime to thy father: but thy father took not thy balls and battledores from thee, nor will he. Cheer up, for thou hast nought to fear."

"Please, Sir," saith Kate, "shall all our brothers and sisters be made monks and nuns, whether they like or no?"

Sir Thomas roared with laughter. His comrade saith gently, "Nay, my little damsel, the King's will is not so. It is but that they shall be kept safe there during his pleasure."

"And will they get any dinner and supper?" saith Maud.

"Plenty!" he answered: "and right good learning, and play in the convent garden at recreation-time, with such other young damsels as shall be bred up there. They will be merry as crickets, I warrant."

Kate fetched a great sigh of relief. She told me afterwards that she had felt quite sure we should every one of us be had to separate convents, and never see each other any more.

So matters dropped down again into their wonted course. For over two years, our mother tarried at Skipton, and then she was moved into straiter ward at Pomfret, about six weeks only (Note 2) before Queen Isabel landed with her alien troops under Sir John of Ostrevant, and drave King Edward first from his throne, and finally from this life. Our father came with her. And this will I say, that our mother might have been set free something earlier (Note 3), if every body had done his duty. But folks are not much given to doing their duties, so far as I can see. They are as ready as you please to contend for their rights—which generally seems to mean, "Let me have somebody else's rights;" ay, they will get up a battle for that at short notice: but who ever heard of a man petitioning, much less fighting, for the right to do his duty? And yet is not that, really and verily, the only right a man has?

It was a gala day for us when our mother returned home, and our brothers and sisters were gathered and sent back to us. Nym (always a little given to romance) drew heart-rending pictures of his utter misery, while in ward; but Roger said it was not so bad, setting aside that it was prison, and we were parted from one another. And Geoffrey, the sensible boy of the family, said that while he would not like a monk's life on the whole, being idle and useless, yet he did like the quiet and peacefulness of it.

"But I am not secure," said our mother, "that such quiet is what God would for us, saving some few. Soldiers be not bred by lying of a bed of rose-leaves beside scented waters. And I think the soldiers of Christ will scarce be taught o' that fashion."

Diverse likewise were the maids' fantasies. Meg said she would not have bidden at Shuldham one day longer than she was forced. Joan said she liked not ill at Sempringham, only for being alone. But Isabel, as she sat afore the fire with me on her lap, the even of her coming home—Isabel had ever petted me—and Dame Hilda asked her touching her life at Chicksand—Isabel said, gazing with a far-away look into the red ashes—

"I shall go back to Chicksand, some day, if I may win leave of mine elders."

"Why, Dame Isabel!" quoth Dame Hilda in some surprise. "Liked you so well as that?"

"Ay, I liked well," she said, in that dreamy fashion. "Not that I did not miss you all, Dame; and in especial my babe here,—who is no longer a babe"—and she smiled down at me. "And verily, I could see that sins be not shut out by convent walls, but rather shut in. Yet—"

"Ay?" said Dame Hilda when she stayed. I think she wanted to make her talk.

"I scarce know how to say it," quoth she. "But it seemed to me that for those who would have it so, Satan was shut in with them, and pleasure was shut out. And also, for those who would have it so, God was shut in with them, and snares and temptations—some of them—were shut out. Only some: but it was something to be rid of them. If it were possible to have only those who wanted to shut out the world, and to shut themselves in with God! That is the theory: and that would be Heaven on earth. But it does not work in practice."

"Yet you would fain return thither?" said Dame Hilda.

Isabel looked into the fire and answered not, until she said, all suddenly, "Dame Hilda, be there two of you, or but one?"

"Truly, Dame Isabel, I take not your meaning."

"Ah!" saith she; "then is there but one of you. If so, you cannot conceive me. Thou dost, Ellen?"

"Ay, Dame Isabel, that do I, but too well."

"They have easier lives, methinks, that are but one. You look on me, Dame Hilda, as who should say, What nonsense doth this maid talk! But if you knew what it was to have two natures within you, pulling you diverse ways, sometimes the one uppermost, and at times the other; and which of the twain be *you*, that cannot you tell—I will tell you, I have noted this many times"—Isabel's voice sank as if she feared to be overheard—"in them whose father and mother have been of divers dispositions. Some of the children may take after the one, and some after the other; but there will be one, at least, who partaketh both, and then they pull him divers ways, that he knoweth no peace." Isabel's audience had been larger than she supposed. As she ended, with a weary sigh, a soft hand fell upon her head, and I who, sat upon her knees, could better see than she, looked up into my Lady's face.

"Sit still, daughter," said she, as Isabel strove to rise. "Nay, sweet heart, I am not angered at thy fantasy, though truly I, being but one like Dame

Hilda, conceive not thy meaning. It may be so. I have not all the wit upon earth, that I should scorn or set down the words of them that speak out of other knowledge than mine. But, my Isabel, there is another way than this wherein thou mayest have two natures."

"How so, Dame, an' it like you?"

"The nature of sinful man, and the nature of God Almighty."

"They must be marvellous saints that so have," said Dame Hilda, crossing herself.

"Some of them," said my Lady gently, "were once marvellous sinners."

"Why, you should have to strive a very lifetime for that," quoth Dame Hilda. "I should think no man could rise thereto that dwelt not in anchorite's cell, and scourged him on the bare back every morrow, and ate but of black rye-bread, and drank of ditch-water. Deary me, but I would not like that! I'd put up with a bit less saintliness, *I* would!"

"You are all out there, Dame," my Lady made answer. "This fashion of saintliness may be along with such matters, but it cometh not by their help."

"How comes it then, Dame, an't like you?"

"By asking for it," saith our mother, quietly.

"Good lack! but which of the saints must I ask for it?" quoth she. "I'll give him all the wax candles in Ludlow, a week afore I die. I'd rather not have it sooner."

"When go you about to die, Dame?"

"Our Lady love us! That cannot I say."

"Then you shall scarce know the week before, I think."

"Oh, no! but the saint shall know. Look you, Dame, to be too much of a saint should stand sore in man's way. I could not sing, nor dance, nor lake me a bit, if I were a saint; and that fashion of saintliness you speak of must needs be sorest of all. If I do but just get it to go to Heaven with, that shall serve me the best."

"I thought they sang in Heaven," saith Isabel.

"Bless you, Damsel!—nought but Church music."

"Dame Hilda, I marvel if you would be happy in Heaven."

"Oh, I should be like, when I got there."

My Lady shook her head.

"For that," quoth she, "you must be partaker of the Divine nature. Which means not, doing good works contrary to your liking, but having the nature which delights in doing them."

"Oh, ay, that will come when we be there."

"On the contrary part, they that have it not here on earth shall not win there. They only that be partakers of Christ may look to enter Heaven. And no man that partaketh Christ's merits can miss to partake Christ's nature."

"Marry, then but few shall win there."

"So do I fear," saith my Lady.

"Dame, under your good pleasure," saith Dame Hilda, looking her earnestly in the face, "where gat you such notions? They be something new. At the least, never heard I your Ladyship so to speak aforetime."

My Lady's cheek faintly flushed.

"May God forgive me," saith she, "all these years to have locked up his Word, which was burning in mine own heart! Yet in good sooth, Dame, you are partly right. Ere I went to Skipton, I was like one that seeth a veiled face, or that gazeth through smoked glass. But now mine eyes have beheld the face of Him that was veiled, and I have spoken with Him, as man speaketh with his friend. And if you would know who helped me thereto, it was an holy hermit, by name Richard Rolle, that did divers times visit me in my prison at Skipton. And he knows Him full well."

"Dame!" saith Dame Hilda, looking somewhat anxiously on my mother, "I do trust you go not about to die, nor to hie in cloister and leave all these poor babes! Do bethink you, I pray, ere you do either."

My Lady smiled. "Nay, good my Dame!" saith she. "How can I go in cloister, that am wedded wife?"

"Eh, but you might get your lord's consent thereto—some wedded women doth."

I was looking on my Lady, and I saw a terrible change in her face when Dame Hilda spoke those words. I felt, too, Isabel's sudden nervous shiver. And I guessed what they both thought—that assent would be easy enough to win. For in all those months since Queen Isabel came over, he had never come near us. He was ever at the Court, waiting upon her. And though his duties—if he had them, but what they were we knew not—might keep him at the Court in general, yet surely, had he been very desirous to see us, he might have won leave to run over when the Queen was at Hereford, were it only for an hour or twain.

Our mother did not answer for a moment. When she did, it was to say—"Nay, vows may not be thus lightly done away. 'Till death' scarce means, till one have opportunity to undo."

"Then, pray you, go not and die, Dame!"

"I am immortal till God bids me die," she made answer. "But why should man die because he loveth Jesu Christ better than he was wont?"

"Oh, folks always do when they get marvellous good."

"It were ill for the world an' they so did," saith my Lady. "That is bad enough to lack good folks."

"It is bad enough to lack *you*," saith Dame Hilda.

My Lady gave a little laugh, and so the converse ended.

The next thing that I can remember, after that, was the visit of our father. He only came that once, and tarried scarce ten days; but he took Nym and Geoffrey back with him. I heard Dame Hilda whisper somewhat to Tamzine, as though he had desired to have also one or two of the elder damsels, and that my Lady had so earnestly begged and prayed to the contrary that for once he gave way to her. It was not often, I think, that he did that. It was four years good ere we saw either of our brothers again—not till all was over—and then Geoff told us a sorry tale indeed of all that had happed.

It was at the time when our father paid us this visit that my marriage and that of Beatrice were covenanted. King Edward of Caernarvon had contracted my lord that now is to the Lady Alianora La Despenser, daughter of my sometime Lord of Gloucester (Hugh Le Despenser the Younger), who was put to death at Hereford by Queen Isabel. But she—I mean the Queen—who hated him and all his, sent the Lady Alianora to Sempringham, with command to veil her instantly, and gave the marriage of my Lord to my Lord Prince, the King that now is (Edward the Third). So my father, being then at top of the tree, begged the marriage for one of his daughters, and it was settled that should be me. I liked it well enough, to feel myself the most important person in the pageant, and to be beautifully donned, and all that; and as I was not to leave home for some years to come, it was but a show, and cost me nothing. I dare say it cost somebody a pretty penny. Beatrice was higher mated, with my Lord of Norfolk's son, who was the King's cousin, but he died a lad, poor soul! so her grandeur came to nought, and she wedded at last a much lesser noble.

Thus dwelt we maids with our mother in the Castle of Ludlow, seeing nought of the fine doings that were at Court, save just for the time of our marriages, which were at Wynchecombe on the day of Saint Lazarus, that is the morrow of O Sapientia (Note 4). The King was present himself, and the young Lady Philippa, who the next month became our Queen, and his sisters the Ladies Alianora and Joan, and more Earls and Countesses than I can count, all donned their finest. Well-a-day, but there must have been many a yard of velvet in that chapel, and an whole army of beasts ermines must have laid their lives down to purfile (trim with fur) the same! I was donned myself of blue velvet guarded of miniver, and wore all my Lady's jewels on mine head and corsage; and marry, but I queened it! Who but I for that morrow, in very sooth!

Ay, and somebody else (Queen Isabelle, the young King's mother) was there, whom I have not named. Somebody robed in snow-white velvet, with close hood and wimple, so that all that showed of her face was from the eyebrows to the lips,—all pure, unstained mourning white. Little I knew of the horrible stains on that black heart beneath! And I thought her so sweet, so fair! Come, I have spoken too plainly to add a name.

So all passed away like a dream, and we won back to Ludlow, and matters fell back to the old ways, as if nought had ever happened—the only real difference being that instead of "Damsel Agnes" I was "my Lady of Pembroke," and our baby Beatrice, instead of "Damsel Beattie," was "my Lady Beatrice of Norfolk." And about a year after that came letters from Nym, addressed to "my Lady Countess of March," in which he writ that the King had made divers earls, and our father amongst them. Dame Hilda told us the news in the nursery, and Jack turned a somersault, and stood on his hands, with his heels up in the air.

"Call me Jack any more, if you dare!" cries he. "I am my Lord John of March, and I shall expect to be addressed so, properly. Do you hear, children?"

"I hear one of the children, in good sooth," said Meg, comically. And Maud saith—

"Prithee, Jack, take no airs, for they beseem thee but very ill."

Whereon Jack fell a-moaning and a-crying out, that Dame Hilda thought he was rare sick, and ordered Emelina to get ready a dose of violet oil. But before Emelina could so much as fetch a spoon, there was Jack dancing a hornpipe and singing, or rather screaming, at the top of his voice, till Dame Hilda put her hands over her ears and cried for mercy. I never did see such another lad as Jack.

We heard but little, and being children, we cared less, for the events that followed—the beheading of my Lord of Kent, and the rising under my Lord of Lancaster. And the next thing after that was the last thing of all.

It was in October, 1330. We had no more idea of such a blow falling on us than we had of the visitation of an angel. I remember we were all gathered—except the little ones—in my Lady's closet, for after my marriage I was no longer kept in the nursery, though Beattie, on account of her much youth, was made an exception to that rule. My Lady was spinning, and her damsel Aveline carding, and Joan and I, our arms round each others' waists, sat in the corner, Joan having on her lap a piece of finished broidery, and I having nothing: what the others were doing I forget. Then came the familiar sound of the horn, and my Lady turned white. I never felt sure why she always turned white when a horn sounded: whether she expected bad news, or whether she expected our father. She was exceeding afraid of him, and yet she loved him, I know: I cannot tell how she managed it.

After the horn, we heard the tramp of troops entering the court-yard, and I think we all felt that once more something was going to happen. Aveline glanced at my Lady, who returned the look, but did not speak; and then Lettice, one of the other maidens, rose and went forth, at a look from Aveline. But she could scarcely have got beyond the door when Master Inge came in.

"Dame," said he, "my news is best told quickly. The Castle and all therein is confiscate to the Crown. But the King hath sent strict command that the wardrobe, jewels, and all goods, of your Ladyship, and of all ladies and children dwelling with you, shall be free from seizure, and no hand shall be laid on you nor any thing belonging to you."

My Lady rose up, resting her hand on the chair from which she rose; I think it was to support her.

"I return humble thanks to the Lord King," said she, in a trembling voice. "What hath happened, Master Inge?"

"Dame," quoth he, "how shall I tell you? My Lord is a prisoner of the Tower, and Sir Edmund and Sir Geoffrey with him—"

If my Lady could turn whiter, I think she did. I felt Joan's hand-clasp tighten upon mine, till I could almost have cried out.

"And Dame Isabel the Queen is herself under ward in the Castle of Berkhamsted, and all matters turned upside down. Man saith that the great men with the King be now Sir William de Montacute and Sir Edward de Bohun, and divers more of like sort. And my Lord of Lancaster, man saith, flung up his cap, and thanked God that he had lived to see that day."

My Lady had stood as still and silent as an image, all the while Master Inge was speaking, only that when he said the Queen was in ward, she gave a sort of gasp. When he had done, she clasped her hands, and looked up to Heaven.

"Dost Thou come," she said, in a strange voice that did not sound like hers, "dost Thou come to judge the earth? We have waited long for Thee. Yet—Oh, if it be possible—if it be possible! Spare my boys to me! And spare—"

A strange kind of sob seemed to come up in her throat, and she held out her hands as if she could not see. I believe, if Master Inge and Lettice had not been quick to spring forward and catch her by the arms, she would have fallen to the floor. They bore her into her bedchamber close by; and we children saw her not for some time. Dame Hilda was in and out; but when we asked her how my Lady fared, she did nought save shake her head, from which we learned little except that things went ill in some way. When we asked Lettice, she said—

"There, now! don't hinder me. Poor children, you will know soon enough."

Aveline was the best, for she sat down and gathered us into her arms and comforted us; but even she gave us no real answer, only she kept saying, "Poor maids! poor little maids!"

So above a month passed away. Master John de Melbourne was sent down from the King as supervisor of the lands and goods of my Lady and her children; but he came with the men-at-arms, so he brought no fresh news: and it was after Christmas before we knew the rest. Then, one winter morrow, came a warrant of the Chancery, granting to my Lady all the lands of her own inheritance, by reason of the execution of her husband. And then she knew that all had come that would come.

We children, Meg except, had not yet been allowed to see our mother, who had never stirred from her bedchamber. One evening, early in January, we were sitting in her closet, clad in our new doole raiment (how I hated it!), talking to one another in low voices, for I think we all had a sort of instinct that things were going wrong somehow, even the babies who understood least about it: when all at once, for none of us saw her enter, a lady stood before us. A lady whom we did not know, clad in white widow-doole, tall and stately, with a white, white face, so that her weeds were scarcely whiter, and a kind of fixed, unalterable expression of intense pain, yet unchangeable peace. It seemed to me such a strange look. Whether the pain or the peace were the greater I knew not, nor could I tell which was the newer. We girls sat and looked at her with puzzled faces. Then a faint smile broke through the pain, on the white face, like the sun breaking through clouds, and a voice we knew, asked of us—

"Don't you know me, my children?"

And that was how our mother came back to us.

She did not leave us again. Ever since he died, she has lived for us. That white face, full of peace and yet of pain, abides with her; her colour has never returned. But I think the pain grows less with years, and the peace grows more. She smiles freely, but it is faintly, as if smiles hardly belonged to her, and were only a borrowed thing that might not be kept; and her eyes never light up as of old—only that once, when some months after our father's end, Nym and Geoff came back to us. Then, just for one moment, her old face came again. For I think she had given them up,—not to King Edward, but to Christ our Lord, who is her King.

Ay, I never knew woman like her in that. There are many that will say prayers, and there are some that will pray, which is another thing from saying prayers: but never saw I one like her, that seemed to do all her work and to live all her living in the very light of the Throne of God. Just as an impassioned musician turns every thing into music, and a true painter longs to paint every lovely thing he sees, so with her all things turn to Jesu Christ. I should think she will be canonised some day. I am sure she deserves it better than many an one whom I have heard man name as meriting to be a saint. Perhaps it is possible to be a saint and not be canonised. Must man not have been a saint before he can be declared one? I know the Lady Julian would chide me for saying that, and bid me remember that the Church only can declare man to be saint. But I wonder myself if the Lord never makes saints, without waiting for the Church to do it for Him. The Church may never call my Lady "Saint Joan," but that will she be whether she be so-called or no. And at times I think, too, that they who shall be privileged to dwell in Heaven will find there a great company of saints of whom they never heard, and perchance some of them that sit highest there will not be those most accounted of in the Calendar and on festival days. But I do not suppose—as an ancestress of my mother did, in a chronicle she wrote which I once read; it is in the possession of her French relatives, and was written by the Lady Elaine de Lusignan, daughter of Geoffroy Count de la Marche, who was a son of that House (Note 5)—I do not suppose that the saints who were nobles in this world will sit nearest the Throne, and those who were peasants furthest off. Nay, I think it will be another order of nobility that will obtain there. Those who have served our Lord the best, and done the most for their fellow-men, these I think will be the nobles of that world. For does not our Lord say Himself that the first shall be last there, and the last first? And I can guess that Joan de Mortimer, my Lady and mother, will not stand low on that list. It is true, she was a Countess in this life; but it was little to her comfort; and she was beside that early orphaned, and a cruelly ill-used wife and a bereaved mother. Life brought her little good: Heaven will bring her more.

But I wonder where one Agnes de Hastings will stand in that company. Nay, rather, will she be there at all?

It would be well that I should think about it.

Note 1. A word which then included uniform and all lands of official garb.

Note 2. On August 3rd she left Skipton, arriving at Pomfret on the 5th.

Note 3. I find no indication of the date: only that she was at Ludlow on October 26, 1330.

Note 4. The precise date and place are not recorded, but it was about this time, and the King, who was present, was in the West only from December 16th to the 21st. It is asserted by Walsingham that Beatrice was married "about" 1327.

Note 5. The Lady Elaine's chronicle is "Lady Sybil's Choice."

Part 3

Chapter 1
Wherein Sister Alianora La Despenser Maketh Moan (1371)

Caged

"But of all sad words by tongue or pen,
The saddest are these—
'It might have been!'"

Whittier.

"I marvel if the sun is never weary!"

Thus spoke my sister Margaret (Note 1), as she stood gazing from the window of the recreation-room, and Sister Roberga looked up and laughed.

"Nay, what next?" saith she. "Heard I ever such strange fancies as thine? Thou wilt be marvelling next if the stars be never athirst."

"And if rain be the moon weeping," quoth Sister Philippa, who seemed as much amused as Roberga.

"No, the moon weepeth not," said Margaret. "She is too cold to weep. She is like Mother Ada."

"Eh dear, what fancies hast thou!" saith Sister Roberga. "Who but thou would ever have thought of putting the moon and Mother Ada into one stall!"

"What didst thou mean, Sister Margaret?" saith the quiet voice of Mother Alianora, as she sat by the chimney corner.

Mother Alianora is our father's sister—Margaret's and mine; but I ought not to think of it, since a recluse should have no kindred out of her Order and the blessed saints. And there are three Sisters in the Priory named Alianora: wherefore, to make diversity, the eldest professed is called

Alianora, and the second (that is myself) Annora, and the youngest, only last year professed, Nora. We had likewise in this convent an Aunt Joan, but she deceased over twenty years gone. Margaret was professed in the Order when I was, but not at this house; and she hath been transferred hither but a few weeks (Note 2), so that her mind and heart are untravelled ground to me. She was a Sister at Watton: and since I can but just remember her before our profession, it seems marvellous strange that we should now come to know one another, after nearly fifty years' cloistered life. There is yet another Sister named Margaret, but being younger in profession we call her Sister Magota.

When Mother Alianora spoke, Margaret turned back from the window, as she ought when addressed by a superior.

"I mean, Mother, that he never hath any change of work," she said. "Every morrow he has to rise, and every night must he set: and always the one in east and the other in west. I think he must be sore, sore weary, for he hath been at it over five thousand years."

Sister Roberga and Sister Philippa laughed. Mother Alianora did not laugh. A soft, rather sorrowful, sort of smile came on her aged face.

"Art thou so weary, my daughter, that the thought grew therefore?" saith she.

Something came into Margaret's eyes for a moment, but it was out again, almost before I could see it. I knew not what it was; Margaret's eyes are yet a puzzle to me. They are very dark eyes, but they are different in their look from all the other dark eyes in the house. Sister Olive has eyes quite as dark; but they say nothing. Margaret's eyes talk so much that she might do very well without her tongue. Not that I always understand what they say; the language in which they speak is generally a foreign one to me. I fancy Mother Alianora can read it better. I listened for Margaret's reply.

"Dear Mother, is not weariness the lot of all humanity, and more especially of women?"

"Mary love us!" cries Philippa. "What gibberish you talk, Sister Margaret!"

"Sister Philippa will come here and ask Sister Margaret's forgiveness at once," saith Mother Gaillarde, the sub-Prioress.

Sister Philippa banged down her battledore on the table, and marching up, knelt before Margaret and asked forgiveness, making a face behind her back as soon as she had turned.

"Sister Philippa will take no cheese at supper," added the sub-Prioress.

Sister Philippa pulled another face—a very ugly one; it reminded me somewhat too much of the carved figure of the Devil with his mouth gaping on the Prior's stall in our Abbey Church. That and Sister Philippa's faces are the ugliest things I ever saw, except the Cellarer, and he looks so good-tempered that one forgets his ugliness.

"Sister Philippa is not weary, as it should seem," saith Mother Alianora, again with her quiet smile. "Otherwise, to speak thereof should scarcely seem gibberish to her."

I spoke not, but I thought it was in no wise gibberish to me. For I never had that vocation which alone should make nuns. Not God, but man, forced this veil upon me; for, ah me! I was meant for another life. And that other life, that should have been mine, I never cease to long for and to mourn over.

Only six years old was I—for though my seventh birthday was near, it was not past—when I was thrust into this house of religion. My vocation and my will were never asked. We—Margaret and I—were in Queen Isabel's way; and she plucked us and flung us over the hedge like weeds that cumbered her garden. It was all by reason she hated our father: but what he had done to make her thus hate him, that I never knew. And I was an affianced bride when I was torn away from all that should have made life glad, and prisoned here for ever more. How my heart keeps whispering to me, "It might have been!" There is a woman who comes for doles to the convent gate, and at times she hath with her the loveliest little child I ever saw; and they smile on each other, mother and child, and look so happy when they smile. Why was I cut off thus from all that makes other women happy? Nobody belongs to me; nobody loves me. The very thought of being loved, the very wish to be so, is sin in *me*, who am a veiled nun. But why was it made sin? It was not sin aforetime. *He* might have loved me, he whom I never saw after I was flung over the convent wall—he who was mine and not hers to whom I suppose they will have wedded him. But I know nothing: I shall never know. And they say it is sin to think of him. Every thing seems to be sin; and loving people more especially. Mother Ada told me one day that she saw in me an inclination to be too much drawn to Mother Alianora, and warned me to mortify it, because she was my father's sister, and therefore there was cause to fear it might be an indulgence of the flesh. And now, these weeks past, my poor, dry, withered heart seems to have a little faint pulsation in it, and goes out to Margaret—my sister Margaret with the strange dark eyes, my own sister who is an utter stranger to me. Must I crush the poor dry thing back, and hurt all that is left to hurt of it? Oh, will no saint in Heaven tell me why it is, that God, who loveth men, will not have monks and nuns to love each other? The Lord Prior saith He is a jealous God, and demands that we give all our love to Him. Yet I may love the blessed saints without any derogation to Him—but I must not love mine own sister. It is very perplexing. Do earthly fathers forbid their children to love one another, lest they should not be loved themselves sufficiently? I should have thought that love, like other things, increased by exercise, and that loving my sister would rather help me to love God. But they say not. I suppose they know.

Ah me, if I should find out at last that they mistook God's meaning!—that I might have had His love and Margaret's too!—nay, even that I might have had His love and that other, of which it is so wicked in me to think, and yet something is in me that will keep ever thinking! O holy and immaculate Virgin, O Saint Margaret, Saint Agnes, and all ye blessed maidens that dwell in Heaven, have mercy on me, miserable sinner! My soul is earth-bound, and I cannot rise. I am the bride of Christ, and I cannot cease lamenting my lost earthly bridal.

But hath Christ a thousand brides? They say holy Church is His Bride, and she is one. Then how can all the vestals in all the convents be each of them His bride? I suppose I cannot understand as I ought to do. Perhaps I should have understood better if that *might have been* had been—if I had not stood withering all these years, taught to crush down this poor dried heart of mine. They will not let me have any thing to love. When Mother Ada thought I was growing too fond of little Erneburg, she took her away from me and gave her to Sister Roberga to teach. Yet the child seemed to soften my heart and do it good.

"Are the holy Mother and the blessed saints not enough for thee?" she said.

But the blessed saints do not look at me and smile, as Erneburg did. She doth it even now, across the schoolroom—though I have never been permitted to speak word to her since Mother Ada took her from me. And I must smile back again,—ay, however many times I have to lick a cross on the oratory floor for doing it. Why ought I not? Did not our Lord Himself take the little children into His arms? I am sure He must have smiled on them—they would have been frightened if He had not done so.

They say I have but a poor wit, and am fit to teach only babes.

"And not fit to teach them," saith Mother Ada—in a tone which I am sure people would call cross and snappish if she were an extern—"for her fancy all runs to playing with them, rather than teaching them any thing worth knowing."

Ah, Mother Ada, but is not love worth knowing? or must they have that only from their happy mothers, who not being holy women are permitted to love, and not from a poor, crushed, hopeless heart like mine?

There is nothing in our life to look forward to. "Till death" is the vow of the Sisterhood. And death seems a poor hope.

I know, of course, what Mother Ada would say: that I have no vocation, and my heart is in the world and of the world. But God sent me to the world: and man—or rather woman—thrust me against my will into this Sisterhood.

"Not a bit better than Lot's wife!" says Mother Ada. "She was struck to a pillar of salt for looking back, and so shalt thou be, Sister Annora, with thy worldly fancies and carnal longings."

Well, if I were, I am not sure I should feel much different. Sometimes I seem to myself to be hardening into stone, body and soul. Soul! ah, that is the worst of it.

Now and then, in the dead of night, when I lie awake—and for an hour or more after lauds, I can seldom sleep—one awful thought harrieth and weareth me, at times almost to madness. I never knew till a year ago, when I heard the Lord Prior speaking to Mother Gaillarde thereanent, that holy Church held the contract of marriage for the true canonical tie. And if it be thus, and we were never divorced—and I never heard word thereof—what then? Am I his true wife—I, not she? Is he happy with her? Who is she, and what is she? Doth she care for him, and make him her first thought, and give all her heart to him, as I would have done, if—

How the convent bell startled me! Miserable me! I am vowed to God, and I am His for ever. But the vow that came first, if it were never undone— *Mater purissima, Sancta Virgo virginum, ora pro me*!

Is there some tale, some sad, strange story, lying behind those dark eyes, in that shut-up heart of my sister Margaret? Not like mine; she was never betrothed. But her eyes seem to me to tell a story.

Margaret never speaks to me, unless I do it first: and I dare not, except about some work, when Mother Gaillarde or Mother Ada is present. Yet once or twice I have caught those dark eyes scanning my face, with a wistful look. Maybe she too is trying to crush down her heart, as I have done. But I cannot help thinking that the heart behind those eyes will take a great deal of crushing.

Mother Alianora is so different from the two I named just now, I am sure there is not a better nor holier woman in all the Order. But she is always gentle and tender; never cold like Mother Ada, nor hard and sarcastic like

Mother Gaillarde. I am glad my Lady Prioress rules with an easy hand—("sadly too slack!" saith Mother Gaillarde)—so that dear Mother Alianora doth not get chidden for what is the best part of her. I should not be afraid of speaking to Margaret if only she were present of our superiors.

At recreation-time, this afternoon, Sister Amphyllis asked Mother Alianora how long she had been professed.

"Forty-nine years," saith she, with her gentle smile.

I was surprised to hear it. She hath then been in the Order only five years longer than I have.

"And how old were you, Mother?" saith Sister Amphyllis.

"Nineteen years," saith she.

"There must many an one have died since you came here, Mother?"

"Ay," quoth Mother Alianora, with a far-away look at the trees without. "The oldest nun in all the Abbey, Sister Margery de Burgh, died the month after I came hither. She remembered a Sister that was nearly an hundred years old, and that had received the holy veil from the hand of Saint Gilbert himself."

Sister Amphyllis crossed herself.

"Annora," saith Mother Alianora, "canst thou remember Mother Guendolen?"

What did I know about Mother Guendolen? Some faint, vague, misty memories seemed to awake within me—an odd, incongruous mixture like a dream—dark eyes like Margaret's, which told a tale, but this seemed a tale of terror; and an enamelled cross, which had somewhat to do with a battle and a queen.

"I scarcely know, Mother," said I. "Somewhat do I recall, yet what it is I hardly know. Were her eyes dark, with an affrighted look in them?"

"They were dark," said Mother Alianora, "but the very peace of God was in them. Ah, thou art mixing up two persons—herself and her cousin, Mother Gladys. They were near of an age, and Mother Guendolen only outlived Mother Gladys by one year: but they were full diverse manner of women. Thou shouldst remember her, Annora. Thou wert a maiden of fifteen when she died."

All at once she seemed to flash up before me.

"I do remember her, Mother, if it please you. She was tall, and had very black hair, and dark flashing eyes, and she moved like a queen."

"I think of her," saith Mother Alianora, "rather as she was in her last days, when those flashing eyes flashed no longer, and the queen was lost in the saint."

"If it please you, Mother," I said, "had she not an enamelled cross that she wore? I recollect something about it."

Mother Alianora smiled, somewhat amusedly.

"She had; and perchance thy memory runneth back to a battle over that cross betwixt her and Sister Sayena, who laid plaint afore my Lady Prioress that Mother Guendolen kept to herself an article of private property, which should have gone into the treasury. It had been her mother's, a marriage-gift from the Queen that then was. Well I remember Mother Guendolen's words—'I sware to part from this cross alone with life, and the Master granted me to keep it when I entered the Order.' Then the fire died out of her eyes, and her voice fell low, and she added—'ah, my sister! dost thou envy me Christ's cross?' Ay, she had carried more of that cross than most. She came here about the age thou didst, Annora—a little child of six years."

"Who was she in the world, Mother?" quoth Sister Nora.

I was surprised to see Mother Alianora glance round the room, as if to see who was there, afore she answered. Nor did she answer for a moment.

"She was Sister Guendolen of Sempringham: let that satisfy thee. Maybe, in the world above, she is that which she should have been in this world, and was not."

And I could not but wonder if Mother Guendolen's life had held a *might have been* like mine.

I want to know what 'carnal' and 'worldly' mean. They are words which I hear very often, and always with condemnation: but they seem to mean quite different things, in the lips of different speakers. When Mother Ada uses them, they mean having affection in one's heart for any thing, or any person, that is not part of holy Church. When Mother Gaillarde speaks them, they mean caring for any thing that she does not care for—and that includes everything except power, and grandeur, and the Order of Saint Gilbert. And when Mother Alianora says them, they fall softly on the ear, as if they meant not love, nor happiness, nor any thing good and innocent, but simply all that could grieve our Lord and hurt a soul that loved Him. They are, with her, just the opposite of Jesus Christ.

Oh, if only our blessed Lord had been on earth now, and I might have gone on pilgrimage to the place where He was! If I could have asked Him all the questions that perplex me, and laid at His feet all the sorrows that trouble me! For I do not think He would have commanded the saints to chase me away because I maybe have poorer wits than other women, — He who let the mothers bring the babes to Him: I fancy He would have been patient and gentle, even with me. I scarce think He would have treated sorrow — even wrong or mistaken sorrow, if only it were real — as some do, with cold looks, and hard words, and gibes that take so much bearing. I suppose He would have told me wherein I sinned, but I think He would have done it gently, so as not to hurt more than could be helped — not like some, who seem to think that nothing they say or do can possibly hurt any one.

But it is no use saying such things to people. Once, I did say about a tenth part of what I felt, when Mother Ada was present, and she turned on me almost angrily.

"Sister Annora, you are scarce better than an idiot! Know you not that confession to the priest is the same thing as to our Lord Himself?"

Well, it may be so, though it never feels like it: but I am sure the priest is not the same thing. If I were a young mother with little babes, I could never bring them to any priest I have known save one, and that was a stranger who confessed us but for a week, some five years gone, when the Lord Prior was ill. He was quite different from the others: there was a soul behind his eyes — something human, not merely a sort of metallic box which sounded when you rang it with another bit of metal.

I never know why Margaret's eyes make me think of that man, but I suppose it may be that there was the same sort of look in his. I am not sure that I can put it into words. It makes me think, not of a dry bough like my heart feels to be, but rather of a walled recluse — something alive, very much alive, inside thick, hard, impenetrable walls which you cannot enter, and it can never leave, but itself soft and tender and sweet. And I fancy that people who look like that must have had histories.

Another person troubles me beside that man and Margaret, and that is Saint Peter's wife's mother. Because, if the holy Apostle had a wife's mother, he must have had a wife; and what could a holy Apostle be doing with a wife? I ventured once to ask Mother Ada how it was to be explained, and she said that of course Saint Peter must have been married before his conversion and calling by our Lord.

"And I dare be bound," added Mother Gaillarde, "that she was a shocking vixen, or something bad, so as to serve for a thorn in the flesh to the holy Apostle. He'd a deal better have been an unwedded man."

Well, some folks' relations are thorns in the flesh, I can quite suppose. I should think Mother Gaillarde was, and that her being a nun was a mercy to some man, so that she was told off to prick us and not him. But is every body so? and are we all called to be thorns in the flesh to somebody? I should not fancy being looked on by my relations (if I were in the world) as nothing but a means of grace. It might be good for them, but I doubt if it would for me.

I wonder if Margaret ever knew that priest whose eyes looked like hers. I should like to ask her. But Mother Ada always forbids us to ask each other questions about our past lives. She says curiosity is a sin; it was curiosity which led Eve to listen to the serpent. But I do not think Mother Ada's soul has any wings, and I always feel as if mine had—something that, if only I were at liberty, would spread itself and carry me away, far, far from here, right up into the very stars, for aught I know. Poor caged bird as I am! how can my wings unfold themselves? I fancy Margaret has wings—very likely, stronger than mine. She seems to have altogether a stronger nature.

Mother Alianora will let us ask questions: she sometimes asks them herself. Well, so does Mother Gaillarde, more than any body; but in such a different way! Mother Alianora asks as if she were comforting and helping you: Mother Gaillarde as though you were a piece of embroidery that had been done wrong, and she were looking to see where the stitches had begun to go crooked. If I were a piece of lawn, I should not at all like Mother Gaillarde to pull the crooked stitches out of me. She pounces on them so eagerly, and pulls so savagely at them.

I marvel what Margaret's history has been!

Last evening, as we were putting the orphans to bed—two of the Sisters do it by turns, every week—little Damia saith to me—

"Sister Annora, what is the matter with our new Sister?"

"Who dost thou mean, my child?" I asked. "Sister Marian?"

For Sister Marian was our last professed.

"No," said the child; "I mean Sister Margaret, who has such curious eyes—eyes that say every thing and don't tell any thing—it is so funny! (So other folks than I had seen those eyes.) But what was the matter with her yesterday morning, at the holy Sacrament?"

"I know not, Damia, for I saw nothing. A religious, as thou knowest, should not lift her eyes, save for adoration."

"O Sister Annora, how many nice things she must lose! But I will tell you about Sister Margaret. It was just when the holy mass began. Father Hamon had said '*Judica me*' and then, you know, the people had to reply, '*Quia Tu es.*' And when they began the response, Sister Margaret's head went up, and her eyes ran up the aisle to the altar."

"Damia, my child!" I said.

"Indeed, Sister, I am not talking nonsense! It looked exactly like that. Then, in another minute, they came back, looking so sorry, and so, *so* tired! If you will look at her, you will see how tired she looks, and has done ever since. I thought her soul had been to look for something which it could not find, and that made her so sorry."

"Had ever child such odd fancies as thou!" said I, as I tucked her up. "Now say thy Hail Mary, and go to sleep."

I thought it but right to check Damia, who has a very lively imagination, and would make up stories by the yard about all she sees, if any one encouraged her. But when I sat down again to the loom, instead of the holy meditations which ought to come to me, and I suppose would do so if I were perfect, I kept wondering if Damia had seen rightly, and if Margaret's soul had been to look for something, and was disappointed in not finding it. I looked at her—she was just across the room,—and as Damia said, there was a very sorrowful, weary look on her face—a look as if some thought, or memory, or hope, had been awakened in her, only to be sent back, sorely disappointed and disheartened. Somebody else noticed it too.

My Lady Prioress was rather late last night in dismissing us. Sister Roberga said she was sure there had been some altercation between her and Mother Gaillarde: and certainly Mother Gaillarde, as she stood at the top of the room by my Lady, did not look exactly an incarnation of sweetness. But my Lady gave the word at last: and as she said—"*Pax vobiscum, Sorores!*" every Sister went up to her, knelt to kiss her hand, took her own lamp from the lamp-stand, and glided softly from the recreation-room. Half-way down stood Mother Alianora, and at the door Mother Ada. Margaret was just behind me: and as I passed Mother Alianora, I heard her ask—

"Sister Margaret, art thou suffering in some wise?"

I listened for Margaret's answer. There was a moment's hesitation before it came.

"No, Mother, I thank you; save from a malady which only One can heal."

"May He heal thee, my child!" was the gentle answer.

I was surprised at Margaret's answering with anything but thanks.

"Mother, you little know for what you pray!"

"That is often the case," said Mother Alianora. "But He knoweth who hath to answer: and He doeth all things well. He will give thee, maybe, not the physic thou lookest for; yet the right remedy."

I heard Margaret answer, as we passed on, in a low voice, as if she scarce desired to be heard—"For some diseases there is no remedy but death."

There are two dormitories in our house, and Margaret is in the west one, while I sleep in the eastern. At the head of the stairs we part to our places. That I should speak a word to her in the night is impossible. And in the day I can never see her without a score of eyes upon us, especially Mother Gaillarde's, and she seems to have eyes, not in the back of her head only, but all over her veil.

I suppose, if we had lived like real sisters and not make-believe ones, Margaret and I would have had a little chamber to ourselves in our father's castle, and we could have talked to each other, and told our secrets if we wished, and have comforted one another when our hearts were sad. And I do not understand why it should please our Lord so much more to have us shut up here, making believe to be one family with thirty other women who are not our sisters, except in the sense that all Christian women are children of God. I wonder where it is in the Gospels, that our Lord commanded it to be done. I cannot find it in my Evangelisterium. I dare say the holy Apostles ordered it afterwards: or perhaps it is in some Gospel I have never seen. There are only four in my book.

If that strange priest would come again to confess us, I should like very much to ask him several questions of that sort. I never saw any other priest that I could speak to freely, as I could to him. Father Hamon would not understand me, I am sure: and Father Benedict would rebuke me sharply whether he understood or not; telling me for the fiftieth time that I ought to humble myself to the dust because my vocation is so imperfect. Well, I know I have no vocation. But why then was I shut up here when God had not called me? I had no choice allowed me. Or why, seeing things are thus, cannot the Master or some one else loose me from my vow, and let me go back to the world which they keep blaming me because they say I love?

Yet what should I do in the world? My mother has been dead many years, for her name is in the obituary of the house. As to my brothers and sisters, I no more know how many of them are living, nor where they are, than if they dwelt in the stars. I remember my brother Hugh, because he used to take my part when the others teased me: but as to my younger brothers, I only know there were some; I forget even their names. I think one was Hubert, or Robert, or something that ended in *bert*. And my sisters—I remember Isabel; she was three years elder than I. And—was one Elizabeth? I think so. But wherever they are, I suppose they would feel me a stranger among them—an intruder who was not wanted, and who had no business to be there. I am unfit both for Heaven and earth. Nobody wants me—least of all God.

I do not imagine that is Margaret's history. How far she may or may not have a vocation—that I leave; I know nothing about it. But I cannot help fancying that somebody did want her, and that it might be to put her out of somebody's way—Foolish woman! what am I saying? Why, Margaret was not five years old when she was professed. How can she have had any history of the kind? I simply do not understand it.

Poor little Damia! I think Mother Gaillarde has given her rather hard measure.

I found the child crying bitterly when she came into the children's south dormitory where I serve this week.

"Why, whatever is the matter, little one?" said I.

"O Sister Annora!" was all she could sob out.

"Well, weep not thus broken-heartedly!" said I. "Tell me what it is, and let us see if it cannot be amended."

"It's Erneburg!" sobbed little Damia.

"Erneburg! But Erneburg and thou art friends!"

"Oh yes, we're friends enough! only Mother Gaillarde won't let me give her the tig."

And little Damia indulged in a fresh burst of tears.

"Give her what?" I said.

"My tig! The tig she gave me. And now I must carry it all night long! She might have let me just give it her!"

I thought I saw how matters stood.

"You have been playing?"

"Yes, playing at

"'Carry my tig
To Poynton Brig—'

"and Erneburg gave me a tig, and I can't give it back. Mo—other Gaillarde won't le-et me!" with a fresh burst of sobs.

"Now, whatever is all this fuss?" asked Mother Gaillarde, from the other end of the room. "Sister, do keep these children quiet."

But Mother Ada came to us.

"What is the matter?" she said in her icicle voice.

Little Damia was crying too much to speak, and I had to tell her that the children had been playing at a game in which they touched one another if they could, and it was deemed a terrible disgrace to be touched without being able to return it.

"What nonsense!" said Mother Ada. "They had better not be allowed to play at such silly games. Go to sleep immediately, Damia: do you hear? Give over crying this minute."

I wondered whether Mother Ada thought that joy and sorrow could as easily be stopped as a tap could be turned to stop water. Little Damia could not stop crying so instantly as this: and Mother Ada told her if she did not, she should have no fruit to-morrow: which made her cry all the more. Mother Gaillarde then marched up, and gave the poor child an angry shake: and that produced screams instead of sobbing.

"Blessed saints, these children!" said Mother Gaillarde. "I wish there never were any! With all reverence I say it, I do think if the Almighty could have created men and women grown-up, it would have saved a world of trouble. But I suppose He knows best.—Damia, stop that noise! If not, I'll give thee another shake."

Little Damia burrowed down beneath the bed-clothes, from which long-drawn sobs shook the bed at intervals: but she did contrive to stop screaming. Mother Gaillard left the dormitory, with another sarcastic remark on the dear delight of looking after children: and the minute after, Mother Alianora entered it from the other end. She came up to where I stood, by Damia's bed.

"Not all peace here?" she said, with her tranquil smile. "Little Damia, what aileth thee?"

As soon as her voice was heard, little Damia's head came up, and in a voice broken by sobs, she told her tale.

"Come, I think that can be put right," saith the Mother, kindly. "Lie still, my child, till I come to thee again."

She went away, and in a few minutes returned, with Erneburg. Of course Mother Alianora can go where the Sisters cannot.

"Little Damia," she said, smiling, as she laid her hand on the child's head, "I bring Erneburg to return thee thy 'tig.' Now canst thou go to sleep in peace?"

"Yes, thank you, Mother. You are good!" said little Damia gratefully, looking quite relieved, as Erneburg kissed her.

"Such a little thing!" said Mother Alianora, with a smile. "Yet thou art but a little thing thyself."

They went away, and I tarried a moment to light the blessed Mother's lamp, and to say the Hail Mary with the children. When I came down-stairs, the first voice I heard in the recreation-room was Mother Gaillarde's.

"Well, if ever I did hear such a story! Sister, you ruin those children!"

"Nay," saith Mother Alianora's gentle voice, "surely not, my Sister, by a little kindness such as that."

"Kindness, indeed! Before I'd have given in to such nonsense!"

"Sister Gaillarde, maybe some matters that you and I would weep over may seem full as foolish to the angels and to God. And to Him it may be of more import to comfort a little child in its trouble than to pass a statute of Parliament. Ah, me! if God waited to comfort us till we were wise, little comforting should any of us have. But it is written, 'Like whom his mother blandisheth, thus I will comfort you,'—and mothers do not wait for children to be discreet before they comfort them. At least, my mother did not."

Such a soft, sweet, tender light came into her eyes as made my heart ache. My mother might have comforted me so.

Just then I caught Margaret's look. I do not know what it was like: but quite different from Mother Alianora's. Something strained and stretched, as it were, like a piece of canvas when you strain it on a frame for tapestry-work. Then, all at once, the strain gave way and broke up, and calm, holy peace came instead. If I might talk with Margaret!

Mother Alianora is ill in the Infirmary. And I may not go to her.

I pleaded hard with Mother Ada to appoint me nurse for this week.

"Why?" she said in her coldest voice.

I could not answer.

"Either thou deceivest thyself, Sister," she added, "which is ill enough, or thou wouldst fain deceive me. Knowest thou not that to attempt to deceive thy superiors is to lie to the Holy Ghost as Ananias and Sapphira did? How then dost thou dare to do it? I see plainly enough what motive prompts thee: not holy obedience—that is thoroughly inconsistent with such fervent entreaties—nor a desire to mortify thy will, but simply a wish for the carnal indulgence of the flesh. Thou knowest full well that particular friendships are not permitted to the religious, it is only the lust of the flesh which prompts a fancy for one above another: if not, every Sister would have an equal share in thy regard. It is a carnal, worldly heart in which such thoughts dwell as even a wish for the company of any Sister in especial. And hast thou forgotten that the very purpose for which we were sent here was to mortify our wills?"

I thought I was not likely to forget it, so long as nothing was allowed me save opportunities for mortifying mine. But one more word did I dare to utter.

"Is obedience so much better than love, Mother?"

"What hast thou to do with love, save the love of God and the blessed Mother and the holy saints? The very word savoureth of the world. All the love thou givest to the creature is love taken from God."

"Is love, then, a thing that can be measured and cut in lengths, Mother? The more you tend a plant, the better it flourishes. If I am to love none save God, will not my heart dry and wither, so that I shall not be able to love Him? Sometimes I think it is doing so."

"You think!" she said. "What right have you to think? Leave your superiors to think for you; and you, cultivate holy obedience, as you ought. All the heresies and schisms that ever vexed the Church have arisen from men setting themselves up to *think* when they should simply have obeyed."

"But, Mother, forgive me! I cannot help thinking."

"That shows how far you are from perfection, Sister. A religious who aims at perfection should never allow herself to think, except only how she can best obey. Beware of pride and presumption, the instant you allow yourself to depart from the perfection of obedience."

"But, Mother, that is the perfection of a thing. And I am a woman."

"Sister Annora, you are reasoning, when your duty is to obey."

If holy obedience means to obey without thinking, I am afraid I shall never be perfect in it! I do not know how people manage to compress themselves into stones like that.

I tried Mother Gaillarde next, since I had only found an icicle clad in Mother Ada's habit. I was afraid of her, I confess, for I knew she would bite: and she did so. I begged yet harder, for I had heard that Mother Alianora was worse. Was I not even to see her before she died?

"What on earth does it matter?" said Mother Gaillarde. "Aren't you both going to Heaven? You can talk there—without fear of disobedience."

"My Lord Prior said. Mother, in his last charge, that a convent ought to be a little heaven. If that be so, why should we not talk now?"

Mother Gaillarde's laugh positively frightened me. It was the hardest, driest, most metallic sound I ever heard.

"Sister Annora, you must be a baby! You have lived in a convent nearly fifty years, and you ask if it be a little heaven!"

"I cry you mercy, Mother. I asked if it should not be so."

"That's another matter," said she, with a second laugh, but it did not startle me like the first. "We should all be perfect, of course. Pity we aren't!"

As she worked away at the plums she was stoning without saying either yes or no, I ventured to repeat my question.

"You may do as you are told!" was Mother Gaillarde's answer. "Can't you let things alone?"

Snappishly as she spoke, yet—I hardly know why,—I did not feel the appeal to her as hopeless as to Mother Ada. To entreat the latter was like beseeching a stone wall. Mother Gaillarde's very peevishness (if I dare call it so) showed that she was a woman, and not an image.

"Mother Gaillarde," I said, suddenly—for something seemed to bid me speak out—"be not angry with me, I pray you. I am afraid of letting things alone. My heart seems to be like a dry bough, and my soul withering up, and I want to keep them alive and warm. Surely death is not perfection!"

I was going on, but something which I saw made me stop suddenly. Two warriors were fighting together in Mother Gaillarde's face. All at once she dropped the knife, and hiding her face in her veil, she sobbed for a minute as if her heart were breaking. Then, all at once, she brushed away her tears and stood up again.

"Child!" she said, in a voice very unlike her usual one, "you are too young for your years. Do not think that dried-up hearts are the same thing as no hearts. Women who seem as though they could not love any thing may have loved once too well, and when they awoke from the dream may never have been able to dream again. Ay, thou art right: death is not perfection. Some of us, maybe, are very far off perfection—further than others think us; furthest of all from what we think ourselves. There have been times when I seemed to see for a moment what perfection is—and it was far, far from all we call it here. God forgive us all! Go to the Infirmary: and if any chide thee for being there, say thou earnest in obedience to me."

She turned back to her plum-stoning with a resolute face which might have been a mask of iron: and I, after offering lowly thanks, took the way to the Infirmary.

I fear I have been unjust to Mother Gaillarde, and I am sorry for it. I seem to see now, that her hard, snappish speeches (for she does snap sometimes) are not from absence of heart, but are simply a veil to hide the heart. Ah me! how little we human creatures know of each others' hidden feelings! But I shall never think Mother Gaillarde without heart again.

Note 1. The rule of silence varied considerably in different Orders, but in all, except the very strict, nuns were at liberty to converse during some period of the day.

Note 2. This transferring of Margaret from Watton is purely imaginary.

Chapter 2
Sister Margaret

"Do I not know
The life of woman is full of woe?
Toiling on and on and on,
With breaking heart, and tearful eyes,
And silent lips - and in the soul
The secret longings that arise,
Which this world never satisfies?"

Longfellow.

Mother Alianora was lying in her bed when I entered the Infirmary, just under the window, where the soft light of the low autumn sun came in and lit up her pillow and her dear old face. She smiled when she saw me.

There was another Sister in the room, who was stirring a pan over the fire, and at first I scarcely noticed her. I went up to the dear Mother, and asked her how she was.

"Well, my child," she said, tenderly. "Nearly at Home."

Something came up in my throat that would not let me speak.

"Hast thou been sent to relieve Sister Marian?" she asked.

"I know not," said I, after a moment's struggle with myself: then, remembering what I had been bidden, I added, "Mother Gaillarde bade me come."

We sat silent for a few moments. Sister Marian poured out the broth and brought it to the Mother, and I supported her while she drank a little of it. She could not take much.

Just before the bell rang for compline, Mother Ada came in.

"I bring an order from my Lady," said she. "Sister Marian will be relieved after compline by another Sister, who will be sent up. Sister Annora is to stay with the sick Mother during compline, and both she and the Sister who then comes will keep watch during the night."

I was surprised. I never knew any case of sickness, unless it were something very severe and urgent, allowed to interfere with a Sister's attendance at compline. But I was glad enough to stay.

Mother Ada went away again after her orders were given, and Sister Marian followed her when the bell rang. As soon as the little sounds of the Sisters' footsteps had died away, and we knew they were all shut in the oratory, Mother Alianora, in a faint voice, bade me bring a stool beside her bed and sit down.

"Annora," said she, in that feeble voice, "my child, thou art fifty years old, yet I think of thee as a child still. And in many respects thou art so. It has been thy lot, whether for good or evil—which, who knoweth save God?—to be safe sheltered from very much of the ill that is in the world. But I doubt not, at times, questionings will arise in thy heart, whether the good may not have been shut out too. Is it so, my child?"

I suppose Mother Ada would say I was exceedingly carnal. But something in the touch of that soft, wrinkled hand, in whose veins I knew ran mine own blood, seemed to break down all my defences. I laid my head down on the coverlet, my cheek upon her hand, and in answer I poured forth all that had been so long shut close in mine own heart—that longing cry within me for some real, warm, human love, that ceaseless regret for the lost happiness which was meant to have been mine.

"O Mother, Mother! is it wicked in me?" I cried. "You, who are so near God, you should see with clearer eyes than we, lost in the tangled wilderness of this world. Is it wicked of me to dream of that lost love, and of all that it might have been to me? Am I his true wife, or is she—whoever that she may be? Am I robbing; God when I love any other creature? Must I only love any one in Heaven? and am I to prepare for that by loving nobody here on earth?"

The door opened softly, and the Sister who was to share my watch came in. She must have heard my closing words.

"My child!" said the faint voice of the dear Mother, who had always felt to me more like what I supposed mothers to be than any other I had known—"my child, 'it is impossible that scandals should not come: but woe unto them through whom they come!' It seems to me probable that one sin may be written in many books: that the actor, and the inciter, and the abettor—ay, and those who might have prevented, and did not—may all have their share. Thy coming hither, and thy religious life, having received no vocation of God, was not thy fault, poor, helpless, oppressed child! and such temptations as distress thee, therefrom arising, will not be laid to thy charge as sins. But if thou let a temptation slide into a sin by consenting thereto, by cherishing and pursuing it with delight, then art thou not guiltless. That thou shouldst feel thyself unhappy here, in an unsuitable place, and that thou mightest have been a happier woman in the wedded life of the world,—that is no marvel: truly, I think it of thee myself. To know it is no sin: to repine and murmur thereat, these are forbidden. Thy lot is appointed of God Himself—God, thy Father, who loveth thee, who hath given Himself for thee, who pleased not Himself when He came down to die for thee. Are there not here drops of honey to sweeten the bitter cup? And if thou want another yet, then remember how short this life is, and that after it, they that have done His will shall be together with Him for ever. Dear hearts, it is only a little while."

The Sister who was to watch with me had come forward to the foot of the bed, and was standing silent there. When Mother Alianora thus spoke, I fancied that I heard a little sob. Wondering who she was, I looked up— looked up, to my great astonishment, into those dark, strange eyes of my own sister Margaret.

Margaret and I, alone, to keep the watch all night long! What could my Lady Prioress mean? Here was an opportunity to indulge my will, not to mortify it; to make my love grow, instead of repressing it. I had actually put into my hand the chance that I had so earnestly desired, to speak to Margaret alone.

But now that the first difficulty was removed, another rose up before me. Would Margaret speak to me? Was she, perhaps, searching for opportunities of mortification, and would refuse the indulgence permitted? I knew as much of the King's Court, as much of a knightly tournament, as I knew of that sealed-up heart of hers. Should I be allowed to know any more?

"Annora," said our aunt again, "there is one thine in my life that I regret sorely, and it is that I was not more of a mother to thee when thou earnest as a little child. Of course I was under discipline: but I feel now that I did not search for opportunities as I might have done, that I let little chances pass which I might have seized. My child, forgive me!"

"Dearest Mother!" I said, "you were ever far kinder to me than any one else in all the world."

"Thank God I have heard that!" saith she. "Ah, children—for we are children to an aged woman like me—life looks different indeed, seen from a deathbed, to what it does viewed from the little mounds of our human wisdom as we pass along it. Here, there is nothing great but God; there is nothing fair save Christ and Heaven; there is nothing else true, nor desirable, nor of import. Every thing is of consequence, if, and just so far as, it bears on these: and all other things are as the dust of the floor, which ye sweep off and forth of the doors into the outward. Life is the way upward to God, or the way down to Satan. What does it matter whether the road were smooth or rough, when ye come to the end thereof? The more weary and footsore, the more chilled and hungered ye are, the sweeter shall be the marriage-supper and the rest of the Father's House."

"Ay—when we are there." It was Margaret who spoke.

"And before, let us look forward, my child."

"Easy enough," said Margaret, "when the sun gleameth out fair, and ye see the domes of the city stand up bravely afore. But in the dark night, when neither sun nor star appeareth, and ye are out on a wild moor, and thick mist closeth you in, so that ye go it may be around thinking it be forward, till ye know not whether your face is toward the city or no—"

"Let thy face be toward the Lord of the city," said Mother Alianora. "He shall lead thee forth by the right way, that thou mayest come to His city and to His holy hill. The right way, daughter, is sometimes the way over the moor, and through the mist. 'Who of you walketh in darkness, and there is no light to him? Let him trust in the name of the Lord, and lean upon his God.' Why, my child, it is only when man cannot see that it is possible for him to trust. Faith is not called in exercise so long as thou walkest by sight."

"But when thou art utterly alone," said my sister in a low voice, "with not one footstep on the road beside thee—"

"That art thou never, child, so thou be Christ's. His footsteps are alway there."

"In suffering, ay: but in perplexity?"

"Daughter, when thou losest His steps, thou yet hast Himself. 'If any lack wisdom, let him ask of God.' And God is never from home."

"Neither is Satan."

"'Greater is He that is in you than he in the world.'"

Mother Alianora seemed weary when she had said this, and lay still a while: and Margaret did not answer. I think the Mother dropped asleep; I sat beside her and watched. But Margaret stood still at the foot of the bed, not sitting down, and in the dim light of our one little lamp I could scarcely see her face as she stood, only that it was turned toward the casement, where a faint half-moon rode in the heavens, and the calm ancient stars looked down on us. Oh, how small a world is ours in the great heavens! yet for one soul of one little babe in this small world, the Son of God hath died.

My heart went out to Margaret as she stood there: yet my lips were sealed. I felt, strangely, as if I could not speak. Something held me back, and I knew not if it were God, or Satan, or only mine own want of sense and bravery. The long hours wore on. The church bell tolled for lauds, and we heard the soft tramp of the Sisters' feet as they passed and returned: then the doors closed, and Mother Ada's voice said,

"*Laus Deo!*" and Sister Ismania's replied, "*Deo gratias!*" Then Mother Ada's footsteps passed the door as she went to her cell, and once more all was silence. On rolled the hours slowly, and still Mother Alianora seemed to sleep: still Margaret stood as if she had been cut in stone, without so much as moving, and still I sat, feeling much as if I were stone too, and had no power to move or speak.

It might be about half-way between lauds and prime when the spell was at last broken. And it was broken, to my astonishment, by Margaret's asking me a question that fairly took my breath away.

"Annora, art thou a saint?"

These were the first words Margaret had ever spoken to me, except from necessity. That weary, dried-up thing that I call mine heart, seemed to give a little bit of throb.

"Our Lady love us, no!" said I. "I never was, nor never could be."

"I am glad to hear it," she said.

"Why, Margaret?"

Oh, how my heart wanted to call her something sweeter! *It* said, My darling, my beloved, mine own little sister! But my tongue was all so unwonted to utter such words that I could not persuade it to say them.

Yet more to my surprise, Margaret came out of the window,—came and knelt at my feet, and laid her clasped hands on my knee.

"Hadst thou said 'Ay,' I should have spoken no more. As thou art not— Annora, is it true that we twain had one mother?"

Something in Margaret's tone helped me. I took the clasped hands in mine own.

"It is true, mine own Sister," I said.

"'Sister!' and 'Mother!'" she said. "They are words that mean nothing at all to me. I wonder if God meant them to mean nothing to us? Could we not have been as good women, and have served Him as well, if we had dwelt with our own blood, as other maidens do, or even if—"

Her voice died away.

"Margaret," I said, "Mother Ada would say it was wicked, but mine heart is for ever asking the same questions."

"Is it?" she said eagerly. "O Annora! then thou knowest! I thought, maybe, thou shouldst count it wicked, and chide me for indulging such thoughts."

"How could I chide any one, sinner as I am!" said I. "Nay, Margaret, I doubt not my thoughts have been far unholier than thine. Thou rememberest not, I am sure; but ere we were professed, I was troth-plight unto a young noble, and always that life that I have lost flitteth afore me, as a bird that held a jewel in his beak might lure me on from flower to flower, ever following, never grasping the sweet illusion. Margaret, sister, despise me not for my confession! But thou wilt see I am no saint, nor like to be."

"Despise thee!" she said. "Dear heart, wert thou to know how much further I have gone!"

I looked on her with some alarm.

"Margaret! we are professed religious women." (Note 1.)

"Religious women!" she answered. "If thou gild a piece of wood, doth it become gold? Religious women are not women that wear black and white, cut in a certain fashion: they are women that set God above all things. And have I not done that? Have I not laid mine heart upon His altar, a living sacrifice, because I believed He called me to break that poor quivering thing in twain? And will He judge me that did His will, to the best of my power and knowledge, because now and then a human sob breaks from my woman-heart, by reason that I am not yet an angel, and that He did not make me a stone? I do not believe it. I will not believe it. He that gave His own Son to die for man can be no Moloch delighting in human suffering—caring not how many hearts be crushed so long as there be flowers upon His altar, how many lives be made desolate so long as there be choirs to sing antiphons! Annora, it is not God who does such things, but men."

I was doubtful how to answer, seeing I could not understand what she meant. I only said—

"Yet God permits men to do them."

"Ay. But He never bids them to make others suffer,—far less to take pleasure in doing so."

"Margaret," said I, "may I know thy story? I have told thee mine. Truly, it is not much to tell."

"No," she said, as if dreamily,—"not much: only such an one as will be told out by the mile rather than the yard, from thousands of convents on the day when the great doom shall be. Only the story of a crushed heart—how much does that matter to the fathers of the Order? There be somewhat too many in these cells for them to take any note of one."

I remembered what Mother Gaillarde had said.

"It is terrible, if that be true," I answered. "I thought I was the only one, and that made me unhappy because I must be so wicked. At times, in meditation, I have looked round the chamber and thought—Here be all these blessed women, wrapped in holy meditations, and only I tempted by wicked thoughts of the world outside, like Lot's wife at Sodom."

Margaret fairly laughed. "Verily," said she, "if it were given to us to lift the veil from the hearts of all these blessed women, and scan their holy meditations, I reckon thine amaze would not be small. Annora, I think thou art a saint."

"Impossible!" said I. "Why, I fell asleep in the midst of the Rosary a s'ennight back,—having been awake half the night before—and Father Benedict said I must do penance for it. Saints are not such as I."

"Annora, if the angels that write in men's books have no worse to set down in thine than what thou hast told me, I count they shall reckon their work full light. O humble and meek of heart, thinking all other better than thyself—trust me, they be, at best, like such as thou."

Margaret left her station at my feet, and coming round, knelt down beside me, and laid her head on my shoulder.

"Kiss me, Sister," she said.

So did I, at once, without thought: and then, perceiving what I had done, I was affrighted.

"O Margaret! have we not sinned? Is it not an indulgence of the flesh?"

"Wert thou made without flesh?" asked Margaret, with a short, dry laugh.

"No, but it must be mortified!"

"Sin must be mortified," she answered more gravely. "Why should we mortify love?"

"Not spiritual love: but natural love, surely, we renounce."

"Why should we renounce it? Does God make men sons and brothers, husbands and fathers, only that they may have somewhat to renounce? Can He train us only in the wilderness of Sinai, and not in the land flowing with milk and honey?"

"But we renounce them for Him."

"We renounce for Him that which He demandeth of us." Margaret's voice was low and sorrowful now. "Ay, there be times when He holdeth out His hand for the one dearest earthly thing, and calls us to resign either it or Him. Blessed are they that then, howsoever they shrink and faint, yet love Him more than it, and brace their will to give it up to Him. To them that so do, Annora, He giveth Himself; and He is better than any earthly thing. *'Quid enim mihi est in caelo? et a Te quid volui super terram?'* (Psalm 73, verse 25) But it seems to me that we ought to beware of renouncing what He does not ask of us. If we are in doubt, then let us draw the line on the safe side,—on His side, not on the side of our inclinations. Yet of one thing am I sure—that many a woman mortifies her graces instead of her sins, and resigns to God that which He asks not, keeping that which He would have."

"Mortify graces!" I cried. "O Margaret! how could we?"

"I think thou wouldst, Sister, if thou hadst refused to kiss me," she replied with an amused smile.

"But kisses are such very carnal things," said I. "Mother Ada always says so. She saith we read of none of the holy Apostles kissing any body, save only Judas Iscariot."

"Who told her so? Doth she find it written that they did not kiss any body? Annora, I marvel if our Lord kissed not the little children. And I am sure the holy patriarchs kissed each other. I do not believe in trying to be better than God. I have noted that when man endeavours to purify himself above our Lord's example, he commonly ends in being considerably less good than other men."

"I wish we might love each other!" I said with a sigh. And I am very much afraid I kissed her again. I do not know what Mother Ada would have said.

"I do not wish we might!" said Margaret, sturdily. "I do, and I will."

"But if we should make idols of each other!" said I.

"I shall not make an idol of thee," answered my sister, again in that low sad tone. "I set up one idol, and He came to me, and held out His pierced hands, and I tore it down from over the altar, and gave it to Him. He is keeping it for me, and He will give it back one day, in the world where we need fear no idol-making, nor any sin at all. Annora, thou shalt hear my story."

At that moment I looked up, and saw Mother Alianora's eyes wide open.

"Do you lack aught, dear Mother?" I asked.

"No, my children," she answered gently. "Go on with thy tale, Margaret. The ears of one that will soon hear the harps of the angels will not harm thee."

I was somewhat surprised she could say that. What of the dread fires of Purgatory that must come first? Did she count herself so great a saint as to escape them? Then I thought, perhaps, she might have had the same revealed to her in vision. The thought did not appear to trouble Margaret, who took it as matter of course. Not, truly, that I should be surprised if Mother Alianora were good enough to escape Purgatory, for I am sure she is the best woman ever I knew: but it was strange she should reckon it of herself. Mother Ada always says they are no saints that think themselves such: whereto Mother Gaillarde once added, in her dry, sharp way, that they were not much better who tried to make other folk think so. I do not know of whom she was thinking, but I fancied Mother Ada did, from her face.

Then Margaret began her story.

"You know," she saith, "it is this year forty-seven years since Annora and I were professed. And wherefore we were so used, mere babes as we were, knew I never."

"Then that I can tell thee," I made answer, "for it was Queen Isabel that thrust us in hither. Our father did somewhat to her misliking, what indeed I know not: and she pounced on us, poor little maids, and made us to suffer for his deed."

"Was that how it was done?" said Margaret. "Then may God pardon her more readily than I have done! For long years I hated with all the force of my soul him or her that had been the cause thereof. It is past now. The priests say that man sinneth when, having no call of God, he shall take cowl upon him. What then of those which thrust it on him, whether he will or no? I never chose this habit. For years I hated it as fervently as it lay in me to hate. Had the choice been given me, any moment of those years, I would have gone back to the world that instant. The world!" Her voice changed suddenly. "What is the world? It is the enemy of God: true. But will bolts and bars, walls and gates, keep it out? Is it a thing to be found in one city, which man can escape by journeying to another? Is it not rather in his own bosom, and ever with him? They say much of carnal affections that are evil, and creep not into religious houses. As if man should essay to keep Satan and his angels out of his house by painting God's name over the door! But all love, of whatsoever sort, say they, is a filthiness of the flesh. Ah me! how about the filthiness of the spirit? Is there no pride and jealousy in a religious house? no strife and envying? no murmuring and rebellion of heart? And are these fairer things in God's sight than the natural love of our own blood? Doth He call us to give up that, and not these? May it not be rather that if there were more true love, there were less envy and jealousy? if there were more harmless liberty, there were less murmuring? When man takes God's scourge into his hands, it seems to me he is apt to wield it ill."

"But, Margaret!" said I, "so shouldst thou make Satan cast out Satan. Forbidden love were as ill as strife and murmuring."

"Forbidden of whom?" saith she. "God never forbade me to love my brethren and sisters. He told me to do it. He never forbade me to honour my father and mother—to dwell with them, to tend and cherish them in their old age. He told me to do it. Ay, and He spake of certain that did vainly worship Him seeing they taught learning and commandments of men." (Matthew 15, verse 9, Vulgate.)

"O Margaret! what art thou saying? Holy Church enjoins vows of religion."

"Tell me then, Annora, what is Holy Church? It is a word that fills man's mouth full comely, that I know. But what it *is*, is simply the souls of all righteous men—all the redeemed of Christ our Lord, which is His Body, and is filled with His Spirit. When did He enjoin such vows? or when did all righteous men thus band together to make men and women unrighteous, by binding commands upon them that were of men, not of God?"

"Margaret, my Sister!" I cried in terror. "Whence drewest thou such shocking thoughts? What will Father Benedict say when thou confessest them?"

"It is not to Father Benedict I confess *them*," she said, with a little curl of her lips. "I confess to him what he expects to hear—that I loved not to sweep the gallery this morrow, or that I ate a lettuce last night and forgot to sign the cross over it. Toys are meet for babes, and babes for toys. They cannot understand the realities of life. Such matters I confess to—another Priest, and He can understand them."

"Well," said I, "I always thought Father Hamon something less wise than Father Benedict: at least, Father Benedict chides me, and Father Hamon gives me neither blame nor commendation. But, Margaret, I do not understand thy strange sayings in any wise. Surely thou knowest what is the Church?"

"I know what it is not," saith she; "and that is Father Hamon, or Father Benedict, or Father Anything-Else. Christ and they that are Christ's—the

Head and the Body, the Bridegroom and the Bride: behold the Church, and behold her Priest and Confessor!"

"Margaret," saith Mother Alianora, "who taught thee that? Where didst thou hear such learning?"

She did not speak chidingly, but only as if she desired information. I was surprised she was not more severe, for truly I never heard such talk, and I was sorely afraid for my poor Margaret, lest some evil thing had got hold of her—maybe the Devil himself in the likeness of some Sister in her old convent.

A wave of pain swept over Margaret's eyes when Mother Alianora said that, and a dreamy look of calm came and chased it thence.

"Where?" she said. "In the burning fiery furnace, heated seven times hotter than its wont. Of whom? Verily, I think, of that Fourth that walked there, who was the Son of God. He walks oftener, methinks, in the fiery furnace with His martyrs, than in the gilded galleries with the King Nebuchadnezzar and his princes. At least I have oftener found Him there."

She seemed as if she lost herself in thought, until Mother Alianora saith, in her soft, faint voice—"Go on, my child."

Margaret roused up as if she were awoke from sleep.

"Well!" she said, "nothing happened to me, as you may well guess, for the years of childhood that followed, when I was learning to read, write, and illuminate, to sew, embroider, cook, and serve in various ways. My Lady Prioress found that I had a wit at devising patterns and such like, so I was kept mainly to the embroidery and painting: being first reminded that it was not for mine own enjoyment, but that I should so best serve the Order. I took the words and let them drop, and I took the work and delighted in it. So matters went until I was a maid of seventeen years. And then something else came into my life."

I asked, "What was it?" for she had paused. But her next words were not an answer.

"I marvel," she saith, "of what metal Saint Gilbert was made, that founded our Order. Was it out of pity, or out of bitter hardness, or out of simple want of understanding, that he framed our Rule, and gave us more liberty than other Sisters? Is it more or less happy for a lark that thou let him out of his cage once in the year in a small cell whence he cannot escape into the free air of heaven? Had I been his mother or his sister, when the Saint writ his Rule, I had said to him, Keep thy brethren and sisters apart at the blessed Sacrament, or else bandage their eyes."

"O Margaret!" I cried out, for it was awful to hear such words. As if the blessed Saint Gilbert could have made a mistake! "Dost thou think thyself wiser than the holy saints?"

"Yes," she answered simply. "I am sure I know more about women than Saint Gilbert did. That he did not know much about them was shown by such a Rule, he might as well have set the door of the lark's cage open, and have said to the bird, 'Now, stay in!' Well, I did not stay in. One morrow at mass, I was all suddenly aware of a pair of dark eyes scanning my face across the nave—"

"From the brethren's side of the church! O Margaret!"

"Well, Annora? I am human: so, perchance, was he. He had been thrust into this life, as I had. Had we both been free, we might have loved each other without a voice saying, 'It is sin.' Why was it sin because we wore black and white habits?"

"But the vows, Margaret! the vows!"

"What vows? I made none, worthy to be called vows. I was bidden, a little babe of four years, to say 'ay' and 'nay' at certain times, and 'I am willing,' and so forth. What knew I of the import attaching to such words? I do ensure thee I knew nothing at all, save that when I had been good and done as I was told, I should have a pretty little habit like the Sisters, and be called 'Sister' as these grown women were. Is that what God calls a vow?—a vow of life-long celibacy, dragged from a babe that knew not what vow nor celibacy were! 'Doth God lack your lie?' saith Job (Job 13, verse 7). Yea, the Psalmist crieth, '*Numquid adhaeret Tibi sedes iniquitatis?*' (Psalm 94, verse 20)—Wala wa! the only thing I marvel is that He thundereth not down with His great wrath, and delivereth not him that is in misery out of the hand of him that despoileth."

If it had been any other Sister, I think I should have been horribly shocked: but do what I would, I could not speak angrily to my own sister. I wonder if it were very wicked in me! But it surprised me much that Mother Alianora lay and hearkened, and said nought. Neither was she asleep, for I glanced at her from time to time, and always saw her awake and listening. Truly, she had little need of nurses, for it was no set malady that ailed her— only a gentle, general decay from old age. Why two of us were set to watch her I could not tell. Had I thought it possible that Mother Gaillarde could do a thing so foreign to her nature, I might have fancied that she sent us two there that night just in order that we might talk and comfort each other. If Mother Alianora had been the one to do it, I might have thought such a thing: or if my Lady had sent us herself, I should have supposed she had never considered the matter: but Mother Gaillarde! Well, whatever reason she had, I am thankful for that talk with Margaret. So I kept silence, and my sister pursued her tale.

"He was not a Brother," she said, "but a young man training for the priesthood under the Master. But not yet had he taken the holy vows, therefore I suppose thou wilt think him less wicked than me."

She looked up into my face with a half-smile.

"O Margaret! I wis not what to think. It all sounds so strange and shocking—only that I have not the heart to find fault with thee as I suppose I should do."

Margaret answered by a little laugh.

"In short," said she, "thou canst be wicked sometimes like other folk. Be it done! I ensure thee, Annora, it comforts me to know the same. Because it is not real wickedness, only painted. And I fear not painted sin, any more than I hold in honour painted holiness. For real sin is not paint; it is devilishness. And real holiness is not paint; it is dwelling in God. And God is love."

"But not that sort of love!" I cried.

"Is there any sort but one?" she made answer. "Love is an angel, Annora: it is self-love that is of the Devil. When man helps man to sin, that is not love. How can it be, when God is love, and God and sin are opposites? Tarry until my tale be ended, and then shalt thou be judge thyself how far Roland's love and mine were sin."

"Go on," said I.

"Well," she said, "for many a week it went no further than looks. Then it came to words."

"In the church!"

"No, not in the church, my scrupulous sister! We should have felt that as wrong as thou. Through the wall between the gardens, where was a little chink that I dare be bound we were not the first to find. Would that no sinfuller words than ours may ever pass athwart it! We found out that both of us had been thrust into the religious life without our own consent: I, thou savest, by the Queen's wrath (which I knew not then); he, by a cousin that coveted his inheritance. And we talked much, and at last came to agreement that as neither he nor I had any vocation, it would be more wrong in us to continue in this life than to escape and be we'd."

"But what priest should ever have wedded a Sister to man training for holy orders?"

"None. We were young, Annora: we thought not of such things. As for what should come after we were escaped, we left that to chance. Nay, chide me not for my poor broken dream, for it was a dream alone. The Prioress found us out. That night I was in solitary cell, barred in my prison, with no companions save a discipline that I was bidden to use, and a great stone crucifix that looked down upon me. Ay, I had one Other, but at first I saw Him not. Nay, nor for eight years afterwards. Cold, silent, stony, that crucifix looked down: and I thought He was like that, the living Christ that had died for me, and I turned away from Him. My heart seemed that night as if it froze to ice. It was hard and ice-bound for eight years. During that time there were many changes at Watton. Our Prioress died; and a time of sore sickness removed many of our Sisters. At the end of the eight years, only three Sisters were left who could remember my punishment—it was more than I have told"—ah, poor soul! lightly as she passed it thus, I dare be bound it was—"and these, I imagine, knew not why it was. And at last our confessor died.

"I thought I had utterly outlived my youthful dream. Roland had disappeared as entirely as if he had never been. What had become of him I knew not—not even if he were alive. I went about my duties in a dull, wooden way, as an image might do, if it could be made to move so as to sew or paint without a soul. Life was worth nothing to me—only to get it over. My love was dead, or it was my heart: which I knew not. Either came to the same thing. There were duties I disliked, and one of these was confession: but I went through with them, in the cold, dull way of which I spake. It had to be: what did it matter?

"One morrow, about a week after our confessor's death, my Lady Prioress that then was told us at recreation-time that our new confessor had come. We were commanded to go to him, ten in the day, and to make a full confession from our infancy. My turn came on the second day. So many of our elder Sisters had died or been transferred, that I was, at twenty-five years, one of the eldest (beside the Mothers) left in the house.

"I knelt down in the confessional, and repeated the Confiteor. Then, in that stony way, I went on with my life-confession: the falsehood that I had told when a child of eight, the obstinacy that I had shown at ten, the general sins whereof I had since been guilty: the weariness of divine things which ever oppressed me, the want of vocation that I had always felt. I finished, and paused. He would ask me some questions, of course. Let him get them over. There was silence for a moment. And then I heard myself asked—'Is that all thou hast to confess?'—in the voice I had loved best of all the world.

My tongue seemed to cleave to the roof of my mouth. I only whispered, 'Roland!' in tones which I could not have told for mine own.

"'I scarce thought to find thee yet here, Margaret,' he said. 'I well-nigh feared to do it. But after thy confession, I see wherefore God hath sent me—that I may pour out into the dry and thirsty cup of thine heart a little of that spiced wine of the kingdom which He hath given to me.'

"Mine heart sank down very low. 'Thou hast received thy vocation, then?' I said; and I felt the poor broken thing ache so that I knew it must be yet alive. Roland would care no more for me, if he had received a vocation. I must go on yet alone till death freed me. Alone, for evermore!

"'I have received the blessedest of all vocations,' he answered; 'the call to God Himself. Margaret, art thou thinking that if this be so, I shall love thee no more? Nay, for I shall love thee more than ever. Beloved, God is not stone and ice; He is not indifference nor hatred. Nay, He is love, and whoso dwelleth in love dwelleth in God, and God dwelleth in us, and His love is perfected in us. Open thy heart to that love, and then this little, little life will soon be over, and we shall dwell together beside the river of His pleasures, unto the ages of the ages.'

"'It sounds fair, Roland,' I said; 'but it is far away. My soul is hard and dry. I cannot tell how to open the door.'

"'Then,' said he, 'ask Jesus to lift the latch and to come in. Thou wilt never desire Him to go forth again. I have much to say: but it hath been long enough now. Every time thou prayest, say also, "Lord Jesu, come into mine heart and make it soft." He will come if thou desire Him. And if thou carest not to do this for His sake, do it for thine own.'

"'I care not for mine own, nor for any thing,' I answered drearily.

"'Then,' saith he, and the old tenderness came into his tone for a moment, 'then, Margaret, do it for mine.'

"I believe he forgot to absolve me: but I did not miss it.

"It is four and twenty years since that day: and during all these years I have been learning to know Christ our Lord, and the fellowship of His sufferings. For as time passed on, Roland told me much of saintly men from whom he had learned, and of many a lesson direct from our Lord Himself. Now He has taken Roland's place. Not that I love Roland less: but I love him differently. He is not first now: and all the bitterness has gone out of my love. Not all the pain. For we came to the certainty after a time, when he had taught me much, that we had better bide asunder for this life, and in that which is to come we shall dwell together for evermore. He was about to resign his post as confessor, when the Lord disposed of us otherwise, for the Master thought fit to draft me into the house at Shuldham, and after eighteen years there was I sent hither. So Roland, I suppose, bides at Watton. I know not: the Lord knows. We gave up for His sake the sweet converse wherein our hearts delighted, that we might serve Him more fully and with less distraction. I do not believe it was sinful. That it is sin in me to love Roland shall I never own. But lest we should love each other better than we love Him, we journey apart for this lower life. And I do not think our Lord is angry with me when at times the longing pain and the aching loneliness seem to overcome me, for a little while. I think He is sorry for me. For since I learned—from Roland—that He is not dead, but the Living One—that He is not darkness, but the Light—that He is not cold and hard, but the incarnate Love—since then, I can never feel afraid of Him. And I believe that He has not only made satisfaction for my sins, but also that He can carry my burdens, and can forgive my blunders. And if we cannot speak to one another, we can both speak to Him, and entrust Him with our messages for each other. He will give them if it be good: and before giving, He will change the words if needful, so that we shall be sure to get the right message. Sometimes, when I have felt very lonely, and He comes near me, and sends His peace into my heart, I wonder whether Roland was asking Him to do it: and I pray Him to comfort and rest Roland whenever he too feels weary. So you see we send each other many more letters round by Heaven than we could possibly do by earth. It was the last word Roland said to me—'The road upward is alway open,' and, 'Et de Hierosolymis et de Britannia, aequaliter patet aula caelestis.'" (Note 2.)

Margaret was silent.

Then said Mother Alianora, "Child, thou hast said strange things: if they be good or ill, God wot. I dare not have uttered some of them thus boldly; yet neither dare I condemn thee. We all know so little! But one thing have I learned, methinks—that God will not despise a gift because men cast it at His feet as having no value for them. I say not, He will not despise such givers: verily, they shall have their reward. But if the gift be a living thing that can feel and smart under the manner of its usage, then methinks He shall stoop to lift it with very tender hands, so as to let it feel that it hath value in His eyes—its own value, that nought save itself can have. My children, we are not mere figures to Him—so many dwellers in so many houses. Before Him we are living men and real women—each with his separate heart, and every separate pang that rends it. The Church of God is one: but it is His

Body, and made of many members. We know, when we feel pain, in what member it is. Is He less wise, less tender, less sensitive than we? There are many, Margaret, who would feel nought but horror at thy story; I advise thee not to tell it to any other, lest thou suffer in so doing. But I condemn thee not: for I think Christ would not, if He stood now among us. Dear child, keep at His feet: it is the only safe place, and it is the happy place. Heaven will be wide enough to hold us all, and before long we shall be there."

Note 1. To the mind of a Roman Catholic, a "religious person" is only a priest, monk, or nun.

Note 2. "From Jerusalem, or from England, the way to Heaven is equally near." —Jerome.

Chapter 3
Annora finds it out

"Peace, peace, poor heart!
Go back and thrill not thus!
Are not the vows of the Lord God upon me?"

It would really be a convenience if one could buy common sense. People seem to have so little. And I am sure I have not more than other people.

That story of Margaret's puzzles me sorely. I sit and think, and think, and I never seem to come any nearer the end of my thinking. And some never seem to have any trouble with their thoughts. I suppose they either have more of them, and more sense altogether, so that they can see things where I cannot; or else—Well, I do not know what else.

But Margaret's thoughts are something so entirely new. It is as if I were looking out of the window at one end of the corridor, which looks towards Grantham, and she were looking from the window at the other end, which faces towards Spalding. Of course we should not see the same things: how could we? And if the glass in one window were blue, and the other red, it would make the difference still greater. I think that must be rather the distinction; for it does not seem to lie in the things themselves, but in the eyes with which Margaret looks on them.

Dear Mother Alianora yet lives, but she is sinking peacefully. Neither Margaret nor I have been called to watch by her again. I begged of Mother Gaillarde that I might see her once more, and say farewell; and all I got for it was "Mind your broidery, Sister!"

I should not wonder if she let me go. I do not know why it is, but for all her rough manner and sharp words, I can ask a favour of Mother Gaillarde easier than of Mother Ada. There seems to be nothing in Mother Ada to get hold of; it is like trying to grip a lump of ice. Mother Gaillarde is like a nut with a rough outside burr; there is plenty to lay hold of, though as likely as not you get pricked when you try. And if she is rough when you ask her anything, yet she often gives it, after all.

I have not exchanged a word with Margaret since that night when we watched together. She sits on the other side of the work-room, and even in the recreation-room she rather avoids coming near me, or I fancy so.

Whatever I begin with, I always get back to Margaret. Such strange ideas she has! I keep thinking of things that I wish I had said to her or asked her, and now I have lost the opportunity. I thought of it this morning, when the two Mothers were conversing with Sister Ismania about the Christmas decorations in our own little oratory. Sister Ismania is the eldest of all our Sisters.

"I thought," said she, "if it were approved, I could mould a little waxen image of our Lord for the altar, and wreathe it round with evergreens."

"As an infant?" asked Mother Gaillarde.

"Well—yes," said Sister Ismania; but I could see that had not been her idea.

"Oh, of course!" answered Mother Ada. "It would be most highly indecorous for *us* to see Him as a man."

Was it my fancy, or did I see a little curl of Margaret's lips?

"He will be a man at the second advent, I suppose," observed Mother Gaillarde.

Mother Ada did not answer: but she looked rather scandalised.

"And must we not have some angels?" said Sister Ismania.

"There are the angels we had for Easter, Sister," suggested Sister Roberga.

"Sister Roberga, oblige me by speaking when you are spoken to," said Mother Ada, in her icicle manner.

"There is only one will do again," answered Mother Gaillarde. "Saint Raphael is tolerable; he might serve. But I know the Archangel Michael had one of his wings broken; and the Apostle Saint Peter lost a leg."

"We had a lovely Satan among those Easter figures," said Sister Ismania; "and Saint John was so charming, I never saw his equal."

"Satan may do again if he gets a new tail," said Mother Gaillarde. "But Pontius Pilate won't; that careless Sister Jacoba let him drop, and he was mashed all to pieces."

"Your pardon, Mother, but that was Judas Iscariot."

"It wasn't: it was Pontius Pilate."

"I am sure it was Judas."

"I tell you it wasn't."

"But, Mother, I—"

"Hold your tongue!" said Mother Gaillarde, curtly.

And being bidden by her superior, of course Sister Ismania had to obey. I looked across at Margaret, and met her eyes. And, as Margaret's eyes always do, they spoke.

"These are holy women, and this is spiritual love!" said Margaret's eyes, ironically. "We might have spoken thus to our own brethren, without going into a convent to do it."

I wonder if Margaret be not right, and we bring the world in with us: that it is something inside ourselves. But then, I suppose, outside there are more temptations. Yet do we not, each of us, make a world for herself? Is it not *ourselves* that we ought to renounce—the earthliness and covetousness of our own desires, rather than the mere outside things? Oh, I do get so tired when I keep thinking!

Yesterday, when Erneburg and Damia were playing at see-saw in the garden, with a long plank balanced on the saddling-stone, I could not help wondering how it is that one's thoughts play in that way. Each end seems sometimes up, and then the other end comes up, and that goes down. I wish I were wiser, and understood more. Perchance it was better for me that I was sent here. For I never should have been wise or brilliant. And suppose *he* were, and that he had looked down upon me and disliked me for it! That would have been harder to bear than this.

Ha, chétife! have all religious women such stories as we two? Did Mother Ada ever feel a heart in her? Mother Gaillarde does at times, I believe. As to my Lady, I doubt any such thing of her. She seems to live but to eat and sleep, and if Mother Gaillarde had not more care to govern the house than she, I do—Mother of Mercy, but this is evil speaking, and of my superiors too! *Miserere me, Domine*!

As we filed out of the oratory last night as usual, Mother Gaillarde stayed me at the door.

"Sister Annora, thou art appointed to the Infirmary to-night." And in a lower tone she added—"It will be the last time."

I knew well what last time she meant: never again in life should I see our dear Mother Alianora. I looked up thankfully.

"Well?" said Mother Gaillarde, in her curt way. "Are you a stone image, or do you think I'm one?"

I kissed her hand, made the holy sign, and passed on. No, dear Mother: thou art not a stone.

In the Infirmary I found Sister Philippa on duty.

"O Sister Annora, I am so glad thou art come! I hate this sort of work, and Mother Gaillarde will keep me at it. I believe it is because she knows I detest it."

"Thou art not just to Mother Gaillarde, Sister," I said, and went on to the bed by the window.

"Annora, dear child!" said the feeble voice. Ay, she was weaker far than when I last beheld her, "Thank God I have seen thee yet once more."

I could do little for her—only now and then give her to drink, or raise her a little. And she could not speak much. A few words occasionally appeared to be all she had strength for. Towards morning I thought she seemed to wander and grow light-headed. She called once "Isabel!" and once "Aveline!" We have at present no Sister in the house named Aveline, and when I asked if I should seek permission to call Sister Isabel if she wished for her, she said, "No: she will be gone to Marlborough," and what she meant I know not. (Note 1.) Then, after she had lain still a while, she said, "Guendolen—is it thou?"

"No, dearest Mother; it is Sister Annora," said I.

"Guendolen was here," saith she: "where is she?"

"Perhaps she will come again," I answered, for I saw that she scarcely had her wits clear.

"She will come again," she saith, softly. "Ay, He will come again—with clouds—and His saints with Him. And Guendolen will be there—my Sister Guendolen, the Princess (Note 2), whom men cast forth,—Christ shall crown her in His kingdom. The last of the royal line! There are no Princes of Wales any more."

Then I think she dropped asleep for a time, and when she woke she knew me at first; though she soon grew confused again.

"Christ's blessing and mine be on thee, mine own Annora!" saith she, tenderly. "Margaret, too—poor Magot! Tell her—tell her—" but her voice died away in indistinct murmurs. "They will soon be here."

"Who, dearest Mother?"

"Joan and Guendolen. Gladys, perchance. I don't know about Gladys. White—all in white: no black in that habit. And they sing—No, she never sang on earth. I should like to hear Guendolen sing in Heaven."

The soft toll of the bell for prime came to her dulled ear.

"Are they ringing in Heaven?" she said. "Is it Guendolen that rings? The bells never rang for her below. They have fairer music up there."

The door opened, and Mother Ada looked in.

"Sister Annora, you are released. Come to prime."

Oh, to have tarried only a minute! For a light which never was from sun or moon had broken over the dying face, and she vainly tried to stretch her hands forth with a rapturous cry of—"Guendolen! Did the Master send thee for me?"

"Sister! You forget yourself," said Mother Ada, when I lingered. "Remember the rule of holy obedience!"

I suppose it was very wicked of me—I am always doing wicked things—but I did wish that holy obedience had been at the bottom of the Red Sea, I kissed the trembling hand of the dear old Mother, and signed the holy cross upon her brow to protect her when she was left alone, and then I followed Mother Ada. After prime I was ordered to the work-room. I looked round, and saw that Sister Roberga and Margaret were missing. I did hope Margaret, and not Sister Roberga, had been sent up to the Infirmary. Of course I could not ask.

For two hours I sewed with my heart in the Infirmary. If the rule of holy obedience had been at the bottom of the Red Sea, I am sure I should not have tarried in that work-room another minute. And then I heard the passing bell. It struck so cold to my heart that I had hard work to keep my broidering in a straight line.

A few minutes later, Margaret appeared at the door. She knelt down in the doorway, and made the sign of the cross, saying, "Peace eternal grant to us, O Lord!"

And we all responded, led by Mother Ada,—"Lord, grant to Thy servant our Sister everlasting peace!"

So then I knew that Mother Alianora had been sent for by the Master of us all.

"Sister Margaret!" said Mother Ada.

Margaret rose, went up to Mother Ada, and knelt again.

"How comes it thou art the messenger? I sent Sister Roberga to the Infirmary this morning."

"Mother Gaillarde bade me go to the Infirmary," said Margaret in a low voice, "and sent Sister Roberga down to the laundry."

"Art thou speaking truth?" asked Mother Ada.

Margaret's head went up proudly. "King Alfred the Truth-Teller was my forefather," she said.

"Well! perhaps thou dost," answered Mother Ada, as if unwilling to admit it. "But it is very strange. I shall speak to Sister Gaillarde."

"What about?" said Mother Gaillarde, appearing suddenly from the passage to my Lady's rooms.

"Sister Gaillarde, this is very strange conduct of you!" said Mother Ada. "I ordered Sister Roberga to the Infirmary."

"You did, Sister, and I altered your order. I am your superior, I believe?"

Mother Ada, who is usually very pale, went red, and murmured something which I could not hear.

"Nonsense!" said Mother Gaillarde.

To my unspeakable astonishment, Mother Ada burst into tears. She has so many times told the children, and not seldom the Sisters, that tears were a sign of weakness, and unworthy of reasonable, not to say religious, women—that they ought to be shed in penitence alone, or in grief at a slight offered to holy Church, that I could only suppose Mother Gaillarde had been guilty of some profanity.

"It is very hard!" sobbed Mother Ada. "That you should set yourself up in that way, when I was professed on the very same day as you—"

"What has that to do with it?" asked Mother Gaillarde.

"And my Lady shows you much more favour than she does me: only to-day you have been in her rooms twice!"

"I wish she would send for you," said Mother Gaillarde, "for it is commonly to waste time over some sort of fiddle-faddle that I despise. You are heartily welcome to it, I can tell you! Now, come, Sister Ada, don't be silly and set a bad example. It is all nonsense, and you know it."

Off marched Mother Gaillarde with a firm step. Mother Ada continued to sob.

"Nobody could bear such treatment!" said she. "The blessed Virgin herself would not have stood it. I am sure Sister Gaillarde is not a bit better than I am—of course I do not speak on my own account, but for the honour of the Order: that is what I am anxious about. It does not matter in the least how people tread *me* down—I am the humblest-minded Sister in the house; but I am a Mother of the Order, and I feel Sister Gaillarde's words exceedingly. Pride is one of the seven deadly sins, and I do marvel where

Sister Gaillarde thinks she is going. I shall offer my next communion for her, that she may be more humble-minded. I am sure she needs it."

Mother Ada bit off her thread, as she said this, with a determined snap, as if it had cruelly provoked her. I was lost in amazement, for Mother Ada has always seemed so calm and icy that I thought nothing could move her, and here she was making a fuss about nothing, like one of the children. She had not finished when Mother Gaillarde came back.

"What, not over it yet?" said she, in her usual style. "Dear me, what a storm in a porringer!"

Mother Ada gave a bursting sob and a long wail to end it; but Mother Gaillarde took no more notice of her, only telling us all that Mother Alianora would be buried to-morrow, and that after the funeral we were to assemble in conclave to elect a new Mother. It will be Sister Ismania, I doubt not; for she is eldest of the Sisters, and the one most generally held in respect.

In the evening, at recreation-time, Sister Philippa came up to me.

"So we are to meet to elect a new Mother!" said she, with much satisfaction in her tone. "I always like meeting in conclave. There is something grand about it. For whom will you vote, Sister Annora?"

"I have not thought much about it," said I, "except that I suppose every body will vote for Sister Ismania."

"I shall not," said Mother Joan.

I see so little of Mother Joan that I think I have rarely mentioned her. She is Mistress of the Novices, and seldom comes where I am.

"You will not, Mother? For whom, then?" said Sister Philippa.

"If you should be appointed to collect the votes, Sister, you will know," was Mother Joan's reply.

"Now, is that not too bad?" said Sister Philippa, when Mother Joan had passed on. "Of course the Mothers will collect the votes."

"I fancy Mother Joan meant we Sisters ought not to ask," I said.

"O Sister! did you not enjoy that quarrel between the Mothers this morning?" cried she.

"Certainly not," I answered. "I could not enjoy seeing any one either distressed or angry."

"Oh; but it was so delightful to see Mother Ada let herself down!" cried Philippa. "So proud and stuck-up and like an icicle as she always is! *Ha jolife!* and she calls herself the humblest Sister in the house!"

Margaret had come up, and stood listening to us.

"Who think you is the humblest, Sister Philippa?"

"I don't know," said Sister Philippa. "If you asked me who was the proudest, maybe I could tell—only that I should have to name so many."

"Well, I should need to name but one," said I. "I would fain be the humblest; but that surely am I not: and I find so many wicked motions of pride in mine heart that I cannot believe any of us can be worse than myself."

"I think I know who is the lowliest of us, and the holiest," said Margaret as she turned away; "and I shall vote for her."

"Who can she mean?" asked Sister Philippa.

"I do not know at all," said I; and indeed I do not.

Dear Mother Alianora was buried this afternoon. The mass for the dead was very, very solemn. We laid her down in the Sisters' graveyard, till the resurrection morn shall come, when we shall all meet without spot of sin in the presence-chamber of Heaven. Till then, O holy and merciful Saviour, suffer us not, now and at our last hour, for any pains of death, to fall from Thee!

We passed directly from the funeral into conclave. My Lady sent word to the Master that we were about to elect a Mother, and he sent us his benediction on our labour. We all filed into our oratory, and sat down in our various stalls. Then, after singing the Litany of the Holy Ghost, Mother Gaillarde passed down the choir on the Gospel side, and Mother Ada on the Epistle side, collecting the votes. When all were collected, the two Mothers went up to my Lady, and she then came out of her stall, and headed them to the altar steps, where they all three knelt for a short space. Then my Lady, turning round to us, and coming forward, announced the numbers.

"Thirty-four votes: for Sister Roberga, one; for Sister Isabel, two; for Sister Ismania, eleven; for Sister Annora, twenty. Our Sister Annora is chosen."

It was a minute before I was able to understand that such an unintelligible and astounding thing had happened, as that our community had actually chosen me—me, of all people!—to execute the highest office in the house, next to my Lady Prioress herself. Mother Gaillarde and Mother Ada came up to me, to lead me up to the altar.

"But it cannot be," said I. I felt completely confused.

"Thou art our Sister Annora, I believe," saith Mother Gaillarde, looking rather amused; "and I marvel the less at the choice since I helped to make it."

"I!" I said again, feeling more amazed than ever at what she said; "but I'm not a bit fit for such a place as that! Oh, do choose again, and fix on somebody more worthy than I am!"

"The choice of the community, guided by the Holy Spirit, has fallen on you, Sister," said Mother Ada, in a cold, hollow voice.

"Come along, and don't be silly!" whispered Mother Gaillarde, taking my right arm.

I really think Mother Gaillarde's words helped to rouse me from my stupor of astonishment, better than any thing else. Of course, if God called me to a certain work, He could put grace and wisdom into me as easily as into any one else; and I had only to bow to His will. But I did so wish it had been another who was chosen. Sister Ismania would have made a far better officer than I. And to think of such a poor, stupid, confused thing as I am, being put over her head! But, if it were God's will—that settled the matter.

It all felt so dreamy that I can scarcely tell what happened afterwards. I remember that I knelt before my Lady, and before the altar—but I felt too confused for prayer, and could only say, "*Domine, miserere me!*" for no other words would come: and then the Master came and blessed me, and made a short address to me (of which I believe I hardly took in a word), and appointed the next day for the service of ordination.

I am an ordained Mother of the Order of Saint Gilbert. And I do not feel any difference. I thought I should have done. The Master himself sang the holy mass, and we sang *Veni Creator Spiritus*, and he said in his address afterwards, that when his hands were laid on my head, the Holy Ghost came down and filled me with His presence—and I did not feel that He did. Of course it was all very solemn, and I did most earnestly desire the influences of the blessed Spirit, for I shall never be able to do any thing without them: but really I felt our Lord nearer me in the evening, when I knelt by my bed for a minute, and asked Him, in my own poor words, to keep me in the right way, and teach me to do His will. I think I shall try that again. Now that I have a cell to myself, I can do it. And I sleep in dear Mother Alianora's cell, where I am sure the blessed Lord has been wont to come. Oh, I hope He will not tarry away because I am come into it—I, who am so worthless, and so weak, and need His gracious aid so much more than she did!

I do wish, if so great a favour could possibly be vouchsafed to me, that I might speak to our Lord just once. He has ere this held converse with the holy saints. Of course I am not holy, nor a saint, nor in the least merit any such grace from Him: but I need it more than those who merit it. Oh, if I could know,—once, certainly, and for ever—whether it is earthly, and carnal, and wicked, as people say it is, for me to grieve over that lost love of mine! Sister Ismania says it is all folly and imagination on my part, because, having been parted when we were only six years old, I cannot possibly (she says) feel any real, womanly love for him. But I do not see why it must be grown-up to be real. And I never knew any thing better or more real. It may not be like what others have, but it was all I had. I wish sometimes that I knew if he still lives, and whether that other wife lives to whom I suppose somebody must have married him after I was thrust in here. I cannot feel as if he did not still, somehow, belong to me. If I only knew whether it was wrong!

I have been appointed mistress of the work-room, and I ought to keep it in order. How I can ever do it, I cannot think. I shall never be able to chide the Sisters like the other Mothers: and to have them coming up to me, when they are chidden, and kissing the floor at my feet—I do not know how I can stand it. I am sure it will give me a dreadful feeling. However, I hope nothing will ever happen of that kind, for a long, long while.

What is the good of hoping any thing? Mother Gaillarde says that hopes, promises, and pie-crust are made to be broken. Certainly hopes seem to be. After all my wishes, if something did not happen the very first day!

When I got down to the work-room, what should I find but Sisters Roberga and Philippa having a violent quarrel. They were not only breaking the rule of silence, which in itself was bad enough, but they were calling each other all manner of names.

I was astonished those two should quarrel, for they have always been such friends that they had to be constantly reminded of the prohibition of particular friendships among the religious: but when they did, it reminded me of the adage that vernage makes the best vinegar.

Sister Isabel cast an imploring look at me, as I entered, which seemed to say, "Do stop them!" and I had not a notion how to set about it, except by saying—

"My dear Sisters, our rule enjoins silence."

On my saying this (which I did with much reluctance and some trembling) both of them turned round and appealed to me.

"She promised to vote for me, and she did not!" cried Sister Roberga.

"I did!" said Sister Philippa. "I kept my word."

"There was only one vote for me," answered Sister Roberga.

"Well, and I gave it," replied Sister Philippa.

"You couldn't have done! There must have been more than one."

"Why should there?"

"I know there was."

"How do you know?"

"I do know."

"You must have voted for yourself, then: you can't know otherwise," said Sister Philippa, scornfully.

Sister Roberga fairly screamed, "I didn't, you vile wretch!" and went exceedingly red in the face.

"Sister Roberga," said I—

"Don't you interfere!" shrieked Sister Roberga, turning fiercely on me. "You want a chance to show your power, of course. You poor, white-faced, sanctimonious creature, only just promoted, and that because every body voted for you, thinking you would be easily managed—just like a bit of putty in any body's fingers! And making such a fuss, as if you were so humble and holy, professing not to wish for it! Faugh! how I hate a hypocrite!"

I stood silent, feeling as if my breath were taken away.

"Yes, isn't she?" cried Sister Philippa. "Wanting Sister Ismania to be preferred, instead of her, after all her plotting with Mother Gaillarde and Sister Margaret! I can't bear folks who look one way and walk another, as she does. *I* shouldn't wonder if the election were vitiated,—not a bit!—and then where will you be, *Mother* Annora?"

"Where you will be, Sister Philippa, until compline," said a voice behind me, "is prostrate on the chapel floor: and after compline, you will kiss the floor at Mother Annora's feet, and ask her to forgive you. Sister Roberta, go to the laundry—there is nobody there—and do not come forth till I fetch you. You also, after compline, will ask the Mother's forgiveness."

Oh, how thankful I felt to Mother Gaillarde for coming in just then! She said no more at that time; but at night she came to my cell.

"Sister Annora," said she, "you must not let those saucy girls ride rough-shod over you. You should let them see you mean it."

"But," said I, "I am afraid I don't mean it."

Mother Gaillarde laughed. "Then make haste and do," said she. "You'll have a bear-garden in the work-room if you don't pull your curb a little tighter. You may always rely on Sister Ismania, Sister Isabel, and Sister Margaret to uphold your authority. It is those silly young things that have to be kept in order. I wish you joy of your new post: it is not all flowers and music, I can tell you."

"Oh dear, I feel so unfit for it!" I sighed.

Mother Gaillarde smiled. "Sister, I am a bad hand at paying compliments," she said. "But one thing I will say—you are the fittest of us all for the office, if you will only stand firm. Give your orders promptly, and stick to them. *Pax tibi!*"

I have put Mother Gaillarde's advice into action—or rather, I have tried to put it—and have brought a storm on my head. Oh dear, why cannot folks do right without all this trouble?

Sisters Amie and Catherine began to cast black looks at one another yesterday evening in the work-room, and when recreation-time came the looks blossomed into words. I told them both to be silent at once. This morning I was sent for by my Lady, who said that she had not expected me to prove a tyrant. I do not think tyrants feel their hearts go pitter-patter, as mine did, both last night and this morning. Of course I knelt and kissed her hand, and said how sorry I was to have displeased her.

"But, indeed, my Lady," said I, "I spoke as I did because I was afraid I had not been sufficiently firm before."

"Oh, I dare say it was all right," said my Lady, closing her eyes, as if she felt worried with the whole affair. "Only Sister Ada thought—I think somebody spoke to her—do as you think best, Sister. I dare say it will all come right."

I wish things would all come right, but it seems rather as if they all went wrong. And I do not *quite* see what business it is of Mother Ada's. But I ought not to be censorious.

Just as I was leaving the room, my Lady called me back. It does feel so new and strange to me, to have to go to my Lady herself about things, instead of to one of the Mothers! And it is not nearly so satisfactory; for where Mother Gaillarde used to say, "Do *so*, of course"—my Lady says, "Do as you like." I cannot even get accustomed to calling them Sister Gaillarde and Sister Ada, as, being a Mother myself, I ought to do now. Oh, how I miss our dear Mother Alianora! It frightens me to think of being in her place. Well, my Lady called me back to tell me that the Lady Joan de Greystoke desired to make retreat with us, and that we must prepare to receive her next Saturday. She is to have the little chamber next to the linen-wardrobe. My Lady says she is of good lineage, but she did not say of what family she came. She commanded me to tell the Mothers.

"*Miserere!*" said Mother—no, Sister Ada. "What an annoyance it is, to be sure, when externs come for retreat! She will unsettle half the young Sisters, and turn the heads of half the others. I know what a worry they are!"

"Humph!" said Sister Gaillarde. "Of good lineage, is she? That means, I suppose, that she'll think herself a princess, and look on all of us as her maid-servants. She may clean her own shoes so far as I'm concerned. Do her good. I'll be bound she never touched a brush before."

"Some idle young baggage, I've no doubt," said Sister Ada.

"Marry, she may be a grandmother," said Mo—Sister Gaillarde. "If she's eighty, she'll think she has a right to lecture us; and if she's only eighteen, she'll think so ten times more. You may depend upon it, she will reckon we know nought of the world, and that all the wisdom in it has got into her brains. These externs do amuse me."

"It is all very well for you to make fun of it, Sister Gaillarde," said Sister Ada, peevishly, "but I can tell you, it will be any thing but fun for you and me, if she set half the young Sisters, not to speak of the novices and pupils, coveting all manner of worldly pomps and dainties. And she will, as sure as my name is Ada."

"Thanks for your warning," said Mother Gaillarde. "I'll put a rod or two in pickle."

The Lady Joan's chamber is ready at last: and I am dad. Such a business I have had of it! I had no idea Sister Philippa was so difficult to manage: and as to Sister Roberga, I pity any one who tries to do it.

"You see, Sister Annora," said Sister Gaillarde, smiling rather grimly, "official life is not all flowers and sunshine. I don't pity my Lady, just because she shirks her duties: she merely reigns, and leaves us to govern; but I can tell you, no Prioress of this convent would have an easy life, if she *did* her duty. I remember once, when I was in the world, I saw a mountebank driving ten horses at once. I dare say he hadn't an easy time of it. But, lack-a-day! we have to drive thirty: and skittish fillies some of them are. I don't know what Sister Roberga has done with her vocation: but I never saw the corner of it since she came."

"Well!" I said with a sigh, "I suppose I never had one."

"Stuff and nonsense!" said Sister Gaillarde. "If you mean you never had a liking for the life, that may be true—you know more about that than I; but if you mean you do not fill your place well, and do your duty as well as you know how, and a deal better than most folks—why, again I say, stuff and nonsense! You are not perfect, I suppose. If you ever see any body who is, I should like to know her name. It won't be Gaillarde—that I know!"

I wonder whose daughter the Lady Joan is! Something in her eyes puzzles me so, as if she reminded me of somebody whom I had known, long, long ago—some Sister when I was novice, or perchance even some one whom I knew in my early childhood, before I was professed at all. They are dark eyes, but not at all like Margaret's. Margaret's are brown, but these are dark grey, with long black lashes; and they do not talk—they only look as if they could, if one knew how to make them. The Lady Joan is very quiet and attentive to her religious duties; I think Sister Ada's fears may sleep. She is not at all likely to unsettle any body. She talks very little, except when necessary. Two months, I hear, she will remain; and I do not think she will be any trouble to one of us. Even Sister Gaillarde says, "She is a decent woman: she'll do." And that means a good deal—from Sister Gaillarde.

I have the chance to speak to Margaret now. Of course a Mother can call any Sister to her cell if needful; and no one may ask why except another Mother. I must be careful not to seem to prefer Margaret above the rest, and all the more because she is my own sister. But last night I really had some directions to give her, and I summoned her to my cell. When I had told her what I wanted, I was about to dismiss her with *"Pax tibi!"* as usual, but Margaret's talking eyes told me she had something to say.

I said,—"Well! what is it, Margaret?"

"May I speak to my sister Annora for a moment, and not to the Mother?" she asked, with a look half amused and half sad.

"Thou mayest always do that, dear heart," said I.

(I hope it was not wicked.)

"Then—Annora, for whom is the Lady Joan looking?"

"Looking! I understand thee not, Margaret."

"I think it is either thou or I," she replied. "Sister Anne told me that she asked her if there were not some Sisters of the Despenser family here, and wished to have them pointed out to her: and she said to Sister Anne, 'She whom I seek was professed as a very little child.' That must be either thou or I, Annora. What can she want with us?"

"Verily, Margaret, I cannot tell."

"I wondered if she might be a niece of ours."

"She may," said I. "I never thought of that. There is something about her eyes that reminds me of some one, but who it is I know not."

"Thou couldst ask her," suggested Margaret.

"I scarcely like to do that," said I. "But I will think about it, Margaret."

I was wicked enough to kiss her, when I let her go.

This morning Sister Ada told me that the Lady Joan had asked leave to learn illuminating, so she would spend her mornings henceforth in the illumination chamber. That will bring her with Margaret, who is much there. Perchance she may tell her something.

It would be strange to see a niece or cousin of one's very own! I marvel if she be akin to us. Somehow, since I had that night watch with Margaret, my heart does not feel exactly the dry, dead thing it used to do in times past. I fancy I could love a kinswoman, if I had one.

Sister Gaillarde said such a strange thing to me to-day. I was remarking that the talk in the recreation-room was so often vapid and foolish—all about such little matters: we never seemed to take an interest in any great or serious subject.

"Sister Annora," said she, with one of her grim smiles, "I always looked to see you turn out a reformer."

"Me!" cried I.

"You," said she.

"But a reformer is a great, grand man, with a hard head, and a keen wit, and a ready tongue!" said I.

"Why should it not be a woman with a soft heart?" quoth Sister Gaillarde.

"*Ha, jolife!*" cried I. "Sister Gaillarde, you may be cut out for a reformer, but I am sure I am not."

I looked up as I spoke, and saw the Lady Joan's dark grey eyes upon me.

"What is to be reformed. Mother?" said she.

"Why, if each of us would reform herself, I suppose the whole house would be reformed," I answered.

"Capital!" said Sister Gaillarde. "Let's set to work."

"Who will begin?" said Sister Ismania.

"Every body will be the second," replied Sister Gaillarde, "except those who have begun already: that's very plain!"

"I expect every body will be the last," said Margaret.

Sister Gaillarde nodded, as if she meant Amen.

"Well, thank goodness, I want no reforms," said Sister Ada.

"Nor any reforming?" said Sister Gaillarde.

"Certainly not," she answered. "I always do my duty—always. Nobody can lay any thing else to my charge." And she looked round with an air that seemed to say, "Deny it if you can!"

"It is manifest," observed Sister Gaillarde gravely, "that our Sister Ada is the only perfect being among us. I am not perfect, by any means: and really, I feel oppressed by the company of a seraph. I'm not nearly good enough. Perchance, Sister Ada, you would not mind my sitting a little further off."

And actually, she rose and went over to the other side of the room. Sister Ada tossed her head,—not as I should expect a seraph to do: then she too rose, and walked out of the room. Sister Ismania had laughingly followed Sister Gaillarde: so that the Lady Joan, Margaret, and I, were alone in that corner.

"My mother had a Book of Evangels," said the Lady Joan, "in which I have sometimes read: and I remember, it said, 'be ye perfect,' The priests say only religious persons can be perfect: yet our Lord, when He said it, was not speaking to them, but just to the common people who were His disciples, on the hill-side. Is it the case, that we could all be perfect, if only we tried, and entreated the grace of our Lord to enable us to be so?"

"Did your Ladyship ever know any who was?" asked Margaret.

The Lady Joan shook her head. "Never—not perfect. My mother was a good woman enough; but there were flaws in her. She was cleverer than my father, and she let him feel it. He was nearer perfection than she, for he was humbler and gentler—God rest his sweet soul! Yet she was a good woman, for all that: but—no, not perfect!"

Suddenly she ceased, and a light came in her eyes.

"You two," she said, looking on us, "are the Despenser ladies, I believe?"

We assented.

"Do you mind telling me—pardon me if I should not ask—which of you was affianced, long years ago, to the Lord Lawrence de Hastings, sometime Earl of Pembroke?"

"Sometime!" ah me, then my lost love is no more!

I felt as though my tongue refused to speak. Something was coming— what, I did not know.

Margaret answered for me, and the Lady Joan's hand fell softly on mine.

"Did you love each other," she said, "when you were little children? If so, we ought to love each other, for he was very dear to me. Mother Annora, he was my father."

"You!" I just managed to say.

"Ah, you did, I think," she said, quietly. "He died a young man, in the first great visitation of the Black Death, over twenty years ago: and my mother survived him twenty years. She married again, and died three years since."

Margaret asked what I wanted to hear. I was very glad, for I felt as if I could ask nothing. It was strange how Margaret seemed to know just what I wished.

"Who was your mother, my Lady?"

The Lady Joan coloured, and did not answer for a moment. Then she said,—"I fear you will not like to know it: yet it was not her fault, nor his. Queen Isabel arranged it all: and she hath answered for her own sins at the Judgment Bar. My mother was Agnes de Mortimer, daughter of the Earl of March."

"Why not?" said Margaret.

"Ah, then you know not. I scarce expected a Despenser to hear his name with patience. But I suppose you were so young—Sisters, he was the great enemy of your father."

So they wedded my lost love to the daughter of my enemy! Almost before the indignation rose up within me, there came to counteract it a vision of the cross of Calvary, and of Him who said, "Father, forgive them!" The momentary feeling of anger died away. Another feeling took its place: the thought that the after-bond was dissolved now, and death had made him mine again.

"Mother Annora," said the Lady Joan's soft voice, "will you reject me, and look coldly on me, if I ask whether you can love me a little? He used to love to talk to me of you, whom he remembered tenderly, as he might have remembered a little sister that God had taken. He often wondered where you were, and whether you were happy. And when I was a little child, I always wanted to hear of that other child—you lived, eternal, a little child, for me. Many a time I have fancied that I would make retreat here, and try to find you out, if you were still alive. Do you think it sinful to love any thing?—some nuns do. But if not, I should like you to love the favourite child of your lost love."

"Methinks," said Margaret, quietly, "it is true in earthly as in heavenly things, and to carnal no less than spiritual persons, '*Major horum est caritas.*'" (First Corinthians 13, verse 13.)

I hardly know what I said. But I think Joan was satisfied.

Note 1. Her thoughts wandered to her married sister, Isabel Lady Hastings and Monthermer, who lived at Marlborough Castle.

Note 2. The last native Princess of Wales, being the only (certainly proved) child of the last Prince Llywelyn, and Alianora de Montfort. She was thrust into the convent at Sempringham with her cousin Gladys.

Chapter 4
Mortifying the Will

"L'orgueil n'est jamais mieux déguisé, et plus capable de tromper, que lorsqu'il se cache sous la figure de l'humilité."
Rochefoucauld.

"Oh, you have no idea how happy we are here!" said Sister Ada to Joan. "I often pity the people who live in the world. Their time is filled with such poor, mean things, and their thoughts must be so frivolous. Now our time is all taken up with holy duties, and we have no room for frivolous thoughts. The world is shut out: it cannot creep in here. We are the happiest of women."

I happened to look at Sister Gaillarde, and I saw the beginning of one of her grim smiles: but she did not speak.

"Some of you do seem happy and peaceful," said Joan (she says I am to call her Joan). "But is it so with all?"

Sister Gaillarde gave her little Amen nod.

"Oh dear, yes!" answered Sister Ada. "Of course, where the will is not perfectly mortified, there is not such unbroken bliss as where it is. But when the rule of holy obedience is fully followed out, so that we have no will whatever except that of our superiors, you cannot imagine what sweet peace flows into the soul. Now, if Father Benedict were to command me any thing, I should be positively delighted to do it, because it was a command from my superior. It would not in the least matter what it was. Nay, the more repugnant it was to my natural inclinations, the more it would delight me."

Joan's eyes wandered to two or three other faces, with a look which said, "Do you agree to this?"

"Don't look at me!" said Sister Gaillarde. "I'm no seraph. It wouldn't please me a bit better to have dirty work to do because Father Benedict ordered it. I can't reach those heights of perfection—never understood them. If Sister Ada do, I'm glad to hear it. She must have learned it lately."

"I do not understand it, as Sister Ada puts it," said I, as Joan's eyes came to me. "I understand what it is to give up one's will in any thing when it seems to be contrary to the will of God, and to have more real pleasure in trying to please Him than in pleasing one's self. I understand, too, that there may be more true peace in bearing a sorrow wherein God helps and comforts you, than in having no sorrow and no comfort. But Sister Ada seems to mean something different—as if one were to be absolutely without any will about any thing, and yet to delight in the crossing of one's will. Now, if I have not any wall, I do not see how it is to be crossed. And to have none whatever would surely make me something different from a woman and a sinner. I should be like a harp that could be played on—not like a living creature at all."

Two or three little nods came from Sister Gaillarde.

"People who have no wills are very trying to deal with," said Margaret.

"People who have wills are," said Sister Philippa.

"Nay," said Margaret, "if I am to be governed, let it be by one that has a will. 'Do this,' and 'Go there,' may be vexatious at times: but far worse is it to ask for direction, and hear only, 'As you like,' 'I don't know,' 'Don't ask me.'"

"Now that is just what I should like," said Sister Philippa. "I never get it, worse luck!"

"Did you mean me, Sister Margaret?" said Sister Ada, stiffly.

"I cry you mercy, Mother; I was not thinking of you at all," answered Margaret.

"It sounded very much as if you were," said Sister Ada, in her iciest fashion. "I think, if you had been anxious for perfection, you would not have answered me in that proud manner, but would have come here and entreated my pardon in a proper way. But I am too humble-minded to insist on it, seeing I am myself the person affronted. Had it been any one else, I should have required it at once."

"I said—" Margaret got so far, then her brow flushed, and I could see there was an inward struggle. Then she rose from the form, and laying down her work, knelt and kissed the ground at Mother Ada's feet. I could hear Sister Roberga whisper to Sister Philippa, "That mean-spirited fool!"

Sister Gaillarde said in a softer tone than is her wont,—"*Beati pauperes spiritu: quoniam ipsorum est regnum caelorum.*" (Matthew 5, verse 3.)

"Thank you, Sister Gaillarde," said Sister Ada, quickly. "I scarcely expected recognition from *you*."

"You got as much as you expected, then," said Sister Gaillarde, drily, with a look across at me which almost made me laugh.

"I told you, I got more than I expected," was Sister Ada's answer.

"Did you mean it for her?" asked Joan, in so low a voice that only those on each side of her could hear.

"I meant it for whoever deserved it," was Sister Gaillarde's reply.

Just then Mother Joan came in and sat down.

"Sister Ada," she said, "Sister Marian tells me, that my Lady has given orders for that rough black rug that nobody likes to be put on your bed this week."

"No, has she?" cried Sister Ada, in tones which, if she were delighted, very much belied her feelings. "How exceedingly annoying! What could my Lady be thinking of? She knows how I detest that rug. I shall not be able to sleep a wink. Well! I suppose I must submit; it is my duty. But I do feel it hard that *all* the disagreeable things should come to me. Surely one of the novices might have had that; it would have been good for somebody whose will was not properly mortified. Really, I *do* think—Oh, well, I had better not say any more."

Nor did she: but that night, as I was going round the children's dormitory, little Damia looked up at me.

"Mother, dear, what's the matter with Mother Ada?"

"What did she say, my child?"

"Oh, she didn't say any thing; but she has looked all day long as if she would like to hit somebody."

"Somebody vexed her a little, perhaps," said I. "Very likely she will be all right to-morrow."

"I don't know—she takes a long while to come right when any body has put her wrong—ever so much longer than you or Sister Margaret. The lightning comes into Sister Margaret's eyes, and then away it runs, and she looks so sorry that she let it come; and you only look sorry without any lightning. But Mother Ada looks I don't know how—as if she'd like to pull all the hair off your head, and all your teeth out of your mouth, and wouldn't feel any better till she'd done it."

I laughed, and told the child to go to sleep, and not trouble her little head about Mother Ada. But when I came into my cell, I began to wonder if Sister Ada's will is perfectly mortified. It does not look exactly like it.

Before I had done more than think of undressing, Sister Gaillarde rapped at my door.

"Sister Annora, may I have a little chat with you?"

"Do come in, Sister, and sit down," said I.

"This world's a very queer place!" said Sister Gaillarde, sitting down on my bed. "It would not be a bad place, but for the folks in it: and they are as queer as can be. I thought I'd just give you a hint, Sister, that you might feel less taken by surprise—I expect you'll have a lecture given you to-morrow."

"What have I done?" I asked, rather blankly.

Sister Gaillarde laughed till the tears came into her eyes.

"Oh dear, the comicality of folks in this world!" saith she. "Sister Annora, do you know that you are a very carnal person?"

"Indeed, I have always feared so," said I, sorrowfully.

"Rubbish!" said Sister Gaillarde in her most emphatic style. "Don't, for mercy's sake, be taken in by such nonsense. It is a wonder what folks can get into their heads when they have nothing else in them! Sister Ada is very much concerned about the low tone of spirituality which she sees in you—stupid baggage! She is miserably afraid you are a long way off perfection. I'm more concerned a deal about her."

"But, Sister Gaillarde, it is true!" said I. "I am very, very far from being perfect, and I fear I never shall be."

"Well!" saith she, "if I had to go into the next world holding on to somebody's skirts, I'd a sight rather they were yours than Sister Ada's. I do think some folks were born just to be means of grace and nothing else. Maybe it is as well some of them should get into nunneries."

"Some are rather trying, I must admit," said I. "Sister Roberga—"

"Oh, Sister Roberga! she's just a butterfly and no better. Brush her off—she's good for no more. But she isn't one that tries me like some other folks. You did not hear what happened yesterday between Sisters Ada and Margaret?"

"No. What was it?"

"Some of the Sisters were talking about hymns in recreation. Sister Margaret said she admired the *Dies Irae*. Sister Ada wanted to know what she admired; she could not see any thing to admire; it was just a jingle of words, and nothing else. The rhymes might be good to remember by— that was all. I saw the look on Sister Margaret's face: of course she did not answer the Mother. But I did. I told her that I believed if any one showed her a beautiful rose, she would call it a red vegetable. 'Well,' quoth she, 'and what is it else? I never smell a rose or any other flower. We were put here to mortify our senses.' 'Sister Ada,' said I, 'the Lord took a deal of pains for nothing, so far as you were concerned.' Well, she said that was profane: but I don't believe it. The truth is, she's just one of those dull souls that cannot see beauty, nor smell fragrance, nor hear music; and so she assumes her dulness as virtue, and tries to make it out that those who have their senses are carnal and worldly. But just touch her pride, and doesn't it fly up in arms! Depend upon it, Sister Annora, men are quite as often taken for fools because they can see what other folks can't, as because they can't see what other folks can."

"I dare say that is true," said I. "But—forgive me, Sister Gaillarde— ought we to be talking over our Sisters?"

"Sister Annora, you are too good for this world!" she answered, rather impatiently. "If one may not let out a bit, just now and then, what is one to do?"

"But," said I, "we were put here to mortify ourselves."

"We were put here to mortify our sins," said she: "and wala wa! some of us don't do it. I dare say old Gaillarde's as bad as any body. But I cannot stand Sister Ada's talk, when she wants to make every creature of us into stones and stocks. She just inveighs against loving one another because she loves nobody but Ada Mansell, and never did. Oh! I knew her well enough when we were young maids in the world. She was an only child, and desperately spoiled: and her father joined in the Lancaster insurrection long ago, and it ruined his fortunes, so she came into a convent. That's her story. Ada Mansell is the pivot of her thoughts and actions—always will be."

"Nay," said I; "let us hope God will give her grace to change, if it be as you say."

"It'll take a precious deal of grace to change some folks!" said Sister Gaillarde, satirically. "Hope many of them won't want it at once, or there'll be such a run upon the treasury there'll be none left for you and me. Well! that's foolish talk. My tongue runs away with me now and then. Don't get quite out of patience with your silly old Sister Gaillarde. Ah! perhaps I should have been a wiser woman, and a better too, if something had not happened to me that curdled the milk of my human kindness, and sent me in here, just because I could not bear outside any longer—could not bear to see what had been mine given to another—well, well! We are all poor old sinners, we Sisters. And as to perfection—my belief is that any woman may be perfect in any life, so far as that means having a true heart towards God, and an honest wish to do His will rather than our own—and I don't believe in perfection of any other sort. As to all that rubbish men talk about having no will at all, and being delighted to mortify your will, and so forth—my service to the lot of it. Why, what you like to have crossed isn't your will; what you delight in can't be mortification. It is just like playing at being good. Eh, dear me, there are some simpletons in this world! Well, good-night, Sister: *pax tibi!*"

Sister Gaillarde's hand was on the latch when she looked back.

"There, now I'm forgetting half of what I had to tell you. Father Hamon's going away."

"Is he?—whither?"

"Can't say. I hope our next confessor will be a bit more alive."

"Father Benedict is alive, I am sure."

"Father Benedict's a draught of vinegar, and Father Hamon's been a bowl of curds. I should like somebody betwixt."

And Sister Gaillarde left me.

She guessed not ill, for I had my lecture in due course. Sister Ada came into my cell—had she bidden me to hers, I should have had a chance to leave, but of course I could not turn her forth—and told me she had been for long time deeply concerned at my want of spiritual discernment. "Truly, Sister, no more than I am," said I. "Now, Sister, you reckon me unkindly, I cast no doubt," saith she: "but verily I must be faithful with you. You take too much upon you,—you who are but just promoted to your office—and are not ready enough to learn of those who have had more experience. In short, Sister Annora, you are very much wanting in true humility."

"Indeed, Sister Ada, it is too true," said I. "I beseech you, Sister, to pray that you may have your eyes opened to the discerning of your faults," saith she. "You are much too partial and prejudiced in your governance of the Sisters, and likewise with the children. Some you keep not under as you should; and to others you grant too little freedom."

"Indeed, Sister, I am afraid it may be so, though I have tried hard to avoid it."

"Well, Sister, I hope you will think of these things, and that our Lord may give you more of the grace of humility. You lack it very much, I can assure you. I would you would try to copy such of us as are really humble and meek."

"That I earnestly desire, Sister," said I: "but is it not better to copy our Lord Himself than any earthly example? I thank you for your reproof, and I will try harder to be humble."

"You know, Sister," said she, as she was going forth, "I have no wish but to be faithful. I cannot bear telling others of their faults. Only, I *must* be faithful."

"I thank you, Sister Ada," said I.

So away she went. Sister Gaillarde said when she saw me, with one of her grim smiles—

"Well! is the lecture over? Did she bite very hard?"

"She saith I am greatly lacking in meekness and humility, and take too much on myself," said I: "and I dare say it is true."

"Humph!" said Sister Gaillarde. "It would be a mercy if some folks weren't. And if one or two of us had a trifle more self-assertion, perhaps some others would have less."

"Have I too much self-assertion, Sister?" I said, feeling sorry it should be thus plain to all my Sisters. "I will really—"

Sister Gaillarde patted me on the shoulder with her grimmest smile.

"You will really spoil every body you come near!" said she. "Go your ways, Sister Annora, and leave the wasps in the garden a-be."

"Why, I do," said I, "without they sting me."

"Exactly!" said Sister Gaillarde, laughing, and away. I know not what she meant.

Mother Joan is something troubled with her eyes, and the leech thinks it best she should no longer be over the illumination-room, but be set to some manner of work that will try the sight less. So I am appointed thereto in her stead. I cannot say I am sorry, for I shall see more of Joan, since in this chamber she passes three mornings of a week. I mean my child Joan, for verily she is the child of mine heart. And my very soul yearns over her, for Sister though I be, I cannot help the thought that had it not been for Queen Isabel's unjust dealing, I should have been her mother. May the good Lord forgive me, if it be sin! I know now, that those deep grey eyes of hers, with the long black lashes, which stirred mine heart so strangely when she first came hither, are the eyes of my lost love. I knew in myself that I had known such eyes aforetime, but it seemed to be long, long ago, as though in another world. Much hath Joan told me of him; and all I hear sets him before me as man worthy of the best love of a good woman's heart, and whom mine heart did no wrong to in its enduring love. And I am coming to think—seeing, as it were, dimly, through a mist—that such love is not sin, neither disgrace, even in the heart of a maid devoted unto God. For He knoweth that I put Him first: and take His ordering of my life, as being His, not only as just and holy, but as the best lot for me, and that which shall be most to His glory and mine own true welfare. I say not this openly, nor unto such as should be likely to misconceive me. There are some to whose pure and devoted souls all things indifferent are pure; and they are they that shall see God. And man saith that in the world there are some also, unto whose vile and corrupt hearts all things indifferent are impure; and maybe not in the world only, but by times even in the cloister. So I feel that some might misread my meaning, and take ill advantage thereof; and I keep my thoughts to myself, and to God. I never ask Joan one question touching him of whom I treasure every bye-note that she uttereth. Yet I know not how it is, but she seems to love to tell me of him. Is it by reason she hath loved, that her heart hath eyes to see into mine?

Not much doth Joan say of her mother to me: I think she names her more to others. Methinks I see what she was—a good woman as women go (and some of them go ill), with a little surface cleverness, that she reckoned to run deeper than it did, and inclined to despise her lord by reason his wit lay further down, and came not up in glittering bubbles to the top. I dare reckon she looked well to his bodily comforts and such, and was a better wife than he might have had: very likely, a better than poor Alianora La Despenser would have made, had God ordered it thus. Methinks, from all I hear, that he hath passed behind the jasper walls: and I pray God I may meet him there. They wed not, nor be given in marriage, being equal unto the angels: but surely the angels love.

Strange talk it was that Joan held with me yesterday. I marvel what it may portend. She says, of late years many priests have put forth writings, wherein they say that the Church is greatly fallen away from the verity of Scripture, and that all through the ages good men have said the same (as was the case with the blessed Robert de Grosteste, Bishop of Lincoln, over two hundred years gone, and with the holy Thomas de Bradwardine, Archbishop of Canterbury, and with Richard Rolle, the hermit of Hampole, whose holy meditations on the Psalter are in our library, and I have oft read therein): but now is there further stir, as though some reforming of the Church should arise, such as Bishop Grosteste did earnestly desire. Joan says her lord is earnest for these new opinions, and eager to promote them: and that he saith that both in the Church and in matters politic, men sleep and nap for a season, during which slow decay goes on apace, and then all at once do they wake up, and set to work to mend matters. During the reign of this present King, saith he, the world and the Church have had a long nap; and now are they just awake, and looking round to see how matters are all over dust and ivy, which lack cleansing away. Divers, both clerks and laymen, are thus bestirring themselves: the foremost of whom is my Lord of Lancaster, the King's son (John of Gaunt), among the lay folk, and among the clergy, one Father Wycliffe (Note 1), that was head of a College at Oxenford, and is now Rector of Lutterworth in Leicestershire. He saith (that is, Father Wycliffe) that all things are thus gone to corruption by reason of lack of the salt preservative to be found in Holy Scripture. Many years back, did King Alfred our forefather set forth much of the said Scriptures in the English tongue; as much, indeed, as he had time, for his death hindered it, else had all the holy hooks been rendered into our English tongue. But now, by reason of years, the English that was in his day is gone clean out of mind, and man cannot understand the same: so there is great need for another rendering that man may understand now. And this Father Wycliffe hopes to effect, if God grant him grace. But truly, some marvellous strange notions hath he. Joan says he would fain do away with all endowing of the Church, saying that our Lord and the Apostles had no such provision: but was that by reason it was right, or because of the hardness of men's hearts? Surely the holy women that ministered to Him of their substance did well, not ill. Moreover, he would have all monkery done away, yea, clean out of the realm, and he hath mighty hard names for monks, especially the Mendicant Friars: yet of nuns was he never heard to speak an unkindly word. Strange matter, in good sooth! it nearly takes away my breath but to hear tell of it. But when he saith that the Pope should have no right nor power in this realm of England, that is but what the Church of England hath alway held: Bishop Grosteste did as fervently abhor the Pope's power— "Egyptian bondage" was his word for it. Much has this Father also to say against simony: and he would have no private confession to a priest (verily, this would I gladly see abolished), nor indulgences, nor letters of fraternity, nor pilgrimages, nor guilds: and he sets his face against the new fashion of singing mass (intoning, then a new invention), and the use of incense in the churches. But strangest of all is it to hear of his inveighing against the doctrine of the Church that the sacred host is God's Body. It is so, saith he, in figure, and Christ's Body is not eaten of men save ghostly and morally. And to eat Christ ghostly is to have mind of Him, how kindly He suffered for man, which is ghostly meat to the soul. (Arnold's English Works of Wycliffe, Volume 2, pages 93, 112.)

Here is new doctrine! Yet Father Wycliffe, I hear, saith this is the old doctrine of the Apostles themselves, and that the contrary is the new, having never (saith he) been heard of before the time of one Radbert, who did first set it forth five hundred years ago (in 787): and after that it slumbered—being then condemned of the holy doctors—till the year of our Lord God 1215, when the Pope that then was forced it on the Church. Strange matter this! I know not what to think.

Joan says some of these new doctrine priests go further than Father Wycliffe himself, and even cast doubt on Purgatory and the worship (this word then merely meant "honour") of our Lady. Ah me! if they can prove from God's Word that Purgatory is not, I would chant many thanksgivings thereon! All these years, when I knew not if my lost love were dead or alive, have I thought with dread of that awful land of darkness and sorrow: yet not knowing, I could have no masses sung for him; and had I been so able, I could never have told for whom they were, but only have asked for them for my father and mother and all Christian souls, and have offered mine own communion with intention thereto. Ay, and many a time—dare I confess it?—I have offered the same with that intent, if he should be to God commanded (dead)—knowing that God knew, and humbly trusting in His mercy if I did ill. But for the worship of our Lady, that is passing strange, specially to me that am religious woman. For we were always taught what a blessing it was that we had a woman to whom we might carry our griefs and sorrows, seeing God is a man, and not so like to enter into a woman's feelings. But these priests say—I am almost afraid to write it—this is dishonouring Christ who died for us, and who therefore must needs be full of tenderness for them for whom He died, and cannot need man nor woman—not even His own mother—to stand betwixt them and Him. O my Lord, have I been all these years dishonouring Thee, and setting up another, even though it be Thy blessed mother, between Thee and me? Yet surely He regardeth her honour full diligently! Said He not to Saint John, "Behold thy mother?"—and doth not that Apostle represent the whole Church, who are thereby commanded to regard her, each righteous man, as his own very mother? (This is the teaching of the Church of Rome.) I remember the blessed Hermit of Hampole scarcely makes mention of her: it is all Christ in his book. And if it be so—of which Joan ensures me—in the Word of God, whereof she hath read books that I have missed—verily, I know not what to think.

Lord, Thou wist what is error! Save me therefrom. Thou wist what is truth: guide me therein!

It would seem that I have erred in offering my communions at all. For if to eat Christ's Body be only to have mind of Him—and this is according to His own word, "*Hoc facite in meam commemorationem*"—how then can there be at all any offering of sacrifice in the holy mass? Joan says that Saint

Paul's Epistle to the Hebrews saith that we be hallowed by the oblation of the body of Jesus Christ once, and that where remission is, there is no more oblation for sin. Truly we have need to pray, Lord, guide us into Thy truth! and yet more, Lord, keep us therein! I must think hereon. In sooth, this I do, and then up rises some great barrier to the new doctrine, which I lay before Joan: and as quickly as the sun can break forth and melt a spoonful of snow, does she clear all away with some word of Saint Paul. She has his Epistles right at her tongue's end. For instance, quoth I,—"Christ said He should bestow the Holy Spirit, to lead the Church into all truth. How then can the Church err?"

"What Church?" said she, boldly. "The Church is all righteous men that hold Christ's words: not the Pope and Cardinals and such like. These last have no right to hold the first in bondage."

"But," said I, "Father Benedict told me Saint Paul bade the religious to obey their superiors: how much more all men to obey the Church?"

"I marvel," saith she, "where Father Benedict found that. Never a word says Paul touching religious persons: there were none in his day."

"No religious in Paul's day!" cried I.

"Never so much as one," saith she: "not a monk, not a nun! Friar Pareshull himself told me so much; he is a great man among us. Saint Peter bids the clergy not to dominate over inferiors; Saint Paul says to the Ephesians that out of themselves (he was speaking to the clergy) should arise heretics speaking perversely; and Saint John says, 'Believe not every spirit, but prove the spirits if they be of God.' Dear Mother Annora, we are nowhere bidden in Scripture to obey the Church save only once, and that concerns the settling of a dispute betwixt two members of it. Obey the Church! why, we are ourselves the Church. Has not Father Rolle taught you so much? 'Holy Kirk,' quoth he—'that is, ilk righteous man's soul.' Verily, all Churches be empowered of Christ to make laws for their own people: but why then must the Church of England obey laws made by the Bishop of Rome?"

"Therein," said I, "can I fully hold with thee."

"And for all things," she said earnestly, "let us hold to God's law, and take our interpretation of it not from men, but straight from God Himself. Lo! here is the promise of the Holy Ghost assured unto the Church—to you, to me, to each one that followeth Christ. They that keep His words and are indwelt of His Spirit—these, dear Mother, are the Church of God, and to them is the truth promised."

I said nought, for I knew not what to answer.

"There is yet another thing," saith Joan, dropping her voice low. "Can that be God's Church which contradicts God's Word? David saith 'Over all things Thou hast magnified Thy Name' (Note 2): but I have heard of a most wise man, that could read ancient volumes and dead tongues, that Saint Hierome set not down the true words, namely, 'Over all Thy Name Thou hast magnified Thy Word.' Now, if this be so—if God hath set up His Word over all His Name—the very highest part of Himself—how dare any assemblage of men to gainsay it? What then of these indulgences and licences to sin, which the Popes set forth? what of their suffering them to wed whom God has forbidden, and forbidding it to priests to whom God has suffered it? Surely this is the very thing which God points at, 'teaching for doctrines the commandments of men.'"

"But, Joan," said I, "my dear heart, did not our Lord say, 'Whatsoever ye shall bind on earth shall be bound in Heaven?' Surely that authorises the Church to do as she will."

"Contrary unto God's Word? It may give her leave to do her will within the limits of the Word: I trow not contrary thereto. When the King giveth plenipotentiary powers to his Keeper of the Great Seal, his own deposing and superseding, I reckon, are not among them. 'All things are subject unto Christ,' saith Paul; 'doubtless excepting Him which did subject all things unto Him.' So, if God give power of loosing and binding to His Church, it cannot be meant that she shall bind Himself who thus endowed her, contrary to His own will and law."

I answered nought, again, for a little while. At last I said, "Joan, there is a word that troubles me, and religious folks are always quoting it. 'If a man hate not his father and his mother'—and so forth—he cannot be our Lord's disciple. I think I have heard it from one or another every week since I came here. What say these new doctrine folks that it means?"

"Ours are old doctrines, Mother dear," saith she; "as old as the Apostles of Christ. What means it? Why, go forth to the end, and you will see what it means: he is to hate his own soul also. Is he then to kill himself, or to go wilfully into perdition? Nay, what can it mean, but only that even these dearest and worthiest loves are to be set below the worthier than them all, the love of the glory of God? That our Lord never meant a religious person should neglect his father and mother, is plainly to be seen by another word of His, wherein he rebukes the priests of His day, because they taught that a man might bestow in oblation to God what his father's or his mother's need demanded of him. Here again, he reproves them, because they rejected the command of God in order to keep their own tradition. You see, therefore, that when the Church doth this, it is not ratified in Heaven."

"Then," said I, after a minute's thought, "I am not bidden to hate myself, any more than my relations?"

"Why should we hate one whom God loveth?" she answered. "To hate our selfishness is not to hate ourselves."

I sat a while silent, setting red eyes and golden claws to my green wyvern, and Joan ran the white dots along her griffin's tail. When she came to the fork of the tail, she laid down her brush.

"Mother," she saith—the dear grey eyes looking up into my face—"shall we read together the holy Scripture, and beseech God to lead us into all truth?"

"Dear child, we will do so," said I. "Joan, didst thou ever read in holy Scripture that it was wicked to kiss folks?"

She smiled. "I have read there of one," saith she, "who stole up behind the holiest of all men that ever breathed, and kissed His feet: and the rebuke she won from Him was no more than this: 'Her many sins are forgiven her, and she loved much.' So, if a full sinful woman might kiss Christ without rebuke, methinks, if it please you, Mother dear, you might kiss me."

Well, I knew all my life of that woman, but I never thought of it that way before, and it is marvellous comforting unto me.

My Lady sent this morning for all the Mothers together. Mine heart went pitter-patter, as it always doth when I am summoned to her chamber. It is only because of her office: for if she were no more than a common Sister, I am sorely afraid I should reckon her a selfish, lazy woman: but being Lady Prioress, I cannot presume to sit in judgment on my superiors thus far. We found that she had sent for us to introduce us to the new confessor, whose name is Father Mortimer, he is tall, and good-looking (so far as I, a Sister, can understand what is thought to be so in the world), and has dark, flashing eyes, which remind me of Margaret's, and I should say also of that priest that once confessed us, did I not feel certain that this is the same priest himself. He will begin his duties this evening at compline.

Sister Gaillarde said to me as we came forth from my Lady,—"Had I been a heathen Greek, and lived at the right time, methinks I should have wed Democritus."

"Democritus! who was he?" said I.

"He was named the Laughing Philosopher," said she, "because he was ever laughing at men and things. And methinks he did well."

"What is there to laugh at, Sister Gaillarde?"

"Nothing you saw, Saint Annora."

"Now you are laughing at me," said I, with a smile.

"My laugh will never hurt you," answered she. "But truly, betwixt Sister Ada and the peacock—They both spread their plumes to be looked at. I wonder which Father Mortimer will admire most."

"You surely never mean," said I, much shocked, "that Sister Ada expects Father Mortimer to admire her!"

"Oh, she means nothing ill," said Sister Gaillarde. "She only admires Ada Mansell so thoroughly herself, that she cannot conceive it possible that any one can do otherwise. Let her spread her feathers—it won't hurt. Any way, it will not hurt him. He isn't that sort of animal."

Indeed, I hope he is not.

When my Lady dismissed us, I went to my work in the illumination-room, where Joan, with Sister Annot and Sister Josia, awaited my coming. I bade Sister Josia finish the Holy Family she was painting yesterday for a missal which we are preparing for my Lord's Grace of York; I told Sister Annot to lay the gold leaf on the Book of Hours writing for my Lady of Suffolk; and as Margaret, who commonly works with her, was not yet come, I began myself to show Joan how to coil up the tail of a griffin—she said, to put a yard of tail into an inch of parchment. It appeared to amuse her very much to see how I twisted and interlaced the tracery, so as to fill up every little corner of the parallelogram. When the outline was drawn, and she began to fill it with cobalt, as I sat by, she said suddenly yet softly—

"Mother Annora, I have been considering whether I should tell you something."

"Tell me what, dear child?" quoth I.

"I am afraid," said she, "I shocked you yesterday, making you think I was scarcely sound in the faith. Yet where can lie the verity of the faith, if not in Holy Writ? And I marvelled if it should aggrieve you less, if you knew one thing—yet that might give you pain."

"Let me hear it, Joan."

"Did you know," said she, dropping her voice low, "that it was in part for heresy that your own father suffered death?"

"My father!" cried I. "Joan, I know nothing of my father, save only that he angered Queen Isabel, and for what cause wis I not."

"For two causes: first, because the King her husband loved him, and she was of that fashion that looked on all love borne by him as so much robbed from herself. But the other was that very thing—that she was orthodox, and he was—what the priests called an heretic. There might be other causes: some men say he was proud, and covetous, and unpitiful. I know not if it be true or no. But that they writ him down an heretic, as also they did his father, and Archdeacon Baldok—so much I know."

I felt afraid to ask more, and yet I had great longing to hear it.

"And my mother?" said I. I think I was like one that passes round and round a matter, each time a little nearer than before—wishing, and yet fearing, to come to the kernel of it.

"I have heard somewhat of her," said Joan, "from the Lady Julian my grandmother. She was a Leybourne born, and she wedded my grandfather, Sir John de Hastings, whose stepmother was the Lady Isabel La Despenser, your father's sister. I think, from what she told me, your mother was a little like—Sister Roberga."

I am sorely afraid I ought not to have answered as I did, for it was—"The blessed saints forfend!"

"Not altogether," said Joan, with a little laugh. "I never heard that she was ill-tempered. On the contrary, I imagine, she was somewhat too easy; but I meant, a little like what Mother Gaillarde calls a butterfly—with no concern for realities—frivolous, and lacking in due thought."

"Was your grandmother, the Lady Julian, an admirer of these new doctrines?" said I.

"They were scarcely known in her day as they have been since," said Joan; "only the first leaves, so to speak, were above the soil: but so far as I can judge from what I know, I should say, not so. She was a great stickler for old ways and the authority of the Church."

"And your mother?" I was coming near delicate ground, I felt, now.

"Oh! she, I should say, would have liked our doctrines better. Mother Annora, is there blue enough here, or shall I put on another coat?"

Joan looked up at me as she spoke. I said I thought it was deep enough, and she might now begin the shading. Her head went down again to her work.

"My mother," said she, "was no bigot, nor did she much love priests; I dare venture to say, had Father Wycliffe written then as he has now, she would somewhat have supported him so far as lay in her power. But my father, I think, would have loved these doctrines best of all. I have heard say he spoke against the ill lives of the clergy, and the idle doings of the Mendicant Friars: and little as I was when he departed to God, I can myself remember that he used to tell me stories of our Lord and the ancient saints and patriarchs, which I know, now that I can read it, to have come out of God's Word. Ay, methinks, had he lived, he would have helped forward this new reformation of doctrine and manners."

"Reformation!" cries Mother Ada, entering the chamber. "I would we could have a reformation in this house. What my Lady would be at, passeth me to conceive. She must think I have two pairs of eyes and six pairs of hands, if no more. Do but guess, Sister Annora, what she wants to have done."

"Nay, that I cannot," said I. I foresaw some hard work, for my Lady is one who leaves things to go as they list for ever so long, and then, suddenly waking up, would fain turn the house out o' windows ere one can shut one's eyes.

"Why, if she did not send for me an hour after we came out, and said the condition of the chapel was shameful; how could we have let it get into such a state? Father Mortimer was completely scandalised at the sight of it. All the holy images were all o'er cobwebs, and all—"

"And all of a baker's dozen of blessed times," said Sister Gaillarde, entering behind, "have I been at her for new pails and brushes, never speak of soap. I told her a spider as big as a silver penny had spun a line from Saint Peter's key to Saint Katherine's nose; and as to the dust—why, you could make soup of it. I've dusted Saint Katherine many a time with my hands, for I had them, if I'd nought else: and trust me, the poor Saint looked so forlorn, I fairly wondered she did not speak. Had I been the image of a saint, somebody would have heard of it, I warrant you, when that spider began scuttering up and down my nose."

"And now she bids us drop every thing, and go and clean out the chapel, this very morning—to have done by vesper time! Did you ever hear such a thing?" said Sister Ada, from the bench whereon she had sunk.

"Mother Ada," said Sister Josia, "would you show me—"

"Mercy on us, child, harry not me!" cried Sister Ada.

"But I do not know whether a lily should be in this corner by the blessed Mary," said Sister Josia, "or if the ass should stand here."

"The lily, by all means," said Sister Gaillarde. "Prithee paint not an ass: there's too many in this world already."

"I do wish Father Mortimer would attend to his own business!" cried Sister Ada, "or that we had old Father Hamon back again. I do hate these new officers: they always find fault with every thing."

"Ay, new brooms be apt to sweep a bit too clean," replied Sister Gaillarde. "Mary love us, but I would we had a new broom! I don't believe there are twenty bristles left of the old one."

Joan looked up from her griffin's tail to laugh.

"Well, what is to be done?"

"Oh, I suppose we must do as we are bid," saith Sister Ada in a mournful voice. "But, dear heart, to think of it!"

"How many pails have you, Sister Ada?"

"There's the large bouget, and the little one. The middle-sized one is broken, but it will hold some water."

"Two and a half, then," answered Sister Gaillarde. "Well, fetch them, Sister, and I will go and see to the mops. I think we have a mop left. Perhaps, now, if we din our needs well into my Lady's ears, we may get one or two more. But, sweet Saint Felicitas! is there any soap?"

"Half a firkin came in last week," responded Sister Ada. "You forget, Sister Gaillarde, the rule forbids us to ask more than once for anything."

"The rule should forbid Prioresses to have short memories, then. Come, Sister Annot, leave that minikin fiddle-faddle, and come and help with the real work. If it is to be done by vespers, we want all the hands we can get. I will fetch Sister Margaret to it; she always puts her heart into what she has to do. Well, you look sorely disappointed, child: I am sorry for it, but I cannot help it. I have no fancy for such vanities, but I dare say you like better sticking bits of gold leaf upon vellum than scrubbing and sweeping."

"Sister Annot, I am ashamed of you!" said Sister Ada. "Your perfection must be very incomplete, if you can look disappointed on receiving an order from your superior. You ought to rejoice at such an opportunity of mortifying your will."

"That's more than I've done," said Sister Gaillarde. "Well, Sister Ada, as you don't offer to move, I suppose we had better leave you here till you have finished rejoicing over the opportunity. I hope you'll get done in time to take advantage of it. Come, Sister Annot."

I thought I had better follow. So, having given Joan a few directions to enable her to go on for a time without superintendence, I went to see after the water-bougets, which should have been Sister Ada's work. She called after me—"Sister Annora, I'll follow you in a moment. I have not quite finished my rosary."

I left her there, telling her last few beads, and went to fetch the bougets, which I carried to the chapel, just as Sister Gaillarde came in with her arms full, followed by Margaret and Annot.

"I've found two mops!" she cried. "Mine was all right, but where Sister Ada keeps hers I cannot tell. Howbeit, Sister Joan has one. Now, Sister Annora, if you will bring yours—And see here, these brushes have a few bristles left—this is a poor set-out, though. It'll do to knock off spiders. Now, Sister Margaret, fetch that long ladder by the garden door. Sister Annot, you had better go up,—you are the lightest of us, and I am not altogether clear about that ladder, but it is the only one we have. Well-a-day! if I were Pr— Catch hold of Saint James by the head, Sister Annot, to steady yourself. Puff! faugh! what a dust!"

We were all over dust in a few minutes. I should think it was months since it had been disturbed, for my Lady never would order the chapel to be cleaned. We worked away with a will, and got things in order for vespers. Sister Annot just escaped a bad fall, for a rung of the ladder gave way, and if she had not clutched Saint Peter by the arm, down she would have come. Howbeit, Saint Peter held, happily, and she escaped with a bruise.

Just as things were getting into order, and we had finished all the dirty work, Sister Ada sauntered in.

"Well, really," said Sister Gaillarde, "I did not believe you could truly rejoice in the mortification of your will till I saw how long it took you! Thank you, the mortification is done; you will have to wait till next time: I only hope you will let this rejoicing count. There's nothing left for you, but to empty the slops and wipe out the pails."

Joan told me afterwards, in a tone of great amusement, that "Mother Ada finished her beads very slowly, and then said she would go after you. But she stopped to look at Sister Annot's work, and at once discovered that if left in that state it would suffer damage before she came back. So she sat down and wrought at that for above an hour. Then she was just going again, but she found that an end of the fringe was coming off my robe, and she fetched needle and thread of silk, and sewed it on. The third time she was just going, when she saw the fire wanted wood. So she kept just going all day till about half an hour before vespers, and then at last she contrived to go."

Note 1. I may here ask pardon for an anachronism in having brought Wycliffe forward as a Reformer some years before he really began to be so. The state of men's minds in general was as I have described it; the uneasy stir of coming reformation was in the air; the pamphlet which is so often (but wrongly) attributed to Wycliffe, The Last Age of the Church, had been written some fifteen years before this time: but Wycliffe himself, though then a political reformer, did not come forward as a religious reformer until about six years later.

Note 2. Psalm 138 verse 2, Vulgate. The Authorised Version correctly follows the Hebrew—"Thou hast magnified Thy Word above all Thy Name."

Chapter 5
Waiting

"If we could push ajar the gates of life,
And stand within, and all God's workings see,
We could interpret all this doubt and strife,
And for each mystery could find a key.

"But not to-day. Then be content, poor heart!
God's plans, like lilies pure and white, unfold:
We must not tear the close-shut leaves apart;
Time will reveal the calyxes of gold.

"And if through patient toil we reach the land
Where tired feet with sandals loose may rest,
When we shall clearly see and understand,
I think that we shall say - 'God knew the best.'"

When we came out from the chapel after vespers, my Lady commanded Sister Gaillarde to follow her. The rest of us went, of course, to the work-room, where Sister Gaillarde joined us in about half an hour. I saw that she looked as though she had heard something that greatly amused her, but we could know nothing till we reached the recreation-room.

The minute our tongues were loosed, Sister Ada attacked Sister Gaillarde as to what my Lady wanted with her. With one of her grim smiles, Sister Gaillarde replied—

"My Lady is about to resign her office."

A storm of exclamations greeted the news.

"Why, Sister? Do tell us why."

"She finds," said Sister Gaillarde, gravely, "the burden of her official duties too heavy."

"I marvel what she reckons them to be!" quoth Sister Joan, who, though not sarcastic in the style of Sister Gaillarde, can now and then say a biting thing. "So far as I ever made out, her duties are to sit on cushions and bid other folks work."

"Exactly: and that is too much labour for her."

"Which of us will be chosen in her stead, I marvel!" said Sister Ada, briskly. "I trust it may be one who will look better to her house than the present Lady has done."

"Amen," said Sister Gaillarde, with a mischievous air. "I hope it will be Sister Joan."

"Truly, I hope not," answered the Sister: "for if any such honour came my way (which I expect not), I should feel it my duty to decline it on account of my failing sight."

"Then you see, my Sisters," quoth Sister Ada, quickly, "to vote for Mother Joan would be to no good."

"It would be little good to vote for Mother Ada," I heard a voice whisper behind me; and another replied, "She thinks we all shall, I warrant."

I feel little doubt that Sister Gaillarde will be the one chosen. One of us four it is most likely to be: and the sub-Prioress is oftener chosen than the rest. Sister Gaillarde, methinks, would make a good Prioress.

We had scarcely recovered from our surprise, and had not half finished our talk, when the bell rang for compline: and silence fell on all the busy tongues. All the young Sisters, and the postulants, were eager to catch a glimpse of Father Mortimer; and I saw a good deal of talk pass from eyes to eyes, in the few minutes before the service began. He sings full well, and is most seemly in his ordering of matters. If he be as discreet in the confessional as in his outer ministrations, methinks I shall like him well. Howbeit, he made a deal less impression than he would have done before my Lady's intention was announced. When we filed out of the chapel, and assembled again in the recreation-room, the tongues were set loose, and I could see that the main stream of talk ran on my Lady; only one here and there diverging to Father Mortimer. I sought out Joan, and asked if our new confessor were any kin to her. She could not tell me, beyond saying that she has three uncles and several cousins in the priesthood; but since, saving her uncle Walter, she has never seen any of them, she could not speak certainly without asking himself.

I marvel I have not seen Margaret all this even, now I come to think. I was so taken up with the news concerning my Lady that I never thought to look for her: and in chapel she sits on the Epistle side, as I do, so that I see her not.

This morrow my Lady called us into conclave, and made known her resignation, which she has already tendered to the Master: and bade us all farewell. She will not tarry with us, but goes into the daughter house at Cambridge; this somewhat surprises me, though I see it does not Sister Gaillarde.

"There'll be more stir there," said she.

"Think you my Lady likes stir?" said I. "I have always reckoned her one that loved not to be stirred."

"Soothly," said Sister Gaillarde: "yet she loveth well to sit on her cushions, and gaze on the stir as a peep-show."

A few hours later we were all again assembled in conclave, and the Master himself with us, for election of a new Prioress. And after the mass of the Holy Ghost we Mothers went round to gather up the votes. It fell as I looked, and Sister Gaillarde is elected. In all the house there were only nine that voted otherwise, and of these four were for Sister Joan, two for Sister Ismania, and one each for Sisters Ada, Isabel, and myself. I feel sure that mine was Margaret's: and Joan says she is certain Sister Ada's was her own. I voted, as before, for Sister Gaillarde, for truly I think her fittest of all for the place. Her ordination fallows next week.

"Verily," said Sister Ada, the next time we were at recreation, "I do marvel at Sister Gaillarde's manner of taking her election. Not one word of humility or obedience, but just took it as if it were her right, and she were the most suitable person!"

"Why, that was obedience, was it not?" responded Sister Ismania.

"Obedience it might be, but it was not lowliness!" said Sister Ada, tartly. "If I had been elect—of course I do not mean that I expected such a thing, not for a moment—I should have knelt down and kissed the chapel floor, and protested my sense of utter unworthiness and incapacity for such an office."

Sister Isabel, who sat by me, said in a low voice,—"Maybe some of your Sisters would have agreed with you." And though I felt constrained to give her a look of remonstrance, I must say I thought with her. Sister Ada as Prioress would have been a sore infliction.

But now Sister Gaillarde herself came forward. I do not think Sister Ada had known she was there, to judge from her change of colour.

"Sister Ada," said she, "you are one of those surface observers who always fancy people do not feel what they do not say. Let me answer you once for all, and any who think with you. As a sinner before God, I do feel mine unworthiness, even to the lowest depth: and I am bound to humble myself for all my sins, and not least for the pride which would fain think them few and small. But as for incapacity, I do not feel that; and I shall not say what I do not feel. I think myself quite capable of governing this house—I do not say as well as some might do it, but as well as most would do; and it would be falsehood and affectation to pretend otherwise. I suppose, in condemning hypocrisy, our Lord did not mean that while we must not profess to be better than we are, we may make any number of professions, and tell any number of falsehoods, in order to appear worse than we are. That may be your notion of holiness; but suffer me to say, it is not my notion of honesty. I mean to try and do my duty; and if any of my Sisters thinks I am not doing it, she will confer a favour on me if she will not talk it over with the other Sisters, but come straight to my rooms and tell me so. I promise to consider any such rebukes, honestly, as before God; and if on meditation and prayer I find that I have been wrong, I will confess it to you. But if I think that it was simply done out of spite or impertinence, that Sister will have a penance set her. I hope, now, we understand each other: and I beg the prayers of you all that I may rule in the fear of God, showing neither partiality nor want of sympathy, but walking in the right way, and keeping this house pure from sin."

Sister Ada made no answer whatever. Sister Ismania said, with much feeling—

"Suffer me, Mother, to answer for the younger Sisters, and I trust the Mothers will pardon me if I am over ready. Sure am I that the majority of my Sisters will consent to my reply. We will indeed pray that you may have the grace of perseverance in good works, and will strive to obey your holy directions in the right path. I ask every Sister who will promise the same to say '*Placet*.'"

There was a storm of *Placets* in response. But unless I was mistaken, Sister Ada and Sister Roberga were silent.

It was while she was answering "*Placet*" that I caught sight of Margaret's face. What had happened to make her look thus white and wan, with the expressive eyes so full of tears behind them, which she could not or would not shed? I sat in pain the whole day until evening, and the more because she seemed rather to avoid me. But at night, when we had parted, and all was quiet in the dormitories, a very faint rap came at the door of my cell. I bade the applicant enter in peace: and Margaret presented herself.

"Annora!" she said, hesitating timidly.

I knew what that meant.

"Come to me, little Sister," I said.

She came forward at once, closing the door behind her, and knelt down at my feet. Then she buried her face in her hands, and laid face and hands upon my knee.

"Let me weep!" she sobbed. "Oh, let me weep for a few moments in silence, and do not speak to me!"

I kept silence, and she wept till her heart was relieved. When at last her sobs grew quiet, she brushed her tears away, and looked up.

"Bless thee, Annora! That has done me good. It is something to have somebody who will say, 'Little Sister,' and give one leave to weep in peace. Dost thou know what troubles me?"

"Not in the least, dear Margaret. That something was troubling thee I had seen, but I cannot guess what it was."

"I shall get over it now," she said. "It is only the reopening of the old wound. Thou hast not guessed, then, who Father Mortimer is?"

"Margaret!"

"Ay, God has given my Roland back to me—yet has not given him. It is twenty years since we parted, and we are no longer young—nor, I hope, foolish. We can venture now to journey on, on opposite sides of the way, without being afraid of loving each other more than God. There can hardly be much of the road left now: and when it is over, the children will meet in the safe fellowship of the Father's Home for ever. Dost thou know, Annora dear, I am almost surprised to find myself quite so childish? I thought I should have borne such a meeting as calmly as any one else,—as calmly as he did." There was a little break in her voice. "He always had more self-control than I. Only I dare not confess to him, for his own sake. He would be tempted either to partiality, or to too much severity in order to avoid it. I must content myself with Father Benedict: and when I want Roland's teaching—those blessed words which none ever gave to me but himself—wilt thou give me leave to tell thee, so that thou mayest submit the matter to him in thine own confession?"

I willingly agreed to this: but I am sorry for my poor child. Father Benedict is terribly particular and severe. I think Father Mortimer could scarcely be more so, however hard he was trying not to be partial. And I cannot help a little doubt whether his love has lasted like hers. Sweet Saint Mary! what am I saying? Do I not know that every sister, every priest, in this house would be awfully shocked to know that such a thing could be? It is better it should not. And yet—my poor child!

This house no longer holds a Sister or Mother Gaillarde. She is now Lady Prioress, having been ordained and enthroned this afternoon. I must say the ceremony of vowing obedience felt to me less, not more, than that simple *Placet* the other day, which seemed to come red-hot from the hearts that spake it.

The Sister chosen to succeed her as Mother is Sister Ismania. I am glad of it, for she is certainly fittest for the place. Mother Joan becomes the senior Mother.

Our new Prioress does not let the grass grow under her feet, and is very different from her predecessor. During the first week after her appointment, such quantities of household articles began to pour in—whereof, in sooth, we stood in grievous need—that we Mothers were at our wits' end where to put them. I thought the steward's man would never have done coming to the grating with such announcements as—"Five hundredweight of wax, if you please, ladies; a hundred pounds of candles, ladies; twenty oaks for firewood, ladies; two sacks of seacoal, ladies; ten pieces of nuns' cloth, ladies; a hundred ells of cloth of linen, ladies; six firkins of speckled Bristol soap, ladies,"—cloth of Sarges (serge), cloth of Blanket (Note 1), cloth of Rennes; mops, bougets, knives, beds; cups, jugs, and amphoras; baskets by the dozen; quarters of wheat, barley, oats, beans, peas, and lentils; stockfish and ling, ginger and almonds, pipes of wine and quarts of oil—nay, I cannot tell what there was not. Sister Ada lost her temper early, and sorely bewailed her hard lot in having first to carry and find room for all these things, and secondly to use them. The old ways had suited her well enough: she could not think what my Lady wanted with all this mopping and scouring. Even Sister Joan said a little sarcastically that she thought my Lady must be preparing for the possibility of our having to stand a siege. My Lady, who heard both behind their backs, smiled her grim smile and went on. She does not keep in her own rooms like the last Prioress, but is here, there, and every where. Those of the Sisters who are indolently inclined dislike her rule exceedingly. For myself, I think in truth we have been going along too easily, and am glad to see the reins tightened and the horse admonished to be somewhat brisker: yet I cannot say that I can always keep pace with my Lady, and at times I am aware of a feeling of being driven on faster than I can go without being out of breath, and perhaps risking a fall. A little occasional rest would certainly be a relief. Howbeit, life is our working-day: and there will be time to rest in Heaven.

Joan tells me that she has had some talk with Father Mortimer, and finds that her mother and he were cousins, he being the only son of her grandfather's brother, Sir John de Mortimer, who died young in the tiltyard (Note 2). It is strange, passing strange, that he and Margaret should have been drawn to one another—he the nephew, and she the daughter, of men who were deadly enemies. From what Joan saith, I can gather that this grandfather of hers must have been a very evil man in many ways. I love not to hear of evil things and men, and I do somewhat check her when she speaks on that head. Was it not for eating of the tree of knowledge of good and evil that our first fathers were turned out of Paradise? Yet the Psalmist speaks of God as "He that teacheth man knowledge." I will ask Father Mortimer to explain it when I confess.

The time is not far off now when my child Joan must leave us, and I shrink from it as it draws near. I would either that she were one of us, or that I could go back to the world. Yet neither can be, seeing she is wedded wife and mother: and for me, is not this the very carnal affection which religious persons are bidden to root out of their hearts? Yet the Apostle Saint John saith we are to love our brethren. How can I do both? Is it lawful to love, only so long as we love not one above another? But our Lord Himself had His beloved disciple: and surely one's own mother must ever be more to her daughter than some other woman's mother? This also I will ask Father Mortimer.

Lack-a-day! this world is full of puzzles, or rather it is this life. I would one might see the way a little clearer—might have, as it were, a thread put into one's hand to guide one out of the labyrinth, like that old Grecian story which we teach the children. Some folks seem to lose their way easier than others; and some scarcely seem to behold any labyrinth at all—they walk right through those matters which are walls and hedges to others, and look as though they never perceived that any such things were there. Is it because of recklessness of right, or of single-heartedness and sincerity?

There are three matters to lay before Father Mortimer. I shall think long till the time come; and I hope he will be patient with me.

So soon as I stepped forth of my cell this morrow, I was aware of a kind of soft sobbing at no great distance. I went towards it, and as I turned the corner of the corridor, I came on a young novice, by name Denise, who sat on the ground with a pail before her, and a flannel and piece of soap on one side of it.

"What is the matter, child?" said I.

"Mother Ismania bade me scrub the boards," said she.

"Well! wherefore no?"

Denise fell a-sobbing yet more. For a minute or two might I not come at the reason: but at the last I did—she was a kinswoman of Sir Michael de La Pole, and thought it so degrading to be set to scrub boards!

"Why, dear heart," said I, "we all do work of this fashion."

"Oh yes, common Sisters may," quoth she.

"Well," said I, "we cannot be all uncommon. I ensure thee, Denise, there are here many daughters of better houses than thine. Mother Ismania herself is daughter of an offshoot of the Percys, and Sister Isabel is a Neville by her mother. My Lady is a Fitzhugh of Ravenswath."

"Well, Sisters!" came from behind us in my Lady's most sarcastic voice, "you choose a nice time for comparing your pedigrees. Maybe it were as well to leave that interesting amusement for recreation-time, and scrub the corridor just now."

Sister Denise melted again into tears, and I turned to explain.

"Your pail looks pretty full, Sister," said my Lady grimly: "much more water will make it overflow."

"May it please you, Madam," said I, "Sister Denise is thus distressed because she, being a De La Pole, is set to scrubbing and such like menial work."

"Oh, is she, indeed?" laughed my Lady. "Sister, do you know what Mother Annora is?"

Sister Denise could only shake her head.

"Her mother was grand-daughter to King Edward of Westminster," said my Lady. "If we three were in the world, I should be scantly fit to bear her train and you would be little better than her washerwoman. But I never heard her grumble to scour the corridor and she has done it more times than ever you thought about it. Foolish child, to suppose there was any degradation in honest work! Was not our blessed Lord Himself a carpenter? I warrant the holy Virgin kept her boards clean, and did not say she was too good to scrub. No woman alive is too good to do her duty."

Sister Denise brake forth into fresh sobs.

"A wa—wa—washerwoman! To be called a washerwoman! (Note 3.) Me, kinswoman of Sir Michael de La Pole, and Sir Richard to boot—a washerwo—woman!"

"Don't be a goose!" said my Lady. "De La Pole, indeed! who be these De La Poles? Why, no more than merchants of Lombard Street, selling towelling at fivepence the ell, and coverchiefs of Cambray (Note 4) at seven shillings the piece. Truly a goodly pedigree to boast of thus loudly!"

"But, Madam!" cries Sister Denise—her tears, methinks, burned up by her vexation—"bethink you, Sir Michael my cousin is a knight, and his wife the Lady Katherine heiress of Wingfield, and the Lady Katherine his mother 'longeth to the knights De Norwich. And look you, his sister is my Lady Scrope, and his cousin wedded the heir of the Lord Cobham of Kent."

"Nay, tarry not there," said my Lady; "do go a bit further while thou art about it. Was not my Lady Joan Cobham's mother daughter to my Lady of Devon, whose mother was daughter unto King Edward of Westminster—so thou art akin to the King himself? I cry thee mercy, my Lady Princess, that I set thee to scrub boards.—Sister Annora, prithee, let this princely damsel go to school for a bit—she's short of heraldry. The heiress of Wingfield, *the* Lady Katherine, forsooth! and the daughter of Sir John de Norwich a 'Lady' at all! Why, child, we only call the King's kinswomen *the* Lord and Lady. As to thy cousin Sir Michael, he is a woolmonger and lindraper (linen draper. The *en* is a corruption) that the King thought fit to advance, because it pleased him, and maybe he had parts (talents) of some sort. Sure thou hast no need to stick up thy back o' that count! To-morrow, Sister Denise, thou wilt please to clean the fire-dogs, and carry forth the ashes to the lye-heap.— Come, Sister Annora; I lack you elsewhere."

Poor little Denise broke into bitterer tears than ever; but I could not stay to comfort her, for I had to follow my Lady.

"I do vow, this world is full of fools!" said she, as we went along the corridor. "We shall have Sister Parnel, next, protesting that she knows not how much oats be a bushel, and denying to rub in the salt to a bacon, lest it should make her fingers sore. And 'tis always those who have small reason that make fusses like this. A King's daughter, when she takes the veil, looks for no different treatment from the rest; but a squire's daughter expects to have a round dozen of her Sisters told off to wait upon her.—Sister Egeline, feathers for stuffing are three-farthings a pound; prithee strew not all the floors therewith. (Sister Egeline had dropped no more than one; but my Lady is lynx-eyed.) Truly, it was time some one took this house in hand. Had my sometime Lady ruled it another twelvemonth, there would have been never a bit of discipline left. There's none so much now. Sister Roberga had better look out. If she gives me many more pert answers, she'll find herself barred into the penitential cell on bread and water."

By this time we had reached the kitchen. Sister Philippa was just coming out of it, carrying one hand covered with her veil. My Lady came to a sudden halt.

"What have you there, Sister?"

Sister Philippa looked red and confused.

"I have cut my finger," she said.

My Lady's hand went into her pocket.

"Hold it forth," said she, "and I will bind it up. I always carry linen and emplasture."

Sister Philippa made half a dozen lame excuses, but at last held out her left hand, having (if I saw rightly) passed something into the other, under cover of her veil.

"Which finger?" said my Lady, who to my surprise took no notice of her action.

"This," said Sister Philippa, holding out the first.

My Lady studied it closely.

"It must have healed quick," said she, "for I see never a scratch upon it."

"Oh, then it is that," quoth Sister Philippa, holding forth the second finder.

"I rather think, Sister, it is the other hand," said my Lady. "Let me look at that."

As my Lady was holding Sister Philippa's left hand, she had no chance to pass her hidden treasure into it. She held forth her right hand—full unwillingly, as I saw—and something rustled down her gown and dropped with a flop at her feet.

"Pick that up, Sister Annora," said my Lady.

I obeyed, and unfolding a German coverchief, found therein a flampoynt and three placentae (a pork pie and three cheesecakes).

"What were you going to do with these?" said my Lady.

"It's always my luck!" cried Sister Philippa. "Nothing ever prospers if I do it. Saint Elizabeth's loaves turned into roses, but no saint that liveth ever wrought a miracle for me."

"It is quite as well, Sister, that evil deeds should not prosper," was my Lady's answer. "Saint Elizabeth was carrying loaves to feed the poor. Was that your object? If so, you shall be forgiven; but next time, ask leave first."

Sister Philippa grew redder.

"Was that your intention?" my Lady persisted.

"I am sure I am as poor as any body!" sobbed the Sister. "We never get any thing good. All the nice things we make go to the poor, or to guests. I can't see why one might not have a bite one's self."

"Were you going to eat them yourself?"

"One of them, I was: the others were for Sister Roberga."

"Sister Roberga shall answer for herself. I will have no tale-telling in my house. This evening at supper, Sister, you will stand at the end of the refectory, with that placenta in your hand, and say in the hearing of all the Sisters—'I stole this placenta from the kitchen, and I ask pardon of God and the Saints for that theft.' Then you may eat it, if you choose to do so."

My Lady confiscated the remainder, leaving the placenta in Sister Philippa's hand. She looked for a minute as if she would heartily like to throw it down, and stamp on it: but either she feared to bring on herself a heavier punishment, or she did not wish to lose the dainty. She wrapped it in her coverchief, and went upstairs, sobbing as she went.

My Lady despatched Sister Marian at once to fetch Sister Roberga. She came, looking defiant enough, and confessed brazenly that she knew of Sister Philippa's theft, and had incited her to it.

"I thought as much," said my Lady sternly, "and therefore I dealt the more lightly with your poor dupe, over whom I have suspected your influence for evil a long while. Sister Annora, do you and Sister Isabel take this sinner to the penitential cell, and I will take counsel how to use her."

We tried to obey: but Sister Roberga proved so unmanageable that we had to call in three more Sisters ere we could lodge her in the cell. At long last we did it; but my arms ached for some time after.

Sister Philippa performed her penance, looking very shamefaced: but she left the placenta on the table of the refectory, and I liked her all the better for doing so. I think my Lady did the same.

Sister Roberga abode in the penitential cell till evening, when my Lady sent for the four Mothers: and we found there the Master himself, Father Benedict, and Father Mortimer. The case was talked over, and it was agreed that Sister Roberga should be transferred to Shuldham where, as is reported, the Prioress is very strict, and knows how to hold her curb. This is practically a sentence of expulsion. We four all agreed that she was the black sheep in the Abbey, and that several of the younger Sisters—in especial Sister Philippa—would conduct themselves far better if she were removed. Sister Ismania was sent to tell her the sentence. She tossed her head and pretended not to care; but I cannot believe she will not feel the terrible disgrace. Oh, why do women enter into the cloister who have no vocation? and, ah me! why is it forced upon them?

At last I have been to confession to Father Mortimer, and I think I understand better what Margaret means, when she speaks of confessing to Father Benedict such things as he expects to hear. I never could see why it must be a sin to eat a lettuce without making the holy sign over it. Surely, if one thanks God for all He gives us, He will not be angered because one does not repeat the thanksgiving for every little separate thing. Such thoughts of God seem to me to be bringing Him down, and making Him seem full of little foolish details like men—and like the poorest-minded sort of men too. I see that people of high intellect, while they take much care of details that go to make perfection—as every atom of a flower is beautifully finished—take no care at all for mere trivialities—what my Lady calls fads—such as is, I think, making the sign of the cross over every mouthful one eats. Well, I made my confession and was absolved: and I told the priest that I much wished to ask his explanation of various matters that perplexed me. He bade me say on freely.

"Father," said I, "I pray you, tell me first, is knowledge good or evil?"

"Solomon saith, my daughter, that 'a wise man is strong;' and the prophet Osee laments that God's people are 'destroyed for lack of knowledge.' Our Lord chideth the lawyers of the Jews because they took away the key of knowledge: and Paul counted all things but loss for the knowledge of Jesu Christ. Here is wisdom. Why was Adam forbidden to eat of the tree of knowledge, seeing it was knowledge of good no less than evil? Partly, doubtless, to test his obedience: yet partly also, I think, because, though the knowledge might be good in itself, it was not good for him. God never satisfies mere curiosity. He will tell thee how to come to Heaven; but what thou wilt find there, that He will not tell thee, save that He is there, and sin, suffering, and Sathanas, are not there. He will aid thee to overcome thy sins: but how sin first entered into the fair creation which He made so good, thou mayest ask, but He gives no answer. Many things there are, which perhaps we may know with safety and profit in Heaven, that would not be good for us to know here on earth. Knowledge of God thou mayest have,—yea, to the full, so far as thine earthen vessel can hold it, even here. Yet beware, being but an earthen vessel, that thy knowledge puff thee not up. Then shall it work thee ill instead of good. Moreover, have nought to do with knowledge of evil; for that is ill, altogether."

"Then, how is it, Father," said I, "that some folks see their way so much plainer than others, and never become tangled in labyrinths? They seem to see in a moment one thing to be done, and that only: not as though they walked along a road which parted in twain, and knew not which turn to take."

"There may be many reasons. Some have more wit than others, and thus perceive the best way. Some are less readily turned aside by minor considerations. Some let their will conflict with God's will: and some desire to perceive His only, and to follow it."

"Those last are perfect men," said I.

"Ay," he made answer: "or rather, they are sinners whom Christ first loved, and taught to love Him back. My daughter, love is the great clue to lead thee out of labyrinths. Whom lovest thou—Jesu Christ, or Sister Alianora?"

"Now, Father, you land me in my last puzzle. I have always been taught, ever since I came hither, a little child, that love of God and the holy saints is the only love allowed to a religious woman. All other love is worldly, carnal, and wicked. Tell me, is this true?"

"No." The word came quick and curt.

"Truly," said I, "it would give me great relief to be assured of that. The love of our kindred, then, is permitted?"

"'Whoso loveth not his brother whom he hath seen, how can he love God whom he hath not seen? And this mandate we have from God: that he who loveth God, love his brother also.'"

"Father," said I, fairly enchanted to hear such words, "are those words of some holy doctor, such as Saint Austin?"

"They are the words," saith he softly, "of the disciple that Jesu loved. He seems to have caught a glimmer of his Master."

"But," said I, "doth it mean my mother's son, or only my brother in religion?"

"It can scarcely exclude thy mother's son," saith he somewhat drily. "Daughter, see thou put God first: and love all other as much as ever thou canst."

"*Ha, jolife!*" cried I, "if the Church will but allow it."

"What God commandeth," said he, "can not His Church disallow."

Methought I heard a faint stress on the pronoun.

"Father," said I, "are there more Churches than one?"

"There is one Bride of Christ. There is also a synagogue of Satan."

"Ah! that, I count, is the Eastern Church, that man saith hath departed from the faith."

"They that depart from the faith make that Church. I fear they may so do in the West as well as the East."

"Well, in the most holy universal Church are counted both the holy Roman Church, and our own mother, the Church of England," said I. "I know not if it include the Eastern schism or no."

"All these," saith he, "are names of men, and shall perish. All that is of man must come to nought. The Church Catholic, true and holy, is not of man, but of God. In her is gathered every saved soul, whether he come from the east or from the west, from the north or from the south. She is not Pauline, nor Petrine, nor Johannine, but Christian. The heavenly Bridegroom cannot have two Brides. 'One is My dove, My perfect one,' There are many counties in England; there is but one realm. So there are many so-called Churches: there is but one holy Church."

"But to find her commands," I answered, "we must, I suppose, hearken each to his own branch of the Church?"

"Her Lord's commands are hers. 'Hear thou *Him*.' The day is coming, daughter, when the Scriptures of God's Word shall be all rendered into English tongue, and, I firmly trust, shall be accessible to every man that chooses to know them. Pray thou heartily for that day; and meanwhile, keep thou close following Christ's steps, to the best of thy knowledge, and entreat Him for pardon of all unknown sins. And when the light of day is fully come, and the blessed lamp of Holy Writ placed in the hands of the people, then come to the light that thou mayest clearly see. For then woe, woe upon him that tarrieth in the shadow! 'If the light that is in thee be darkness, what darkness can equal it?'"

"Father," said I, "I thank you, for you have much comforted me. All this while have I been trying not to love folks; and I find it full hard to do."

"Battle with thy sins, Daughter, and let thy love alone. I counsel thee to beware of one thing, of which many need no warning to beware: I think thou dost. A thing is not sin because it is comfortable and pleasant; it is not good because it is hard or distasteful. Why mortify thy will when it would do good? It is the will to sin which must be mortified. When Christ bade His disciples to 'love their enemies,' He did not mean them to hate their friends. True love must needs be true concern for the true welfare of the beloved. How can that be sin? It is not love which will help man to sin! that love cometh of Sathanas, and is 'earthly, sensual, devilish.' But the love which would fain keep man from sin,—this is God's love to man, and man cannot err in bestowing it on his brother."

"But is it sin, Father, to prefer one in love above another?"

"It is sin to love man more than God. Short of that, love any one, and any how, that ever thou wilt. The day *may* come—"

He brake off suddenly. I looked up.

"There were wedded priests in England, not an hundred years ago," (Note 5) he said in a low voice. "And there were no monks nor nuns in the days of the Apostles. The time may come—*Fiat voluntas Tua! Filia, pax tibi.*"

Thus gently dismissed, I rose up and came back into the illuminating-room, where I found Joan gathering together her brushes and other gear.

"The last time!" she said, sadly—for she returns to her home to-morrow. "Why is it that last times are always something sorrowful? I am going home to my Ralph and the children, and am right glad to do it: and yet I feel very mournful at the thought of leaving you, dear Mother Annora. Must it ever be so in this life, till we come to that last time of all when, setting forth on the voyage to meet Christ our Lord, we yet say 'farewell' with a pang to them we leave behind?"

"I reckon so, dear heart," said I, sighing a little. "But Father Mortimer hath comforted me by words that he saith are from Holy Writ—to wit, that he which loveth God should love his brother likewise. I always wanted to love folks."

"And always did it, dear Mother," said Joan with a laugh, casting her arms around my neck, "for all those chains of old rules and dusty superstitions which are ever clanking about you. And I am going to love you, whatever rules be to the contrary, and of whomsoever made. Oh, why did ill folks push you into this convent, when you might have come and dwelt with Ralph and me, and been such a darling grandmother to my little ones? There, now, I did not mean to make you look sorrowful. I will come and see you every year, if it be only for an hour's talk at the grating; and my Lady, who is soft-hearted as she is rough-tongued, will never forbid it, I know."

"Never forbid what, thou losenger?" (Flatterer.)

Joan turned round, laughing.

"Dear my Lady, you are ever where man looketh not for you. But I am sure you heard no ill of yourself. You will never forbid me to visit my dear Mother Annora; you love her, and you love me."

"Truly a pretty tale!" saith my Lady, pretending (as I could see) to look angry.

"Now don't try to be angered with me," said Joan, "for I know you cannot. Now I must go and pack my saddle-bags and mails." (Trunks.)

She went thence with her light foot, and my Lady looked somewhat sadly after her.

"I love thee, do I, child?" saith she in another tone. "Ah, if I do, thou owest it less to anything in thee than to the name they wed thee in. Help us, Mother of Mercy! Time was when I thought I, too, should one day have been a Greystoke. Well, well! God be merciful to us poor dreamers, and poor sinners too!"

Then, with slower step than she is wont, she went after Joan.

My child is gone, and I feel like a bereaved mother. I shall see her again, if it please God, but what a blank she has left! She says when next Lent comes, if God will, she will visit us, and maybe bring with her her little Laurentia, that she named after my lost love, because she had eyes like his. God bless her, my child Joan!

Sister Roberga set forth for Shuldham the same day, in company with Father Benedict, who desired to travel that road, and in charge of two of the brethren and of Sister Willa. I trust she may some day see her errors, and amend her ways: but I cannot felicitate the community at Shuldham on receiving her.

So now we shall slip back into our old ways, so far as can be under a Prioress who assuredly will let none of us suffer the moss to grow upon her, body or soul, so far as she can hinder it. I hear her voice now beneath, in the lower corridor, crying to Sister Sigred, who is in the kitchen to-day—

"Did ever man or woman see the like? Burning seacoal on the kitchen-fire! Dost thou mean to poison us all with that ill smoke? (Note 6.) And wood in the wood-house more than we shall use in half a year! Forty logs came in from the King only yesterday, and ten from my Lord of Lisle the week gone. Sister Sigred, when shall I put any sense in you?"

"I don't know, Madam, I'm sure!" was poor Sister Sigred's rather hopeless answer.

I have found out at last what the world is. I am so glad! I asked Father Mortimer, and I told him how puzzled I was about it.

"My daughter," said he, "thou didst renounce three things at thy baptism—the world, the flesh, and the Devil. The works of the flesh thou wilt find enumerated in Saint Paul's Epistle to the Galatians (Galatians 5, verses 19-21): and they are *not* 'love, joy, peace, long-suffering, gentleness, goodness, faith, meekness, temperance.' These are the fruits of the Spirit. What the Devil is, thou knowest. Let us then see what is the world. It lies, saith Saint John, in three things: the lust of the flesh, the lust of the eyes, and the pride of life. What are these? The lust of the flesh is not love, for that is a fruit of the Spirit. It is self-love: worshipping thyself, comforting thyself, advantaging thyself, and regarding all others as either toys or slaves for that great idol, thyself. The lust of the eye is not innocent enjoyment of the gifts of God: doth a father give gifts to his child in order that she may *not* use and delight in them? It lies in valuing His gifts above His will; taking the gift and forgetting the Giver; robbing the altar of God in order to deck thine idol, and that idol thyself. Covetousness, love of gain, pursuit of profit to thyself—these are idolatry, and the lust of the eye. The pride of life—what is this? Once more, decking thyself with the property of God. Show and grandeur, pomp and vanity, revelling and folly—all to show thee, to aggrandise thee, to delight thee. The danger of abiding in the world is lest the world get into thee, and abide in thee. Beware of the thought that there is no such danger in the cloister. The world may be in thee, howsoever thou art out of the world. A queen may wear her velvet robes with a single eye to the glory of God, and a nun may wear her habit with a single eye to the glory of self. Fill thine heart with Christ, and there will be no room left for the world. Fill thine heart with the world, and no room will be left for Christ. They cannot abide together; they are contrary the one to the other. Thou canst not saunter along the path of life, arm-in-arm with the world, in pleasant intercourse. Her face is not toward the City of God: if thine be, ye must go contrary ways. 'How can two walk together, except they be agreed' what direction to pursue? And remember, thou art one, and the world is many. She is strong enough to pull thee round; thou art not at all likely to change her course. And the peril of such intercourse is that the pulling round is so gradually effected that thou wilt never see it."

"But how am I to help it, Father?"

"By keeping thine eye fixed on God. Set the Lord alway before thee. So long as He is at thy right hand, thou shalt not be moved."

Father Mortimer was silent for a moment; and when he spoke again, it was rather to himself, or to God, than to me.

"Alas for the Church of God!" he said. "The time was when her baptismal robes were white and spotless; when she came out, and was separate, and touched not the unclean thing. Hath God repealed His command thus to do? In no wise. Hath the world become holy, harmless, undefiled—no longer selfish, frivolous, carnal, earth-bound? Nay, for it waxeth worse and worse as the end draws nearer. Woe is me! has the Church stepped down from her high position as the elect and select company of the sons of God, because these daughters of men are so fair and bewitching? Is she slipping back, sliding down, dipping low her once high standard of holiness to the Lord, bringing down her aim to the level of her practice, because it suits not with her easy selfishness to gird up her loins and elevate her practice to what her standard was and ought to be? And she gilds her unfaithfulness, forsooth, with the name of divine charity! saying, Peace, peace! when there is no peace. 'What peace, so long as the whoredoms of thy mother Jezebel and her witchcrafts are so many?' They cry, 'Speak unto us smooth things'—and the Lord hath put none such in our lips. The word that He giveth us, that must we speak. And it is, 'Come out of her, My people, that ye be not partakers of her sins, and that ye receive not of her plagues.' Ye cannot remain and not partake the sins; and if ye partake the sins, then shall ye receive the plagues. 'What God hath joined together, let not man put asunder.'" (Note 7.)

Thank God for this light upon my path! for coming from His Word, it must be light from Heaven. O my Lord, Thou art Love incarnate, and Thou hast bidden us to love each other. Thou hast set us in families, and chosen our relatives, our neighbours, our surroundings. From Thine hand we take them all, and use them, and love them, in Thee, for Thee, to Thee. "We are taught of God to love each other." We only love too much when we love ourselves, or when we love others above Thee. And "the command we have of Thee is that he who loveth Thee, love his brother also"—the last word we hear from Thee is a promise that Thou wilt come again, and take us—together, all—not to separate stars, but to be with Thee for ever. Amen, Lord Jesu Christ, so let it be!

It is several weeks since I have seen Margaret, otherwise than in community. But to-night I heard the timid little rap on my door, and the equally timid "Annora?" which came after. When Margaret says that word, in that tone, she wants a chat with me, and she means to inquire deprecatingly if she may have it.

"Come in, darling," I said.

Since Father Mortimer gave me leave to love any one, any how, so long as I put God first, I thought I might say "darling" to Margaret. She smiled,—I fancied she looked a little surprised—and coming forward, she knelt down at my feet, in her favourite attitude, and laid her clasped hands in my lap.

"Is there some trouble, Margaret?"

"No, dear Annora. Only little worries which make one feel tired out: nothing to be properly called trouble. I am working under Mother Ada this week, and—well, you know what she is. I do not wish to speak evil of any one: only—sometimes, one feels tired. So I thought it would help me to have a little talk with my sister Annora. Art thou weary too?"

"I think I am rested, dear," said I. "Father Mortimer has given me a word of counsel from Holy Writ, and it hath done me good."

"He hath given me many an one," she saith, with a smile that seemed half pleasure and half pain. "And I am trying to live by the light of the last I had—I know not if the words were Holy Writ or no, but I think the substance was—'If Christ possess thee, then shalt thou inherit all things.'"

She was silent for a moment, with a look of far-away thought: and I was thinking that a hundred little worries might be as wearying and wearing as one greater trouble. Suddenly Margaret looked up with a laugh for which her eyes apologised.

"I could not help thinking," she said, "that I hope 'all things' have a limit. To inherit Mother Ada's temper would scarcely be a boon!"

"All good things," said I.

"Yes, all good things," she answered. "That must mean, all things that our Lord sees good for us—which may not be those that we see good for ourselves. But one thing we know—that if we be His, that must be, first of all, Himself—He with us here, we with Him hereafter. And next to that comes the promise that they which are Christ's, with whom we have to part here, will be brought home with us when He cometh. There is no restriction on the companying of the Father's children, when they are gathered together in the Father's House."

I knew what she saw. And I saw the dear grey eyes of my child Joan; but behind them, other eyes that mine have not beheld for fifty years, and that I shall see next—and then for ever—in the light of the Golden City. Softly I said— (Note 8.)

> "'Hic breve vivitur, hic breve plangitur, hic breve fletur;
> Non breve vivitur, non breve plangitur, retribuetur.'"

Margaret's reply sounded like the other half of an antiphon. (Note 9.)

> "'Plaude, cinis meus! est tua pars Deus; ejus es, et sis.'"

Note 1. The early notices of blanket in the Wardrobe Accounts disprove the tradition that blankets were invented by Edward Blanket, buried in Saint Stephen's Church, Bristol, the church not having been built until 1470.

Note 2. Father Mortimer is a fictitious person, this Sir John having in reality died unmarried.

Note 3. Laundresses were very much looked down on in the Middle Ages, and were but too often women of bad character.

Note 4. Cambric handkerchiefs. It was then thought very mean to be in trade.

Note 5. Married priests existed in England as late as any where, if not later than in other countries. Walter, Rector of Adlingfleet, married Alice niece of Savarie Abbot of York, about the reign of Richard the First. (Register of John of Gaunt, volume 2, folio 148); "Emma, widow of Henry, the priest of Forlond," was living in 1284 (Close Roll, 12 Edward the First); and "Denise, daughter of John de Colchester, the chaplain," is mentioned in 1322 (Ibidem, 16 Edward the Second).

Note 6. Coal smoke was then considered extremely unhealthy, while wood smoke was thought to be a prophylactic against consumption.

Note 7. I would fain add here a word of warning against one of Satan's wiliest devices, one of the saddest delusions of our time, for a multitude of souls are led astray by it, and in some cases it deceives the very elect. I mean the popular blind terror of "controversy," so rife in the present day. Let us beware that we suffer not indolence and cowardice to shelter themselves under the insulted name of charity. We are bidden to "strive together for the truth of the Gospel" — "earnestly to contend for the faith" (in both places the Greek word means to *wrestle*); words which presuppose an antagonist and a controversy. Satan hates controversy; it is the spear of Ithuriel to him. We are often told that controversy is contrary to the Gospel precepts of love to enemies—that it hinders more important work—that it injures spirituality. What says the Apostle to whom to live was Christ—on whom came daily the care of all the Churches—who tells us that "the greatest of these is charity"? "Though we, or an angel from Heaven, preach any other Gospel—let him be accursed!" "To whom we gave place by subjection, no, not for an hour: that the truth of the Gospel might continue with you." Ten minutes of friendly contact with the world will do more to injure spirituality than ten years of controversy conducted in a Christian spirit—not fighting for victory but for truth, not for ourselves but for Christ. This miserable blunder will be seen in its true colours by those who have to eat its bitter fruit.

Note 8.

"Brief life is here our portion;
   Brief sorrow, short-lived care:
The life that hath no ending,
   The tearless life, is there."

Note 9.

"Exult, O dust and ashes!
   The Lord shall be thy part:
His only, His for ever,
   Thou shalt be, and thou art."

Appendix

Historical Appendix

I. The Royal Family

King Edward the Second was *born* at Caernarvon Castle (but not, as tradition states, in the Eagle Tower, not then built), April 25, 1284; *crowned* at Westminster Abbey, August 6, 1307, by the Bishop of Winchester, acting as substitute for the Archbishop of Canterbury. The gilt spurs were borne by William le Mareschal; "the royal sceptre on whose summit is the cross" by the Earl of Hereford (killed in rebellion against the King) and "the royal rod on whose summit is the dove" by Henry of Lancaster, afterwards Earl: the Earls of Lancaster, Lincoln, and Warwick—of whom the first was beheaded for treason, and the third deserved to be so—bore the three swords, Curtana having the precedence: then a large standard (or coffer) with the royal robes, was carried by the Earl of Arundel, Thomas de Vere (son and heir of the Earl of Oxford), Hugh Le Despenser, and Roger de Mortimer, the best friend and the worst enemy of the hapless Sovereign: the King's Treasurer carried "the paten of the chalice of Saint Edward," and the Lord Chancellor the chalice itself: "then Peter de Gavaston, Earl of Cornwall, bore the crown royal," followed by King Edward himself, who offered a golden pound as his oblation. The coronation oath was administered in French, in the following terms. "Sire, will you grant and keep and confirm by oath to the people of England, the laws and customs to them granted by the ancient Kings of England, your predecessors, the rights and devotions (due) to God, and especially the laws, customs, and franchises granted to the clergy and people by the glorious King, Saint Edward, your predecessor?" "I grant and promise them," was the royal answer. "Sire, will you preserve, towards God and holy Church, and to the clergy and people, peace and concord in God, fully, according to your power?" "I will keep them," said the King. "Sire, will you in all your judgments do equal and righteous justice and discretion, in mercy and truth, according to your power?" "I will so do." "Sire, will you grant, to be held and kept, the righteous laws and customs which the commonalty of your realm shall choose, and defend them, and enforce them to the honour of God and according to your power?" King Edward's answer was, "I grant and promise them." Twenty years later, chiefly by the machinations of his wicked wife, aided by the blinded populace whom she had diligently misled, Edward was *deposed* at Kenilworth, January 20, 1327; and after being hurried from place to place, he was at last *murdered* in Berkeley Castle, September 21, 1327, and *buried* in Gloucester Cathedral on December 20th.

In the companion volume, *In All Time of our Tribulation,* will be found the story, as told by the chroniclers, of his burial by the Abbot and monks of Gloucester. The Wardrobe Accounts, however, are found to throw considerable doubt upon this tale. We find from them, that the Bishop of Llandaff, three knights, a priest, and four lesser officials, were sent by the young King "to dwell at Gloucester with the corpse of the said King his father," which was taken from Berkeley Castle to Gloucester Abbey on October 21st. (*Compotus Hugonis de Glaunvill,* Wardrobe Accounts, 1 Edward the Third, 58/4). For the funeral were provided:—Three robes for knights, 2 shillings 8 pence each; 8 tunics for ditto, 14 pence each; four great lions of gilt picture-work, with shields of the King's arms over them, for wax mortars (square basins filled with wax, a wick being in the midst), placed in four parts of the hearse; four images of the Evangelists standing on the hearse, 66 shillings, 8 pence; eight incensing angels with gilt thuribles, and two great leopards rampant, otherwise called volant, nobly gilt, standing outside the hearse, 66 shillings, 8 pence... An empty tun, to carry the said images to Gloucester, 21 shillings... Taking the great hearse from London to Gloucester, in December, 5 days' journey; for wax, canvas, napery, etcetera. Wages of John Darcy, appointed to superintend the funeral, from November 22 to December 21, 19 pounds, 6 shillings, 8 pence. New hearse, 40 shillings; making thereof, from November 24 to December 11, 32 shillings. A wooden image after the similitude of the Lord King Edward, deceased, 40 shillings. A crown of copper, gilt, 7 shillings, 4 pence. Vestments for the body, in which he was buried, a German coverchief, and three-quarters (here a word is illegible, probably *linen*); item, one pillow to put under his head, 4 shillings (? the amount is nearly obliterated). Gilt paint for the hearse, 1 shilling. Wages of the painter (a few words illegible) grey colour, 2 shillings, (Wardrobe Accounts, 1 Edward the Third, 33/2). The King *married...*

Isabelle, *surnamed* the Fair, only daughter of Philippe the Fourth, King of France, and Jeanne Queen regnant of Navarre: *born* 1282, 1292, or 1295 (latest date most probable); *married* at Boulogne, January 25, 1308. All the chroniclers assert that on Edward the Third's discovery of his mother's real character, he imprisoned her for life in the Castle of Rising. The evidence of the Rolls and Wardrobe Accounts disproves this to a great extent. It was at Nottingham Castle that Mortimer was taken, October 19, 1330. On the 18th of January following, 36 pounds 6 shillings 4 pence was paid to

Thomas Lord Wake de Lydel, for the expense of conducting Isabel Queen of England, by the King's order, from Berkhamsted Castle to Windsor Castle, and thence to Odiham Castle. (Issue Roll, *Michs.*, 5 Edward the Third.) On the 6th of October, 1337, she dates a charter from Hertford Castle; and another from Rising on the 1st of December following. She paid a visit to London—the only one hitherto traced subsequent to 1330—in 1341, when, on October 27, she was present in the hostel of the Bishop of Winchester at Southwark, when the King appointed Robert Parving to the office of Lord Chancellor. She dates a charter from Hertford Castle, December 1st, 1348. (Close Rolls, 11, 15, and 22 Edward the Third.) The Household Book for the last year of her life is in the British Museum, and it runs from September 30th, 1357, to December 4th, 1358 (Cott. Ms., Galba, E. 14). We find from this interesting document that she spent her final year mainly at Hertford, but that she also made two pilgrimages to Canterbury, visiting London on each occasion; that she was at Ledes Castle, Chertsey, Shene, Eltham, and Windsor. The King visits her more than once, and several of his children do the same, including the Princess Isabel. There is no mention of any visit from the Queen, but she corresponds with her mother-in-law, and they exchange gifts. The most frequent guests are Joan Countess of Surrey, and the Countess of Pembroke: there were then three ladies living who bore this title, but as letters are sent to her at Denny—her pet convent, where she often resided and finally died—it is evident that this was the Countess Marie, the "fair Chatillon who (*not* 'on her bridal morn,' but at least two years after) mourned her bleeding love." Both these ladies were of French birth, and were very old friends of Isabelle: the Countess of Surrey was with her when she died. Her youngest daughter, Joan Queen of Scots—an admirable but unhappy woman, who had to forgive that mother for being the cause of all her misery and loveless life—spent much of this last year with Isabel. Her most frequent male guests are the Earl of Tankerville and Marshal Daudenham, both of whom were probably her own countrymen; and Sir John de Wynewyk, Treasurer of York: the captive King of France visits her once, and she sends him two romances, of which one at least was from the *Morte Arthur*. Oblations are as numerous—and sometimes more costly—as in her earlier accounts. She gives 6 shillings 8 pence to the *head* of the eleven thousand virgins, and 2 shillings to minstrels to play "before the image of the blessed Mary in the crypt" of Canterbury Cathedral. Friars who preach before her are usually rewarded with 6 shillings 8 pence. Her Easter robes are of blue cloth, her summer ones of red mixed cloth. Two of Isabelle's ruling passions went with her to the grave—her extravagance and her love of making gifts. Her purchases of jewellery are vast and costly during this year, up to the very month in which she died: two of the latest being a gold chaplet set with precious stones, price 150 pounds (the most expensive I ever yet saw in a royal account), and a gold crown set with sapphires, Alexandrian rubies, and pearls, 80 pounds, expressly stated to be for her own wearing. Two ruby rings she purchased exactly a fortnight before her death. She was probably ill for some weeks, since a messenger was sent in haste to Canterbury to bid Master Lawrence the physician repair to Hertford "to see the state of the Queen," and he remained there for a month. Medicines were brought from London. Judging from the slight indications as to remedies employed, among which were herbal baths, she died of some cutaneous malady. Her Inquisition states that her *death* took place at Hertford, August 23rd, 1358; but the Household Book twice records that it was on the 22nd. Fourteen poor men watched the corpse in the chapel at Hertford for three months, and in December the coffin (the entire cost of which was 5 pounds, 9 shillings, 11 pence) was brought to London, guarded by 40 torches, and *buried* in the Church of the Grey Friars. It may be stated with tolerable certainty that the Queen was not confined for life at Rising Castle, though she passed most of her time either at Rising or Hertford; that she never became a nun, as asserted by some modern writers, the non-seclusion, the coloured robes, and the crown, being totally inconsistent with this supposition; that if it be true, as is said, that she was seized with madness while Mortimer hung on the gallows, and passed most of her subsequent life in this state, probably with lucid intervals—a story which various facts tend to confirm—this was quite sufficient to account for her retirement from public life, and ordinary restriction to a few country residences; yet that the incidents chronicled in the Household Book seem to indicate that she was generally, if not fully, sane at the time of her death.

Their children:—1. King Edward the Third, *born* in Windsor Castle, November 13, *baptised* 16th, 1312; *crowned* Westminster, February 1, 1327. The Rolls of the Great Wardrobe for 1327 contain some interesting details respecting this ceremony. The King was attired in a tunic, mantle, and cape of purple velvet, price 5 shillings (but this is probably the mere cost of making), and a pair of slippers of cloth of gold, price 6 shillings 8 pence. He was anointed in a tunic of samitelle (a variety of samite), which cost 2 shillings, and a robe of Rennes linen, price 18 pence. A quarter of an ell of sindon (silk) was bought "for the King's head, to place between the head and the crown, on account of the largeness of the crown," at a cost of 12 pence. (*Rot. Gard.*, 1 Edward the Third, 33/2). The "great hall" at Westminster was hung with six cloths and twelve ells of cloth from Candlewick Street and fifteen pieces of cloth were required "to put under his feet, going to the Abbey, and thence to the King's chamber after the coronation." The platform erected in the Abbey to sustain the throne, and the throne itself, were hung with silk cloth of gold; five camaca cushions were placed "under the King and his feet;" and "the King's small chair before the altar" was also covered with cloth of gold. The royal oblation was one cloth of gold of diapered silk. Two similar cloths were laid over the tomb of Edward the first. The Archbishop of Canterbury's seat was covered with ray (striped) silk cloth of gold, and that of the Abbot of Westminster with cloth of Tars. The royal seat at the coronation feast was draped in "golden silk of Turk," and in order to save this costly covering from "the humidity of the walls," 24 ells of canvas were provided. Red and grey sindon hung before the royal table; the King sat on samitelle cushions, and two pieces of velvet "to put under the King" also appear in the account. (*Rot. Magnae Gard., pro Coronatione et in Palatio,* 1 Edward the Third, 33/5.) King Edward *died* at Shene, June 21, 1377, and was *buried* in Westminster Abbey. He *married*—Philippine (called in England Philippa), daughter of William the Third, Count of Hainault and Holland, and Jeanne of France; *born* 1312 or a little later; *married* at York, January 24, 1328; crowned in Westminster Abbey, February 20, 1328. The Wardrobe Accounts tell us that the Queen rode from the Tower to Westminster, the day before her coronation (as was usual) in a dress of green velvet, a cape of the *best* cloth of gold diapered in red, trimmed with miniver, and a miniver hood. She dined in a tunic and mantle of red and grey samitelle, and was crowned in a robe of cloth of gold, diapered in green. She changed to a fourth robe for supper, but its materials are not on record. (Wardrobe Accounts, 4-5 Edward the Third, 34/13.) Red and green appear to have been her favourite colours, judging from the number of her dresses of these hues compared with others. On the occasion of her churching in 1332 (after the birth of her daughter Isabel) she wore a robe of red and purple velvet wrought with pearls, the royal infant being attired in Lucca silk and miniver, and the Black Prince (aged about 2 and a half years) in a golden costume striped with mulberry colour. Some of these items appear rather warm wear for July. (Wardrobe Accounts, Cott. Ms. Galba, E. 3, folio 14 *et seq*). The Queen *died* of dropsy, at Windsor Castle, August 15, 1369; *buried* in Westminster Abbey.

2. John, *born* at Eltham, August 15, 1316; created Earl of Cornwall; *died* at Perth, *unmarried*, September 14, 1336; *buried* in Westminster Abbey.

3. Alianora, *born* at Woodstock, 1318; *married* at Novum Magnum, 1332, Raynald the Second, Duke of Gueldres; *died* at Deventer, April 22, 1355; *buried* at Deventer.

4. Joan, *surnamed* Makepeace, *born* in the Tower of London, (before August 16,) 1321; *married* at Berwick, July 17, 1328, David the Second, King of Scotland; *died* at Hertford Castle, September 7, 1362 (not 1358, as sometimes stated); *buried* in Grey Friars' Church, London.

II. The Despensers

Hugh Le Despenser *the Elder*, son of Hugh Le Despenser, Justiciary of England, and Alina Basset: *born* March 1-8, 1261 (*Inq. Post Mortem Alinae La Dispensere*, 9 Edward the First, 9.); sponsor of Edward the Third, 1312; created Earl of Winchester, 1322; *beheaded* at Bristol, October 27 (Harl. Ms. 6124), 1326. (This is not improbably the true date: that of Froissart, October 8, is certainly a mistake, as the Queen had only reached Wallingford, on her way to Bristol, by the 15th.) As his body was cast to the dogs, he had *no burial*. *Married* Isabel, daughter of William de Beauchamp, Earl of Warwick, and Maud Fitz John; *widow* of Patrick de Chaworth (by whom she was mother of Maud, wife of Henry Duke of Lancaster): *married* 1281-2 (fine 2000 marks); *died* before July 22, 1306. *Issue:*—1. Hugh, *the Younger, born* probably about 1283; created Earl of Gloucester in right of wife; *hanged* and afterwards beheaded (but after death) at Hereford, November 24, 1326; quarters of body sent to Dover, Bristol, York, and Newcastle, and head set on London Bridge; finally *buried* in Tewkesbury Abbey. The Abbot and Chapter had granted to Hugh and Alianora, March 24, 1325, in consideration of benefits received, that four masses per annum should be said for them during life, at the four chief feasts, and 300 per annum for either or both after death, for ever; on the anniversary of Hugh, the Abbot bound himself to feed the poor with bread, beer, pottage, and one mess from the kitchen, for ever. (*Rot. Pat.*, 20 Edward the Second) In the Appendix to the companion volume, *In All Time of our Tribulation*, will be found an account of the petitions of the two Despensers, with the curious list of their goods destroyed by the partisans of Lancaster. Hugh the Younger *married* Alianora, eldest daughter of Gilbert de Clare, The Red, Earl of Gloucester, and the Princess Joan of Acre, (daughter of Edward the First), *born* at Caerphilly Castle, November, 1292; *married* May 20, 1306, with a dowry of 2000 pounds from the Crown, in part payment of which the custody of Philip Paynel was granted to Hugh the Elder, June 3, 1304 (*Rot. Claus.*, 1 Edward the Second). Her youngest child was born at Northampton, in December, 1326, and she sent William de Culpho with the news to the King, who gave him a silver-gilt cup in reward (Wardrobe Accounts, 25/1 and 31/19). On the 19th of April, 1326, and for 49 days afterwards, she was in charge of Prince John of Eltham, who was ill at Kenilworth in April. She left that place on May 22, arriving at Shene in four days, and in June she was at Rochester and Ledes Castle. Three interesting Wardrobe Accounts are extant, showing her expenses at this time (31/17 to 31/19); but the last is almost illegible. "Divers decoctions and recipes" made up at Northampton for the young Prince, came to 6 shillings, 9 pence. "Litter for my Lady's bed" (to put under the feather bed in the box-like bedstead) cost 6 pence. Either her Ladyship or her royal charge must have entertained a strong predilection for "shrimpis," judging from the frequency with which that entry occurs. Four quarters of wheat, we are told, made 1200 loaves. There is evidence of a good deal of company, the principal guests beside Priors and Canons being the Lady of Montzone, the Lady of Hastings (Julian, mother of Lawrence Earl of Pembroke), Eneas de Bohun (son of Princess Elizabeth), Sir John Neville (one of the captors of Mortimer), and John de Bentley (probably the ex-gaoler of Elizabeth Queen of Scotland, who appears in the companion volume). Sundry young people seem to have been also in Lady La Despenser's care, as companions to the Prince:—Earl Lawrence of Pembroke; Margery de Verdon, step-daughter of Alianora's sister Elizabeth; and Joan Jeremy, or Jermyn, sister of Alice wife of Prince Thomas de Brotherton. The provision for April 30, the vigil of Saint Philip, and therefore a fast-day, is as follows (a few words are illegible): *Pantry*:—60 loaves of the King's bread at 5 and 4 to the penny, 13 and a half pence. *Buttery*:—One pitcher of wine from the King's stores at Kenilworth; 22 gallons of beer, at 1 and a half pence per gallon, 2 shillings 6 pence. *Wardrobe*: ... lights, a farthing; a halfpennyworth of candles of cotton ... *Kitchen*:—50 herrings, 2 and a half pence; 3 codfish, 9 and three-quarter pence; 4 stockfish... salmon, 12 pence, 3 tench, 9 pence, 1 pikerel, 12 roach and perch, half a gallon of loaches, 13 and a half pence; one large eel... One and a half quarters pimpernel, 7 and a half pence; one piece of sturgeon, 6 pence. *Poultry*—100 eggs, 5 pence; cheese and butter, 3 and three-quarter pence... milk, one and a quarter pence; drink, 1 penny; *Saltry*:—half a quarter; mustard, a halfpenny; half a quarter of vinegar, three-quarters pence; ... parsley, a farthing. For May 1st, Saint Philip's and a feast-day: *Pantry*: 100 loaves, 22 and a half pence. *Buttery*: one sextarius, 3 and a half pitchers of wine from the King's stores at Kenilworth; 27 gallons of beer, 2 shillings, 8 and a half pence, being 17 at 1 penny, and 12 at 1 and a half pence. One quarter of hanaps, 12 pence. *Wardrobe*:—3 pounds wax, 15 pence; lights, 1 halfpenny; half a pound of candles of Paris, 1 penny. *Kitchen*:—12 messes of powdered beef, 18 pence; 3 messes of fresh beef, 9 pence; one piece of bacon, 12 pence; half a mutton, powdered, 9 pence; one quarter of fresh mutton, 3 pence; one pestle of pork, 3 and a half pence; half a veal, 14 pence. *Poultry*—One purcel, 4 and a half pence; 2 hens, 15 pence; one bird (*oisoux*), 12 pence; 15 ponce, 7 and a half pence; 8 pigeons, 9 and a half pence; 100 eggs, 5 pence; 3 gallons milk, 3 pence... *Saltry*:—half a quarter of mustard, one halfpenny... 1 quarter verjuice, 1 and a half pence; garlic, a farthing; parsley, 1 penny. Wages of Richard Attegrove (keeper of the horses) and the laundress, 4 pence; of 18 grooms and two pages, 2 shillings, 5 pence. (Wardrobe Accounts, 19 Edward the Second, 31/17). When King Edward left London for the West, on October

2nd, he committed to Lady La Despenser the custody of his son, and of the Tower. On the 16th, the citizens captured the Tower, brought out the Prince and the Chatelaine, and conveyed them to the Wardrobe. On November 17th she was brought a prisoner to the Tower, with her children and her damsel Joan (Issue Roll, *Michs.*, 20 Edward the Second; Close Roll, 20 Edward the Second), their expenses being calculated at the rate of 10 shillings per day. Alianora and her children were delivered from the Tower, with all her goods and chattels, on February 25, 1328, and on the 26th of November following, her "rights and rents, according to her right and heritage," were ordered to be restored to her. (*Rot. Claus.*, 2 Edward the Third.) She was not, however, granted full liberty, or else she forfeited it again very quickly; for on February 5, 1329, William Lord Zouche of Haringworth was summoned to Court, and commanded to "bring with him quickly our cousin Alianora, who is in his company," with a hint that unpleasant consequences would follow neglect of the order. (*Rot. Pat.*, 3 Edward the Third, Part 1.) A further entry on December 30 tells us that Alianora, wife of William La Zouche of Mortimer (so that her marriage with her gaoler's cousin had occurred in the interim), had been impeached by the Crown concerning certain jewels, florins, and other goods of the King, to a large amount, which had been "*esloignez*" from the Tower of London: doubtless by the citizens when they seized the fortress, and the impeachment was of course, like many other things, an outcome of Queen Isabelle's private spite. "The said William and Alianora, for pardon of all hindrances, actions, quarrels, and demands, until the present date, have granted, of their will and without coercion, for themselves and the heirs of the said Alianora, all castles, manors, towns, honours, and other lands and tenements, being of her heritage, in the county of Glamorgan and Morgannon, in Wales, the manor of Hanley, the town of Worcester, and the manor of Tewkesbury, for ever, to the King." The King, on his part, undertook to restore the lands, in the hour that the original owners should pay him 10,000 pounds in one day. The real nature of this non-coercive and voluntary agreement was shown in November, 1330, when (one month after the arrest of Mortimer) at the petition of Parliament itself, one half of this 10,000 pounds was remitted. Alianora *died* June 30, 1337, and was *buried* in Tewkesbury Abbey.

2. Philip, *died* before April 22, 1214. *Married* Margaret, daughter of Ralph de Goushill; *born* July 25, 1296; *married* before 1313; *died* July 29, 1349. (She *married*, secondly, John de Ros.)

3. Isabel, *married* (1) John Lord Hastings (2) about 1319, Ralph de Monthermer; *died* December 4 or 5, 1335. Left issue by first marriage. The daughters of Edward the Second were brought up in her care.

4. Aveline, *married* before 1329, Edward Lord Burnel; *died* in May or June, 1363. No issue.

5. Elizabeth, *married* before 1321 Ralph Lord Camoys; living 1370. Left issue.

6. Joan, *married* Almaric Lord Saint Amand. (Doubtful if of this family.)

7. Joan, *nun* at Sempringham before 1337; *dead*, February 15.

8. Alianora, *nun* at Sempringham before 1337; living 1351. *Issue of Hugh the younger and Alianora;—*1. Hugh, *born* 1308. He held Caerphilly Castle (which belonged to his mother) against Queen Isabelle: on January 4 of that year life was granted to all in the Castle except himself, probably as a bribe for surrender, which was extended to himself on March 20; but Hugh held out till Easter (April 12) when the Castle was taken. He remained a prisoner in the custody of his father's great enemy, Roger Earl of March, till December 5, 1328, when March was ordered to deliver him to Thomas de Gournay, one of the murderers of King Edward, and Constable of Bristol Castle, where he was to be kept till further order. (*Rot. Claus.*, 1 and 2 Edward the Third; *Rot. Pat.*, 1 Edward the Third.) On July 5, 1331, he was ordered to be set at liberty within 15 days after Michaelmas, Ebulo L'Estrange, Ralph Basset, John le Ros, Richard Talbot, and others, being sureties for him. (*Rot. Claus.*, 5 Edward the Third) In 1338 he was dwelling in Scotland in the King's service (*Ibidem*, 12 Edward the Third); and in 1342 in Gascony, with a suite of one banneret, 14 knights, 44 scutifers, 60 archers, and 60 men-at-arms. (*Ibidem*, 16 *ibidem*). He *died* S.P. February 8, 1349; *buried* at Tewkesbury. *Married* Elizabeth, daughter of William de Montacute, first Earl of Salisbury, and Katherine de Grandison; (*widow* of Giles Lord Badlesmere, *remarried* Guy de Bryan;) *married* 1338-44; *died* at Astley, June 20, 1359; *buried* at Tewkesbury.

2. Edward, *died* 1341. *Married* (and left issue), Anne, daughter of Henry Lord Ferrers of Groby, and Margaret Segrave (*remarried* Thomas Ferrers): living October 14, 1366.

3. Gilbert, *died* April 22, 1382. *Married*, and left issue; but his wife's name and family are unknown.

4. Joan, *nun* at Shaftesbury, in or before 1343; *died* April 26, 1384.

5. Elizabeth, *married* 1338 Maurice Lord Berkeley; *dead* August 14, 1389; left issue. (Doubtful if of this family.)

6. Isabel, *married* at Havering, February 9, 1321, Richard Earl of Arundel; *divorced* 1345; *buried* in Westminster Abbey. No issue.

7. Alianora, contracted July 27, 1325, to Lawrence de Hastings, Earl of Pembroke: contract broken by Queen Isabelle, who on January 1st, 1327, sent a mandate to the Prioress of Sempringham, commanding her to receive the child and "veil her immediately, that she may dwell there perpetually as a regular nun." (*Rot. Claus.*, 1 Edward the Third.) Since it was not usual for a nun to receive the black veil before her sixteenth year, this was a complete irregularity. Nothing further is known of her.

8. Margaret, consigned by Edward the Second to the care of Thomas de Houk, with her nurse and a large household; she remained in his charge "for three years and more," according to his petition presented to the King, May 1st, 1327 (*Rot. Claus.*, 1 Edward the Third.) On the previous 1st of January, the Queen had sent to the Prioress of Watton a similar mandate to that mentioned above, requiring that Margaret should at once be professed a regular nun. No further record remains of her.

III. Hastings of Pembroke

John de Hastings, second (but eldest surviving) son of Sir John de Hastings and Isabelle de Valence: *born* 1283, *died* (before February 28) 1325. *Married* Julian, daughter and heir of Thomas de Leybourne and Alice de Tony; *born* 1298, or 1303; succeeded her grandfather William as Baroness de Leybourne, 1309; *married* before 1321. By charter dated at Canterbury, March 5th, 1362, she gave a grant to the Abbey of Saint Augustine in that city, for the following benefits to be received: a mass for herself on Saint Anne's Day, with twopence alms to each of 100 poor; a solemn choral mass on her anniversary, and 1 penny to each of 200 poor; perpetual mass by a secular chaplain at the altar of Saint Anne, for Edward the Third, Lawrence Earl of Pembroke, and John his son; all monks celebrating at the said altar to have mind of the said souls. On the day of her anniversary the Abbot was to receive 20 shillings, the Prior 5 shillings, and each monk 2 shillings, 6 pence. (*Rot. Claus.*, 36 Edward the Third.) She died November 1st, 1367, and was *buried* in Saint Augustine's Abbey. (She had *married*, secondly, in 1325, Sir Thomas Blount, Seneschal of the Household to Edward the Second, who betrayed his royal master; and, thirdly, in 1328, William de Clinton, afterwards created Earl of Huntingdon.)

Their son:—Lawrence, born at Allesley, near Coventry, March 20, 1321 (*Prob. Aet.*, 15 Edward the Third, 1st Numbers, 48); in 1326 he was in the suite of Prince John of Eltham, and in the custody of his intended mother-in-law, Alianora La Despenser: he and the young Alianora must therefore have been playfellows up to five years of age, at least. Three pairs of slippers are bought for him, price 20 pence, (Wardrobe Accounts, 20 Edward the Second,

31/18.) On July 27, 1325, Lawrence was contracted to Alianora, daughter of Hugh Le Despenser the younger (*Rot. Pat.*, 19 Edward the Second): which contract was illegally set aside by Queen Isabelle, who granted his custody and marriage in the King's name to her son Prince Edward, December 1st, 1326 (*Rot. Pat.*, 20 Edward the Second). The marriage was re-granted, February 17, 1327, to Roger Earl of March. We next find the young Earl in the suite of Queen Philippa; and he received a robe from the Wardrobe in which to appear at her churching in 1332, made of nine ells of striped saffron-coloured cloth of Ghent, trimmed with fur, and a fur hood. In the following year, when the Queen joined her husband at Newcastle, she left Lawrence at York, desiring *"par tendresce de lui"* that the child should not take so long and wearying a journey. He was therefore sent to his mother the Countess Julian, "trusting her (says the King's mandate) to keep him better than any other, since he is near to her heart, being her son." She was to find all necessaries for him until further order, and the King pledged himself to repay her in reason. (*Rot. Claus.*, 7 Edward the Third, Part 1.) Lawrence was created Earl of Pembroke, October 13, 1339; he *died* in the first great visitation of the "Black Death," August 30, 1348, and was *buried* at Abergavenny. *Married* Agnes de Mortimer, (see next Article) *married* 1327 (Walsingham); *died* July 25, 1368; *buried* in Abbey of Minories. (She *remarried* John de Hakelut, and was first Lady in Waiting to Queen Philippa.)

Their children:—1. Joan, *married* Ralph de Greystoke, after October 9, 1367.

2. John, 2nd Earl of Pembroke, *born* 1347, *died* at Arras, France, April 16, 1375; *buried* Grey Friars' Church, London. *Married* (1.) Princess Margaret, daughter of Edward the Third; *born* at Windsor, July 20-21, 1346; *married* in the Queen's Chapel (Reading?), 1359; *died* S.P. (after October 1st), 1361; *buried* in Abingdon Abbey. (2.) Anne, daughter and heir of Sir Walter de Mauny and Margaret of Norfolk: *born* July 24, 1355; *married* 1363; *died* April 3, 1384.

IV. The Mortimers of Wigmore

Edmund De Mortimer, Lord of Wigmore, son of Roger de Mortimer and Maud de Braose: *born* March 25, 1266; *died* at Wigmore Castle, July 17, 1304; *buried* in Wigmore Abbey. *Married* Margaret, daughter of Sir William de Fienles: *married* September 8, 1285; sided warmly with her son, and gathered various illegal assemblies at Worcester, where she lived, and at Radnor. On December 28, 1325, the King wrote, commanding her to retire to the Abbey of Elstow without delay, and there dwell at her own cost till further order: "and from the hour of your entering you shall not come forth, nor make any assembly of people without our special leave." She was commanded to write and say whether she intended to obey! The Abbess of Elstow was at the same time ordered to give convenient lodging to her in the Abbey, but not to suffer her to go forth nor make gatherings of persons. (Close Roll, 19 Edward the Second.) Nothing further is known of her except that she was alive in 1332, and was *dead* on May 7, 1334, when the mandate was issued for her *Inq. Post Mortem*. The latter contains no date of death. Margaret was *buried* at Wigmore. *Their children:*—1. Roger, *born* April 25 or May 3, 1287; created Earl of March, 1328; *hanged* at Tyburn, November 29, 1330: *buried* in Friars' Minors Church, Coventry, whence leave was granted to his widow and son, in November, 1331, to transport the body to Wigmore Abbey. *Married* Jeanne de Geneville, daughter and co-heir of Peter de Geneville (son of Geoffroi de Vaucouleur, brother of the Sieur de Joinville, historian of Saint Louis) and Jeanne de Lusignan: *born* February 2, 1286; *married* before 1304. On hearing of her husband's escape from the Tower in August 1323, she journeyed to Southampton with her elder children, intending to rejoin him in France: but before she set sail, on April 6, 1324, the King directed the Sheriff of Southampton to capture her without delay, and deliver her to the care of John de Rithre, Constable of Skipton Castle. A damsel, squire, laundress, groom, and page, were allowed to her, and her expenses were reckoned at 13 shillings 4 pence per day while travelling, and after reaching Skipton at 13 shillings 4 pence per week, with ten marks (6 pounds, 13 shillings 4 pence) per annum for clothing. (Close Roll, 17 Edward the Second.) These details appear afterwards to have been slightly altered, since the account of the expenses mentions 37 shillings 6 pence for the keep of two damsels, one laundress, one chamberlain, one cook, and one groom. Robes were supplied to her at Easter and Michaelmas. She remained a prisoner at Skipton from May 17, 1324, on which day she seems to have come there, till August 3, 1326. (*Rot. de Liberate*, 19 Edward the Second, and 3 Edward the Third.) By mandate of July 22, 1326, she was transferred to Pomfret (Close Roll, 20 Edward the Second), which she reached in two days, the cost of the journey being ten shillings 10 pence, (*Rot. Lib.*, 3 Edward the Third.) When her husband was seized in October, 1330, the King sent down John de Melbourne to superintend the affairs of the Countess, with the ladies and children in her company, dwelling at Ludlow Castle, with express instructions that their wardrobes, gods, and jewels, were not to be touched. (*Rot. Pat.* and *Claus.*, 4 Edward the Third.) The lands of her own inheritance were restored to her in the December and January following, with especial mention of Ludlow Castle, (*Rot. Claus., ibidem*). Edward the Third always speaks of her with great respect. In August, 1347, there were suits against her in the Irish Courts (the Mortimers held large estates in Ireland), and it is noted that she was not able to plead in person on account of her great age, which made travelling perilous to her. (*Rot. Claus.*, 21 Edward the Third.) She was then 63. On the 19th of October, 1356, she died (*Inq. Post Mortem*, 30 Edward the Third 30)—the very day of her husband's capture, 26 years before—and was *buried* in the Church of the Friars Minors, Shrewsbury. (Cott. Ms. Cleop., C, 3.)

    2. Edmund, Rector of Hodnet.

    3. Hugh, Rector of Old Radnor.

    4. Walter, Rector of Kingston (Dugdale) Kingsland (Cott. Ms. Cleop. C, 3).

    5. Maud, *married* at Wigmore, July 28, 1302, Theobald de Verdon; *died* at Alveton Castle, and *buried* at Croxden, October 8, 1312. Left issue.

    6. Joan, *nun* at Lyngbroke; living September 17, 1332.

    7. Elizabeth, *nun* at Lyngbroke.

    8. John, *born* 1300, *killed* in tilting, at Worcester, January 3, 1318, S.P.; *buried* at Worcester.

Issue of Roger, first Earl of March, and Jeanne de Geneville:—1. Edmund, *born* 1304, *died* at Stanton Lacy, December 28, 1331; *buried* at Wigmore. He is always reckoned as second Earl, but was never formally restored to the title, for which he vainly petitioned, and the refusal is said to have broken his heart. He *married* Elizabeth, third daughter, and eventually co-heir, of Bartholomew Lord Badlesmere, and Margaret de Clare: *born* 1313, *married* in or before 1327; (*remarried* William de Bohun, Earl of Northampton;) *died* June 17, 1355.

    2. Roger, *died* 1357. *Married* Joan, daughter of Edmund de Boteler, Earl of Carrick, and Joan Fitzgerald; contract of *marriage* February 11, 1321.

    3. Geoffrey, Lord of Cowith. He was one of the King's Bannerets in 1328 (*Rot. Magne Gard.*, 33/10), was taken with his father and his brother Edmund in 1330, and was kept prisoner in the Tower till January 25, 1331 (Issue Roll, *Michs.*, 5 Edward the Third). On the following March 16, he obtained leave to travel abroad. (*Rot. Pat.*, 5 Edward the Third, Part 1.) He was living in 1337, but no more is known of him.

    4. John, *killed* in tilting at Shrewsbury, and *buried* there in the Hospital of Saint John. He *married* (and left one son).

Alianora (family unknown), *buried* with husband.

5. Margaret, *married* Thomas Lord Berkeley; *died* May 5, 1337; *buried* at Bristol.

6. Joan, *married* James Lord Audley of Heleigh.

7. Isabel, *nun* at Chicksand. These three girls accompanied their mother to Southampton, and were captured with her. By the King's order they were sent to separate convents "to dwell with the nuns there;" there is no intimation that they were to be made nuns, and as two of them afterwards married, it is evident that this was not intended. Margaret was sent to Shuldham, her expenses being reckoned at 3 shillings per day while travelling, and 15 pence per week after arrival; Joan to Sempringham, and Isabel to Chicksand, their expenses being charged 2 shillings each per day while travelling, and 12 pence each per week in the convent. One mark per annum was allowed to each for clothing. (*Rot. Claus.*, 17 Edward the Second.) Isabel chose to remain at or return to Chicksand, since she is mentioned as being a nun there in February 1326. (Issue Roll, *Michs.*, 19 Edward the Second.)

8. Katherine, *married* about 1338, Thomas de Beauchamp, Earl of Warwick; *died* August 4, 1369.

9. Maud, *married* about 1320 John Lord Charleton of Powys; living July 5, 1348.

10. Agnes, *married* (1) 1327, Lawrence de Hastings, Earl of Pembroke; (2) before June 21, 1353, John de Hakelut; *died* July 25, 1368; *buried* in Abbey of Minories.

II. Beatrice, *married* (1) about 1327, Edward son of Prince Thomas de Brotherton, Earl of Norfolk; (2) 1334 (?) Thomas de Braose (*Rot. Claus.* 8 E. three.) (who appears to have purchased her for 12,000 marks—8000 pounds): *died* October 16, 1383 (*Inq. Post Mortem*, 7 Richard the Second, 15).

12. Blanche, *married*, before March 27, 1334, Peter, third Lord de Grandison; *dead* July 24, 1357. Either she or her husband was *buried* at Marcle, Herefordshire.

V. Chronological Errata

The accounts given by the early chroniclers, and followed by modern historians, with respect to the movements of Edward the Second and his Queen, from September, 1326, to the December following, are sadly at variance with fact. The dates of death of the Despensers, as well as various minor matters, depend on the accurate fixing of these points.

The popular account, generally accepted, states that the Queen landed at Orwell in September—the exact day being disputed—that the King, on hearing of it, hastened to the West, and shut himself up in Bristol Castle, with his daughters and the younger Despenser; that the Queen hanged the elder Despenser and the Earl of Arundel before their eyes, on the 8th of October, whereupon the King and the younger Despenser escaped by night in a boat: some add that they were overtaken and brought back, others that they landed in Wales, and were taken in a wood near Llantrissan. Much of this is pure romance. The King's Household Roll, which names his locality for every day, and is extant up to October 19th, the Wardrobe Accounts supplying the subsequent facts, distinctly shows that he never came nearer Bristol on that occasion than the road from Gloucester to Chepstow; that on the 8th of October he was yet at Cirencester; that he left Gloucester on the 10th, reaching Chepstow on the 16th, whence he departed on the 20th *"versus aquam de Weye"* and therefore in the contrary direction from Bristol. On the 27th and 28th he dates mandates from Cardiff; on the 29th and 30th from Caerphilly. On November 2nd he left Caerphilly (this we are distinctly told in the Wardrobe Accounts), on the 3rd and 4th he was at Margan Abbey, and on the 5th he reached Neath, where he remained up to the 10th. He now appears to have paid a short visit to Swansea, whence he returned to Neath, where, on the 16th, his cousin Lancaster and his party found him, and took him into their custody, with Hugh Le Despenser and Archdeacon Baldok. They took him first to Monmouth, where he was found by the Bishop of Hereford (sent to demand the Great Seal), probably about the 23rd. Thence he was conveyed to Ledbury, which he reached on or about the 30th; and on the 6th of December he was at Kenilworth, where he remained for the rest of his reign.

The Queen landed at Orwell in September: Speed says, on the 19th; Robert of Avesbury, the 26th; most authorities incline to the 22nd, which seems as probable a date as any. The King, at any rate, had heard of her arrival on the 28th, and issued a proclamation offering to all volunteers 1 shilling per day for a man-at-arms, and 2 pence for an archer, to resist the invading force. All past offenders were offered pardon if they joined his standard, the murderers of Sir Roger de Belers alone excepted: and Roger Mortimer, with the King's other enemies, was to be arrested and destroyed. Only three exceptions were made: the Queen, her son (his father omits the usual formula of "our dearest and firstborn son," and even the title of Earl of Chester), and the Earl of Kent, "queux nous volons que soent sauuez si auant come home poet." According to Froissart, the Queen's company could not make the port they intended, and landed on the sands, whence after four days they marched (ignorant of their whereabouts) till they sighted Bury Saint Edmunds, where they remained three days. Miss Strickland tells a rather striking tale of the tempestuous night passed by the Queen under a shed of driftwood run up hastily by her knights, whence she marched the next morning at daybreak. (This lady rarely gives an authority, and still more seldom an exact reference.) On the 25th, she adds, the Queen reached Harwich. Robert de Avesbury, Polydore Vergil, and Speed, say that she landed at Orwell, which the Chronicle of Flanders calls Norwell. If Froissart is to be credited, this certainly was not the place; for he says that the tempest prevented the Queen from landing at the port where she intended, and that this was a mercy of Providence, because there her enemies awaited her. The port where her enemies awaited her (meaning thereby the husband whom she was persecuting) was certainly Orwell, for on the second of September the King had ordered all ships of thirty tuns weight to assemble there. Moreover, the Queen could not possibly march from Orwell at once to Bury and Harwich, since to face the one she must have turned her back on the other. The probability seems to be that she came ashore somewhere in Orwell Haven, but whether she first visited Harwich or Bury it is difficult to judge. The natural supposition would be that she remained quiet for a time at Bury until she was satisfied that her allies would be sufficient to effect her object, and then showed herself openly at Harwich were it not that Bury is so distant, and Harwich is so near, that the supposition seems to be negatived by the facts. From Harwich or Bury, whichever it were, she marched towards London, which according to some writers, she reached; but the other account seems to be better authenticated, which states that on hearing that the King had left the capital for the West she altered her course for Oxford. She certainly was not in London when the Tower was captured by the citizens, October 16th (*Compotus Willielmi de Culpho*, Wardrobe Accounts, 20 Edward the Second, 31/8), since she dates a mandate from Wallingford on the 15th, unless Bishop Orleton falsified the date in quoting it in his Apology. Thence she marched to Cirencester and Gloucester, and at last to Bristol, which she entered on or before the 25th. Since Gloucester was considerably out of her way—for we are assured that her aim was to make a straight and rapid course to Bristol—why did she go there at all if the King were at Bristol? But we know he was not; he had then set sail for Wales. Her object in going to Bristol was probably twofold: to capture Le Despenser and Arundel, and to stop the King's supplies, for Bristol was his commissariat-centre. A cartload of provisions reached that city from London for him on the 14th (Note 2.) (*Rot. Magne Gard.*, 20 Edward the Second, 26/3), and his butler, John Pyrie, went thither for wine, even so late as November 1st (*Ibidem*, 26/4). Is it possible that Pyrie, perhaps unconsciously, betrayed to some adherent of the Queen the fact that his master was in Wales? The informer, we are told by the chroniclers, was Sir Thomas le Blount, the King's Seneschal of the Household. But that suspicious embassage of the Abbot of Neath and several of the King's co-refugees, noted on November 10th in terms which, though ostensibly spoken by the King and dated from Neath, are unmistakably the Queen's diction and not his, cannot be left out of the account in estimating his betrayers. From October 26, when the illegally-assembled Parliament, in the hall of Bristol Castle, went through the farce of electing the young Prince to the regency "because the King was absent from his kingdom," and October 27th, which is given (probably with truth) by Harl. Ms. 6124 as the day of the judicial murder of Hugh Le Despenser the Elder, our information concerning the Queen's movements is absolutely *nil* until we find her at Hereford on the 20th of November. She then sent Bishop Orleton of Hereford to the King to request the Great Seal, and he, returning, found her at Marcle on the 26th. It was probably on the 24th that the younger Despenser suffered. On the 27th the Queen was at Newent, on the 28th at Gloucester, on the 29th at Coberley, and on the 30th at Cirencester. She reached Lechlade on December 1st, Witney on the 2nd, Woodstock on the 3rd. Here she remained till the 22nd, when she went to Osney Abbey, and forward to Wallingford the next day. (Wardrobe Accounts, 20 Edward the Second and 1 Edward the Third, 26/11.) She was joined at Wallingford by her younger son Prince John of Eltham, who had been awaiting her arrival since the 17th, and losing 3 shillings at play by way of amusement in the interim (*Ibidem*, 31/18). By Reading, Windsor, Chertsey, and Allerton she reached Westminster on the 4th of January (*Ibidem*, 26/11).

I have examined all the Wardrobe Accounts and Rolls likely to cast light on this period, but I can find no mention of the whereabouts of the two Princesses during this time. Froissart says that they and Prince John were delivered into the Queen's care by the citizens of Bristol; which is certainly a mistake so far as concerns the Prince, whose compotus just quoted distinctly states that he left the Tower on October 16th (which fixes the day of its capture), quitted London on December 21st, and reached Wallingford on the 24th. He, therefore, was no more at Bristol than his father, and only rejoined his mother as she returned thence. The position of the royal sisters remains doubtful, as even Mrs Everett Green—usually a most faithful and accurate writer—has accepted Froissart's narrative, and apparently did not discover its complete discrepancy with the Wardrobe Accounts. If the Princesses were the companions of their royal father in his flight, and were delivered to their mother when she entered Bristol—which may be the fact—the probability is that he sent them there when he left Gloucester, on or about the 10th of October.

VI. The Order of Sempringham

The Gilbertine Order, also called the Order of Sempringham, was that of the reformed Cistercians. Its founder was Gilbert, son of Sir Josceline de Sempringham; he was Rector of Saint Andrew's Church in that village, and died in 1189. The chief peculiarity of this Order was that monks and nuns dwelt under the same roof, but their apartments were entered by separate doors from without, and had no communication from within. They attended the Priory Church together, but never mixed among each other except on the administration of the Sacrament. The monks followed the rule of Saint Austin; the nuns the Cistercian rule, with Saint Benedict's emendations, to which some special statutes were added by the founder. The habit was, for monks, a black cassock, white cloak, and hood lined with lambskin; for nuns, a white habit, black mantle, and black hood lined with white fur. There was a Master over the entire Order, who lived at Sempringham, the mother Abbey also a Prior and a Prioress over each community. The Prior of Sempringham was a Baron of Parliament. The site of the Abbey, three miles south-east from Folkingham, Lincolnshire, may still be traced by its moated area. The Abbey Church of Saint Andrew alone now remains entire; it is Norman, with an Early English tower, and a fine Norman north door.

But few houses of the Gilbertine Order existed in England, and those were mainly in Yorkshire and Lincolnshire. The principal ones—after Sempringham, which was the chief—were Chicksand, Bedfordshire; Cambridge; Fordham, near Newmarket; Hitchin, Hertfordshire; Lincoln, Alvingham, Bolington, Cateley, Haverholme, Ormesby, Newstead (not the Abbey, which was Augustinian), Cotton, Sexley, Stikeswold, Sixhill, Lincolnshire; Marmound and Shuldham, Norfolk; Clattercott, Oxfordshire; Marlborough, Wiltshire; Malton, Sempringham Minor, Watton, and Wilberfosse, Yorkshire.

The Gilbertine Order "for some centuries maintained its sanctity and credit; afterwards it departed greatly from both."

VII. Fictitious Persons

In Part One, these are Cicely's daughters, Alice and Vivien, and her damsels, Margaret and Fina; Meliora, the Queen's sub-damsel; Hilda la Vileyne, and her relatives. Of all others, the name and position at least are historical facts.

The fictitious persons in Part Two are more numerous, being all the household of the Countess of March (except John Inge the Castellan): and Nichola, damsel of the Countess Agnes.

The three Despenser nuns, Mother Alianora, and the Sisters Annora and Margaret, and Lady Joan de Greystoke, are the only characters in Part Three which are not fictitious.

A difference in the diction will be noticed between Part Three and the earlier parts, the last portion being more modern than the rest. Sister Alianora must not be supposed to write her narrative, which she could not do except by order from her superiors; but rather to be uttering her reflections to herself. Since to her the natural language would be French, there was no need to follow the contemporary diction further than, by a quaint expression now and then, to remind the reader of the period in which the scene is laid.

It may be remarked that the diction of Parts One and Two is not strictly correct. This is true: because to make it perfectly accurate, would be to make it also unintelligible to nine out of ten readers, and this not so much on account of obsolete words, which might be explained in a note, as of the entirely different turn of the phraseology. An imaginary diary of the reign of Elizabeth can be written in pure Elizabethan language, and with an occasional explanatory note, it will be understood by modern readers: but a narrative prior to 1400 at the earliest cannot be so treated. The remaining possibilities are either to use as much of the correct diction of the period as is intelligible, employing modern terms where it is not, or else to write in ordinary modern English. Tastes no doubt differ on this point. I prefer the former; since I extremely dislike to read a mediaeval story where modern expressions alone are used in the dialogue. The reader, if himself acquainted with the true language, finds it impossible to realise or enter into the story, being constantly reminded that he is reading a modern fiction. What I object to read, therefore, I object to write for the reading of others. Where circumstances, as in this case, make perfect accuracy impossible, it seems to me the next best thing is to come as near it as they will permit.

The biographical details given in this Appendix, with few exceptions, have not, I believe, been previously published. For such information as may readily be found in Dugdale's Baronage, extinct peerages, etcetera, I refer my readers to those works.

> Note 1. This document is mistakenly headed and catalogued as a Compotus of Leonor, Queen of Edward the First. It certainly belongs to Queen Philippa. The internal evidence is abundant and conclusive—*eg*, "the Countess of Hainault, the Queen's mother."

Note 2. The details of this cartload are not uninteresting:—203 quarters, 12 pounds wax; 774 pounds broken sugar, 11 pence per pound; 200 almonds; 100 pounds of rice; 78 ells of Paris napery, 10 pence per ell; 6 and a half ells of Rouen napery, same price; 18 short towels; 15 and a half ells of "cloth of Still;" 100 ells of linen, 100 ells of canvas; 200 pears, at 4 shillins per 100, bought of Isabel Fruiterer; 2000 large nuts, at 1 shilling per 1000; four baskets for the fruit, 10 pence. The journey from London occupied five days, and the travelling expenses were 14 pence per day.